SAY *you'll* STAY

Say You'll Stay – Special Edition

CORINNE MICHAELS

Editor:
Lisa Christman, Adept Edits

Proofreading:
Ashley Williams, Adept Edits

Cover Design:
Sarah Hansen, Okay Creations

Dedication

To the love that let me go so I could find the one worth holding on to.

And to my father, who showed me the kind of man I don't want in my life. You may not have thought I was good enough for you, but it was you who wasn't good enough for me.

"The rain will stop, the night will end, and the hurt will fade. Hope is never so lost that it can't be found." – Mandy Hale

One

"Why don't you head home, Presley? I can close up," Angie offers from behind the counter.

We run a small cupcake shop in Media, Pennsylvania. It's been a long few days with our two bakers being sick. I've worked almost forty hours in three days, and I'm beyond tired. Angie doesn't bake, but she runs the business side of things, which means I've had to fill in both spots by myself.

"Are you sure?"

"Yes." She laughs. "Now go before I call Todd and make him drag you out."

"You're lucky I love you."

She kisses my cheek. "I love you more, even if you drive me nuts with your need for perfection."

Angelina, or Angie as we all call her, is my sister-in-law and former college roommate. My husband is her brother, who I fell in love with when he was there for me during a dark time in my life. Of course, at first she didn't love the idea of us dating, but she came around when she saw how well we fit together.

"I'll see you in the morning." I grab my coat and head to my car before I find a reason to stick around.

I call my house, but the boys don't answer. I picture Logan

with his headphones on, playing some mindless game, and Cayden refuses to move for anything. It's a daily adventure with those two. It's hard to believe they'll both be in middle school next year. It feels like they were infants only yesterday.

The machine beeps, and I pray one of them or my husband hears it. "Hey boys, I'm on my way home. I hope your homework is done. I'd like to maybe go out for dinner? Love you! Oh, and Todd . . . don't forget to call your mother, she's called eight times this week."

I turn out of the lot and head to where I'm sure chaos is in full effect. We own a beautiful row home about ten minutes from the bakery. His parents moved to Florida to escape the cold winters, and there was no way in hell I was moving back to Tennessee after college. I'd have to be dragged there in cuffs. So, my in-laws sold it to us after we got married. We gutted it, and now it's everything I could want. The remodel ended up costing more than buying a new place, but we wanted to live here.

Once I park, I check myself quickly. My face is covered in various baking products, and thanks to the bowl of flour I sent flying earlier today, my dark brown hair is sprinkled with white powder. Typical day.

"Hello?" I call out as I enter the house. Papers are thrown around, shoes are left where they landed, and coats are dropped right where the boys walked in. I swear, getting anyone to hang something up is like pulling teeth. "Boys! Clean this mess!" I yell, but no one responds.

I walk toward the family room where, exactly as I assumed, they're playing a game with their headphones on. I lift one side off each of their ears. "Hey!"

"Mom!" they both grumble. "We're playing a game."

"I see that. How about you play clean the hallway? I think that sounds like a fun game." I smile and kiss them each on the cheek, which grants me another protest. "Aww, don't you want your Mommy—"

"Stop!" They pause the game and jump up. "You love to embarrass us," Logan complains.

"It's my mission in life." I shrug. "Where's your dad?"

"We haven't seen him since we got home. I guess he's upstairs."

"Go clean up, and then we'll talk about how school was." I point to the door as they drag their feet.

Mama always said boys are easier. Maybe having only one is, but twins are a whole new world of fun. They use the other to bargain for what they want. Todd and I are always on our toes. That being said, I have no doubt that being a parent is the most rewarding job in the world.

"Babe?" I call toward the bedroom.

No answer.

"Todd! I'm home."

He's probably in his office or on the phone. We have a relationship that all our friends envy. No matter what obstacles we face, we have each other. He's truly the most loving and caring man I've ever met. He's never strayed or been anything but supportive. When I said that Angie and I wanted to open the store, he didn't blink. We took out loans, and he stood behind me. I know that I can always count on him. He loves me more than I deserve.

I climb the stairs but don't see him in the office or the boys' room.

"Babe, are you here?" I ask again with no response. "Todd?" I look around the bedroom, but he's not here.

I walk toward the bathroom. "Hun, are you in here? You can at least answer me." I laugh and open the door.

My body goes still.

My heart shatters.

My world crumbles.

"No!" I scream, rushing toward him. His body hangs limp on a rope tied to the beam in the ceiling. His lips are blue, eyes bloodshot, and there's not a sound coming from him. "God, no!" I grab his legs, trying to hold him up as my body shakes. I need to get him down. Fear grips me as I use all my strength to keep him from hanging.

He doesn't respond or move. "Todd, please. You can't. Why?" I cry as tears fall relentlessly. I fight with everything I have to wake him.

I need to call 911, but I know. I know with everything inside me that it's too late. There's no sound of breathing. No movement. I can't save him. He's gone. But I refuse to give up. I rush to the other room and grab the phone.

I fumble as I dial, and my hands shake so hard I can barely press the buttons. As the call goes through, I return to trying to bring him back to me.

"911, what's your emergency?"

"M-my husband!" I scream into the receiver as I keep trying to hold him. "He tried . . . I mean, I t-think he's d-dead. He's not breathing."

"Okay, ma'am, remain calm and tell me your address?"

I rattle off what I hope is the correct address. I can't see as the tears blind me. "How could you leave me?" I sob as my arms cramp. "He's not breathing!" I tell the operator frantically. I hoist him up as much as I can with one arm and press my fingers to his wrist, but I feel nothing.

"Ma'am, can you tell me what happened?"

I'd like to know the same thing. He would never do this to me and the boys. Yet, here I stand with my arms around his legs and his lifeless body. My chest aches as I think of Logan and Cayden unaware of what's happening. "He's h-hanging. I can't get him down. I'm trying to push up, but I-I . . ." Every part of me breaks apart as I say the words. Then it hits me. "Oh, God." I shake even harder. "My boys. They're in the house. They don't know," I explain to the 911 operator.

"Can you tell me your name?"

"Presley. Presley Benson."

"Okay, Presley. I'm Donna, and I'm going to stay on the line with you until the police and paramedics arrive. Is he moving at all?" Donna asks.

"No. He's not moving. He's not waking up. He . . . he's . . . I can't let the boys see this."

"Is he breathing or making any sounds?"

I shake my head as I hear her words but can't respond. This can't be real. This is just a fucking dream. There's no way this is real. *Wake up, Presley.* I shake my head, but nothing changes.

"Presley, are you there?"

"He's not breathing. He has no pulse," I say as the fear sharpens every nerve in my body. I'm breaking apart as the words spill from my mouth.

She talks as I fall back on my heels. "Take a few deep breaths. Can you have your children open the door for the police?"

"No." I have to protect them. He's dead. My husband of thirteen years just took his own life. "They can't see this. I can never let them see him like this."

Why would he do this? How am I going to tell them? How? I can't do this. I'm not strong enough.

"All right, Presley, I need you to open the front door. The officers are almost there."

"My boys. I-I have to . . ."

"Go to the front door, shield the boys as much as you can. They'll be there in less than three minutes. Can you do that?"

Can I do anything?

Can I move?

Tears fall as I release my arms. "Why, Todd?" I whisper. A sob erupts from my chest as I stand there unable to move. "Why?"

"Are you still there?" Donna asks.

"I'm here. I can't breathe. They can't see him like this. He's just . . ."

"I know, Presley. Take a deep breath, help is almost there. Can you go downstairs and bring them to a neighbor?"

I fall to the ground. My knees hit the unforgiving floor, but it's nothing compared to the pain in my chest. I sit, unmoving, as my life falls apart. I have to think of those precious boys whose lives are about to be altered. The only thing I can do is be certain they're protected. I wipe my face and try to pull myself together as much as I can.

"I'm heading there now."

"Okay, I'll remain on the phone with you until the officer arrives if you'd like."

Right now, Donna is the only person that knows. If I disconnect the call, then this is it. It's irrational and ridiculous, but once this call disconnects . . . it's all real. "Please. I can't do this alone."

"Of course. I'm right here. You're not alone, Presley."

I manage to lift myself off the floor. My feet somehow move forward. I head to the living room, and Logan looks up.

"Mom?" He stands.

"I need you boys to go out the back and knock on Mrs. Malgieri's door. Play with Ryan until I come get you," I instruct on autopilot. My eyes close as I fold my arm around my torso.

Logan rushes over. He's always been my more sensitive soul. This is going to crush him. "What's wrong?"

I place my hand against his cheek as a tear falls. "You and Cayden go, and I'll be there in a bit." My voice cracks as the pain rips through me. My boys. My sweet, innocent, and loving boys will never be the same. Cayden's eyes well as I'm sure he hears the pain in my words.

"You're doing great, Presley," Donna encourages. "They're one minute out."

"You're scaring me, Mom." He looks at me with his big, green eyes.

"I need to handle something and you don't need to be here." I fight back the sob building inside me, knowing that my children are about to be destroyed.

Logan's arms encircle my middle, and Cayden pulls him back. "Is it Dad?" he asks.

"Go! Now!" I'm no longer able to maintain my composure. I just need them to go. I know I've scared them, and I can see they're freaking out inside, but I can't catch my breath. "I'm sorry. I need you both to get up right now and go over to Ryan's house."

"Come on, Logan, let's go." Cayden has always been more perceptive. He reads between the lines and can often see things that most kids his age can't.

There's no fooling them. My face must be red and my eyes

swollen from crying. Cayden stares at me as my chin quivers. "We're going to be okay."

"Mom?" Logan asks as I can no longer hold back the tears.

A tear falls from Cayden's face as I pull them into my arms. "I love you."

I stare at them, praying I can find a way to make this okay. Reluctantly they release me and head out the back door. I watch them go and cry. I cry for them. For me. And for how much pain this is going to cause them.

When they disappear from my view, I walk to the front door and open it. The police car approaches, lights blazing, and the hollowness swallows me.

Two

"Presley!" Angie calls out as she enters the house. I'm sitting on the couch where I've been for the last forty minutes. The police called Angie and asked her to come before they had even finished taking my statement. I went over everything I knew, and they handed me tissues as I struggled with my agony. The paramedics are upstairs taking care of the body.

She rushes forward. "Ang?" I stare at her, watching the fear in her eyes. My heart breaks knowing I'm about to tear her world apart.

"Is it the boys?"

I shake my head.

"No!" She sinks next to me as I pull her into my arms. "Oh, God," Angie cries and we cling to each other.

I lean back as she wipes her eyes. "I don't . . . I don't know how to tell you this." It's so much worse.

"Tell me what?"

"He . . . he . . . he hung himself." My chest heaves as I say the words aloud.

"No, no, no, no," she says over and over. "Why? How? No! He would never! You're lying!"

"He did."

Her eyes fill with confusion. "No. You're wrong!" Angie stands and moves around. "Not Todd. He loves you. He loves those boys more than anything. I don't believe you. He wouldn't do this!"

I don't really believe it either. "I wish I was lying. I wish this was a bad dream, but it's not. He . . . he . . ." My breaths come in small bursts as I struggle to inhale. This is too much. "I saw him h-h-hanging f-from the bathroom beam!" I scream and sob hysterically. "I'm not lying! I'm . . . I'm . . ."

The officer that sits beside me grips my shoulders and instructs me to inhale slowly. In through the nose. Out through the mouth. I repeat this process until I'm not on the verge of a panic attack.

Angie cries with me, letting out her own sounds of devastation. We clutch each other and mourn the loss of a man we love.

Twenty minutes later, just as Angie and I have settled together and calmed into quiet weeping, the paramedics appear on the staircase. A black bag lies on the gurney, holding the man I planned to grow old with, the father of my children, and all the hopes of the life I'd imagined. No more dinners. No more kisses. No more laughs can be shared between us. Because he decided he couldn't. And I don't even know why.

We have a beautiful home, stable jobs, smart and healthy kids. I'm so confused. I keep waiting for Todd to walk down the stairs and tell me it's all going to be okay.

I stand, staring at the blackness that fills my view.

The emptiness drains the parts of me that were once so full. It takes over the hope I once had, making it black and ugly. They wheel him out as I crumple to the floor. Angie rushes over to me, enveloping me in her arms, and holds on.

"I'm so sorry, Pres."

"I'm sorry, too." I release her and know what I have to do now. "I have to go get the boys."

"Oh, God," she gasps, covering her mouth. "What do they know?"

"They know something's wrong and it's about their father. I

have to go get them. They're probably terrified."

I manage to pull myself up as the last police officer lingers by the back door. He walks over as I squeeze my arms around my stomach. "Here's my card, Mrs. Benson. If you need anything, please give me a call."

I nod and close my eyes. I need for this to not be real, but he can't do that. "Thanks."

Angie's hand rests on my back. "Do you want me to stay?"

"Please," I say and she heads to the couch. I hear her moan break free as I walk the officer out.

"I can stay here if it'll help," he offers.

"I appreciate it. I don't think anything is going to help." I grip the card in my hand as a lifeline. "How do I tell them?" I ask this man who is a stranger. I need someone to tell me what to do.

"I wish I could tell you, Mrs. Benson. I don't know that there is a right way." He loses a sigh. "I've made too many notifications, and it's never easy. Just be honest, and be there for them."

"Thank you, Officer . . . ?" I realize I don't know his name. This man comforted me for the last hour, and I don't even know his name.

"Walker. Michael Walker."

"Thank you for your help, Officer Walker. I don't know how I'm going to do this alone. I've never been alone." As the word leaves my lips, it hits me. Alone. Yeah, I have the boys, but my husband is gone.

"We'll tell them together," Angie says from behind me.

The officer nods, gets in his car, and we head over to do the last thing in the world I want to do—tell the boys. I look at Angie, whose face is covered in black streaks. She loved her brother so much. He had so much love and support around him. So many people to talk to, and he chose this? I can't get my head around this.

I wipe my face and then knock. Mrs. Malgieri opens the door. Her hands fly to her mouth as my eyes close again. "Oh, Presley." She pulls me into her arms. "Please tell me he's okay. We saw the lights and the boys said something was wrong."

I remove myself from her embrace. If it's hard to tell her, it's going to be pure agony with the boys. My face falls as my eyes close. "Are the boys here? I-I . . ."

"I'm so very sorry, honey."

This is going to be the first in a long line of apologies. "Thank you. I need to talk to them."

"They're watching television, but they're very quiet and scared." Her eyes fill with sorrow.

I hold my breath, trying to stay strong. "Thank you for keeping them."

Logan must hear my voice, because next thing I know, he's barreling toward me crying. "Mom, I saw the lights. Where's Dad?"

I crouch down, grip his hand in mine, and see Cayden standing behind him, unmoving. "Cay, come here." I extend my other hand.

He shakes his head as I battle all emotions I'm feeling. I have to be strong for them. "Cayden," Angie says from behind me, unable to stop her steady stream of tears. "Come here, buddy."

He heads into his aunt's arms. They've always had a special bond, and I'm grateful she's here for him. I look at both of them and decide right then that I can't tell them everything. I don't want to lie to them, but I have to protect their hearts. If they know this was his choice, I don't know that they'll ever recover. How could he not think they were worth living for? I won't let them feel that.

"Boys." I struggle to speak. "Your Daddy . . . his heart . . . it . . . it stopped . . . the paramedics, they tried so hard but they couldn't . . ." I inhale slowly and deeply, trying to compose myself before I completely shatter their world. "I'm so sorry, babies. I'm so sorry, but Daddy went to Heaven."

Logan's arms drape around my neck as he sobs. I rub his back, trying to soothe him. I can no longer hold inside the agony I feel. I sob. We hold each other and he soaks my shirt. I look over at Cayden, who's being comforted by Angie. He cries and shakes his head back and forth.

Logan pushes back, balling his fists. "He was upstairs! He has to be okay, Mom!" He shakes his head. "He . . . he's . . . he's strong, and the doctors need to try harder!"

"They tried, buddy." I attempt to pull him into my arms, but he moves so I can't grab him. "Th-they tried . . . so many times." I fall apart as I watch my son grapple with the truth.

"Try again!" Logan screams as he rushes out the door and across the yard. "He needs help!"

Cayden doesn't say anything. Angie tilts her head, letting me know it's okay for me to go after Logan.

"Dad!" Logan calls out as he reaches the front door. "Dad!" he screams as tears fall down his face. "Daddy! No . . . no, Daddy!" He heads toward the stairs, but I grab him before he can get that far.

My heart breaks into a million pieces. I pull him into my arms as he fights to get out. I don't let go, and he doesn't stop attempting to get where his father last was. He cries and calls out for Todd, struggling with his grief. With each scream, I cry harder. After a few minutes, his screams stop, he turns into my chest, and his body goes limp. I hold him tight and murmur words that are useless in this moment.

"H-he can't be gone, Mom. He . . . he was supposed to help me with my project. He promised. He wouldn't break a promise."

I kiss the top of his head, rocking to soothe both of us. "I know, baby. I'm sorry." I sit on the hardwood floor, staring at the ceiling and wishing he would come back. If this could all be a joke, then I could put my boys back together. I could fix this. Hearing their cries is killing me.

"Make him come back. Please, please, just make him come back." His voice cracks as he begs.

If only I could. God, if only.

Cayden and Angie make their way to the front door. They both wrap their arms around Logan and me on the floor. We hold each other in the hallway, each trying to find some comfort. Time passes, darkness falls, but we stay huddled and take turns crying.

Eventually, we move to the living room. I call my parents,

telling them to come here right away. Angie calls her parents and brother in Florida. I can hear my mother-in-law's screams through the phone.

Getting through the next few days is going to take a miracle. Everyone is on their way while we try to get from one minute to the next.

Cayden and Logan won't leave my side. We're curled up on the couch, each on one side of me. They barely speak. The television is on, but no one is watching. Each of us drowning in our grief.

Angie makes some soup, but I can't eat.

"What happens now?" Cayden asks.

"What do you mean?"

My tears have finally dried. I don't have any left. I'm numb and lost.

His eyes are filled with fear. "Will we have to move? Do we get to see Daddy again?"

"No, honey, we won't have to move. I have to make arrangements, and we'll have a service for your dad." I don't know how to answer him about seeing his father. "I'm not sure if you'll see him again, baby."

"Oh." He looks away despondently. "I'm sorry, Mom."

"Sorry? What could you be sorry for, sweetheart?"

Cayden's green eyes close as a tear falls. "I should've gone upstairs. I could've—"

"No, baby. This isn't anything you could've stopped."

Logan sniffles. "I sat here playing video games, too. Dad needed us."

"Boys." I get up, turning to face them. "I need you to listen to me." I wait for them to acknowledge me before I continue. "You did nothing wrong. You couldn't have saved him. Do you understand me?"

Neither says a word—they just cry. And the tears I thought dried, become rivers down my cheeks. *Why, Todd? Why?*

Three

"I'm so sorry for your loss," says a nameless face who is standing in front of me after the burial. Everyone is nice, all sympathetic, but I don't care. I'm sure they're sorry. They all wish me and the boys the best. But I see the pity in their eyes.

Maybe it's my paranoia, but I hear their whispers to each other on why it was a closed casket when it was a heart attack. I feel their gazes as they watch me stand motionless over the gravesite, unable to place my rose there.

If they only knew. They didn't have to take the call from the funeral home saying they couldn't cover the bruises or ligature marks. They don't understand the way my heart clenches each time someone asks how he passed. The bitter lie I utter. They're all praying for us, and I'm praying they leave us alone. I shake their hands and allow their hugs, but I'm empty.

More people leave, but all I focus on is the body lying in the casket.

"How could you do this?" I grasp the flower in my hand. "How could you think this was the answer?" The thorn pricks at my skin. "We had a life. We had a family." A tear falls. I look around and see Angie by her car and my mother standing by hers. Cayden and Logan sit in the car with my daddy. He's been the only person they want to be around. Cayden still won't speak much, but Logan won't stop. They're coping—barely.

Everyone gives me some time alone as I bid farewell to my husband.

"You're really gone." I brush my hand across the smooth wood casket, rubbing my fingers back and forth. "I feel so many things right now. I guess this is goodbye." My voice cracks. "I guess this is where I leave you and the life we had in the ground." I catch my breath. I lift the rose and place it down. The single rose stands apart from the rest, which sit in a pile. "Goodbye, Todd."

Tears fall, and my knees give out. My hand rests against the wood as I sob.

Minutes pass, and my tears dry, but I can't move. When I leave this place, it'll be the end of us. He's been gone for a week, but this will really be it.

"You ready, sugar?" Mama asks. She squats before taking my hand in hers.

"No," I say, staring at the hole in the ground where my husband's body will rest.

"You're going to be okay, Presley." She leans back and reassures me, "I know it's hard, but you're a strong woman."

I look at my mother, begging with my eyes for her to give me something to help with the pain. "Mama?"

Her lips purse as she rubs the side of my face. "I can't take this away from you. Lord, how I wish I could." Her eyes fill with moisture as her hand drops, gripping each of mine. "You're strong, though. You always were the strongest of all of us. Not many have the guts to chase something they want. Look at what you did. Moving on, going to school, makin' something of your life."

"Look where that got me."

"Hey, now." Her stern, Southern voice leaves no room for debate. "You got those boys. You have a home, a business, and you've done well for yourself. Things that you might not have if you'd stayed on the ranch. You couldn't wait to get out of Bell Buckle, and while it wasn't the way you planned, it led you to

Todd. That man loved you all more than anything. He didn't leave this world or you willingly."

I can't stop the hysterical laugh that escapes me. My chest constricts as I feel the first twinge of anger. I stand quickly while balling my fists at my side. "Mama, if that were the truth I—" I stop, realizing that I almost told her that it wasn't a heart attack. "Let's just go."

"What aren't you telling me?" She stands slowly with her eyes never leaving mine.

"Nothing, Mama."

"Don't lie to me, Presley Mae. I know when you're hiding something."

Her eyes study me. She's one of those women who sees too much. She was always able to tell if my brother, Cooper, and I were lying. That is, until I started dating. Then it was a whole new world. I perfected telling half-truths and leaving out details she didn't need to know. "There's nothing worth repeating." I release her hand and walk to the car. This isn't the end of it, but I'm not ready to tell anyone yet.

Thankfully, my father doesn't say a word as I climb in. Our relationship suffered when I left the ranch. He hoped that Cooper and I would run it together. His was not a dream I shared. There was a lot of anger when I decided to go to college out of state. Daddy refused to help contribute anything for school, and when I said I wasn't coming back . . . he was livid. Bell Buckle was like living in a vacuum cleaner. It sucked the life out of me. I wanted more. I wanted it all.

"Mom?" Cayden's small hand rests on my arm.

"Yes, buddy?"

"Why did God take my dad?"

My shoulders rise and fall as my head shakes. I answer him with as much honesty as I can—as though he'd asked why his father killed himself. "I don't know. I really don't. Sometimes things just don't make sense. Sometimes we never have answers to these questions."

I hear Logan sniff and then say, "I miss him."

"I miss him too, baby. You have no idea how much."

Cayden leans his head against my arm and I kiss his hair. This one event will shape so much of who they are. For all my father's shortcomings, he loved me so deeply. His determination to fight for what he believed in is what I learned from him. But Daddy always told me and Cooper that anything worth fighting for is worth everything you have. He wished I didn't want to run as fast as I could out of Tennessee. I'm sure he still hasn't forgiven me.

"Sometimes, boys." My father's deep voice cuts through the silence as he continues, "There's no comprehending why things happen. People leave you before you're ready for them to go, but you have to keep livin'." I can't help but think he's also talking about me. His green eyes stare at me through the reflection in the rearview mirror. "That doesn't mean you won't miss them though."

"Daddy." I start, but he shakes his head, stopping my words.

"And you'll always love them. No matter what."

I squeeze my hands together and close my eyes. Daddy is a man of few words, but when he speaks—people listen.

My mother gets in the car with disappointment rolling off her. There's so much to be said between all of us. Years of disappointment and resentment hang in the air. Right now, though, I don't care about any of it. I can't see past my own anguish.

I look at my sweet boys. I see their pain and wish I could take it away. But I can't. All I can do is let them know that they have so many people here who love them. People who will always be here. Even if their father didn't think we were worth living for. "I want you to know something. We all love you boys . . . so much. Nana and Papa, Grandma and Grandpa, Aunt Angie, and of course, me. You're surrounded by people who would do anything for you." I glance at my father, hoping he'll hear my message to him. "Loving someone doesn't stop just because you don't see them anymore."

Both boys nod and busy themselves with their video games. As much as I hate those things, I'm grateful the boys can get lost in them for a little bit.

We return to the house, and I head to my room. Logan and

Cayden convinced my parents to take them to dinner, so I'm alone for the first time since Todd . . . died. My mother never eats out. Everything comes from scratch. Cooking is her true love. Getting her to agree to let someone else touch her food is not an easy feat. Those boys know how to get what they want.

I flop on the bed with my black dress still on. Black. That's how I feel—void of any light or color.

I stare at the bathroom door. I rise and my feet move of their own accord to the place where he was last. My knees touch the cold tiles, then my hands, before my entire body presses against the floor. I'm so cold, but I don't move. Needing to feel close to him, my body touches the last place he was. "We had so much left to do, Todd. We had children to raise, vacations to take, and love still left to make. Our time wasn't up. You promised me forever." I curl my legs. "Forever wasn't over. I'm still here, dammit. What do I do now, huh? How do I keep this home together? You've set fire to every part of our life! You've killed me alongside of you!" I shout as cries shudder through me. My chest heaves as I cling to my legs. "I'm so mad. I'm so confused. No note? No explanation why? Fuck you! I needed you! I gave up everything for you and then you do this? I hate you right now." I close my eyes, allowing the tears to leak out as I fall asleep.

~

"Presley." A familiar voice causes my eyes to open. "Presley, honey, wake up."

I pull the covers over my head. "Go away. I don't want to talk to anyone."

It's been a little over a week since the funeral. Eighteen days since Todd took his own life. I alternate between being awake and angry and sleeping. That's all I can manage now. I know I'm not providing what the kids need, but I can't find my way through the fog. There's nothing guiding me. The haze is too thick, and my heart is too heavy.

"Too bad." Angie rips the blanket off. "You've been asleep for a while. My parents are downstairs. They'd like to see you before they head to the airport."

Fighting her on this is pointless. I grumble as I get out of bed, throwing on my oversized sweater and squeezing my midsection.

We descend the stairs as they both give me sad smiles. My mother-in-law's eyes are puffy from all the crying she's done. She doesn't want to leave the boys and me—or Todd. She's gone to the gravesite every morning. "We can't stay any longer. I wish we could, honey," Pearl says.

"I understand."

My father-in-law steps forward, "Presley, there are a few things you'll need to take care of. The insurance agent that I set Todd up with called. You'll need to get in touch with him first thing tomorrow. If you have any questions about any paperwork, call me."

I nod.

"Thank you, Martin. I appreciate it." He and Angie are the only ones who know the truth surrounding Todd's death.

"You come visit with the boys, okay?" Pearl's eyes tear as she pulls me into her arms. "We love you all very much. I'm just . . ."

I console her before Martin pulls her back. "We're always here for you. You're like our own daughter."

"Thank you."

Cayden and Logan rush over to them, wrapping their arms around their grandparents. "I'll miss you, Grandma."

They say their goodbyes and I make my way to the couch. Angie heads over with a mug of coffee to where I sit. "Here. Drink it." I take it in my hands but can't muster the strength to take a sip. "Boys, can you go play in the back for a few minutes?"

I glance at their faces, taking in the small smiles I haven't seen recently as they head out the door.

"I'm going to say this to you, and I need you to listen." Angie sits next to me. "Know that I love you."

My eyes meet hers. There's a dark rim around her blue irises. The bags under her eyes are darker than I remember.

"Presley?" she says, breaking my trance.

"Yeah, I'm listening."

She lets out a heavy sigh. "Are you listening? I mean, are you doing anything?"

Excuse me? "What the hell does that mean?"

"The boys need you. Your parents are leaving tomorrow, and I have to go back to work. You have to pull yourself out of this . . . I don't even know what to call it. You look like shit. You aren't eating, all you do is sleep, and this isn't you."

My anger boils. "Have you lost a husband? Have you walked in to find your spouse hanging dead in your bathroom? Did you cry out for him to wake up? Huh? Have you?" I taunt her as my rage grows. "No? Oh, that's right . . . it was me!"

"I know you're angry. So be angry! Be anything!"

"I am!" I yell as my hands shake. "I'm so fucking angry! How could he do this, Angie? How could he think this was the goddamn answer?"

"I don't know, babe. I don't. I'm livid, too. I hate that he did this. My own brother!" She balls her hands into fists. "It makes no fucking sense, but you can't lie here paralyzed. The boys need you."

I'm not insensitive to her feelings. This is hard for her, too. I have a brother and even though we're not close anymore, I would be broken if I lost him. But I'll never get the images out of my mind. My life will never be the same. When my eyes close, I remember the events of that day in vivid detail.

"Don't tell me what they need. Don't tell me what you think I should do! You're not me. You're stronger than I am, apparently. I can't stop questioning this. I can't make sense of it. Why would he do this to me?"

"All I can come up with is that he felt hopeless."

"Well, I really appreciate that feeling right now."

Angie stands and rakes her hands through her hair. "You're going to get in the shower. You're going to get dressed in something other than sweatpants, and you're going to function."

Who the hell does she think she is? How dare she talk to me

like this? I'm in misery right now. Everything hurts. My head, my heart, my soul are aching. "You have no idea how I feel."

"Then tell me."

The idea of trying to articulate any of this makes me tired. "Confused. I'm so confused. All I keep asking is why? Why, why, why? I go from denial to anger and back to denial. I keep waiting for him to open the door or send me a text. I can't stop myself from calling his phone." I start to cry again. "I call and listen to his voice. I play it over and over because I'll never hear it again."

"Shhh." She enfolds me in her arms. "Did something happen with him or between you guys?"

That's the million-dollar question. I went through all his belongings, searching for an answer, but there was nothing. His home office held nothing. Everything he owned was in its place.

"I have no idea." My voice is thick with emotion. "This isn't the man I knew. My husband, your brother, their father—wouldn't do this. He would've talked to me, or I don't know."

She takes my hand in hers. "When are you going to tell the boys the truth?"

I close my eyes and release a long breath. "I can't tell them everything. I know they're not babies, but they can never know the details."

Her eyes widen. "Pres."

"They don't ever need to know he chose to leave us. I won't lie, but I'm going to protect them. I need you to do the same."

"Pres," she interjects, but I raise my hand to stop her.

"No." My voice leaves no room for discussion. "They're my kids. They're already apologizing for not saving him, and I'm thanking God they never walked upstairs. So, no. We protect the kids. I never want them to know what he did. The emotions I feel, the anger, disappointment, and confusion—they shouldn't have to battle it, too. No one else can know either. Not your mother, not my parents, no one."

She leans back with disapproval written all over her face. "One day they'll find out, and then what?"

"Then I'll handle it."

I probably shouldn't be making these kinds of choices right now. I'm not in the right state of mind, but this . . . I feel confident about. Those babies are all I have left. My heart is torn apart, not only from losing him, but also from knowing how. Why couldn't he talk to me? When did he decide this?

"Okay," she says with disappointment. "I don't agree, but I won't say a word."

We sit in awkward silence. Angie has been my best friend since I left Tennessee. She's helped me in so many ways, but right now, she can't. I have to do this on my own.

~

I grab the phone off my nightstand. "Hello?" My voice is still heavy with sleep despite it being after two in the afternoon.

"Mrs. Benson, this is John Dowd. I was Todd's insurance agent."

"Oh, yes." I sit up, wiping my eyes. "Thank you for calling me back."

"I wanted to go over some information with you. Is now a good time?"

The boys are at school, I'm in bed, and I'm not planning on moving from this spot today, so I guess it's as good a time as any. "Sure, Mr. Dowd. Now is fine."

He releases a deep breath. "I'm calling to let you know the status of the insurance payout. Your father-in-law started the process on your behalf. About a year ago, Todd had me revise his life insurance plan. He upped it from $500,000 to $750,000. He wanted to ensure you had enough income, if something should happen, once your business started."

"Oh. I guess that was nice of him." How nice that he was planning for the future, I want to scoff.

"Yes, well, the issue is that there's a suicide clause. Martin explained the circumstances surrounding Todd's death. The thing is . . . if the plan isn't two years old, the insurance policy won't pay out."

The floor drops out from under me all over again. "But he was the primary breadwinner. I don't understand. We'll get nothing?"

He clears his throat. "I'm afraid so. I tried, but with the policy being only a year old, they're refusing to pay anything other than what Todd paid in. We rolled the premium over, but honestly, Mrs. Benson, it's not much."

Oh, my God. "I-I," I stutter, trying to find the words. "But my kids. Our home. How are we going to survive? How do I pay the mortgage and the bills?"

"I'm truly sorry. I would call the bank, plead your case. Sometimes they'll work with you. I'll call Martin as well, explain the situation. But I tried all the appeals I could. There's really nothing the insurance agency can offer you."

"I don't know how I'm supposed to handle this." I feel sick. "You're positive there's nothing else? If I obtained a lawyer?"

Mr. Dowd sighs. "I wish it would help. But the policy is very clear."

"Okay, then," I reply with defeat.

"If I can do anything, I will. I'm sorry again."

"Thank you."

I hang up the phone, bearing yet another blow. They just keep coming.

Four

Of course. That's all I can keep thinking. Of course this is happening. If he hadn't changed the plan, we would have money to pay our bills. Now, I don't know how we're going to afford the mortgage. Our bakery is barely breaking even, let alone paying me enough to survive.

I spend the next hour going through our home office. There's nothing financial anywhere. I can't find a bank statement, credit card bill, paystub . . . nothing. I don't know if maybe he kept all the bills at work. I find the phone numbers on the back of the cards and start dialing.

"What do you mean we have an outstanding bill?" I ask the fourth credit card company.

"I'm sorry, Mrs. Benson," the woman on the phone says for the tenth time. "The notes state that your husband arranged a payment plan but has been unable to keep up with it. If you don't pay the minimum balance by the end of the week, we're going to be sending the account to collections."

The blood drains from my body. It's the same speech from every account we have. Dozens of apologies. Hundreds of tears. And zero answers on how to get through this. I decide to call the office. Maybe Jeff will have some answers about where the hell Todd's paychecks have been going.

"Sterling, Dodd, and March Investment," Kyla's sweet voice rings in my ear.

"Hi, Kyla." I let out a shaky breath. "It's Presley Benson. Is Jeff available?"

I haven't had time to think about much, but I don't remember seeing him at the funeral. It's all a blur though, a horrible nightmare.

"Oh, I'm so sorry to hear about Todd," her concern floats through.

"Thank you," I say on autopilot. I hear this so much that it's lost its meaning. Sorry for what? Sorry that I'm in pain? Sorry that the boys are now without a father? Sorry that you didn't see it coming? What exactly is everyone fucking sorry for?

She clears her throat. "I wanted to call."

"It's fine," I pacify her. "Is Jeff available?"

"Umm, he's . . . he isn't . . . well," she stutters. "He's actually out of the office."

"Okay," I say with confusion. "Are any of Todd's supervisors there? I'm trying to get some information about his paychecks."

Todd handled all our bills. There wasn't a need for me to worry because he was an investor. It made sense for him to control the finances.

"I'm sorry, Mrs. Benson." Her voice drops. "Todd hasn't worked here in a while. He received his last paycheck months ago."

"What?"

"I don't . . . I can put you through to payroll, but I don't know what they'll say."

"I don't understand. He went to work the day he died."

"Let me put you through to Jeff's voicemail," she replies quickly.

Before I can say anything, I hear Jeff's voice and then a beep. "Jeff, it's Presley. I need you to call me. I'm . . . just call." I hang up the phone and sit here stunned.

He lost his job? Did he change companies and that was why we were late? What the fuck is going on? I can't take much more. There's no money coming in from anywhere, and I have to pay bills that I didn't know we had. I have to worry about food and how we're going to keep a roof over our heads.

Oh, my God. The house.

I grab the phone and call the lender.

"How far behind are we on the mortgage?" I ask. I close my eyes and pray he's paid at least this one.

"The house is set to go into foreclosure this week."

I grab my throat as I struggle to inhale. How could he do this to us? It's one blow after another. He lied all this time. Anger takes hold and my fingers shake. This man was supposed to be my rock, and this is what he does? He spends months living some alternate life? I stand and begin to pace.

"But—" I close my eyes and let out a breath. "I have two small kids, my husband has passed away, and I'm afraid I don't have any way to pay all of the outstanding amount." I'm breaking apart as the reality of my financial situation unravels.

"I understand, ma'am." Her voice is full of sympathy I don't want. "I can put you through to my supervisor, but there's not much we can do unless we can get at least four months caught up."

"Please," I beg. "I can't lose this house."

I go over everything again with the supervisor. She's able to give me another month, but I need to come up with a lot of money.

There's no way it can happen.

Even if I were to get lucky enough to find a job, I won't make that much money. I don't know anyone that pays a twelve-years-out-of-work stay-at-home mother with a little baking experience great money.

After getting off the call, I text Angie and ask her to come over. This is a disaster.

My world implodes again.

I'm screwed. And alone.

I hear the door open ten minutes later.

"I'm in the kitchen," I call out.

"Hey, what's up?" Angie asks.

I go over what the insurance agent said. Her jaw falls slack as I tell her our conversation. I feel the ground beneath me caving in, and my hopes drain like the sand in an hourglass. Time is running out, just like our money.

"Did you call the bank?"

"Yeah," I say with rage flowing through my veins. "It seems that Todd hasn't paid the mortgage in four months. Did you know he doesn't work for Sterling anymore?" I ask, hoping maybe she knew and I'm suffering from amnesia.

"No, he was there last week. He called me from the office to see if we could have lunch."

"What?" I ask completely lost. "I don't get it. Kyla said that he hasn't worked there in a while. What the hell is going on?" I start to shake.

"I don't know, Pres. I don't know what to think."

That makes two of us. "We're completely maxed out on all our credit cards, and the bank is already starting the foreclosure process."

"Oh, my God."

"He lied to me. He told me we were fine. He went to work every day for Christ's sake! I'm fucked. I can't afford this house. I can't even pay the utilities."

She steps forward and grips my shoulders. I can see the fear splayed across her face. "You can live with me. You and the boys come live at the apartment."

I close my eyes while holding her arms. "We can't."

"I'll take out a loan. I'll do something."

"Angie." I sigh. "You can't do any of that. Your apartment is a one bedroom in downtown Philly. You're in as much debt as we are. The bakery isn't making us any real money."

With each ounce of truth that falls from my lips, there is a bit of knowledge of what's going to happen that falls with it. The life I fought so hard to escape is going to become my reality again.

"You can't go back to Tennessee. You can't leave here."

"Trust me, I'd rather cut off my arm than go back to Bell Buckle. I have maybe a month or two to figure out how to dig us out of the hole we're in before I can't find a way out."

She nods. "We'll figure it out. I can't lose you, too."

I sure as hell hope so, because if I can't magically produce a large sum of money, the life I've known for the last eighteen years is about to become a distant memory.

"I'm very sorry, Mrs. Benson. At this time the bank isn't able to offer any more extensions," the slender woman explains to me again.

I've exhausted all my options. I was able to borrow some money to get one month caught up, but now we're back to square one. There won't be enough funds to make another payment. No more help is available.

"So, I have no other options?"

"I'm afraid not."

My mind can't process all that's happening. I continue to suffer loss after loss. I've spent the last few weeks trying to find a way to make ends meet. I start to make progress, get one thing paid off, only to learn about a half dozen new credit cards that he took out in my name. Thanks to online accounts, all he needed was my social and date of birth. I'm legally responsible for all of it. It's a never-ending nightmare that I can't wake from.

I stand, grab my purse, and walk out without another word. Nothing I can say will change anything. My kids and I will be homeless, we're broke, and we have no other option. I can't get a loan with no income and ruined credit. And I don't have time to explore other options.

Once I arrive back home, I look around feeling conflicted. I don't want to leave, but I also don't want to be here. The boys don't understand why I sleep on the couch most nights. But being in that king-size bed reminds me that he left.

Slowly, I climb the stairs to my bedroom. I remove the pearl earrings, which Todd bought me on our wedding day, and clutch them in my hand, feeling the prick from the backs before I launch them across the room. "Damn you!" I scream as I grab the photo of us that sits on my dresser.

"Lies! You lied! You broke me!" I yell at the man in the photo. "I loved you! I believed you when you said you'd never hurt me." My voice cracks. "You didn't hurt me! You destroyed me. You destroyed the boys because you're selfish! Selfish!" I throw the photo to the ground and the glass splinters into tiny shards. "You!" Tears fall. "You did this. You couldn't stick it out, so you leave us to deal with it? Is that it?" My head falls back as I talk to the ceiling.

I've tried so hard to keep myself together. Each day I gather enough strength to get Cayden and Logan to school before I crawl back to bed. I've lived my entire life with someone taking care of me. I don't know how to be this woman. My father, *him*, and then Todd have defined who I am. Now, I'm the widow.

I'm the girl whose husband tragically died.

If they only knew.

My eyes close as I try to get my emotions in check. The boys will be home in a few hours, and I need a plan.

The doorbell rings before I have a chance to even think.

"Jeff," I say quietly. "I didn't expect to see you."

"Can I come in, Presley?"

I open the door and wave my arm, inviting in Todd's old boss. "What can I do for you?"

He looks at the mess, and for the first time, I see it all. Dishes stacked, clothes in piles, and open chip bags. I cringe. Chips are all I've been eating for two weeks.

"How are you holding up?"

Jeff and Todd were extremely close. They helped turn the investment firm into what it is. Each of them were promoted around the same time and handled top accounts. For their ages, the money they made was remarkable.

"What do you care?" I ask with disdain dripping from each syllable.

He lets out a heavy sigh before his hands grip the back of his neck. "I'm sorry I didn't come to the funeral. I couldn't believe he . . . I mean, I never thought he would . . ."

Only Angie and my in-laws know it was suicide. His words now tell me that he knows as well.

My lips part as my chest aches. "You knew this was possible?" I struggle to intake air. "You knew he was thinking about this?"

"I didn't think he was serious, Presley. Not him. Not like this."

Each breath is labored. I step back, the backs of my knees hit the couch, and I sink down. "You could've stopped him." My vision becomes blurred with tears. "You could've told me or anyone. If you had, maybe this wouldn't be my goddamn life."

"If I thought for one second he was serious, I would have," he explains. I look at him as he crouches in front of me with a pained expression. "I swear."

My body shakes as I feel everything come rushing forward. It's as if I walked in on him all over again. All I can do is sit here in disbelief. He went to Jeff and didn't come to me. But Jeff didn't tell us. All of this is so fucked-up. I fight back the urge to scream. Why couldn't he trust me?

Jeff grips my hand. "He came to the office and begged me to rehire him. I explained that I couldn't. The investors didn't want to work with him after the money he lost on a bad tip. No accounts were going to trust him, but he begged still. He told me he was desperate and he hadn't told you he was fired," he pauses, drawing in a deep breath. "I explained that my hands were tied, but if I could help—I would."

I can tell he wants to say more. I squeeze my eyes as the beads of moisture fall down my cheeks. "Go on," I murmur.

"He said he probably wouldn't see me again but made me promise I'd check in on you and the boys. I had no idea why the hell he would say that, so I asked him, but he said he'd be leaving."

A howl comes from my throat as I fall apart. My hands cover

my face and Jeff's arms encircle me. "Why?" I ask again, trying to make sense of this.

"I thought he meant leaving town, not this. When I heard, I couldn't face you." He rubs my back. "I'm so sorry. I never thought he was serious. I didn't think he meant this."

Jeff sits with me for the next hour as I process everything he says. He's struggling with guilt, and I'm battling to get through another minute. We talk about how bad off I am financially, and Jeff offers to help, but when he hears the numbers, his face says it all. There's no way to fix this. It's not just a simple cut, it's an artery ripped apart. The utilities will be off soon, the bank will take the house, and there's no way to stop it.

It's clear that from this day forward, I have to leave the dependent girl I was behind and stand on my own feet.

Five

~THREE MONTHS LATER~

"I'm not going." Cayden stands at the door with his arms crossed. "I don't want to move. I hate this."

He's not the only one. I feel the same way. Logan has been the only one handling it somewhat well. Since being told that we had to vacate our home within sixty days, our lives have fallen apart. I'm barely keeping us together with Scotch tape and bubble gum.

"I know you don't want to go. But we have nowhere to live, Cay. Nana and Papa have a big home, and as soon as we have enough money to get out of there, we will. This is temporary."

At least that's what I'm deluding myself into believing. Last night I spent two hours sobbing as I packed the rest of our things. I had to sell all our furniture and anything we couldn't fit in the small trailer. Basically, we're bringing nothing but clothes and personal items.

"You're making us go! This is where we lived with Dad! This is where he was. Why are you trying to make my life miserable?"

"Yes, Cayden. That's my goal, to make you miserable. We have no choice. We have nowhere to live."

He grumbles under his breath before he puts his headphones back on. This is the new normal with him. All he does is watch videos or listen to music. He's angry, while Logan is depressed and clingy. At times, I wish I could behave like them, but there's been no time for me to feel. I've spent hours trying to find a way to avoid having to go back to Tennessee.

But, it's inevitable. I have to live with my parents, work on the ranch, and face every person who told me I'd be back. The only good thing is that *he's* not there. It's going to be bad enough, at least I won't have to face the boy I ran away with.

Angie grabs the last box as Cayden and Logan reluctantly get in the car. I stand in the doorway with conflicting emotions. This is the home we brought the twins to. It's where they took their first steps, learned to ride bikes, it's where so many memories were made and where I saw our future, but it's also filled with pain. I haven't used the master bathroom since I found my husband there. I can't go in there. I see his body, even though I know it's not there. My heart races from simply touching the doorknob. Instead, I use the one in the hallway, where no memories haunt me.

I close the door with tears in my eyes. No matter what the last few months have brought into our lives, this was home.

Angie leans against my car door with her sunglasses over her eyes, even though it's overcast. "Hey." She attempts a smile.

"This isn't forever," I say the words with such conviction I almost believe them. "I'll be back."

Angie steps forward. "I know."

"I swear I will. I want updates on the bakery, even though I'm not an owner anymore." It was the first thing I had to sell. Since we aren't really profitable, there wasn't much to make off the deal, but it got me through until now.

"It will always be part yours!" she admonishes me.

"Tell Patty to lay off the extra sugar. Remind Beth that she has to make smaller batches for the banana cupcakes," I ramble, trying to avoid saying goodbye. "Oh, and get a dog or something so you don't become a recluse."

She smirks and wipes away the tears under her glasses. "I remember when you showed up from bumfuck Tennessee. You had your cowboy boots, painted-on jeans, and your hair was . . . well." We both laugh. "You had the year we don't talk about, and then you met Todd. I remember wishing we could be sisters. I never knew it would come true. I'm sorry I couldn't help you. I would give anything to keep you here. You're my best friend."

A tear falls from behind her glasses and I step closer. "You're my best friend, too. You're my sister. And I know you want us to be here. Lord knows I don't want to go back there. But I don't regret anything. Even if I knew it would've been this way . . . I wouldn't change anything."

Her arms wrap around me as sadness falls around us. The blanket of despair has been covering us for too long. "Promise me that you'll call once a week. And that I can come visit."

"I promise." A tear falls from my eye. "And I'll be back as soon as I can."

"Anytime you need to come here, I'll make room. Who needs a living room?"

We both giggle, and it hits me . . . I may not see her for a long time. I don't know when I'll be able to afford to make the trip. I have enough money to get to Tennessee and that's about it. There's so much to tell her. Things I never got a chance to say.

"Listen." I wait until she looks up before I continue, "You need to open your heart. I know that dickhead broke it, but let it heal. Don't work too hard, take some time to enjoy things. Also, your hair looked better brown. Fix that." I wink.

"Asshole."

"You saved me when my world fell apart before. You're doing it again whether you know it or not."

"I think you have that backward, my friend."

She smiles before pulling me into her arms. "Take care of yourself. I already miss you and the boys."

Now it's my turn to cry. "I wish . . ."

"Me too."

"I'll call you soon."

We hug once more before I get in my car that was paid off a year ago. Thank God for that. The boys wave as we leave the past behind us, only to have to come face to face with my childhood. I watch the house I built a family in, along with the life I thought I would have, fade away in the rearview mirror.

~

"Are we there yet?" Logan asks for the hundredth time.

"If you ask me again, I'm going to tie you to the roof," I grumble as we cross the Tennessee state line.

"Do it again!" Cayden taunts. They then begin to annoy each other, which drives me crazy.

We drive for hours before we enter Belford County. The knots in my stomach constrict with each passing mile. The place is beautiful. It's quaint, loving, and all up in your business. It's the quintessential small town. Memories of why I left cause me to tense. My fingers grip the wheel as the muscles in my back squeeze tighter. Being here brings the memories front and center. I can feel the air getting heavy. I keep telling myself we had no choice and that it's just until we can get on our feet.

My mother and father didn't hesitate to ask us to come live with them when I told them about our financial situation. My childhood home sits on over four hundred acres of land with a house that could fit practically everyone that lives in the town. Daddy built it himself from close to nothing. His parents owned the land, but he vowed to give Mama a place to be proud of. When I was born, they finished the first round of renovations. Each time Daddy could, he built her more.

Driving into town, I see a few store owners come to their windows. I try not to slink down in my seat. They most likely knew I was coming home the minute Mama hung up. While she's not the town gossip, there's no doubt she'd be singing this from the rooftops. Her baby girl and grandbabies moving here is everything she ever wanted.

"Boys." I call their attention. "We're here."

"What is that?" They both have their noses to the glass as they take in where I grew up. "It looks like an old Western movie!"

I laugh. "It's downtown."

Cayden groans and puts his headphones back on. Logan keeps watching as thirty seconds later we're out of downtown. "That's it?"

"Yup," I state matter-of-factly. "Don't blink or you'll miss it."

"Where's Target? Or the mall?"

I sigh. "About four towns over." The life they know is gone. Out here, there's no hours of video games, but there's also no risk of ever being bored. When you live on a ranch, there's always work to be done. I grew up reining in cattle, harvesting the eggs, and milking cows. They've never seen a horse, let alone ridden one.

Logan's voice rises a notch. "Four towns? Mom! What if we need something?"

"Well." I chuckle as I speak, "You wait until we can take the ride."

Cayden mumbles under his breath about hating life. When I told him we had to move, he called his best friend and asked if he and Logan could live there. Of course that was never going to happen, but he pleaded. Leaving their friends and school hasn't been something either one has accepted well. I sympathize—it's not easy for me either.

I get to the edge of the driveway and park. "Townsend Cattle Ranch," Logan reads the large white sign above us. "Are we going to be Townsends now?"

"No," I say immediately. "You're a Benson, always will be. Your daddy gave you that name. It's a gift you'll never have to return." I smile in the mirror. That's something Mama said to Cooper when we were kids.

Logan lets out a sigh of relief. "I didn't know."

Cayden removes his headphones as I turn in my seat to face them. "Listen, I know you're not happy about this. It's been a lot of change for you in a short amount of time. But there's a lot of fun

things to do around here." Lie. "And the schools aren't bad."
Another lie. "Plus, you'll make some new friends that might even
be better than the ones you left." God, I'm getting good at this.
"Promise me you'll *try* to make the best of it."

They both nod. Whether or not they actually will is another
story. I put the car in drive and head down the longest road I've
ever been on. Each inch feels like a mile. The rotations of the
wheels have a link to the pit in my stomach, forcing it to tighten as
we move.

Mama and Daddy are on the porch watching us approach.
"There you are!" Mama yells out as we exit the car.

"Mama, Daddy." I smile as I look at my house. I've only been
here once since I left seventeen years ago. The boys were less than
a year old, and we visited for no more than two days. The entire
town told stories about how my ex and I were destined to be
together in front of Todd. It was extremely uncomfortable. After
that, Todd paid for my parents to visit us twice a year. "You painted," I muse.

"It's been almost eighteen years, Presley. Of course we
painted."

It amazes me how my mother can scold me while she kisses
my cheek.

The boys look around in wonder. They knew I was raised in
the country, but I think their version of country and mine are a
little different. Todd thought we lived in a rural area in Pennsylvania. I would laugh and roll my eyes. These boys have no idea.

Logan and Cayden assault my father with questions.

"Do you have a lot of horses, Papa?"

"Can we ride a horse?"

"Do you eat the cows you have here?"

"Is this a petting zoo?"

"Does the rooster wake you up or do you have electricity?
What about Wi-Fi?"

"Boys, boys." I place my hands on their shoulder. "Easy. Yes,
we have electricity. Yes, we have a few horses, and Papa doesn't
kill the cattle here, he sells them." Then they kill them. Minor

detail. "Let's get our stuff inside and then I can show you around, okay?"

"Presley!" Cooper calls out as he walks toward us. I haven't spoken to my brother much. I'm praying this won't be too awkward.

"Cooper!" I smile as he gets closer. I walk toward him and he yanks me into his arms. He's freaking huge! "Holy crap, are you bench-pressing the cows? You're like a bear." I don't remember him being this tall. I'm not short, but he's well over six foot. His chest is wide and his arms are insane. My little brother is all grown.

"I'm sorry to hear about your husband. I would've been there, but I had to run the ranch."

I look at the ground and wish people would stop talking about him. I'm tired of people's sympathy. I don't want to be this grieving widow who's lost and sad. No one can even begin to understand the anger I have, especially since I have to hide the truth. I can't help but hate him for what he's done to the three of us. He set off a bomb and left me with the fallout. "I understand, Coop. Thanks."

He tickles my sides and becomes animated again. "But look at you, all city girl."

"Look at you, all country," I say, giggling.

He laughs. "Not all of us got to experience life outside of here. Someone had to run the ranch when you left to be with your boyfriend."

Well, that took a lot less time than I thought. "Cooper."

"You left, and I stayed. It's just the truth."

I roll my eyes and bite my tongue. I have a feeling the teeth impressions I'll have on my tongue will become permanent. Cooper got the short end of the stick according to him. When I left, he was forced to take over the ranch. He had big dreams of leaving here and moving to a city. He was smart and could've done it, but then Daddy needed to retire, and I left. He's resented me ever since.

"It wasn't like that," I try to defend myself.

He shakes his head. "You ran off with him and never came back. It's exactly like that." Cooper walks toward Mama who watches me with sad eyes.

Looks like it's going to be a long few months . . . or longer.

Six

I can't sleep. I stare at the ceiling in my room. The same room I lived in for eighteen years. I figured they would've at least taken my posters off the wall, but no. It's a time warp in here. This whole house is. The boys almost cried when they saw their room. Flowers everywhere, on the walls, the sheets, the border . . . you'd think a florist vomited in there.

I glance at the clock—five a.m.—might as well get up.

I head downstairs to where Mama already has breakfast started. "Mornin', Mama."

"Mornin', sugar. You sleep well?"

"I did. What's for breakfast?" It's a lie, I'm getting really good at them now. If she knows, she doesn't say anything, though.

She whips something in the bowl and my stomach rumbles. This will be the one thing about being home that won't suck. "Just the normal things. Go on out to the coop and grab us some eggs."

"Okay." I've always hated the chickens. There was one hen who is evil and always tried to attack me. Mama used to make me go if she needed a good laugh.

I grab the basket that has sat by the back door since I can remember and head out toward the animals who are not my friends. It's like time has stood still out here too. Everything is the same, and it makes me want to scream.

I grab a half dozen eggs with no drama and head back to the house.

"Presley?" A deep, familiar voice stops me in my tracks.

My heart pounds, and my blood runs cold. It can't be him. I turn slowly, praying it isn't. He shouldn't be here, not here, not now. Slowly my gaze lifts and relief floods me. It's not the blue eyes and dark brown hair I expect to see. Instead, it's a pair of honey eyes and light brown hair that I'd know anywhere. The one person in this town I actually am happy to see. "Wyatt!" My smile is automatic.

"I'll be damned! I thought that was you, but I didn't know you were visiting!" He rushes forward and then hoists me in the air. He smiles while shaking his head. "I can't believe it. Presley Townsend in the flesh."

"Benson now." I laugh as he squeezes me tight. "What are you doing on the ranch?" I ask as he puts me down.

"I'm the new foreman."

I slap his chest in excitement. "Foreman? Here?" That makes no sense.

"I didn't want to work for my family, so I came to work for your brother. You know how that goes, don't ya?"

Wyatt Hennington has been a part of my life since birth. His mama and mine have been best friends since they were kids. He's also the younger brother of the boy I ran away with. The boy who gave me my first engagement ring, my first broken heart, and the reason I never wanted to return to this town.

"That's . . . " I struggle to find the right thing to call it. "Understandable, I guess?"

Wyatt shrugs with his irresistible grin still in place. "I think it's good."

I fight against asking the next logical question, but I don't want to know. "How are your parents?"

He laughs as if he knows what I'm avoiding. "Good. They're traveling a lot since they retired."

"That's good. And Trent?"

"Trent's the sheriff now."

"Sheriff?" I ask in disbelief. "They let him be in charge of people?"

"Who would've thought, right? He's still an idiot, though."

"Oh, I'm sure that's true." We both chuckle. "Still, to give the kid who stole a cop car when we were kids a gun and a badge . . . is crazy."

Wyatt shakes his head. "I figure he liked pretending he was a cop so much that he decided to do it for real."

"Sounds like Trent."

"Yup." He rocks on his heels. "And Zachary is—"

"Glad everyone's doing well." I cut him off. Right now my heart can't handle hearing his name. When I think about Zach, I think about college. When I think about college, I think about Todd piecing me back together after I was shattered. Then I think about how Todd went and shattered me himself. It's better to not think.

"Right," he draws out the word. "You lost your accent."

"Well, seventeen years in the North will do that to you." I smile. "God, it's so good to see you."

Wyatt's eyes go from my head to my toes and he smiles. "You look good too, Pres. You doin' all right up there in the big city?"

He doesn't know? "I'm . . . well . . . I'm sorta back here for a while."

I shouldn't be surprised that he doesn't know. Wyatt was always the guy who ignored the town gossip. He's the youngest of the Hennington brothers and was always into trouble. He and Trent were always creating some kind of town uproar while—the other brother—was on the field. And I was in the bleachers.

"I feel like I'm missing something." His light brown eyes study me as if he were trying to solve a puzzle.

"I honestly can't believe no one told you." My mother isn't one to blab anyone's business, but she and my father leaving town for a week would've been big news. Especially if they were heading to the city.

His brow furrows. "Heard what?"

I might as well get it out now. "Four months ago, my husband passed away."

He steps forward and places his hands on my shoulders. "I'm so sorry, Pres." Wyatt's voice is filled with compassion. "I'd heard something, but you know how it is here. I figured it was bullshit."

I wish that were the case. I shrug him off and let out a heavy sigh. "It's true. He died, and it turns out we were struggling financially. So, I'm here. Back where I swore I'd never be again."

"You know you love it here." His grin tells me he knows I'd rather be homeless.

"Oh, yeah." I roll my eyes. "It's paradise."

He laughs and then raises his brow. "Well, it's something. You should probably get dressed before some of the handlers get here. They're not used to this view."

"Huh?" I look at my tiny shorts and tank top—with no bra. Immediately my hands cross over my chest. "I'm off to a great start."

"I'll see you around, Presley Townsend. Homecoming queen. Thank you for returning and reminding us of your beauty." He clutches his heart and laughs as he walks away.

"Jerk!"

Mama's standing at the door with a blank expression. It's way too early for this. I can feel her eyes studying me. "Wyatt's grown to be a good man." My mother always wished it were Wyatt I loved. Our parents practically tried an arranged marriage.

"Mama," I warn. "Don't."

She smiles with her hands in the air. "I'm not sayin' a thing."

It's what she's not saying that has me worried. She doesn't believe in a woman being without a man. She met my daddy when they were eleven and told him they were going to be together forever. He laughed and walked away. The next day some boy threw a rock at her, he punched him, and they've been together since. Daddy tells it different, but my mother says a woman knows. I can remember feeling the same way at twelve.

Seeing *him* and knowing we'd be married someday. Then he left me. Just like Todd. I'll never do this again.

"It hasn't even been six months since Todd died. I'm in no way ready. I have to battle to get to sleep and I have to pry myself out of bed every morning."

Her hand rests on my forearm. "I'm just sayin' it would be good to have a friend. I feel like there are demons you're battling, sugar. You need to have a shoulder to cry on."

I don't want friends here. I don't want to *be* here. This town will slowly close in on me again. There's no way I'm residing here long enough to warrant trying to be nice to anyone. I have to keep my vision clear. Make some money, get out of the immense debt, and get back to my life.

"I'm not the most popular person here, Mama. And I don't need any friends. I have enough back home."

"This is your home." The hurt in her voice is clear.

I sigh. "I didn't mean . . ."

"Presley, I've been understanding that you're not happy about this. But it'll be better if you make peace with your life now. I'm not happy that Todd dying and you havin' no money is what brought you back to Bell Buckle, but I'd be lyin' if I said I wasn't glad to have you back. I'll let you keep your secrets because every woman has them." She looks away. "Just know I'm here."

"It's not that simple."

My mother's eyes close as she lets out a breath. "I wish you would talk to me. You give me half answers. Your father and I want to help you. Cooper too."

Right.

"Like I said, Mama. I'm here to get on my feet."

"It makes no sense that you lost everything, Presley. Didn't y'all save?"

"Mama, please." I'm not ready to tell her. I'm not ready to admit this to anyone. My parents would never understand this. Hell, I don't understand it. "I don't want to talk about all this. The sooner we can get out of Bell Buckle the better."

"Why do you hate it here so much?" Mama asks with a tinge of anger. "Were we that bad of parents?"

"God, no!" I say quickly. "I never wanted to be a rancher or live out in the country. I wanted to live in the city, have a different life. It wasn't you or Daddy."

"Is it about Zachary? Is he what kept you away all these years?"

My breathing stops at hearing his name. It's been seventeen years since I saw his face, but it still hurts. "No." That's not entirely true, but I won't allow myself to go down a road that has a caution sign glaring at me. Shattered glass, shredded metal, and broken bones are what wait for me if I let my heart go back there. I loved him so much.

Her eyes tell me she doesn't believe me. "You know he—"

"I don't want to hear it." I don't need to hear anything about him. He doesn't exist in my life anymore.

Mama's lips purse and her head shakes. "All right then. Just know that I love you and I'll always be here to listen."

"Thanks, Mama."

"Now," she says, wiping her hands on her apron. "Why don't you whip up those eggs while I get the bacon going?"

Thankful for her dropping the subject, I smile and get to work. Now, to figure out how I'm going to stop everyone I see from bringing him up. That's the thing about young love in a small town—it never dies.

The rest of the day passes with the boys off with Cooper. He promised them a day of fun. They wanted to see the ranch, and Cooper was all too happy to not have to see me. He had big dreams and he blames me for crushing them, but it's time to get over it. We're going to have to deal with this—and soon. I've been going over all the books trying to make sense of Cooper's accounting methods, which is difficult since a lot of his book-keeping is on Post-it notes.

I start tossing around papers, and folders tumble to the ground. Awesome.

As I'm gathering my mess, I hear the screen door shut. "One second," I call out from my spot on the floor.

"You need help, baby girl?"

I stand with my arms full and almost drop them again. "I'm okay, Daddy."

"Are you?"

No. "Yeah, I'm good."

"Okay." He clearly doesn't believe me. "Cooper hasn't done much with this side of the business. I know I'm retired, but would you let me know if he screwed up real bad?"

I don't think that's really why he's here, but it's sweet. My dad and I were always close when I was a kid. I was the only girl, and he hung the moon. "Of course, Daddy. I'll make sense of it soon."

"You were always the one with the brains," he chortles.

"Well." I stop. "Not when it comes to certain things."

Daddy nods with a knowing grin. "Boys were always your downfall, sugar. But I think you got it right with my grandbabies."

Yeah, I sure did. They're great boys with a lot of love to give. "I was lucky with them."

"Nah." He waves his hand. Daddy walks over to a shelf where all my rodeo ribbons and trophies are. "Remember how mad your mama would get when I'd take you out to practice?"

"I do. She would refuse to let you eat anything she cooked for the day."

My mother's sister died when she was a little girl from a riding accident. My mother was dead set against me barrel racing, but my father would sneak me out. It was in my blood, my mind, and it lived deep in my heart. I think my father saw that and knew I would find a way regardless of what my mama wanted.

It was our thing. We'd wake up real early and ride out to the edge of the property. Cooper and Daddy had their hunting and crap, but the bond between me and my father was special. At least I thought so.

My father's eyes pierce me. "I would've gone hungry if it meant I got to see your smile when you rode."

"Daddy," I murmur.

"None of that." He looks away.

I come around the desk, place my hand on his shoulder, and squeeze. "Maybe we could go for a ride?"

His eyes fill with joy as he looks at me.

Finally, after a second he answers, "I think we could arrange something."

"Good." I smile. "Let me know."

"How about tomorrow?" he asks with hope laced in his voice.

"Perfect."

Daddy pulls me into his arms. "I've missed you, darlin'. I missed you so much."

I grab on, holding him close and fighting back the tears. It feels good having a sense of forgiveness between me and my parents. I didn't realize how much I needed it. They love me, and they love the boys. My desire to keep away was never fully about them though. It was about the town, the feeling of failure, and the whispers about how I belonged with Zach. There's not a place I turn here that doesn't remind me of him, which means that my parents, Cooper, and this town are all tied to him. And he made it clear he didn't want to be tied to me when he made the choice to leave me. Now I need to find a new rope to hold on to.

Seven

"Why would you do this, Todd? Why would you choose to leave us like that?"

"I thought I was helping." His sad voice washes over me.

I look at him, only now I see him differently. This time I notice the sadness around his eyes. The way he really doesn't look at me, more like through me. My tears fall when I see the pain I'm feeling reflected back at me.

"It hurts so much. I'm so angry with you," I tell him as we sit on our knees.

Todd sits beside me and cries as well. "I'm angry with me. I wish I could've been a better man. I tried so hard to make things right, but I couldn't do it anymore, Pres. I couldn't keep going."

"Not even for me? Or for Logan and Cayden?" I ask through my sobs.

"I miss them. I knew I would, but I would've failed them far worse if I stayed."

"No!" I shake my head in denial. "You broke us! I don't know how to do this. I've never felt so alone or scared."

His hand rises as if he's going to touch my cheek, but drops it. "You'll be fine, my love. You were always so strong. So beautiful. I left knowing you'd be okay."

"You left us with nothing!" My emotions ping pong back and forth as I try to get my answers. *"I had to leave our home, our lives have been flipped upside down. Do you know what this has done to the boys? You were selfish to think this was the answer. You had options!"*

Todd's tears fall as he listens to me weep. *"I knew you'd hate me. But I knew you'd move on. You'll be fine, Presley."*

"Do you think I'm fine? I'm not fine, Todd! Why didn't you just talk to me?"

His lips purse. *"Would you have listened?"*

These dreams are killing me. Each night it's something. It's been a week since we've been at the ranch and I haven't slept peacefully once. I sit up with tears running down my face—tears of rage.

Rage that he did this.

That he gave me so much and then took it away. I loved him for so long, and now I feel like I never knew him. It would've been difficult for him to face the mess he put us in, but those two boys sleeping in the other room were all the reason he needed.

They don't deserve this. And for the pain he inflicted on them . . . I'll never forgive him.

I grab my phone to check the time. *Ugh, three in the morning.* I'll never be able to fall back asleep. I get up, grab my phone, and head out to walk off the anxiety building inside me.

My mind races with my dream conversation with him. *Would I have listened?* What the hell is that? I comprehend this was a dream and this is all in my mind, but that last line has my stomach in knots.

As my feet carry me, my thoughts begin to settle. My anger abates, and I'm left with the knowledge that it was just a dream. A very vivid dream, but it wasn't real.

I find myself standing in front of the stall of my beautiful horse. "Hi, Casino." I smile as he walks toward the door. "Sorry I haven't been here to see you." His head comes over the opening and I rub his nose. "Aww, I missed you too. You look tired, boy. Are they taking good care of you, huh?"

He's so much older now, as am I, but I can't help but travel back in time. I got him the year before I left for college. I think my parents hoped I would stay close to home for him. I spent hours training him between Zach's ball games.

Life was simple then. School, horses, Zach, and leaving here as soon as I could. I worked hard to get into the college where Zach was on a full ride. I promised him I would go where he went after two years of long distance, we'd have a few years together, and then he'd enter the draft. I kept my end of the deal. Followed through on it all. He promised me eternal love and broke it with one decision. Funny how that works.

I rub Casino's neck, soothing both him and me.

"Well, why don't you saddle him up?" a familiar voice says from behind me.

"You're the foreman." I smile as I turn to see Wyatt. "Isn't that your job?"

His navy blue jeans and white shirt cling to him, and the Stetson on his head makes him look rugged. "Aren't you spunky this morning? What are you doing awake at this hour?"

"I could ask you the same."

"You could. But you've probably guessed I'm coming home from a hot date."

Wyatt was always a playboy. He was young, sexy, and came from the Hennington family line, which bought him about anything he wanted. The same could be said about being a Townsend.

"Couldn't have been too hot if you're standing here talking to me." I challenge him.

Suddenly I remember the last time I saw him. I quickly check to see what I'm wearing, and catch Wyatt doing the same. "I'm not a cuddle after sex kind of guy."

"I figured."

Trent and Wyatt were notorious for breaking hearts. Each naïve girl would swear they'd be the one to tame them. I was the lucky one. Zach is three years older than Wyatt and me. He was always the sensible, loyal, and responsible one of the brothers.

"Let's go for a ride, Presley Mae."

I loathe my damn name. "You do mean horseback, right?"

One can never tell with this lot.

He lets out a long, booming laugh. "Like I would ever dream of that happening. My brother would cut my dick off."

"Your brother has no claim on me."

"Never said he did, darlin'. Never said he did." Wyatt slaps my ass as he walks past and saddles the horses.

"Pig."

Once he's done, he hands me the reins for a horse I've never ridden. "You getting on the horse or are you gonna stand there and look at it?" he says from the back of our largest horse.

"I haven't ridden in a long time," I admit with fear.

"Your instincts will kick in. Hop up," Wyatt encourages.

He's probably right. I put my foot in the stirrup and get seated. "What's the horse's name?"

"Shortstop."

I inwardly groan. "Of course it is." Wyatt chuckles, knowing I already hate this horse. "Surprised you didn't give me one named Zach."

Zach was a shortstop. My fantastic, talented, gorgeous, base-ball playing, and going somewhere boyfriend. Scouted by every college and promised the world. I loathe baseball. It stole every-thing from me.

"Thought about it but figured you'd kick it too much."

"I'm about to kick you."

"I might like it." He winks and then heads out of the barn.

I rub the horse's neck and familiarize myself with him. "All right, Shortstop. I'm Presley. I haven't ridden in a while, so be gentle, okay?"

Shortstop bobs his head, and I smile. I exit the barn, hoping that maybe I can breathe again.

Wyatt doesn't say anything as we move through the fields in the moonlight. He silently walks beside me on his horse, allowing me some time to quietly reflect. He always knows when to push and when to back off. It's the one thing I love most about him.

We ride along the property for a while, the sun is peeking over the horizon. No words are spoken until we reach a field I know well. "What do you say?" I can hear the dare in his voice.

I bite my lip as I think about it. If we allow the horses to open up, it'll require some galloping, which I haven't done in seventeen years. I can be scared or I can plunge in head first. "Let's go."

Once we break through the clearing, we get a few yards out and Wyatt nods. My nerves flutter as the horse pushes through. It's been so long. But I remember the feelings as if it were yesterday. I close my eyes and draw in a deep breath before the trees part. As I exhale, Shortstop flies.

I smile as I hold the reins and lean forward. My legs move with his gallop and I feel alive. My heart can't contain any pain as I fly. Each push of his legs sends me to a place where there is no sadness. No death haunting my thoughts, just air. The struggle to breathe lifts. All I am is free. Freedom breaks the chains that have bound me. Chains that have crippled me.

We ride for miles through the Tennessee countryside. I glance over and see Wyatt staring back. He smiles as if he can read my thoughts. He pulls back, slowing his horse to a trot, and I follow.

"There she is," he says innocently. I know Wyatt, and nothing he says is offhanded. He's a man who says what he means.

"You see too much."

"I know you. I've known you since we were infants. So yeah, I see you. You going to tell me what's really going on?"

I jerk back on the reins and the lightness I felt moments ago dissipates. "I'm just trying to get my bearings."

Wyatt doesn't say anything, but I can feel the air thicken. "I've never known you to give up." I look over quickly and his eyes stay on mine. "Don't start now. Fight hard, because there's nothing you can't do."

So many thoughts float through my mind, but I can't seem to get them to come out. I want to cry, scream, confess, and run as fast as I can. I don't want to feel anymore. Why can't I be numb?

Isn't there a way for me to hold onto that feeling of weightlessness? Because I really need it. I deserve it.

"Not today. Give me today," I say and then spur the horse forward.

As we race back toward the ranch, there is no peace. The high that I was chasing is gone. Freedom is an intoxicating emotion that I want to drown in. But I'm not free. I've been condemned to live back in Bell Buckle.

Wyatt follows me to the barn and holds the horses as I climb down. "Thanks for this," I say, touching his arm.

He smiles and tips his head. "Anytime, Cowgirl."

"You know, you're one of the few things I missed."

He laughs. "I always knew you liked me best."

"I wouldn't go that far."

"I'm glad you're back. I know you're not, and I get why you stayed away." He pauses for just a second. "But I'm glad you're in Bell Buckle, where you belong. Next we'll work on getting you to smile more."

"Don't get too comfortable with me being around. I'm not staying forever." I turn and head out.

"Presley?" Wyatt's voice stops me.

"Yeah?"

"There's not a soul who doesn't have a skeleton of some sort, but the longer you keep it locked up, the longer it's going to hold you down."

Tears pool and I fight back the words. I want to blurt it out. Tell him, or hell, *anyone*, the truth. No one understands the visions that I can't stop seeing. His eyes. The way he didn't move. The black bag he left in. It's there all the damn time. I want it to go away, but it won't.

"I want—" I start. "I can't yet. I want to, but I can't."

He nods. "Well, anytime you wanna ride my stallion . . . feel free to let me know."

"Oh, my God." I laugh. Leave it to Wyatt to soften the mood.

"That's what they call me."

"What lucky girls." I snort in disgust.

"Hey," he says as an afterthought. "What are you doing tonight?"

I pretend to have to think. "Not a damn thing."

"Be ready at seven. I need someone to take a ride with me."

I look at him as if he sprouted a third head. That's all I need. Being seen in this damn town riding around with another Hennington brother. No, thank you. "On second thought, I *am* busy."

"Get un-busy."

"It doesn't work that way. I have the boys."

Cooper's voice breaks our mini argument. "I've got the boys. You need to leave this property before people say we're holding you hostage."

I look at my brother, wishing I could punch him in the balls. What is with the damn men in my life? All of them think they know what's best for me. Pains in my damn ass.

"I'm not up to it."

"Good," Wyatt says and claps his hands. "I'll see you later."

"I said no."

"I don't accept."

"I'm not going," I say with my arms crossed.

Wyatt steps forward. "I've carried your tiny ass out of that bedroom window once before. I'll do it again. Be ready or you're going in whatever you're wearing." He taps my nose and saunters off with me scowling.

There's not a doubt in my mind he'll do it. And not a freaking person in my house who would stop him. Damn him.

Eight

"Presley! Wyatt is here!" Mama calls out.

"So is this a date?" Cayden asks.

"No. Not at all," I reassure him. There's no way I want to date anyone, and certainly no one from here. I'll never go through that again. Besides, Wyatt is like a brother to me. "Wyatt is a friend that I went to school with. He just needs someone to go run some errands with."

Logan walks over and then clutches his arms around me. "I miss Daddy."

I cup his face and kiss his nose. "I know, baby. I miss him too."

As angry as I am . . . I still miss him. Sure, throughout the years we had ups and downs like any other couple, but I loved him. Todd understood me. He wasn't the burn-the-sheets type of love, but he was a reliable love. There wasn't a moment I felt like he would abandon me. Until he did.

"I don't want a new dad." Cayden stands to the side with a scowl. "You can't do this."

"Cayden." I walk over to him. "No one said you're getting a new dad. This is a friend. And I don't need your permission."

This isn't easy on them. They've endured a boatload of changes, none of which they asked for. At the same time, I feel like we're all in purgatory. None of us are living. And if I don't start moving forward, they'll never follow. Instead of Wyatt carrying me out of my room, I'm going to walk out on my own.

Cayden shakes his head with a pout on his face. "I hate it here!"

"I know you do. But being around Uncle Cooper is pretty fun. He said you boys have been a big help on the ranch." I bend so I'm eye level with them. "I know how hard it is to live somewhere you don't want to be. I've been where you boys are. It's a big change from home. But I promise, Bell Buckle is a great place to live." For the first time since being here, I feel like maybe this isn't the worst thing that could've happened to us. My parents, my brother, Wyatt, and this ranch could save us all.

"We haven't even left the house! There's nothing to do here! I hate it!" Cayden is by far the angrier of the two. He wears it on his face. Daddy said to let him have his anger. A boy needs it sometimes. I don't know what to think. "I want to go back. I can live with Aunt Angie."

"That's not happening, buddy. This is how it has to be for now."

A tear leaks from his eye. I want to make this better for him. I would take all of their pain and carry it, but I can't. I have to stand strong and hope that by living, they'll do the same. Right now, all they see is me moping around and angry at the world. I'm going to do better for them. "We need to make the best of it. Is it ideal?" I pause. "No. But we have to live here for the foreseeable future. So we have two choices: we make the most of it or we suffer the entire time. You choose."

"Whatever." Cayden crosses his arms while shaking his head.

"I love you both very much, and believe me, I want to be back home too."

"We miss our friends," Logan says. "Cayden is boring."

"I promise you'll make new friends as soon as school starts." Logan looks away with a dejected look on his face. "Will you try a little bit harder?" His back straightens a little, and he nods. "What about you, Cay?" Logan nudges Cayden, but he doesn't look at me. "Cayden?" He looks at the wall, refusing to meet my eyes. "Okay, you can be mad. I won't push you right now, but you are not allowed to be disrespectful to me. I'll let this go now, but we're going to have this talk."

Cayden continues to silently loathe me. I kiss the tops of both their heads and try to keep myself from crying. All of this was so unnecessary. That's all I can think. The catalyst to our new life could've been handled so differently.

I put my dark brown hair in a side braid, put my boots on, and head downstairs. Wyatt sits at the table with my parents. "Damn, I was hoping I was going to have to drag you out."

I roll my eyes. "I'm so sorry to disappoint you."

"There's always next time."

"Ass."

"Presley!" my mother gasps. "I raised you better than that."

If she knew the language that we all used as kids, she'd fall over. "Sorry."

"You should be." Wyatt smirks at me. "I'm so disappointed that the city has ruined my sweet friend."

Now I want to choke him. "Let's go before I change my mind."

He laughs and throws his arm over my shoulder. "You can't say no to me. I know all your games."

After we have driven a few miles, I realize I have no idea where we're going. Wyatt doesn't inform me either, which is typical. I've never been good with this, and he damn well knows it. I swear these boys love to torture me—always have. Zach and Trent would thrive on scaring the shit out of me. Wyatt never did that. Instead, he would give me the silent treatment when I wanted to know something, which was equally frustrating.

He turns into the local bar and every part of me locks. "No way!" I yell and try to figure a way out of this. "No. I'm not going in there. You knew. You knew this is the last place in this damn town I would want to be."

"Rip the Band-Aid off."

"I'm gonna rip something off!" I glare at him.

He shrugs. "Would you rather it be now so they can all stop their bullshit speculating or wait for it to get worse?"

Like I give a shit what they all think. I ball my hands and ignore him.

"We can sit out here and let people talk too. I'm all for steaming up the windows. I have a rep to protect." Wyatt leans back in the seat and puts his hat over his face.

If I weren't me and he weren't him, I wouldn't mind that either. To let myself get lost in the arms of another for just a moment. To feel not so completely alone. Wyatt always has been hot, and when he flashes that smile, girls fawn over him. But Zach was always where my heart was. We had it all, or so I thought. Zach would walk in a room and every part of me would awaken. He was everything, and I was everything to him. Our souls touched when we were around each other. I couldn't see anything but him, which put a damper on any chance Wyatt ever had.

"Fine," I finally say as the windows start to fog. "Let's go."

He grabs my hand. "I'm with you the whole time. But I think you'll be fine."

"Who's going to be here?"

"Just invited some friends." He winks and opens the door.

The entire damn town is here. When I walk in, there are hoots and hollers all around the bar. I smile and duck my head at the unwanted attention. Nothing like being famous in this place. I glare at Wyatt. He's dead meat.

People approach me with arms open as we all reunite. I can't stop smiling at the first to reach me. "If it isn't the town trouble-maker!" Trent Hennington jerks me into his arms and spins me around.

"I'm still in shock they let you have a gun," I say, laughing.

He puts me down and cups my face. "You should be scared."

"Oh, I am."

We both grin. Trent is two years older than Zach. He was always that annoying older brother who thrived on making my life hell. He would sneak in on me and Zach and mess with us. It was his mission to embarrass me, and he often succeeded.

"I won't monopolize you, darlin'. You better stop by this week so you can test out my cuffs."

I snort. "You're still a moron."

"One you love."

"You damn Henningtons need to learn humility," I say. Trent and Wyatt are so full of themselves. It's a wonder anyone talks to them. "Married?"

"Hell no, woman. Chicks dig a badge."

I start to reply but my best friend from high school squeals and looks like she's going to cry. Trent steps back at the sound. "You didn't call!" Grace says as she rushes forward. "I didn't know you were back until Cooper said something." She pulls me close, squeezing as she continues on. "I've missed you so much. It was like you disappeared."

I lean back and smile. "I did. I needed to. I'm sorry though, I should've kept in touch."

"Honey, if I could've done it . . . I would've. But you know how it goes for most of us." I do know. There's safety in staying, and sometimes people can't cut the cord that's holding them. "Tell me why in the hell you came back."

Before I can respond my eyes look toward the bar. Everything stops. My heart. My breathing. My entire world stands still. Zachary Hennington stands there staring at me. He doesn't move and neither do I. A tsunami of memories floods the room. Our first kiss, the first time we made love, the promises, the proposal, the love that filled our lives, and the pain when he left me. Not a muscle on him moves as he looks at me. I can see the questions pass between us.

Is that really you?

How are you?

Why are you here?

Why didn't you call?

Why did you leave me?

Why didn't you come with me?

Where have you been?

Do you feel this?

What does it mean?

Grace shakes my arm, and I want to scream. She must see the panic in my eyes and realizes what's holding my attention. "Did you know?" she asks.

"Know?"

"That he lives here?"

My head is light as I try to comprehend her words. "What do you mean?"

She turns me so I can't see him and loops her arm around mine. "He's been back here for a while now. Probably about eight years or so. He took over his family's business."

"I don't—" I look over and this time he's not alone. A woman with long black hair hangs on his arm. She runs a finger down his cheek and then looks right at me. I nearly choke when I realize who she is—Felicia Hayes. She gives a self-satisfied smile before returning her attention to Zach.

Grace lets a puff out her nose. "She sunk her talons in quickly."

"They're together?" I ask, already knowing the answer. Of all of the people in the world, it had to be her. Although I don't have a right to care. She's the devil, and in some small recess of my heart—he's still mine.

"About five years now. They're not married though, which of course keeps us all talkin'. After that long why wouldn't you? My guess is there's someone else he's still pining for."

I look back over, and he's not there. My heart beats erratically as I look for him. Instead, I see Felicia heading our way.

"Shit. The witch is coming," Grace says as Felicia approaches.

I turn and look at the girl I never wanted to lay eyes on again. She's aged but is still pretty. We both appraise each other in an instant. Her hair is almost jet black and hangs down right past her shoulders, bangs frame her emerald eyes, and she's definitely had implants.

"Hello, Presley." Her sweet Southern voice does nothing to cover the bitch in her.

"Hello, Felicia." The smile on her face is fake, but then again, so is mine.

She looks over at Grace with a scowl. "Grace."

"Bitch," Grace replies without hesitation.

This is another reason I vowed never to return. Felicia Hayes is the devil. I swear the girl has horns. Her life's mission is to make people miserable. If anyone is happy, they are a target. I can't imagine living with a black heart.

She steps forward with a smug grin. "I heard you were back in town, and I couldn't believe it. Bell Buckle hasn't been the same without you here."

"It was tough staying away so long. I mean, living in the city with so much to do." I shrug. She always talked about wanting to leave too. She planned to marry her way out of here, preferably with my then fiancé. I never understood her need for rivalry when it came to Zach.

"I bet you were just lovin' your perfect life. Which brings me back to wondering why you're here now. Things not work out for you?"

It takes every ounce of control I have not to slap her. She's always been so high and mighty. She spent our entire childhoods trying to bring someone down. I never understood why she was so hateful. It seems that time has only intensified that trait. "I guess you could say not."

Her shoulder lifts as she turns her head to the side in a shrug. "So sad."

I could tell her that my husband died. But she wouldn't care. Her fake sympathy is the last thing I want or need. I won't give her ammunition to use against me later.

"Well, Grace and I have some catching up to do," I say dismissively.

"Oh." She looks over at the bar where Zach is standing. "I'm sure you do. Zach and I were saying a few weeks ago how much we've missed you."

"Bless your heart." I clutch my chest. "I'm so honored you all were thinkin' of me," I reply with heavy sarcasm.

"I bet you were." Felicia turns and walks away.

Looks like some people never change, although I didn't expect much from a heartless wench. The thing about this town is that trying to avoid someone is like trying to dodge the rain—it's impossible.

Grace and I chat a little, a lot of people come say hello, and I begin to relax. Trent gets me to dance with him for a slow song, but I spend half the time looking over his shoulder at Zach. I can't believe he's here. If I'd known, I would've never come back, which is probably why no one told me.

I head back to the table where Grace is sitting. Wyatt is flirting with some bimbo from another town—typical.

"So why aren't you married?" I ask, noticing she has no ring.

She shrugs and holds up her left hand. "I'm picky."

We laugh and she tells me all about the guy she has been talking to. I can almost pretend that my life isn't a mess right now. The atmosphere of the bar allows me to forget for a bit.

"Is he from here?" I ask.

"Pres." Grace's eyes nearly bug out of her head.

"What?" Her gaze is locked on something behind me, and I can see it in her eyes. He's here.

"Presley." His deep voice slides my name out like silk. I fight my body from responding like it wants to. He can't have this control. I won't let him.

"Zachary." I turn and struggle to keep it together.

He's the same boy I fell in love with at twelve. His eyes still hold the same intensity when he looks at me. My fingers tingle as Zach stands before me. He's paralyzed me with one look. His light brown hair is a little shorter, his five o'clock shadow makes him more rugged, and his body is so much more filled out. Age has only made him better than I remember.

Grace clears her throat. "I'll let you two catch up."

I try to grab her arm, but she moves too quickly.

"You look great, Pres." He smiles, and I fight the urge to slap him. I don't look great. I don't feel great. I'm a mess, and I'm trying to find a way to get up in the mornings. But there's not a snowball's chance in hell I'm telling him that. The Zach I knew would've already seen that. "How are you?" he asks.

I have a voice somewhere, but I can't seem to get it to cooperate. "Okay," I murmur. Damn it. *Pull it together, Presley. You're a grown ass woman who doesn't need or want to ever be hurt like that again.* "You?" Great. One word is all I can manage.

"I'm doing good. Wyatt said you were back in town, but I didn't believe him. You were pretty clear about never coming back."

Wyatt. That son of a bitch. He knew this was going to happen. "I sure was. Wonder why?"

"Right." He's thrown off by something. Probably my hostility. But he continues our very uncomfortable conversation. "I thought about stopping by the ranch. I didn't think you wanted to see me, though."

I let out a heavy breath. "I didn't know you were here, Zach. He failed to mention that, as did everyone else. If I had known . . . " I trail off while I collect myself a little more. "I don't know. I'm kind of surprised right now. I didn't expect to see you."

I didn't want to see him either. I never wanted to lay my eyes on him again. There wasn't a doubt in my mind that he'd affect me this way. It's always been like this for me. I've never been able to control my heart where Zach is concerned. He has some kind of special hold on me.

"We should talk."

There's nothing to talk about.

"Why are you in Bell Buckle?" I ask with an edge to my voice.

"Blew out my shoulder," he says, and I want to laugh. I literally want to laugh in his face. He broke my heart. He left me in Maine to go play pro baseball and winds up back here. "I came back to rehab it, but ended up settling here when my dad had a stroke."

Felicia slithers behind him, the whole time watching me. "There you are, baby." Her fingers slowly glide up his arm before reaching his shoulder. "I was hoping we'd get to talk to you together, Presley. I was telling Zach how long it's been since the three of us were in the same room. Of course the dynamic has changed a little now."

I let out a short laugh. "Yup. It has."

Zach's eyes stay on me. He doesn't even acknowledge her. "There's a lot that's changed."

Felicia rests her head on his arm. He looks at her and then back to me. She perks right up. "I would love to have lunch or something. Wouldn't that be fun, Presley? We could talk all about your life and how Zach and I are doing."

"You know." I let out a dramatic sigh. "I'm really busy these days."

"I'm sure you are."

I clench my fists, ready to let out months of hostility, but Zach interjects. "Felicia."

She, of course, doesn't take well to him defending me. "Really, Zachary?" She rips her arm away before raking her fingers through her hair.

Wyatt comes to stand next to me and tosses his arm over my shoulder, hauling me against his side. "There you are, Cowgirl. I need to put one of those tracking things on you."

Felicia snorts. "Like one of the cows."

I want to claw her eyes out. Wyatt must sense it because his hand clasps my shoulder. "I meant to ask you, Felicia," he says with indifference. "Did you get what you wanted for your anniversary? You know, the day after Presley got back in town?"

"Why don't you grab us a few beers?" Zach urges Felicia.

She shoots daggers at him. I have a feeling I'm missing something. "What?" she whines. "You're kidding me?"

Wyatt tugs me closer. "Grab us one too, would you?"

"Fuck you," she snips before turning to Zach. "Babe, let's go back to the bar."

I glance at Zach, whose eyes are zeroed in on Wyatt's hand. He rubs up and down, and I turn into him a little more. I'm being infantile. I'm fully aware of this. I'm nothing to Zach, and he's nothing to me. We're just two old lovers who are now face to face. Of course, the history between us could fill a library, but he's moved on. I've moved on. I have two boys and a life to get back to. I wish he weren't here, though, and I wish more than anything I didn't feel this pit in my stomach.

Wyatt coughs and waves his hand in front of his brother's face. "Earth to Zach."

"What?"

Felicia's lips slant down, and I fight back a smile. She's pissed. "I said let's go. But you were staring off into space."

Zach looks at her and then back to Wyatt and me.

"You should go, Zach." Wyatt smiles and kisses my cheek. "Presley is my hot date, and I need a dance before someone else tries to swoop on in."

My eyes widen when he says date. Zach zeroes in on that too. "Date?" he asks.

"Well, yeah. She's single. I'm single. That doesn't bother you, does it, brother?" Wyatt goads him.

He looks at me and shakes his head. "Of course not. All I've ever wanted is for her to be happy."

If I hadn't known Zachary my entire life, I might actually believe the bullshit he just spewed. There's nothing he likes about this. My being here, his brother touching me, him having to see me —it's all eating him up, and I'm glad. I hope this makes him hurt because the scars he left from ripping my heart apart are starting to ache.

"Zach!" Felicia practically yells. "Now!"

I can see the struggle in his eyes. He watches me before letting out a sigh. "Have a good night."

"You too, buddy," Wyatt says to his back.

Once again, Zach walks away.

Now to decide how many ways I can kill Wyatt. He knew this was going to happen. It was bad enough seeing Zach, but seeing him with Felicia—torture.

"Dance with me." I step out of his grasp.

"I'm about to pay for this, aren't I?"

"Yup." I turn without another word.

We head off to the dance floor and a part of me crumbles

again. Wyatt takes my hand in his and pulls me against his body. "Don't knee me in the balls or something, please."

Our bodies move to the music as he leads me around the floor. He's lucky I haven't stomped on his feet. "Why would you let me walk in like this?" My voice is filled with anger. "How could you not tell me?"

He spins me as our feet shuffle in time. "Would you have come?"

"No! That's the damn point." I shove his hand, and he laughs.

"Look, you were going to see him eventually. This town is way too small, and this way, Trent and I were here."

"I'm so mad at you. You have no idea. You should've warned me. You should've told me he was here. If you were my friend," I pause, "I wouldn't have been blindsided."

He shakes his head, clearly not agreeing. "I've always been your friend. I'll always be your friend. But you've got a thick head, and sometimes you're going to have to trust me." Wyatt looks over toward the bar and smirks. "Right now, my brother is ready to rip my arms off and feed them to me." I glance over where Zach is shooting daggers at Wyatt as we dance. Wyatt's hands move lower toward my ass as he spins us again, breaking my view. "Payback's a bitch."

"That's what this is?"

Wyatt's light brown eyes bore into mine. "I would never use you for payback. Ever. I wouldn't think of you that way. You'd be the reward." My breath hitches, and I try to decipher what he means. Is he saying he thinks of me as more? Does he have feelings for me still? No. He couldn't. He must sense my panic, because he continues, "I'm just saying this isn't some game. Your friendship isn't something I'd fuck up for fun."

"I know that."

"Good."

When the music stops, he bends in a dramatic bow. "I'm still pissed."

He chuckles. "You'll get over it. Just like you're over him." His chin raises in the direction of the bar. I'm a fool if I look, but I've always been stupid when it comes to Zach. He leans against the railing, staring at me while Felicia vies for his attention. When our gazes lock, everything disappears.

There's no one else in the room, this town, or this world right now.

Zach and I might be over, but my heart doesn't seem to care. I'm deluding myself if I think otherwise.

But I'll never go there again.

I remember why I'm here. The reason my life is now on the path I'm traveling. Zach left, I met Todd, and this is the consequence.

Nine

I awake the next morning with a killer headache. It was exhausting trying to avoid Zach all night. I ducked out pretty early. Thankfully Grace offered to take me home.

Not wanting to wallow in my fury of conflicting emotions, I decide to head into town to get a few office supplies. I'm lucky that most of the town is at church so I can get around undetected.

Or maybe not.

"Oh, my God! Presley?" a woman shrieks as I exit my car. "Is that you?"

I turn to see one of my high school girlfriends. "Emily Young!" I pull her into a hug. "You look amazing!" Her blonde hair hangs to the middle of her back, and she's ridiculously skinny. She was always pretty, but she's stunning now.

"Thanks." She fixes her shirt. "I've been singing up in Nashville, so lookin' good kind of helps get you a gig in that town."

"That's awesome. I know you loved to sing when we were kids."

She sang in every play, chorus, and at church for as long as I can remember. Her mother and mine are close friends. Well, everyone who's the same age here are close friends.

Emily shrugs. "I can't seem to stop. It's my passion."

We start to walk down the sidewalk. "That's really great, Em. I'm so happy you've found something you love."

"Thanks." She smiles. "What about you? What the *hell* are you doing back in Bell Buckle?"

Oh, just trying to not go insane. "Had some things happen, needed a change." I don't want to explain it anymore.

"Good for you. Oh, my God!" Her voice gets very dramatic. "Have you seen Zach?" Her eyes alight with wonder. "He's gotten *so* good looking. I mean, he's with the town bitch, but." She sighs. "Now that you're back . . ."

Now that I'm back what? He's got his girlfriend. I've got my miserable life. End of story.

"Did I mention I have two boys that are almost eleven now?" I try to throw her off the topic.

She stops and stands in front of me. "Oh, nice try, Presley Townsend. You're not going to give me the questions with a question thing. You know you can't pull that crap down here."

I sigh and decide to give her a tiny piece of information. "I saw him. He was with Felicia. We said hello, I said goodbye."

I have to remember to answer only the question. I don't know how anyone tries to get away with anything here. My mother could've been a detective with the way she's able to wring out information. You think they're asking one thing, but the follow up question is what gets you.

She smirks. "Were the sparks there?"

"Can we not talk about this?" I beseech her. "I'm sorry, it's been a long day, and I'm out of coffee." And I don't want to think about him. It's bad enough he starred in my dream last night; I don't need that becoming reality.

"Oh, let's go to the coffee shop," she suggests. "We can talk more about all the things you've been doing since you've been gone."

Yay! Not.

"Sounds great."

We get some coffee, which immediately makes me feel more human. Everyone looks as I walk in, and I hear the whispers. God,

I miss Philly. At least there I could walk into a Starbucks and no one would even notice.

"You should come to Nashville soon. I have a few gigs lined up," Emily says as she sips her coffee.

"I would love that."

"I'm sure this is a tough change from the city life."

I laugh. "That's an understatement."

"Even though you were raised here?"

"It's different from what I remember. I've become so used to having everything close. The boys have had a major culture shock."

"I bet."

We spend time filling each other in on our lives, and people stare as if I'm an apparition. My mother had to have told her friends. It baffles me that anyone is shocked at this point. Then again, I've been pretending it wasn't real by staying at the ranch.

"I need to head out." Emily checks her watch. "I hope you and Zach get a chance to talk."

"Em, it's over. It's been over for almost two decades." I wish my heart would accept that. Seeing him again, knowing he's close, has me all torn up inside.

It's like I'm fourteen all over again and he's asking me to go on our first horseback ride. The assured grin he wore, the tight jeans that made his butt look great, and the way his eyes would convey everything he wouldn't say. We were so young, so in love, and so idealistic.

"Sure, it is. You know, this town isn't ready to believe that. We all watched you both. There's not a single memory I have without you two in it. Your love is the kind people write songs about."

Great, my life is a country song. I'm a widow, living on a ranch, driving a truck, and the long-lost "love of my life" and I are face to face. All I need is a dog.

"I think you all remember things very different. And we're not in love anymore. Besides, if our love was so special, we would still be together."

Emily grabs my hand. "I'm serious, Pres. You'll see. Y'all are soul mates."

I give her hand a squeeze as I shake my head. "There's no such thing."

She stands and grins. "I'm going to pretend I didn't hear that."

I get out of my seat and give her another hug. "I think it's time everyone lets it go."

"Whatever. Love doesn't let go, it grows stronger. I'll see you soon?" she asked, leaning in to give me a kiss on the cheek.

"Definitely."

I open the door to leave and see the truck I'd know anywhere. There's no way I want to see him. I yank my sweatshirt hood over my head and rush to my car. The more I can avoid him, the safer my heart will be.

⁓

A knock on my office door causes me to stop working. "Zach?" I push my glasses up the bridge of my nose and stand. I should've known avoiding him wasn't really going to work when he can roll up any ol' time he wants. It was only a matter of time.

"Sorry to stop by without callin', but the other night wasn't exactly the best place for us to talk." He removes his hat and tosses it on the chair. "I saw you in town yesterday trying to be incognito. Figured we should try to be civil."

Civil? He can't just show his face when he wants. He doesn't belong here. I don't want to see him at all, much less in my home, the one place that's my safe haven. Damn him for not taking the fucking hint.

"Your mother said you were out here. She didn't throw something at me, so I took that as a good sign."

"What are you doing here?" I stand, slamming my hand on the desk. "My mother may not have thrown anything because she's a proper Southern woman, but I'm not anymore. I've spent enough time in the North to not give a shit if I pelt you in the head with a stapler!" I grab it off the desk and rear back.

"Whoa! Whoa!" he says with his hands raised. "I'm not coming to start anything. I just want to see how you are. I've missed you."

"Asshole!" I throw the stapler at his head. "You don't get to miss me!"

He ducks as it makes a loud bang against the wall. Zach's eyes widen as his lips turn up. "Seems all those years watching me play ball taught you how to throw."

I grab the next thing I see. "You apparently sucked at teaching!"

"Felicia and I wanted to invite you over for dinner."

He has lost his damn mind.

Zach lets out a sigh and moves closer. "I know it could be awkward, but I figured if . . ."

"If what? That there's a chance we could be friends? Hang out even? You need your head examined if you think that'll happen." I don't know if maybe he forgot how we ended things.

"Pres," he chides.

"Don't 'Pres' me! You have some nerve showing up here."

"It was a long time ago." I want to sock him in the face.

"Leave," I demand.

Zach walks closer and crosses his arms across his chest.

"I'm not leaving until we settle this. I want us to get things out in the air."

"Fine." I grab the paper clip holder and toss it. I miss again. "That was in the air." I look for something else to launch at him.

"Stop throwing things!" He moves closer with his hands raised in surrender.

I glare at him. "Don't tell me what to do. We have nothing to say to each other."

Zach half laughs as he grips my arms. "I think there's a lot to say, Pres. It's been a long time." He releases my arms and gives me a look that says: "Don't throw anything."

"I have nothing to say to you."

"If we're both living here now, I think we owe it to each other to air out the past."

I fight the hundreds of snarky comments that sit on my tongue. "Right. Just like that. We can hash out the fact that you cut me to pieces faster than a hot knife through butter. What was I thinking?" I clutch my chest in mockery. "Please, by all means, sit." I motion for the chair in front of him. "Let's air out the fucking past."

He looks at me with a smug grin. "You haven't lost your sarcasm." Zach moves around to the chair in front of my desk and sits slowly, keeping his eyes on me. At least I have him scared I'm going to chuck something at him. Next thing to go flying is my boot.

"I haven't lost my temper either."

"First," he says, leaning forward and resting his elbows on his knees. "I'm truly sorry. I never wanted to hurt you. I loved you so much, and leaving you that day was the hardest thing I've ever done. I've lived my whole life regretting that choice."

I sit back as the air expels from my lungs. "That's what you start off with? For Christ's sake, Zach, let's not waste any time getting to the heavy stuff."

"If I didn't say it now, I don't know if you'd let me have that chance." His fingers run through his hair, which means he's nervous. At least it's not just me. "I've never forgiven myself for hurting you."

I roll my eyes. "You didn't hurt me. You killed me. But that's all in the past. I'm over it, and you."

"Was the stapler itchin' to be thrown?"

"Are you saying I'm not over you? Do you think I've spent all this time pining for you?" I ask with my arms crossed. Idiot.

"I didn't mean—" He stops. "I didn't think you were."

Years I've wanted to hear those words. I wanted to know how it was so easy for him to choose baseball over me. I was his fiancée. He made me promises. I've never loved anyone like Zach. First love is naïve. I was open and trusting. I didn't hold back on how much love I gave; he got every ounce inside of me. He took over every nook and cranny. There are spaces inside that Todd never could touch because they were Zach's. I hate him for that. I hate that I would look at Todd sometimes and wish he acted like Zach. It is irrational and unfair, but that's the truth.

"So, Felicia, huh?"

"She's changed," he says.

"I'm sure." She hasn't.

Zach rubs his hands on his legs. This is uncomfortable for both of us. "Can we not talk about her? Please," he pleads. "I didn't come here to fight."

"What do you want to talk about?"

It's not like I even want to have this conversation, but it seems it's unavoidable. "This used to not be so hard," he says as he grabs the back of his neck. "We used to talk about anything."

"Zach," I say with a sigh. "I don't know what you want here. It's been almost eighteen years since we last saw each other. And when we said goodbye it wasn't on good terms. There's a shit ton unresolved between us. If you came here for forgiveness—I forgive you. If you came here for a friendship—I can't do that."

He sits back and doesn't respond. I wait for him to say something after my tirade, but I get nothing.

Well, I refuse to say another word.

Finally, he clears his throat. "I didn't come here looking for anything. I came here because Wyatt said you have no plans of leaving. I thought you were passing through, so I stayed away. I knew you didn't want to see me. And if we're being honest, I didn't know if I wanted to see you."

"Gee, thanks."

"Let me finish." He groans. "You bring up a whole lot of shit I buried."

"Well, sorry to make you suffer."

"Fucking hell, Presley." His voice grows more agitated. "I'm trying to be nice here."

I couldn't give a shit what he's trying to do. "Seventeen years! Seventeen years! Nice? You think being nice is going to erase all of that? Did you really think I was going to be happy to see you? I've avoided this damn town because it hurts too much." I let out a long breath through my nose. "I'm not in love with you. I don't need to clear anything up. Everyone keeps talking about you, and I don't want to! Every single place here has something that reminds me of you. Hell, this damn desk does!"

His eyes go to it as his grin forms. Bastard. "I live with the memories too. You're not the only one who lost here. I wanted a future, but you closed that door when I left."

"Say that last part again."

"I didn't leave you because I didn't love you. I wanted to build a life with you! It didn't have to be over!"

My heart skips a beat. As much as I will try to fight the draw—it's there. Zach holds a string that's tied inside of me. If he pulls, I'll unravel. I'm praying I can keep enough tension to prevent that pain. I've had enough in the last few months.

"Yeah." I sigh. "It really did." So many things he doesn't even have a clue about. What I went through when he left. The heartache I endured . . . he doesn't have an inkling of what I suffered.

"I know I hurt you. I hate that I broke your heart. I also know you're married."

I look at my hand. He heard Wyatt say I was single. He's fishing, but the truth is already out there. "My husband passed away, but I'm guessing you know something about that." I challenge him. "I highly doubt your mama didn't mention it."

"I'm sorry. I really am," he says, leaning forward. "All I knew was that you were back because of something with him, but I was trying to let you say it."

So many years. So many memories between us. It's easy to look at him and recall them all. Zach reminds me of a time when life was just—easy. We lived as if nothing could touch us. We had passion, trust, love, and hope for the future we dreamed of. I still see the boy who had the world at his feet. He's deep inside this man who I don't know anymore.

"I really need to get back to work."

"Mom!" Logan barrels through the door. "Cayden took my iPad and deleted all the pictures." His face is red from either running or crying.

"I'm sure we'll get them back," I reassure him.

Logan pants, trying to catch his breath. "They had all my pictures of Dad."

I stand and come around the desk as he holds the tablet out. "I have photos of your daddy. Don't worry."

The chair shifts and Zach stands as Logan and I look over. My chest constricts at the sight of my son standing before the man that could've been my husband. My eyes shift between them.

Zach steps forward with a smile. "Hey there. I'm Zach Hennington." He extends his hand. "You know my brother, Wyatt?"

"Oh! I'm Logan," Logan exclaims and puts his hand in Zach's. "Wyatt is fun. He took us out on the horses this morning. He and Uncle Cooper are going to teach us to shoot a gun today!"

"The hell they are!" I scoff. I swear, these damn men in my life.

"Stop being a baby, Mom."

Zach smirks. "Wyatt really likes when you tell him how bad he missed."

Logan grins as if they're in some secret pact. "Thanks, man."

"Any time."

Logan runs off, completely forgetting about the iPad issue. Zach's entire demeanor shifts. His eyes fill with some emotion I can't place. "Logan?"

"Yeah? And his twin brother is Cayden." I have no clue where he's going with this.

"You named your son Logan?" He moves around the room, stopping and then starting again.

"Zach?"

He takes two steps, and his body is almost touching mine. I stop breathing from his proximity, and that light-headed feeling floods back. His hand lifts and drops before he touches me. "I need to leave."

I muster all the strength I have. "You always do."

The hurt flashes in his eyes, but he recovers quickly. "I'm not the same man I was then. I wasn't even a man. I was twenty-two years old with a lot of dreams." Zach steps back and I can breathe again.

I get that we were kids. Deep down I'm fully aware I'm being unjust. Zach was offered the chance of a lifetime. He took it. But in the wake of that decision, I was left to pick up the pieces. Alone in a town away from my family, with a broken promise, and a lot of heartache. When he followed his dream, he annihilated mine of a life together.

"I know, and if it weren't for those choices, I wouldn't have the life I do now."

As I say the words, I'm unsure if I'm happy about that or angry again. Funny how there can be so many meanings to one sentence.

"I'm sorry you lost your husband. I truly am."

"I'm glad you found Felicia," I reply. I'm completely full of shit. Of all the people in the world, she's the worst of them. Right now, I don't want anything from him but for him to leave me the hell alone.

I'm barely holding on. Being around him like this . . . hurts. I miss him. I've missed him for so long. Yes, I loved my husband very much. Yes, my life was fine without Zach. But Zach knew me without having to say a word.

There were never questions about what was wrong. He just knew. And God how I miss that level of friendship. Even after a decade of being with Todd, he never had that with me. It was different.

Zach steps closer, and I retreat. His proximity isn't a good thing. "I'm not going to hurt you, Presley."

But like old times, his blue eyes tell me he doesn't know if he can keep that promise. He's testing me. Testing himself. We both feel the electricity between us. It was there long ago, and it apparently hasn't ebbed at all. His body moves with ease toward me. My heart races and I'm sure he can see my breathing quicken. "Zach," I say as a plea.

"I just want to get this part over," he explains.

Slowly his hands extend toward my arms. As soon as his skin

touches mine, a tear falls. I swallow a whimper as his fingers clasp my shoulders. It's an innocent touch, but it ruins me. Zach doesn't stop though. He pulls me into his body. He breaks me apart. He puts me together. He's my poison and my antidote. My arms wrap around his torso without hesitation. We remain like this for who knows how long, but for the first time since Todd killed himself, I feel safe.

And that's not a good thing to feel in Zach's arms.

Ten

"I know," I say to Angie while trying to clean the boys' rooms. "I miss you too."

It's been hard going from seeing her every day to this. She has no idea what hearing her voice does to me. Part of me wants to smile and be happy to talk to her. I miss her terribly. The other part of me wants to curl up and cry.

"I can't believe this is the first time we're talking. I knew you'd be busy, but I figured you'd call a few times." Her wounded tone tells me everything.

I sit on the edge of the bed, feeling deflated. "I'm sorry." I won't lie to her and tell her some bullshit excuse, which she'd let me use.

"I get it, Pres, but you're missed here." Her voice cracks. I'm not the only one who had their life flipped upside down. Angie lost her brother, and then me and the kids. "When do you think you'll come home?"

I don't think she fully understands. The credit card bills and the equity line he took out, and all of it with my name as a co-signer. I either file for bankruptcy, which I want to avoid at all costs, or I live here and pay the payment plans they've allowed me.

A tear falls as I wrestle with the truth. "I don't know. Short of winning the lottery, it's going to be a while."

"This is such bullshit. You know that, right?" She pauses and then begins her own tirade. "You shouldn't have to be punished because of him. He did all this. He opened new credit cards. Not you. It's ridiculous and unfair. So now you and the kids had to move, sell your part of the bakery, and work for your parents? You didn't do this, so why the hell do you have to pay it back?"

My anger builds as I listen to her. I grip the shirt in my hand and rage consumes me. "Because he was a fucking coward! He did this to us! You want the answer? It lies at Todd's feet."

Angie gasps. "I . . . I'm," she struggles to speak.

I know I've hurt her, but it's why we haven't spoken. My anger turns to sadness as I decide to lay it all out for her. She didn't do this to me and doesn't deserve my hostility. "I'm sorry. He was your brother, which is why talking to you is so hard. I'm really angry, Ang. I mean, deep in my soul kind of anger." A tear falls. "I'm not sad or longing for him anymore. Then I feel guilty for feeling that way," I confess the feelings I keep bottled up.

"I'm sorry. You're allowed to feel," she says.

"It's different for me now. And when I talk to you, I remember the life I had. The job I always wanted, the house I loved, the friends and PTA I had to leave." She doesn't say a word, but I can hear the hiccup through the line. "You remind me of him. You remind me of the happiness I once had. It hurts to talk to you, and it hurts to know that."

"I'm angry too, Presley. I've lost everyone." She's sobbing now. "He tore a hole in my life too. I'm dealing with the same emotions. I just want you back here. I want my best friend and my sister back."

The agony in her voice breaks me. Hurting her is the last thing I would ever want to do. "I wish it were different."

"I wish a lot of things."

We both sit quietly, coming down from the emotional outbursts and raw truths.

Angie clears her throat. "How's Bell Buckle? Are you holding up okay?"

"It's . . . the same."

"How do the boys like it?"

I smile. "Surprisingly well after the shock wore off. They're loving being around Cooper and Wyatt. Cayden has really taken to the horses. And you know Logan, he's easy." That's the one thing I have to be most grateful for. They may have lost their father, but they've gained two male role models.

"Wyatt is on your ranch?"

Shit. "Yeah, he's the foreman."

I can imagine the wheels turning in her head. I give her five seconds before the next question comes.

Five.

Four.

"What about Zach? Is his stupid ass still in Los Angeles or wherever the fuck he left you to go?"

Angie is not a fan of Zach. She'd have castrated him if she could've back then. He has no clue about the mess I was in. But Angie does. She picked me up off the floor and forced me to live.

"Zach's here."

"Well, I hope you kneed him, slapped him, or some other form of physical pain. It must've been great to let it out on him though."

"Yup."

I can't tell her what I'm feeling. It feels like every part of my life is lying to the other. The tangled web is so immense—I don't know where the beginning is anymore. The lies about how Todd died. The lies about how seeing Zach makes me feel. The lies about how badly I'm in debt. It's suffocating me.

"I gotta run, Ang. I'll call soon. I promise."

"Okay," she says with disappointment in her voice. "Love you."

"Love you too."

I disconnect the call and wipe my face. I've never kept secrets from her. I've never lied to her, but this isn't something I can share. I don't even know what it is anyway. I have old feelings. That's normal. I mean Zach was my first love. He was my world for so long, of course seeing him would make me nostalgic. That's all this is.

~

Of course my mother asks me to head into town to get her some things she needs for dinner. Apparently, she and Wyatt are in on the same plan. Push me off the ranch and force me to deal with living here. I was doing fine pretending otherwise.

I head to the general store, which is no bigger than a 7-11 but packs more items than a major chain grocery store. It baffles me.

I grab the things I need and head to the register. "Well," Mrs. Rooney says as she looks up with a smile. "I was wondering when you were going to come see me." She comes around and draws me in her arms. "Get over here and let me get a look at you."

She hasn't changed much. She's still under five foot, her hair still hangs to her mid back, only now it has a lot more gray in it, but it's her eyes that I remember most. She has the kindest eyes. One look and I instantly feel better.

"I'm sorry it wasn't sooner," I say, hugging her back.

Mrs. Rooney was the only one who didn't try to hold me back. She was easily my favorite person in this town. I can remember coming in here as a kid and sitting on the stool and telling her everything. She was the kind of friend that you could bare your soul to and she'd never judge you. I feel guilty for not coming to see her before now.

She pulls back with a smile. "I understood why you've stayed in hiding, darlin'."

"I'm not hiding," I defend myself.

"No? What do you call a month of living here and only leaving your house a handful of times?"

"Adjusting."

Mrs. Rooney laughs and shakes her head. "You're something

else. Your mama talks about those two little boys constantly. Tell me how old they are now."

I fill her in a little bit more about my life. She tells me how her husband took a bad fall and broke his leg. She's been working extra hours to help out. I tell her all about the boys, Philadelphia, and my bakery—all the good things.

However, the elephant in the room is only growing with each passing minute.

"Presley," she says in a soft voice. "I'm really sorry about your husband passing."

My lips form a thin line. It's like every time someone else brings it up, I'm forced back there. Grief is a never-ending battle that drains you of who you once were. I'll never be the same person I was five months ago. I've been forced to toughen up, face life head on, and protect myself at all costs.

"I appreciate that."

"What happened, honey? You're so young to have such great loss this early in life."

I force out a laugh to avoid the question. "I don't feel that young. I remember everyone saying that your thirties are the best years. I'm thirty-five but feel seventy." I hope she doesn't pick up on the deflection. She's one of the few people I don't want to give a half-truth. At the same time, it's the only way to protect my kids, and myself.

"Wait till you're sixty!" She grins. "Did you see that Zach is living here too? It's like fate brought you back together. Oh he's with that Felicia who is still the same scheming girl she always was." She gives a dramatic sigh. "Have you seen him at all?"

The phone rings, giving me the perfect excuse to not answer her. She hops up and tugs me into her arms again before pushing back to take a look at me. "You always were a pretty girl, but you sure grew to be a beautiful woman. No matter how old you feel, you're still gorgeous."

She heads to the back to grab the phone, and I place a twenty on the counter. This place is so different from the city. It's much more forgiving here. They don't worry about money because everything is the I'll-get-you-later mentality.

"You know she's right," the voice I'd know anywhere says from behind me.

I turn, grabbing the bag of groceries. "Right about what?"

His deep chuckle slides from his lips. I hold on to the annoyance I felt a few seconds ago. We go from not seeing each other for weeks to him being everywhere. I prefer option A. "That you're still gorgeous."

"Really, Zachary?" I say with condescension. "Where's your girlfriend?" I look around him, pretending I actually want to see the evil bitch. "Leave her at the plastic surgeon? Psychiatrist? Either one is appropriate."

I insult Felicia for several reasons, but mainly because I want to see what he does. Does he defend her? Does he ignore me again? It seems he doesn't like bringing her up, and I'd like to know why. Wyatt clearly hates her, as do most people who've had to endure being around her.

"Felicia's at work. I'm sure she'd love for you to stop by." He raises his brow.

"I'd rather gnaw on my arm. Besides, she didn't like you and me talking before."

He grins before leaning in. My heart races as he gets closer. He places a five-dollar bill on top of the bill I put down. "There's a good reason for that, darlin'." He's so close I can't stop myself from breathing him in. All I can sense is him. The sun, grass, dirt, and all Zach. He smells like home.

The bag in my arms begins to slide out of my grip.

"You need help with that?" he asks.

I was so lost in him that I forgot I was holding something. Dammit. I hike the bag over my shoulder and attempt a smile. "I'm good."

"Yeah, Pres. You sure are." I would swear he's hitting on me.

"Are you trying to make this worse than it is?"

His eyes study me. "By saying you're still beautiful or by

saying you're doing good? I don't see how I'm making anything worse."

Maybe I'm being stupid. "Sorry."

I need to get away from him. I walk toward the door, but Zach follows. He pushes the door open, forcing me to have to squeeze past him. I pray that Wyatt stayed and will save me.

No such luck.

"How'd you get here?" Zach asks when he notices there are no other cars but his.

Wyatt had to run a few towns over to get some things for Cooper. I needed the truck and he did too. So he said he'd drive me and either pick me up on the way back or I could walk. Of course going a few towns over meant hours that I'd be stuck in town, so I chose to walk. It's only a few miles and would give me some time to think. But I secretly hoped he would wait.

"Wyatt. Before he apparently left."

"I just saw him. He said since I was here he could go. I didn't know he was waiting for you."

Fucking Wyatt. I swear the bastard planned this. He's dead. "How nice of him."

"I can take you back to the ranch," Zach offers. "It's your call."

I don't really want to walk, but there's no way I'm getting in that truck. That truck is *the* truck. The place where so many nights were spent doing things we shouldn't have been doing. A lot of love was exchanged in that front seat. I don't think I can be in there with him.

Zach looks over where my eyes are and his shoulders slump. It's as if we've both had the same realization.

"I can walk." My life is painful and complicated already. I'm not going to make this harder on myself. Being close to him is hard enough because I keep going backward. I know we don't have a shot. I don't even want one, but he's familiar. And I'm alone. He reminds me of comfort.

He looks over with a hint of disappointment. "You sure?"

I smile and nod. "Thanks for the offer."

He tosses his keys in the air and catches them as he walks

away. I take two steps, and the sky opens up. Rain falls hard and fast, soaking my hair and clothes.

I rush to get under the awning, but Zach jumps back out of his truck and grabs the bag from me. "Come on. You're not walking in this."

Defeat flows through me. He wins again.

Eleven

"You cold?" Zach asks as I climb in. I'm shaking, but it has nothing to do with being cold. My body is pressed against the door, trying to keep as much distance as possible between us.

"I'm just fine."

The drive isn't long, but each second feels like an hour. I look around and smile. "You're kidding me." I laugh as my fingers touch the sticker on the dash. When Zach was playing a game in Nashville, I wanted to give him something that would make him remember me. It was only two nights, but I was young and dumb. There was a sticker that read: Love Your Cowgirl. I stuck it on the dash, hoping he wouldn't get pissed.

Before leaving, he came to my house, took me in his arms, and kissed me till I couldn't breathe. He never said a word. Just got back in his truck, winked, and drove off. He was always doing things like that. He would tell me he needed to feel something real.

"I refused to remove it at first," he says with warmth in his voice. "Then it had been there so long, it wouldn't come off."

"Sorry I permanently defaced your truck. I didn't realize it would still run after this long."

The roar of the engine vibrates through the silence. I

remember it was always loud, but I swear I never felt it like this. Zach clears his throat. "I don't think it'll ever die. It's tough as hell."

He puts the truck in drive and heads down the small road toward my house. "This looks really bad," I say, squinting.

Zach drives slowly as rain pelts the truck harder than before. I can barely see anything out the windshield. He pulls over to the side of the road. "I can't see. I'm going to wait until this lets up a little."

Mother Nature is a cold-hearted bitch. Doesn't she know how much I don't want to be in this truck? Couldn't she give me one freaking break? Of course not. Nope. We should make this as awkward and uncomfortable as humanly possible. The thunder booms behind us, causing me to jump. Great. Now we're going to have the storm from hell.

"So?" I say after a minute of silence.

"You never could handle the quiet." Zach smirks as I fight the urge to punch him in the leg.

"Yes, I could!"

"No. You always needed either music or talking. Good to see some things are still the same."

"I'm a lot different."

So much has changed since he left me. Not only in my life, but who I am. Loving someone the way I loved him changed me deep inside. But losing my husband took a part of my heart and tarnished it beyond repair.

"We both are, Pres." He's right. He's not the same boy I remember. "Since we're stuck here, tell me how you're different."

"We don't have to talk." I cross my arms and look out the window.

He chuckles. "No. But who knows how long before the rain stops."

I don't want to let my guard down with him. It would be so easy to let go and be his friend. I'm not prepared to be trapped in a car with him. I continue to gaze out at the road, trying to find a break in the downpour.

"Suit yourself," Zach says as he opens a candy bar.

Son of a bitch. "You're going to eat that in front of me?" I have no restraint when it comes to chocolate and peanut butter.

"Want some?" He tilts the chocolaty goodness close and then jerks it back. "I only ask for one thing."

"What's that?" I ask, snatching the candy out of his hand.

"You can't ignore me while we're stuck here."

I snap off a piece, pop it in my mouth, and grin. "Fine. Tell me how you're so different."

"Well, first of all, I wouldn't ever play chicken on the covered bridge. I would never try to tip a bull again. Most of all, I would never try to steal a candy bar from Mrs. Rooney."

Just remembering us as the kids we were makes me smile. "God, we did some dumb stuff when we were younger."

"Yeah, we sure did."

"I mean, do you remember the time we snuck out at one in the morning to ride horses out in the woods? We got so lost I swear we found ourselves three towns over. Mama and Daddy almost killed you that day."

Zach nods. "I thought your daddy was going to. He came out on the porch with that shotgun pointed at me. But nothing was as bad as my dad when I got home. He was pissed."

"You were grounded for a week."

"I still snuck out to see you."

I smile. "I know. I remember."

"Do you remember how we tried to light a bonfire and we ended up needing to call the fire department?"

We had no understanding of consequences. "So many times we could've gotten hurt or worse. Now that I have Logan and Cayden, I think about the dumb crap they're going to do. It scares the shit out of me."

"Well, at least they don't have Trent feeding them ideas."

I smile as I roll my eyes. "Yet."

Zach wipes the fog off the window and another memory rips through my heart. *It's like we're sixteen all over again.*

"Huh?"

"What?"

"You said something about being sixteen." He stares into my eyes.

"I didn't mean to say that out loud."

He smiles and shifts his body toward me. "What were you thinking about?"

"Nothing. Just something you did reminded me of when we were kids."

Zach's eyes never leave mine, and I swear he's reading my thoughts. The intensity in his eyes only grows, and again, I'm thrown back in time.

"Zach," I moan as my hands search for something to grip. "Please, don't stop this time."

We've been dancing around this for months now. I love him. I want to be with him for the rest of my life. I want to share this with him, but he keeps saying no.

His tongue swipes up, and my hips buck. "I love you, Presley."

I lift his face and hold it in my hands. "I love you, Zachary. Please, make love to me. I want you to be my first."

Zach hovers above me on one arm, and he uses the forearm of his other arm to wipe away the fog that covers the window. Heat consumes the cab of the truck, and all I want is to steam it up more. "We'll make love, Pres. We'll make love more times than we can count. But it sure as hell ain't going to be in this truck with my brother in the car next to us."

I cover myself and sit up. "Trent is here?"

He laughs and then kisses me. "It's make-out lake. Of course Trent is here, and from the looks of it . . . half our senior class is too."

"I hate this town. I can't wait till we're both out of here." I groan, pulling my shirt over my head while Zach zips his pants.

After both of us are dressed, he takes my hand. "We're out of here soon enough, baby. I head off to college, and you'll come there. We'll both finish with school, I'll get picked up by a pro team, and we'll have everything. You and me, Presley. You and me. I'll give you the world."

Zach waves his hands in front of my face. "Earth to Presley."

I blink.

"What were you thinking about?" he asks.

Like I'm going to tell him that. Not on his life. "The boys," I lie.

"The boys?"

"Yeah, I have two of them, remember?" I play coy, hoping to change the subject. I try to focus on bringing my heart rate back to normal. If being this close to him triggers these things, I need to figure out a way to stay far, far away. Zach extracts too many memories that I buried a long time ago.

He studies me but lets me have my lie. "I was thinking about the things we did and the time we spent in this truck."

My head turns toward him. Is he really bringing this up? "Oh?"

"Yeah." Zach's voice is layered with confliction. "A lot of memories on this front seat. Being around you makes it hard to forget."

I turn my body in his direction. The thunder rumbles in the background and the lightning flashes, illuminating the sky. It feels a lot like the storm raging inside me. "You didn't have a hard time forgetting me."

He moves forward slightly, and our knees touch. Once again, the electricity charges between us. "You think I forgot about you?" The tone of his voice lets me know he's truly confused.

"What else could I think?" I shrug. "I begged you to stay. You left. You never came back."

He shakes his head. "How can two people remember the same thing so differently? I never forgot you. I tried to call, but you wouldn't answer."

"I was mad. I was hurt and confused."

The space between us closes as we gravitate to one another. The anger, the emotion, the frustration of seventeen years comes to a head. "You think I wasn't?"

"Please enlighten me on what you could've been mad at."

Zach's face inches closer and closer. The heat in the car rises as the conversation intensifies. His eyes tell me everything. There's a war raging inside him, and I'm about to be his first casualty.

"I was angry with myself." His voice is low, but his words aren't. "I watched your face disappear, and with each mile between us, I hated myself. I never got over that. I've looked back every single day, wondering why." Our breaths mingle as I listen to things I've longed to hear. "I wanted to come back to you. It's why I sent letters when you wouldn't answer my calls. It's why I went to Cooper, Wyatt, or anyone who would talk to you. But you —" He stops. My breathing stops as I wait for him to continue. "You didn't care. You were dating and getting engaged like we never mattered."

"What did you expect? For me to wait around until you decided I was worth it?" I try to scoot back, but he follows.

"I thought . . ." He runs his hands through his hair. "I thought you'd give me another chance. I didn't think you'd move on so fucking quickly!"

I see the anger in him for the first time. "I didn't betray you, Zach. I didn't choose someone or something else over you."

"No?" He laughs. "You chose *him* over me. You got married and never even gave us another chance."

My mouth falls open. He has no idea. "Don't you dare judge me. I was alone in a college that you chose for *us*. I followed you everywhere, Zach! I gave up the college of my dreams for you. Then you get an offer within the first two months that I got there, and less than twenty-four hours later, you're driving off. I loved you so much that I thought my heart was dead when you left! I needed you."

"And I needed you!" His hands grip my cheeks and I hold on to his arms. "I needed you, Presley. I've always needed you. I'll always need you."

Before I can respond, his mouth is on mine. He kisses me without any apologies. I can't think. Everything becomes foggy as my heart beats uncontrollably. How can this be happening? I'm confused as to whether I want this or not. He clouds my judgment. His touch is all consuming. I don't know when my brain disconnects from my body, but I kiss him back. It's soft and rough, slow and quick, all at the same time. My lips tingle as he holds me still.

When his tongue presses against my mouth, I snap. No! No, I won't do this. I will never let him in again. I can't endure losing anyone else. He had his chance and he threw me away.

I push against his chest as his eyes lock on mine. I'm filled with anger at him, but more so at myself. How could I let him kiss me? More than that, how could I kiss him back? Damn him for doing this to me! I'm a widow. I've lost my husband, my home, my life. I'm not about to go messing things up any further.

My hand rises, and I slap him across the face. "Don't ever do that again. You don't get to kiss me."

"I don't . . ." He looks away with shame. "I should've never done that."

"No," I say with a shaky breath. "You shouldn't've."

"I'm sorry."

"Take me home, Zach."

"Please," he begs. "Forgive me."

"Now." I turn in my seat and close my eyes. If I can hold myself together for a few minutes, I can lose it later.

"Why the fuck do I keep screwing up with you? It's so easy to forget how much you hate me."

My fingers press against my lips as guilt overwhelms me. All I could think when he touched me was how much I've missed that feeling. The way a man's mouth felt against mine. I've been lonely, and hating him is the absolute last thing I feel. I've never hated him—not even when that was all I prayed I would feel. I've loved him my whole life, and there's a part of me that knows that will never stop. "I just want to go home."

He puts the truck in drive and doesn't say another word. I keep my gaze forward as we approach my house. As soon as we get there, he parks. "Presley, I'm sorry."

There's nothing to say, so I keep quiet. If I were to speak, he'd hear it in my voice. I won't let him see how much he's rattled me.

But he has. He's rocked me to my core. That kiss reminded me of how much I truly love him. How my world clicks with him, and how much power Zachary Hennington has over me.

I hop out not caring if I get drenched. In fact, I welcome the rain. At least it's real. Unlike anything Zach and I could ever have. I've been left by him once before. It's a recurring theme in my life, it seems. I can't be vulnerable now, and that's exactly what Zach makes me.

Twelve

ZACHARY

Kissing her again solidified it. I've never stopped loving her. I knew I never had, but now there's no way I can deny it.

I've moved on in some ways, but Presley . . . she's everything.

Even with her throwing things at me, slapping me, and being angry right now . . . I don't care, because she's here. She's the reason I haven't been able to move forward in my life. I've tried to live, love again, but it never compared.

She fucking ruined me.

I sit in my truck outside her house and let my head fall back. What the hell am I going to do now? She clearly doesn't feel the same way. No, Presley still hates me.

"Fuck!" I slam my hand on the steering wheel. "Dammit, Zach," I say to myself. "You can't go there. You can't think of that woman, because you don't have a chance. You blew it." I say the words I need to remember. "I'm so fucking screwed."

"Yeah, you sure are."

I jump at the sound of my brother outside my window. "How much did you hear?"

"All of it. You must like talking to yourself." Wyatt opens the passenger side door and climbs in. "Next time try words of encouragement. I hear that makes people smarter."

"By all means," I grumble. "And fuck off. You're the one who keeps making these situations happen."

"Dude, what the hell did you think? It's why I told you that she was here weeks ago. It's why I keep telling you to make things right. Presley has always been your biggest regret."

I shake my head, wishing he were wrong. "I regret leaving her, not lovin' her."

"Brother," he says as he runs his hand down his face, "I warned you years ago that you need to stop this shit. You pining away, thinking that one day she'd show back up and love you again. You blew that chance a long time ago."

"I know."

"Do you?" He pauses, and I could punch his smug face. "She was married and has twins. Did you know that?"

"Yeah," I inform Wyatt. "I saw him."

"Who?" he says confused.

"Her son, Logan."

That name. Of all the fucking names she picks. And then for her not to remember . . . crushed me. She ripped my heart out, and she doesn't even know it.

"They're good boys. Been through hell," he says pointedly. "They lost their father and everything they've known, so you can't be fucking with their mama's heart."

Wyatt is usually pretty quiet about other people's business, but he has no issue when it comes to mine. He loves Presley. He always has, but he's protective of her too. She's family to all of us. I wanted her to be a different family member for me.

"She slapped me!" I yell.

"Well, from the look on her face you deserved it."

I hate my brother. "I kissed her."

He laughs and rolls his eyes. "Of course you did. She's Presley, and you damn well can't help yourself. You want to be with her."

"I'm with Felicia," I remind him.

"Sure, you are."

"What the fuck does that mean?"

He shakes his head and sighs. "You're going to sit here and tell me you love her? The way you love Presley?" He pauses, and I don't say a word. "I didn't think so." I open my mouth to argue, but he goes right back into his monologue. "You never stopped hoping she'd come back. Hoping she'd give you a second chance. But so help me God, Zach. If you hurt her, I'll fuck you up. I don't care if we're brothers, I'll beat the ever loving shit out of you."

"I'm not going there again," I state. There are some things people can come back from, but not sixteen years of anger. That's a lot of forgiveness, and there are things I'm still pissed off about too.

"Right."

"Get out of my truck," I demand. "Why aren't you in there telling her all this shit?"

Wyatt throws his feet on the dash. "What makes you think I haven't?"

"I need to get home." I'm done with this conversation. "Leave."

"I'm telling you to be careful, Zach. Not just because of her, but because you were a miserable son of a bitch too. I'd be willing to bet a lot of your injuries, and the reason you came back home, was for her."

"What?" He's way off. I came home because of our parents. I got hurt because that's what fucking happens in baseball.

"You heard me."

"I swear to God if you don't get out of this fucking truck right now . . ." I let him figure out the rest.

"Tell Felicia I said hello." He climbs out of the truck. There's no love lost between those two. She hates him as much as he despises her. It's why my brother is the foreman here and not at our own ranch.

I flip him off and get the hell off Townsend property. I decide my head is too jumbled to go back home. Felicia isn't dumb. She's been watching me since Presley returned. Her timing though, who the hell could've planned it? The day I'm going to propose to Felicia, she returns to Bell Buckle.

I love Felicia, but it's not fair to her. Not when I look at her and wish she were Presley. I have to figure out what the hell I want to do. So, I head to the one place that I can always feel at home—the field.

I step out of my truck, smell the fresh cut grass, and I relax. There's no one here but me. I walk to my position and step over a puddle. "So much of my life was spent right here," I talk to the baseball gods. They're real in my head. "I asked you to let me play in the majors, but at what cost? I had to lose her? You couldn't let me keep both?" I walk in circles. "You had to make me choose, and now look where I am. No baseball. No Presley. And no answers."

My mind fills with memories. But one that I've fought back for so long, hits me like a ball to the face.

Holy shit. Holy fucking shit! I'm going to play in the major leagues. I can't believe this. All these years are finally paying off. The money, the traveling, the life I can give her is at my fingertips. Presley. I have to tell her.

"Just sign these papers and we're all set." The team manager is already sliding the contract over.

"I need to talk to my fiancée." I hesitate for a second.

He sighs. "I'm sorry, son. You need to sign now or the deal is off the table. If we come back." He pauses. "I won't be able to get you as much."

I'm not letting this pass. I'm going to play in the majors. It's all I've ever wanted, and it's here. Presley would slap me for letting this much money go. I reach for the pen. "I'll sign."

"Well, Zach." The team manager stands and smiles. "We're happy to have you as a member of the Dodgers organization. You'll need to report to LA by the end of the week."

"The end of the week?" I clarify.

"Yes, the season is already in full swing. The coach wants you there as soon as possible."

I finish with the papers and rush out to find her. I can't wait to see her face when I tell her all our dreams are coming true.

"Pres!" I yell as she's exiting her class.

"Hey." Her smile is bright as she walks toward me. You'd think after all this time she'd be less beautiful to me, but she's not. I don't

even notice the girls that pass by. None of them are close to what I have. "You okay? You never meet me outside of class." Her green eyes are full of concern.

"Darlin'," I say, stopping right in front of her. "It's happening." Her eyes widen and her lips part. "What's happening?"

"I got offered a deal!"

"Zach! That's amazing!" She leaps into my arms as I fall back a little with a laugh. "Where? What team?" she asks with excitement. "Oh, my God! What are they offering? Wait, who offered?" She shoots the questions off in rapid fire.

She steps back and takes my hand. I can't believe this is really happening. "LA for the Dodgers."

"California?" she gasps. "That's the other side of the country. I . . ." Her breath hitches. "When do you have to give them an answer?"

And it hits me—I'm going to leave her again. After we spent the last two years apart.

"I already signed the contract."

Presley steps back and clutches her stomach as if I've just punched her. "You already signed? I thought we were going to wait. I didn't think you'd take it, especially without talkin' to me."

"It won't be that bad." I explain to her. "I leave this week, and I'll find us a great house. You can come as soon as you finish this semester. I promise, it'll be fine." Maybe I can convince her this isn't going to be that rough.

She doesn't say a word. Her eyes fill with tears, and I'm no longer happy. "I can't go with you now . . . I'm not leaving school, Zach. You . . ." She starts, but then she turns. "I can't believe you didn't talk to me."

"Pres." I try to get her to look at me. "I know it'll be hard, but we can make it work."

"I'm in the first semester of my freshman year. I can't quit. I'm happy for you, but I don't know." She chews her lip for a second and then continues, "I'm hurt."

I take her hand. "He told me if I didn't sign now, I could lose the contract."

"We're supposed to be partners. How could you not talk to me?"

"I wanted to. But I figured you'd be fine with transferring schools and moving."

Clearly, I was wrong.

"And then what if you get traded? What if in three weeks you get called up? We've been apart for so long. I can't do this again." Her voice hiccups in the middle.

"Yes, we can. We'll still see each other, and you only have three years left of school. You can come out and live with me after that or transfer to California whenever you want."

We'll be fine, she just needs to calm down. Presley is my fiancée. She's my world, and we'll work through this.

"You want me to wait three years? You want me to sit here while you're all over the country with these girls who are waitin' for a chance to bang the ball player? No. No way. You can't possibly think that's fair. I have already waited two years just to get here." There's no anger in her words, just sadness.

"Then come with me."

She shifts her books into her other arm and stares at me. "For me to sit alone in California while you travel the country? How is that going to work?"

"We'll make it work."

"Zach." She sighs and wipes her face. "You don't get it. I came to this school for you. I gave up my scholarship, moved, had to take out more loans so we could be together. I understand that this is your dream." Her eyes water again. "But do my dreams not matter? I worked so hard to get in here. This culinary program is one of the best in the country. I can't follow you wherever you go. That's not fair. And I don't have it in me to do long distance again so soon. The last two years were unbearable. If you leave, you'll be focused on baseball, you aren't going to have time for us. We both know you'll be traveling most of the year. Not to mention all the girls that will be all over you. I'm sorry, I'm not ready to live through that."

We had plans, but this doesn't mean those can't change. We

*made it through the two years she was still in high school. This will
be easier. I can afford to fly her out and visit.*

*I'm not sure what she expects, but baseball is my life too. This
is my chance, and I won't walk away from it. We'll figure out a way
to make it work.*

"Yes, but this is my dream, Presley. Right now I can play ball
for a living. I can't give it up. I won't. I leave tomorrow."

"Tomorrow?" she practically yells. "You're kidding me! Tomorrow, Zach?"

I nod.

"I guess we're done then." She chokes on the words.

"Done?" I yell. "The hell we are. We're not breaking up over
this. We're engaged!"

The tears she fought back are now streaming down her face. I
hate making her cry. I try to step forward but she puts her hand up.

"No, Zach. I can't be away from you like this again. I almost
went crazy back in Tennessee, but Wyatt, Grace, and Emily were
there. Who do I have now? Angie is my only friend. I'm only here
because you promised me we'd be together." Her voice cracks.
"We're supposed to get married, start a family, and you didn't even
talk to me before you signed that deal!" Presley grows more upset
with each word. "I'm happy that you've gotten this chance, but this
isn't just your life. I'm the other half in this too!"

"We have plenty of time to start a family. We can still do all
that, just not now. Not when my career is about to take off."

"So all the plans we had are gone, like that?"

"Plans change, Presley." I want to take her in my arms, but
each time I move forward, she moves back. "Don't," I plead.
"You're not looking at the whole picture!"

"You painted the picture of us spending the next two years with
you finishing school, getting married, living together, and then
entering the draft. You did all this behind my back."

"But now I don't have to do that. I can go play ball now," I
explain. She's missing that this is my chance. "And what if I get
hurt this year playing here? Then I might not get this opportunity
again."

"I get that. I know the risks, and you're right that this is your chance. You already signed it and you're going, but I can't do this. I can't spend four years sitting here waiting for you. I won't move to California now either. You'll be training or playing, which means you'd never be around. It's not fair to me either."

I can't lose her, but I can't quit baseball either. "I won't give you up, Presley. I lived the last two years without you."

"I know. I lived through missing my prom and having to see you only on breaks, and even then, you were training. I was the one who dealt with the drunken phone calls and heard about girls hanging on you while I was a thousand miles away."

"I never—"

"Don't. I'm not done, Zachary." I let her continue on, trying to think of ways to fix this. "I struggled through two years of waiting for you. I did it all because of how much I love you—and at the end of it, I thought we'd finally be together. And then you do this? Am I supposed to just up and move each time you decide something?"

I try telling myself that she's in shock. She doesn't mean this. As soon as the dust settles, she'll see. "This is my dream. I mean it's pro. It's everything I worked for. There's no way I can walk away from this. You've always known this was the end game."

Her chest heaves as she looks me in the eye. "Then go." She tries to catch her breath.

"I feel like you're making me choose between you and baseball. I can't do that. Don't you see I can't choose?" To give up my dream or her . . . I can't. But I know Presley, she's upset, but she loves me.

"No, Zach." She sniffles and I can see a multitude of emotions playing across her face. "You're choosing what you want. And that's fine. I'm choosing what's best for me. I'm not changing colleges. And I'm not going to live my next three and a half years in misery while you tour the country. I'm happy you got picked up." Hope starts to form. "I really am proud of you. I love you so much it hurts." This is the Presley I've loved my whole life. "But that doesn't mean I can be with you while you do this. I want you to be happy, but I need to make sure that I'm not being stupid either. I'm eighteen years old, so maybe this is for the best."

Yeah, we had a different plan, but this is a chance of a lifetime. There's a thousand people in line behind me who would kill for this deal. I step closer, and she doesn't retreat. "I love you."

"I love you too."

"Then tell me this isn't over. We can find a way."

She steps close, kisses me, and then takes a huge step back. "I wish we could. But I've lived the last two years in a long-distance relationship with you. I know what it takes. I won't do that again."

"Fine, then we'll take a break while you finish."

"A break?" *She closes her eyes.* "And what? We see other people?"

"I don't know. We can see how it goes." *In the back of my mind, I know it won't work. Not because we don't love each other, but it's a whole different world. I've talked to guys who went to the majors and none of their relationships lasted.* "I'm willing to try."

She wipes the tears that fall. "I want a life with you, Zach. Not to spend the next few years apart while I sit around waiting for phone calls again." *Presley places the engagement ring in my hand.* "I will always love you, but goodbye, Zach."

Before I can say anything else, she's running away. I could chase her. I want to chase her, but my feet don't move. I watch the love of my life leave, and I don't do a damn thing.

Thirteen

PRESLEY

"Can you head over to the Hennington ranch today?"

I look at Cooper as if he's grown another head. He knows that's the last place I want to go. "Why can't Wyatt go get the horses? It's his family."

"Listen, it's business. We bought two more horses from the Henningtons. I need Wyatt out in the pasture. The other men are busy, and you work for me." Cooper tries so hard to be stern.

I giggle. "That was almost convincing."

"I'm not joking. You need to be there before five."

It's been two weeks since the last time I saw Zach. Two weeks and not a peep. It's like one step forward and two steps back with us. I thought we were getting somewhere in the truck, and then he ruined it by kissing me. We have these moments of clarity only to have it eclipsed by the past.

"Coop, I can't." I go through possible excuses in my mind. He'll know that I'm lying, but there's not a chance in hell it's happening.

"I'm not asking."

"I'm not going."

"It's not all about you and your love life, Presley. Some of us had no choice. Some of us had to give up our dreams to face reality. Now it's time for you to grow up and face yours."

What does he know about reality? I've been in hell, waiting for things to be a little easier. But no, every time I feel an ounce of relief, something else happens. "Wow, it must be nice to sit in your ivory tower and judge me. You think I haven't had to grow up? Live a real life? You think I didn't have dreams that didn't pan out? Wake the fuck up."

I stand and Cooper rolls his eyes. "So what if you had to come back home?"

"I didn't come back home, Cooper. I lost *everything*. Every single thing that I had in my life. I lost it all. My husband, bakery, home, friends, the kids' school, you name it . . . it's gone. So tell me what reality you think I'm not facing, *dear* brother."

Cooper and I were close as kids. Being only two years apart meant we spent a ton of time together. Between him dating my girlfriends and teaming up with the Hennington boys to torment me, we were always in the same space. Plus, we had to help with the ranch. But this guy. This angry man isn't the Cooper I knew.

"I'm not going to argue with you."

"Yes," I demand, "you are. I want my brother back."

"Fine." His hands rise and fall. "You left all of us, Presley. You didn't just leave to go to college. You left. You never came back to visit or check on your family. I didn't even know your husband until after you were married. Let alone ever get to know my nephews. They're how old? This is the first time I've spent any time with them—ever."

I can imagine it hurt him. But I never knew it did this much. I always assumed Cooper was mad about not being able to leave here. "You were welcome at my home any time."

"I didn't want to come there. I wanted you to come home. This is your home. This is where you had an entire life you've pretended didn't exist." As angry as he appears to be, I can hear the underlying sorrow.

Tears pool as his words cut like knives. I never wanted to hurt my brother or my family. I couldn't come back here. I didn't want to face the people who said Zach and I were crazy and too young. Seeing the pity and hearing their whispers was something I knew I couldn't endure.

"It wasn't like that. I couldn't come home and deal with the rumors."

"Who cares what the hell people think? If you would've given anyone a chance, you would've known everyone was sad for you. But you never gave anyone a damn chance to show you that. You hid away and created a new life where none of us were welcome."

Cooper's right. I should've come home after the first time I visited. I excluded everyone in this town from my life. My parents, my brother, and anyone who had any connection to Zachary. I didn't want to think about him. Just hearing his name was like someone ripping my heart from my chest.

I've gone from hearing apologies for months to saying them constantly. "I'm sorry, Coop. I really am. I love you." I step forward and grab his arm. "It was easier to avoid."

I see the fight go out in Cooper's eyes. "It might have been for you. But it hurt like hell to lose my sister."

All I want is to feel normal again. I don't want tension with Cooper or anyone else. My brother has been there for the boys since we've been back. I want us to be back to what we once were. "I'm so sorry I hurt you." My honesty is in each syllable. "Can we move on? Can we find a way to be close again?"

"Yeah," he says with a smile. "You can shovel the stables for the next month, and I'll find a way to love you again."

"No way!" I laugh.

Cooper tugs me into his embrace. "I would've been there for you. I'm always here. Stop being so stubborn and let us help you."

I sink into my brother's arms and let go. "I'm so angry. I'm so sad."

He holds me tight. "I know, Pres. It's going to be okay."

I let him console me because I'm too tired to pretend anymore. And with Cooper, I don't have to.

Fourteen

"You didn't really think you could hide forever, did you?" Wyatt asks, leaning against the post. "That's the best part about small towns—they're small."

I've been able to dodge him for the most part. Keeping things really short and business oriented. "I'm not hiding."

He flashes a quick grin. "You're hiding a lot more than you're willing to admit."

"Well, if I told you then it would defeat the purpose."

It's five thirty in the morning, and I thought I'd be safe out here. My dreams have been getting worse and worse since the kiss. Now, Todd comes and accuses me of loving Zach all along. I know it's all my subconscious playing tricks on me, but I wake in a pool of sweat every morning. Now, I fight even falling asleep. It's better than the damn nightmares. But when I think about Todd, I grow extremely sad. All of our memories are tainted by the façade he was feeding me. I think about him waking up for work, getting dressed, and kissing me goodbye all the while knowing it was a lie. I wonder how many other lies he told me. Then my sadness shifts back to anger. It's exhausting.

"We're all hiding something, aren't we?"

"And what are you hiding?" I ask as he walks forward.

Wyatt studies me as if he can figure it out. "We're not talking about me. I know you, Pres. You've gotta tell someone, darlin'. It's eating you up."

"You don't know what the hell you're talking about."

He laughs. "You're a whole lot of angry. It seeps from you. It's keeping you from really being here."

I shake my head in annoyance. Why does he have to push me? Everyone has let me grieve in my own way, but not Wyatt. "You don't get to dictate how I handle my life. You're damn right I'm angry. I'd like you to find someone in my situation who wouldn't be."

"You're not the first person to deal with death." His voice is layered in sympathy even if his words aren't. "You're not grieving, Pres. You're barely living. Those boys," he points to the window of their bedroom, "they're living. They're helping on the farm, laughing, getting to know a family they didn't know. They're actually living, but you?" He pauses as my chest aches. Wyatt stands face to face with me. His brown eyes are open and honest. "You're just going through the motions."

Wyatt's hands brush up and down my arms.

"I don't know how to feel anything but anger."

He nods. "Anger I understand."

"I want it to stop."

"Take a walk with me," Wyatt urges. "There's a place you'll want to see."

My choices are simple—either go back to bed and get accosted later or face it now. Well, that's if Wyatt even lets me go anywhere. He's pretty damn good at getting his way. And the truth is, there's a part of me that doesn't want to be alone. "Fine, but I'm doing it under protest."

"When have you ever done anything willingly?" He laughs at his own joke and lightens the mood.

I shrug. "Maybe once."

We walk through the property out toward the creek as the sun is just starting to peek over the horizon. When we were kids, this was our spot. Wyatt and I would come sit out on the big rock in the middle of the water. We'd talk about all the things we were going to do, the way we'd live next to each other and our kids would be inseparable. The dreams of small town best friends.

"You know?" he says as we get close enough to hear the water. "I keep waiting for you to come home."

I look over with confusion. "Umm," I say. "I am home."

"No, you're still there," he states. "You've got half your heart still gone, Cowgirl." He tilts his head back looking at the stars. "You ever wonder what else is out there? It's a big universe, filled with so many people all searching for something else. His eyes meet mine, and he continues, "Tell me, what are you wishing for?"

My heart cracks as the reality that my wishes won't ever be possible flows through my veins. "It doesn't matter what I wish for, none of it will ever come true."

"I don't know about that. You can always wish, but it doesn't mean your wishes will get answered. Sometimes you have to choose whether what you're wishin' for is really what you want."

"Okay, Yoda."

We stand at the edge of the water as I look above me, wondering where Todd is. If he can see and hear this. I question if he knows what's in my and the boys' hearts. I ruminate about all the choices I've made and their outcomes. Choices are something we take for granted until we no longer have any options, and then we want to go back in time.

"Hop on," Wyatt says, squatting in front of me.

I scoff. "I'm not getting on your back."

"Woman, you always have to be a pain in the ass."

He turns around, crouches back down, and grips my knees. I don't have a moment to respond before I'm thrown over his shoulder. "Wyatt Hennington! You put me down!"

He trudges into the creek. "You sure about that?"

"No," I groan. "One day you'll let me have my way the first time."

"I doubt that. You usually pick wrong. I figure I'm saving us both a headache by doing it this way."

"You should talk."

A few more steps and we're at the rock. He puts me down, and I curl my legs so he has room. "Let's talk. You're stuck out here until you get over your shit."

I don't mention that I could walk my way back. I mean, it's two feet of water. However, I don't think that's the point. "What do you want me to say?"

He inches closer and nudges me with his arm. "Start with why you came back."

"My husband." I hesitate, needing to breathe a few times before I can continue. "He put us in a really bad spot."

"How so?"

Oh, the ways are never ending. This is the part I struggle with. How much information can I actually disclose? Why am I hiding all of his transgressions? Todd clearly didn't give a shit, so why do I? Part of it is pride, I know this. I don't want people to see how oblivious I was. Because only a fool doesn't know how bad their life is falling apart. "I was in the dark about every part of my life. I didn't know that Todd had lost his job or that we were in debt. So when he died, I had a mountain of problems dropped in my lap."

Wyatt rubs my back. "So you came back to put yourself on track?"

"I came back homeless. We lost it all. Literally. I was so stupid, Wyatt."

"You weren't stupid. If your husband didn't tell you, how would you know?"

I let out a half laugh. "Only someone so selfish and wrapped up in themselves wouldn't know their husband was out of work. I had no idea how bad things were. I could've helped out, but Todd went on like everything was fine. But it wasn't. It was—is—so bad."

"I don't know if you were selfish or just didn't want to know."

It's true, I didn't want to know anything. I let him handle every aspect of our financials because that was what he did for a living. It was natural for him to take the bills, and I ran the rest of our home. Looking back now, I was ignorant. I should've known at least something about our situation. And if I were being completely honest, the writing was on the wall, but I covered it with paint so I didn't have to see it.

"Do you think I'm pathetic?"

"Of course I don't!"

"I'm a thirty-five-year-old widow with two boys, and I live with my mother and father."

He sighs. "Okay, maybe a little."

I elbow him and he laughs. "Jerk."

"Look, life is a gamble. You played your cards and lost. Doesn't make you a loser. Means you need to find a new dealer."

I shake my head and grin at him. "You need to stop watching *The Hangover*. You've never even been to Vegas."

"I don't need to go to Vegas to learn about gambling."

"I guess it's better than quoting Kenny Rogers lyrics."

"I'm serious." Wyatt's tone shifts. "You're not stupid for loving someone or trusting them. Sometimes the other person loves you back, other times they love your brother."

"Wyatt," I say softly.

"You know I've loved you since I can remember. I know we'll never be. I accepted that a long time ago, but I like to give you shit when I can. One day you'll get your heads out of your asses and fix this mess you both made."

Wyatt told me about how he felt when Zach left for college. It wasn't in a leave-my-brother-for-me type of way. He explained that he had to tell me so he could move on. I cried as he clarified his feelings. I loved him, but not in that way. He also told Zach, which didn't go over well.

My hand finds his and he squeezes. "It would've been easier if it was you," I admit.

"It would've been easier if it wasn't you."

We both fall quiet as the water rushes past us. I yawn and Wyatt pulls me close. I rest my head on his shoulder with my eyes closed. It would've been so different if I had chosen him. Wyatt would've grounded me. He never had intentions of leaving here. He wanted to run his family's horse ranch, settle down, and have kids. Somehow we've both drifted so far off our paths we're not even in the same state.

Wyatt clears his throat waking me from the half-dazed state I fell under. "The sun is coming up. Time to head back."

I groan. "Five more minutes."

Cold water pelts me as I squeal. "Stop!"

I jump up as he continues. "Good morning, Cowgirl. Glad to see you're ready to head back. I was worried you were going to want to sleep here forever."

"It's a wonder why some girl hasn't married you yet," I tease.

"Am I throwing you over my shoulder or are you going to be a good girl?"

I climb on his back, and we head to the property. He moves with such ease as I rest my head on his shoulder. Wyatt doesn't put me down when we get to the creek bank like I expect. He keeps going, and I relax. "Thanks for this," I say as he gets closer to the house.

"If it's not going to be me you talk to, find someone. There's no shortage of people who love you. Even my half-wit brother—either of them."

We get to the house, and I climb off his back. "I don't think Zach and I will be talking any time soon."

He looks up and smiles. "Don't be so sure of that, darlin'."

I turn and find Zach sitting on the step. His hat covers his face and it's clear he's asleep. Son of a bitch. "Why?" I ask the sky. "Why do you torture me?"

Wyatt kisses my cheek before pushing me toward him. "Either you wake him or I do."

"I'm going inside. Let him know I have nothing to say to him."

I'm not dealing with him. That kiss was two weeks ago, and he's been radio silent since. And there's no gossip about him and the evil bitch breaking up. So it's clear that once again, Zach chose something else. I shouldn't be surprised. I shouldn't be hurt. I'm nothing to him. Hell, I'd be the homewrecker in this situation. Well, if I had instigated it.

Whatever, it doesn't matter. I don't want to talk to him, and I don't have to.

"I swear," Wyatt mutters as I walk around to the front of the house. I don't care if he thinks I'm being a child. I wonder if he knows what his brother did on the ride he manipulated to happen. I would've loved to have seen that, then I could've had the pleasure of watching him kick Zach's ass.

～

I gasp as I sit up in my bed. The clock reads twelve o'clock in the afternoon. I don't remember going to sleep, but I clearly did.

Quickly I get dressed and head downstairs. "Hello there, sugar," Mama says as she peels potatoes. "I was wondering when you were going to join us."

"Sorry, Mama. I must've fallen back asleep."

She smiles and goes back to cooking. "You haven't been sleeping. I figured you could use the rest."

My eyes snap up at her words. I thought I'd been hiding it well. Apparently not. "My mind never stops."

She puts the knife on the board, wipes her hands, and comes around the counter. "You could take today and go into town. Maybe get your hair done?"

I fight back the groan. Going to the beauty shop here is like stepping back into 1980. And not just because they haven't remodeled since then, the hair styles seem to have been stuck there as well. The thing is, I can't keep hiding out. "Maybe I'll head to Nashville," I say casually.

She scoffs. "I think you get much better service in town. I'll call over and see if Victoria has any openings."

Mama doesn't waste any time as she heads over to the phone. "Mornin'," Daddy says as he walks in.

My mother yaps on the phone as Daddy flashes a grin. "Save me, Daddy."

He laughs and kisses my cheek. "Oh, baby girl, there's no

saving you when she gets her mind set. The boys are planning to help Cooper with baling hay later if you want to help."

"My most dreaded chore."

"They seem to like it here." He tosses his hat on the table.

I sit and grab a muffin.

As much as I subconsciously wanted them to hate it here, I'm glad they're fitting in. They've had as much change and hard times as I have. I'm grateful for my brother, Wyatt, and my father being here to help guide them.

"They're trying. I think it's hard going from the city to here."

"It's been great watching them with the horses. They're naturals. They didn't even hesitate with helping Zachary."

The muffin falls to the floor. "What?" I almost scream. "What do you mean helping him?"

I stand and try to calm myself, but every muscle in my body is tight.

"Zach brought the horses that you refused to go get. If you would stop being so damn obstinate, he wouldn't have had to come all this way."

I scoff. "All this way?" Please. It's less than a mile and he used to walk it every day. "When did he leave?"

Daddy stands, puts his hat back on, and lets out a long breath. "He's with the boys now."

I don't say a word. I leave and head right out the door. He's not allowed near my kids. I don't want him anywhere around us. If they were to ever find out the truth about Zach and me, it would drum up too many questions. Plus, I don't want them to like him.

I get out to the corral where the boys are sitting on the fence. Their feet dangle and they both lean forward. Zach stands in front of them with a horse, and I hear their laughter. It stops me in my tracks. Both boys are laughing. I've missed that sound so much. A tear falls as I clutch my chest. It's been so long since any of us have been happy. So many months of feeling nothing.

Zach's eyes raise and lock with mine.

As angry as I was a few minutes ago, right now I can't find that feeling. Cayden and Logan have been sad or entirely vacant with me, and here they are, once again, seemingly whole.

"He's not always a dipshit." Wyatt nudges me as he sees what I'm looking at.

"Debatable."

Zach and the boys start laughing again. He gives the boys the reins, and I watch them walk around with huge smiles.

"When are you going to wake up, Pres?"

I look over at him with frustration. I'm so tired of him pushing. "Don't."

He raises his hands in surrender. "I'm not saying a word." He stops talking for only a second before opening his mouth again. "But I will say this . . ."

"You can't help yourself."

"I think those boys need to see their mama smile and laugh. They need to see that it's okay to be happy."

Wyatt's arm wraps around my waist. He holds me against him and Zach's eyes find mine again. "They love you, Presley. They see you and watch how you're barely holding on. It's hard for kids to see their mama like that. So, go show them you're happy they're allowed to be."

He's probably right. I don't want them to think it's not okay to live. I want happiness for them. Hell, I want it for me too. I want to stop seeing that night. It's killing me. I have dark circles under my eyes, my clothes are loose, and I'm so damn tired.

I walk slowly over toward the corral and hold myself together. "Boys," I say with a smile.

"Mom!" Logan rushes over. "Look! This is mine and that's Cayden's new horse!"

"Whoa!" I'm taken aback. "I didn't know you got your own horses."

"Isn't it awesome?"

"It sure is! Did you name them?"

"No! Cay!" Logan yells over to his brother. "We have to name them!"

The boys run off, trotting them around the ring. I smile. Each time the horse does something new, they both come to life. It reminds me of the Christmas that Todd and I got them each the bikes they wanted. We had to bundle them in five layers so they could ride in the freezing cold.

"I can't believe Cooper and my daddy could afford this," I say to myself.

I look at Zach, and he smiles. "Well, your dad bought two new horses, but I thought that maybe the boys would like their own too."

"You did this?" I ask. "You gave them two horses?"

"They can't live on a farm without a horse."

"Zach," I whisper, "it's too much."

My heart swells with appreciation. Horses are not cheap. The Hennington Horse Farm has always been extremely lucrative. They breed, train, board, and sell some of the top horses in the state. The gesture is beyond anything I deserve. The last time we saw each other, I slapped him. Yet, here he is, giving each of my kids a horse. It reminds me of the boy I fell in love with.

"I remember being a kid. I can't imagine this is easy for them. A horse can be a great therapy tool. Think about how many nights we'd take off just to free our minds. I figured with their dad, a new home, and not knowing anyone . . ."

I feel like such a bitch. Here he is going out of his way for my kids, and I wanted to come out here and punch him in the face. I look over at the boys as they pet their new horses. "Thank you, Zach. I truly don't know what to say. I'm really blown away."

"Just say, 'Thank you, Zachary.'" He pauses, smiling. "'You're the kindest, most handsome man I've ever known.'"

I laugh. "Still living in a delusional world."

We both stand there, watching the boys. Wyatt hops in the ring with them and shows them a few tips.

"Are you sure about this? It's a lot of money. If it's a problem, we can work something out."

"Absolutely not."

"You really didn't have to do this."

"I really did. I wanted to do this for them. And for you."

He doesn't even know them, but he always had a big heart and a soft spot for kids.

"I wish I could pay you."

Zach's hand grips my upper arm. "I wouldn't let you."

I look at where his skin touches mine, and we both step back.

"Look, what happened two weeks ago—"

"Let's not," I reply quickly. The last thing I want to do is talk about that damn car ride home. It's only going to bring up unwanted emotions.

He sighs and looks away. "The more we keep pretending, the worse this keeps getting. I shouldn't have kissed you."

"No. You shouldn't've."

"I know you're not ready."

"Not ready?" I laugh. "Not ready for what? For the fact that you have a girlfriend? Not ready because my husband died less than six months ago? Or maybe it's because we haven't seen each other in, ohhh." I pause, counting off in my head. "seventeen years."

"I'm not saying I want to be together, Presley. I mean, you're not ready to forgive me for something that you know was the right choice. Or at least the choice anyone would've made."

I sigh and close my eyes. 'Round and 'round we go.

"Right for you, Zach. It was the right choice *for you*. It's a common theme in my life." It hits me right then. I love men who choose themselves above me.

"What does that mean?"

"It means that it wasn't the best choice for us. It wasn't what I wanted. It was what you wanted. If you hadn't dragged me out there and left, it could've been different. I'm not angry because you took it, I'm angry because you decided our life without even talking to me."

He shakes his head and pushes the air from his lungs. "You couldn't be any more wrong about that. You think that choice wasn't for the both of us? I could've given you everything. The money I was going to make would've given us the life we dreamt of."

He's being delusional. Zach wouldn't have started in the majors. He thought the money would have been there, but he forgets that Triple-A ball players barely make a living wage. Plus, I wasn't ready to live that life. We had talked about him entering the draft after his senior year, not the beginning of his junior year. We would've had almost three years together by the time everything had worked out. Then, to find out he did it all without a word—hurt.

All I wanted was a say in how our life would go.

I don't speak as my chest heaves. I am so tired of this goddamn merry-go-round. I want off. This is in the past, yet we keep bringing it to the present. "Can we stop? Please? There's a lot I would change about how we handled things in our past. I don't want to be angry anymore."

He steps forward. "I was thinking of you." His voice is hushed. "I thought about how I could finally be the man you saw."

"I don't want to do this."

"I was ready to give you everything. I *could* give you everything."

"Now you can give it to Felicia."

Zach rears back. "I told her everything."

My heart races. "She forgave you?"

He studies me. "She understands this is difficult for both of us. Felicia isn't the girl you remember."

"Maybe not. I don't know . . . she seems the same to me."

"I get it now." Zach's deep voice seems amused.

"Get what?"

"You don't want me. You've made that clear, but you don't want anyone else to have me. Did you think I'd live alone and pine over you, Presley?"

Again, we go one step forward and two steps back. Of course I didn't think that. I wished it, but I didn't think it would happen. I tried very hard not to think of Zach. Because loving him nearly broke me apart. Even all these years later when I think of him, my heart yearns for him. Zach is the piece of my soul that's been missing. But he's not mine anymore.

"Thank you for the horses. Maybe one day we'll be able to keep things civil." I raise my brow and pat his chest.

Zach steps closer. "I know you may not want to hear this, but I will always be here for you. You have been a part of my life since I can remember. I hated not having you in it. I missed you." His eyes stay trained on me. "I don't know a day that's gone by when I haven't thought of you. So, if you want me to be the bad guy . . . fine. I'll be that because I think you need someone to hate."

I gasp while shaking my head. "I never wanted to hate you."

"But you do, and I can take it. I spent enough years hating myself. Just remember what I said."

There's no way we can go back. I'm not the girl I once was. I appreciate his gesture, whether it was sincere or spawned from guilt. But when it comes to me, there's a line he's not welcome to cross. I don't know that I can be friends with someone I loved—love—so much.

Fifteen

There's a stack of papers sitting on my desk that need to be handled. I head to the office where Cooper sits in a chair with his hat over his face. I creep over and jump, making a loud *bang*. He leaps out of his seat ready to fight. I burst out laughing as he glares at me.

"So not funny."

"Oh, I beg to differ."

He slaps the dirt off his leg and sits back down. "Revenge is a sport I'm a champion of."

I know this all too well. Cooper and I had full-out wars throughout our childhood and adolescence. Mama was always warning us she'd paddle our asses. One time, I took all of Coop's clothes, put them in a garbage bag, and buried them. He wore the same nasty pants and shirt for four days, then Daddy threatened to sell my horse if I didn't tell him where it was.

"I'm not exactly a loser either, dear brother."

"Ha! You'll never beat me."

"Whatever." I dismiss his antics. "What brings you to the office?"

Cooper and Wyatt never have time to stop here during the day. I honestly don't know how they were managing anything before. Since I've gotten here, I've been able to make sense of their nonexistent filing system. My mother has been doing her best to help, but when my father retired, so did she. Instead of Cooper finding someone to run the office, he pretended the problem wasn't there.

"No one is here nagging me."

"Ahh." I smirk. "Mama and Daddy are at it again?"

They want more grandbabies. They want my brother to get married. And when they can corner him, they let him have it.

"She's trying to set me up with some girl a few towns over."

"She pretty?" His face says it all. "Okay, then."

"Anyway, I'm here because the boys want to go camping and explore. I thought I'd take them out for a three-day ride. You good with that?"

I've been on these rides. They're not easy. "Why don't you start with a one-day camp out?"

"Because they're going to be men. Stop babying them."

"I don't baby them."

"Sure, you don't." His exasperation is clear in his tone. "Look, we'll ask them. If they want to go, which they will because I'm pretty fucking fun, then you let them."

All of the dangers flood my brain. I went on a hundred of these trips, but I knew how to shoot a coyote. I was aware of what to watch for. Logan and Cayden have never gone camping. Todd didn't like being outside in the wilderness, and I never pushed. I was happy with our vacationing to major cities and staying in hotels. Todd's idea of roughing it was a hotel with no room service.

"I don't know . . ."

"Go ahead, Pres. Raise a bunch of pussies. They'll do great when they start school in a month. You want to send them to school not knowing how to bait a hook?"

Asshole has a point. "Fine. We'll ask them." Wyatt clears his throat from the door. "Let me guess . . . you think this is a good idea?"

"Cowgirl, it *was* my idea."

I should've known.

As Cooper had predicted, the boys were ecstatic. They ran out of my room and were throwing things in bags before I even said yes. I made Cooper promise me a few things before I was fully on board. First, they take experienced horses. Those boys haven't ridden, and we don't know the personalities of their new horses. Second, either my father or Wyatt had to go with them too.

My father agreed to ride out, but he said he was too old to sleep out there with the "youngins." Wyatt said he had plans, but Trent was off this weekend and would be happy to go. When I shot that down, they pointed out he was the sheriff. And my argument was lost. It's like they've all forgotten the stories about Trent.

They left about an hour ago, and Mama left to go play cards with Mrs. Hennington and Mrs. Rooney, which I know she does when she tells Daddy she's going to practice singing for the church choir. Those women haven't practiced in thirty years.

Taking my mother's, well, everyone's unsolicited advice, I called Grace for a girls' night. Thanks to my stress, I've lost a ton of weight and can wear some pretty cute things. I'd gone online and ordered some clothes that are a little more form fitting than I've been able to wear since having twins. Those kids destroyed my body.

Once in my black shorts and one-shoulder shirt, I head over to the mirror and look myself over. Staring at my reflection, I smile and let out a deep breath. I feel beautiful. More than that, I feel like a woman. My curves are smooth, my hair hangs in soft curls, my eyes are bright green thanks to my makeup, and my ass looks fantastic. At least one good thing has come of this. I throw on my cowboy boots and head to the porch.

"You got a hot date or somethin'?" Grace calls from the window of the car.

"You know it." I laugh and climb in.

She demanded that she drive so I could relax for a little bit. It's insane for her to think I'm going to need a designated driver, but I'm tired of fighting everyone and everything, so I go with it. That's my plan for tonight . . . let loose and smile.

Grace puts the car in drive, practically bouncing in her seat.

"I'm so glad you called. I needed to get out. Since I ended things with Trent, I haven't been out."

I've wondered about that. "What happened?"

She snorts. "You know better than anyone about dating a Hennington."

"I'm sorry, Gracie."

She grips my hand. "Please, I'm over it. He's hot and all, but I'm not going to beg a man to love me."

Grace has had her eyes on that man since we were kids. He was by far the hottest of the three, but he knew it. Looking at him now, he's definitely not the sexiest anymore. At least not to me. He's still built and in shape, but there's something missing. Why couldn't they be ugly? Have one of their nuts missing or something? Instead, they're all perfect in their own ways. Wyatt's humor makes him more attractive, plus his job keeps him fit. Zach has only gotten better with age, plus his heart is still huge. And Trent's authority is damn right sinful. Stupid Hennington boys.

We park in front of the local bar and my head falls back. "Not here, Grace."

"Zach isn't going to be here. And it's easy if we both drink too much."

How she knows Zach won't be here is beyond me. But I look around the parking lot and don't see his truck. "Let me guess." I smirk as I think I figure it out. "Another guy will be?"

"Trent is with your boys, isn't he?" she asks.

"I didn't say Trent."

She groans. "Look, there's a guy I like, but he won't talk to me when Trent is around. Bastard made it like he owns me or something. So, you can be my wingman-girl-whatever."

It's been a really long time since I've done this. But if there's anyone I want to still be close with, it's Grace. She's not once pried or made me feel uncomfortable. She's been here for me without pushing, which is a damn gift in this town.

"Fine, let's go snag us some country boys."

We exit the car, and I try to tug my shorts down. "Does this make me look slutty?" I ask her.

Grace lets out a giggle before covering her mouth. "Honey, any shorter and those are panties."

"Oh, my God." I start to head toward the car, but she grabs my arm.

"You look amazing, Presley. I was kidding," she tries to reassure me. "I mean it. I only wish I had your body . . . and I never had kids."

"Now you're just lying."

"Never. Please," she begs, "if he's not here we can drive to another town."

Grace's pouty face reminds me of the boys. One day I'll stop being a sucker. "Fine."

We head in where everyone is hanging around. Grace grabs my hand and leads me through the crowd. Thankfully there aren't a lot of people I recognize. We find a spot at the bar and grab our beers. It's funny how since Todd is gone, I remember things I used to like. When he was alive, I drank wine or vodka, now I'm grabbing beer and whiskey. I hated wearing boots or anything tight, yet here I am in both. I don't know if it was him that I changed for, or if I was fighting so hard to not be the country girl I am.

Morphing into something else didn't hide who I really am.

"Look what the cat dragged in." I hear Felicia's unpleasant voice from behind me.

I turn with a scowl. "Hi there, Felicia."

Grace side eyes me.

"Good to see you," Felicia says.

"I thought you and Zach were in Nashville," Grace tacks on.

"We were, but Wyatt called sayin' there was some emergency at the farm. You know how it is with our farm."

Our? Grace grabs my arm before I can say anything. "We're having a girls' night, so we'll catch you later." She whisks me away.

"What the hell?"

"She's delusional, and you don't need to worry about the crap she shits out of her mouth."

I laugh at the visual she paints. "Do you see the cowboy you have your eyes on?" If she doesn't, we're leaving.

"Yup, I do!" Grace practically bounces. "How do I look?"

I give her a once over, fluff her hair, and pull one sleeve off her shoulder. She always was beautiful. Her hair is woven to a side braid and her deep blue eyes pop with the dark liner. "You look perfect."

"Trent—" She starts to say something and then stops, shaking her head. "No, I'm not thinking about that man. He had his chance. I'm over him."

The Hennington boys don't seem to think their hold runs out though.

I glance around her, trying to see who the cowboy she set her sights on could be, but my eyes land on Zach. Dammit.

"Grace, he's here."

Her breath catches. "Who? Trent?"

"No, Zach."

"So what? You're not with him. You don't even like him."

I know Grace and she knows me. I may not like him. I may not want even a second of time with him, but there's no denying how we still look at each other. We both try to fight the rope that binds us, but the knots are too tight.

"Right. Not a big deal." I try to play it off, but the slight lift of her lip tells me she doesn't buy it. "Shut up."

Her hands rise. "I didn't say a word."

She turns her head and lets out a heavy sigh. "What is it?" I ask.

"I need a shot. I'm being a chicken."

I shake my head. She's always been shy. It was always one of us pushing her out of her comfort zone. Good to see some things are still like I remember. "Okay, shots it is."

Nothing like some liquid courage.

Grace gets a Buttery Nipple whereas I get Jameson on the rocks from the bartender, Brett. He graduated high school with us and was always the one throwing parties. Funny that he chose this line of work. He hands us the drinks with a smile and lingering eyes.

"No fair that I'm the only one doing shots!" Grace complains.

"Wanna trade?" I offer her, but she shakes her head.

"I don't know how you drink that stuff anyway."

"Bottoms up!" I raise my glass.

We clink, and she chugs. I sip my whiskey, looking around and enjoying the music. She stares at the dance floor looking forlorn. I feel bad that she's unhappy, so I quickly finish my glass and order us another round. Grace's mood perks up as we keep drinking.

Two more glasses down, and somehow Grace gets me to do a few of her nasty shots. I'm feeling light and free. It's like floating . . . albeit with cement blocks on my feet.

Zach and Felicia slow dance, and it takes everything within me not to pitch a fit. The feeling I was enjoying dissipates. I hate her. Self-righteous bitch. I hate him. Reckless boy. I hate men because they're assholes who break your heart and then make you live a life you didn't want.

I chug the remnants of my Jameson and thank God for the one man who always keeps me feeling good.

Then I look over at Zach, who smiles. *Fuck you and your dumb smile. I hate you.* I fake smile back and then turn toward Grace with a grimace.

"Why the long f-face?" Grace stutters.

I close my eyes so I don't have to see them. "I hate her. I really hate her. And she's ugly."

Grace looks over and laughs. "Inside and out."

"Right." I giggle. "Whatever, I don't want him anyway. He can keep his stupid girlfriend with her stupid hair and her stupid lips. I don't even like him."

"Suuure," she slurs while falling off the chair. "Crap!"

We burst out in loud fits. Shit, I'm drunk as hell. "How much have we drank?"

"Not enough! Bartendeeeeer!" Grace slams her hand on the bartop. "Get my girl and me another round."

We take another round of shots, which some very nice man at the end of the bar pays for. Grace and I are now completely blitzed. "Let's dance!" she yells, or at least I think she does.

Bouncing to the dance floor, we hold on to each other as we do what I think are the right steps. I've been doing this my whole life. I'm functioning solely on muscle memory.

At the end of the song, a handsome cowboy grabs me. "Wanna dance?"

"Why the hell not?" I smile.

He holds me close against his body and leads me around the floor. I giggle and rest my head on his chest so I don't get sick. His hands are strong and firm. Everything I remember about these kind of guys. They're rough and rugged with muscles to die for. But this cowboy doesn't know my current baggage, so I let him roam the range a little. Plus, right now . . . I don't even care.

"You're Presley Townsend, right?"

"Benson, but yes."

"Well, you're as pretty as I remember."

That stops me for a second. "I know you?"

He laughs as his hand grabs right above my butt cheek. "Honey, I've known you my whole life. You were always untouchable though."

I lift my head to find Zach glaring at me and my dance partner. I return the look briefly before giving my attention back to him. "Well, I'm not untouchable anymore." I move my hand up his chest slowly.

His lips close in and brush against my cheek. "I see that."

I turn my head so I can look back at the man who held that role for so long. He gazes down at Felicia, and then she grabs his neck and kisses him. I start to shake and drop my hands. "I don't feel good. I'll be back," I explain and rush to the bathroom. I feel sick, but it's not the booze.

I take a few minutes to collect myself. He was kissing her, but she's his girlfriend. It's irrational and completely insane to think I should care. I was married. I have two kids and clearly had a life after him. But I didn't ever consider him having the same. My hands hold the sink as I try to get a freaking grip.

My mind goes to the way he stared at me. The way he kissed me. Zach is engrained so deep in my soul I don't know how to expunge him. I don't want him in there, because he doesn't belong to me anymore.

I promise myself I won't let myself acknowledge any of those feelings. This is just my loss and pain reflecting on the past. The sands of time have fallen and buried Zach and me. Now it's up to me to find a new hourglass.

I close my eyes and step back, ready to live this new drunken life.

"Watch it." I hear from behind me.

"Did I step on your foot? Poor thing." I want to say sorry, but it's Felicia, so I don't. I couldn't care less about hurting her right now. Plus, I'm not really certain that I'm speaking in coherent sentences.

Grace opens the door. "Pres! There you are!"

Felicia looks at her before returning to me. "Zach'll rub it. He rubs all my pains away." She shrugs. "I bet you remember how that feels. Or maybe you don't."

I go from annoyed to hostile in no time. "Fuck you." I step toward her with my fists balled. "I'm pretty sure he'd much rather be rubbing me than you."

Oh, my God. I actually said that.

By the sound of Grace's gasp, I really did. She comes around behind me and tries to pull me away.

"That's why he's here with me?"

"Is that why he kissed me?" *Keep it up, Presley. You're on a roll.* I want to punch myself. I shouldn't have said that. I shouldn't be letting her bother me. I need to leave and get sober. But for this one second, it feels so good. I'm not bottling anything up or thinking about anything. I'm letting it all out.

Grace yanks me harder toward the door. "Pres, let's go dance."

"He already told me." She crosses her arms. "He told me how he felt nothing when it happened. It reaffirmed you're his past."

It hurts me in the depths of my soul where I've been hiding all my emotions. It was a stupid mistake that meant nothing. Maybe it was just old times. Maybe it was something else, but there is a small part of me that still loves him. And her saying that . . . cuts me deep.

"You're a bitch," Grace says over her shoulder as she pulls me out of the bathroom.

"I want another drink," I say to Grace. She nods and rubs my back.

Zach is standing right outside the door when we exit. His eyes meet mine, and I'm sure he sees it. "Presley. Are you okay?" The sound of his voice soothes me, even though I don't want it to. I look at him and remember the good things. The way Zach could make me feel so protected. His heart that he wore on his sleeve. His heart that was mine. I remember the nights he'd hold me in his arms, promising me we'd always be together. The way his lips felt against mine, and how I never wanted to lose that.

I close my eyes as a tear falls. I won't let him see me though. "No." I say the word as we walk away.

It's honest.

It hurts.

But it's the first real thing I've said to him.

Grace pulls me against her, and we move. The tears don't stop. The alcohol has unleashed the things I've hidden. I plop into a chair with my head in my hands. "I'm so foolish," I say as Grace rubs my arms.

"Go grab her some water, Grace. I'll take her outside for some air." Zach's deep timbre is close to my ear.

I look up with blurry vision, but I know it's him. I would be able to see him if I were blind.

"Let's go outside. You don't need eyes on you." His hand extends, and I don't hesitate. When our skin touches, my chest aches. I don't want to feel anymore. Why can't I close myself off? The confusion whips around in my head, tying me up and fusing me to him. Zach's touch spurs a myriad of reactions.

Once we get out back, I rip my hand from his. "Why are you here? Why do you have to be here? Why can't you leave me alone?"

"Why are you so hell-bent on pushing me away?"

"Because you mess with my head!" The tears fall as I look in the blue eyes I've missed. "Why do you care? Why are you out here with me and not with her?"

"Because you're in pain," he says as if that makes any sense.

"You have no idea, Zach. You can't even begin to imagine how much pain I'm in."

"Tell me. I'm always your friend. Just talk to me and tell me. Get it out, Presley. What has you in so much pain that you can't even see what you have here?"

Anger flows from the pit of my stomach. Hate, regret, fear, devastation all bubble to the surface. I look at him and want him to understand. He did this. Todd did this. "Because of you and him! You're the same. You leave. You take and take, and then you both threw me away like I was nothing." The agony pours out from every fiber of me. "Am I that bad? Am I worth nothing? Don't you see, Zach?" I choke on the words. "You left me alone and scared. Then Todd put me together only to fucking hang himself because I wasn't worth the time to talk about it. He left me and those boys like we meant nothing. God!" I grip the side of my head as I explode from every cell in my body. I can't stop crying or feeling. My words are like a volcano erupting. "Selfish! You're both selfish!"

"Presley." He steps forward, but when he touches me, I flinch back. "It wasn't like that with me."

His words only enrage me more. "It was exactly like that! I'm not healing because you all have cut me so deep, there's no cure. I needed you to stay! I loved you so much that a part of me died when you left me. You broke me so much more than I even knew! I got better though. I picked myself up and found my second chance. I needed him to stay! I needed you to stay!" I step back as a sob erupts from my chest. "Why couldn't you have stayed?"

That's the thing though, no one ever stays.

Zach's arms are around me before I can say another word. I cling to him like he's my savior. I need him so much right now. I don't know why. I can't grasp anything except the pain I feel and the comfort he's offering. In this moment, he feels safe. He holds me close as I weep.

"I'm sorry," he says as he tightens his embrace. "I'm so sorry I hurt you, Presley. I loved you more than you ever knew." He doesn't loosen his hold as he continues. "I never wanted to leave you. I wanted to figure it out."

He's keeping me together. I can't speak or even think. I allow his arms to envelop me. I don't want him to let go because I fear that I'll fall apart.

Zach pulls back, gripping my face in his hands. His thumbs wipe the tears that fall. "Your husband, though, he must've been desperate. No one would ever leave you unless they had no choice."

"Don't," I plead. "I should've never said anything." In all these months I've never said the words aloud. The lie of his death has been my own load to carry, and I'm being crushed by it.

"You've been keeping this in all this time?" My lips quiver as I see the pain in his eyes. He may not have known Todd, but he can see the agony I'm in. "Pres, who else knows?"

My body shakes as the reality of what I've revealed truly hits. I told the last person I'd ever want to confess my secret to. I start to backpedal. "That's not what I meant."

His eyes widen. "What part?"

"Nothing. I'm drunk and didn't mean what I said."

Zach steps back and the door flies open. "There you are!" Felicia's eyes narrow in on Zach's hands on my wrists. "Baby?" She saunters over. "I was looking for you."

I tug my arms back and wipe my face. I will not let her see anything.

"Hey," he says with a tremble in his voice. "Presley was upset. I was checking on her."

She rolls her eyes and her arms slither around his torso. "She looks fine now." I hear his sigh as she continues to twist the knife. "Let's head home."

The bile churns inside my stomach, and I want to throw up. I hate this girl. "Give me a few more minutes out here," Zach says, looking back at me as he pushes her arms off him. "I'll be right in." Her arms fall. She's clearly pissed. But a fragment of my fractured heart just became Zachary Hennington's. One look, one choice, one moment of time was all it took to reaffirm all the reasons I loved him once upon a time. He dismissed her—for me.

"Zach," I say as Felicia crosses her arms. "I'm fine." It's the furthest thing from the truth, but I don't want to talk anymore. I don't want the pity that comes with him knowing my secret.

Grace comes through the door, stumbling a little. "Good Lord! Where the hell have you been?" She clutches her chest.

"Sorry." I plaster on a fake smile.

Felicia takes this distraction to attach herself to Zach, and he clearly looks uncomfortable.

"I thought you left when you weren't out front, or I don't know."

I head toward her, hoping to calm her down. "Everything is good. We were all just coming inside."

She loops my arm in hers, and we walk toward the door. I pause for a second, look back at Zach, and mouth the words, "Thank you."

He nods, and I pray he'll keep my secret. The last thing I need is for people to find out what really happened. There are enough rumors and people talking now. If they know . . . there's no way I can contain it.

Sixteen

Grace does her best to get my mind off things. We dance, but my head spins with how easy it was for me to tell him. And how good it felt to be in his arms. It scares me because it would be effortless to let myself go back there. He's the boy who taught me to love. He's the boy I saw myself growing old with, having children with, and yet he destroyed me.

"You having fun?" Grace asks slightly out of breath.

"Tons." I smile at her. The truth is . . . I want to go crawl in bed and cry. As much as I hate that I told Zach, it hurts more that I said it at all.

"Liar."

"Little bit."

She rests her head on my shoulder. "We can go."

"No, it's fine. We can stay a bit longer. Besides, your man is heading this way."

The guy who Grace has been eyeing all night asks her to dance. She's so funny. I know she doesn't really like him, but I also know what trying to move on from a Hennington is like. God help her.

I look over at the dance floor where Zach has Felicia in his embrace. I imagine myself as her. The way his body feels, the ridges of his chest, the strength of his arms, and how he can make you forget all your pain. When we were young, he was able to take my worries away. I never felt scared. I loved that so much about him. I think that was the worst part of losing him—the uncertainty. Watching Felicia share that with him is difficult. Does she know the person he is? Does she know how much better he is than her?

My eyes open to see him watching me. My breathing stops as we share something in this stare. All I feel is his regret, and all I give him back is my forgiveness. I turn away, hoping to break the connection, but it feels as if my heart is no longer in my chest.

I can do this.

I'm not falling for him again. Nope. I'm drunk and not thinking straight.

Unable to stop myself, I look back at him. He gives me a smile, then looks at Felicia as she turns and glares at me. I get up and head to the bar. I don't need to witness their lover's quarrel.

"Looks like trouble in paradise." The bartender smirks as he hands me my drink.

"I wouldn't know." I refuse to look over, but I'm sure he's talking about Zach and Felicia.

He laughs. "I could give you the play by play. He doesn't look happy to see us talking." Brent grips my hand and leans in. "I'll give him a little push." His hand brushes across my lips, and I worry he's going to kiss me. "Just go with it," he murmurs.

I close my eyes and slightly turn my head so that he doesn't actually kiss me. When I open them, Brent whispers, "He just pushed Felicia away."

"I-I don't." There's nothing that I can say to even express what I'm feeling. So many damn things go through my head. I glance at them and clearly Felicia is pissed.

I quickly turn my head, and Brent smirks. "That one's on the house."

Minutes go by, and I force myself not to look. He didn't come over here, so Brent obviously knows nothing. And why am I even wanting him to come over?

"Pres." A hand touches my shoulder, and I gasp. My stomach clenches at the feel of his touch.

I turn as Zach is staring at me.

I don't know what to say.

"Presley, there's a problem. We have to go."

Confusion washes over me. "What do you mean?"

"I got a call from Wyatt."

"Is he okay?" I jump up as panic sets in. "What's wrong?"

Zach looks away and fear takes hold. "Wyatt's okay," he says quickly. "But something's happened, and we need to get to the ranch."

"You're confusing me."

He lets out a deep breath. "It's Cayden."

My mouth falls open as my body goes numb. "What?" I ask breathlessly. "Cayden? What about Cayden?" I practically scream.

I can't handle anything happening to my sons. I can't endure another loss. I will die with them. I won't be able to recover from anything else. I'm already on the fringe of losing it.

"Trent and Cooper were working on the campsite and the boys took off on the horses. They went after them, but they can't find Cayden. They've searched everywhere, and nothing."

"Oh, my God!" I cry out. "We have to go! Now!" I scream and grab my purse. Here I was out drinking and one of my kids is lost in the woods. I sober up immediately. I can't think of anything but finding my son. Panic and anger swirl together as my emotions conflict. This can't be happening.

"Brent, get a bunch of guys together. We need as much help as we can get," Zach instructs.

It's one of those moments where it feels like nothing is moving. I'm paralyzed with fear. It's as if my feet are stuck to the ground. I stand still while people move around me. Zach touches my shoulder and I flinch. "I'm leaving." I snap out of my trance and blurt out.

"Let's go. I'm coming with you," he says as he follows behind me. I rush to get my car.

"Zach!" Felicia calls out. "What the hell are you doing?"

I don't stop. I don't have time. I burst through the door and realize I don't have my car. "Fuck!"

I turn to go get Grace and see Zach pushing Felicia's arms off him. She's yelling at him as he tries to move toward me. "God damn it, Felicia!" he shouts. "I'm going. No one knows those woods like me. Get a ride with someone or walk. We'll finish our conversation later." He runs toward me and points to his truck. "Get in."

I don't hesitate. We both hop in, and Zach throws the truck in reverse. I don't say anything as we fly down the dirt roads. All I can think is Cayden must be so scared. He's alone in the dark, out in the woods. There are so many things that can go wrong. He's never been camping and doesn't know what to do if you get separated. There's so much I should've told them before I agreed to this.

"I can't—" My breathing comes rapidly and my heart pounds. "He must be so alone."

"He's going to be okay." Zach tries to reassure me. "We'll find him."

"You don't know that."

"We'll find him, Presley."

I shake my head because he can't guarantee anything. I know he wants to help, but with my luck . . . "Don't make me promises, Zachary. You've broken them before."

"I won't break this one."

We get to my house faster than I could've imagined, or maybe it just feels that way. I jump out of the truck and Zach follows. My father is waiting at the barn.

"Daddy!" I rush toward him.

"It's going to be okay, sugar." His strong arms cocoon me.

"What about Logan?" I look around as my breathing turns even more erratic.

Daddy holds my shoulder and touches my cheek with his other hand. "He's upstairs with your mama. He's okay, but worried."

I look and see Mama in the window. I start to head inside, but she shakes her head and puts her finger to her lips.

"Let him sleep," Daddy says quietly. "We'll find him, Presley. Cooper, Trent, Wyatt, and all my ranch hands are out looking now." My father has always been so confident, but even he looks a little shaken.

I can't stand here any longer. If Logan is safe, then I have to focus on Cayden. I need to go look for him. "We're heading out too."

"I figured as much. I had the horses saddled with the gear you need. There's another group of us going in twenty minutes to take a different route."

I take off running toward the barn. Zach is on my heels as we both know there's no time to waste. "Are you okay to ride?" he asks.

I mount the horse and glare at him. "Let's go."

"All right."

We head out toward the area they're in. It'll take us about a half hour to get close. My nerves are frayed as I think about the time we're wasting. But it's much easier to get through this area on horseback than in a car. I don't say anything to Zach. A part of me doesn't even realize he's with me. I just want to find my son.

Finally, we get into the general area around the falls where we usually camp. "Presley!" Zach calls from behind and comes alongside me.

"What?" I ask as the adrenaline pulses through me. "We don't have time. We have to find him." My words come out like bullets as I spur my horse forward, but he grabs the reins.

"Stop."

"Let go," I say between gritted teeth. "This is my son!" I don't care about anything else. Standing here and talking is wasting time. I want to find Cayden. I'm so stupid to have let him go on this trip. I should've known that Cooper and fucking Trent couldn't handle them.

"You need to stop. We need a plan. Think for a second."

Part of me wants to knee him in the balls, but he's right. If we start wandering through the woods, we'll never find him. "I don't know what to do," I say feeling more helpless than ever.

"Where would he go? What does he like?"

I try to focus on what he asked. I don't know what the boys saw during the day. I'm not sure if they went along any special trails, but Cooper and Trent probably checked those first. What else is out here? Logan would follow an animal, but Cayden has always loved the water. "The falls!"

Zach takes off ahead of me, ducking and turning, avoiding the trees and branches. My horse follows him, and I focus on not losing him. My father put lights on the back of our saddles, so I can see a dot. "Cayden!" I call out as I ride. Hoping he hears me.

I can faintly hear Zach doing the same.

We ride for what seems like forever until I can hear the rushing water. I slow down and shine the flashlight, calling out, "Cayden!"

"Go to the right, I'll take the left," Zach instructs.

I search all over the falls area. The full moon is bright and helps illuminate the normally dark woods.

"Please, Cayden!" At some point my screaming becomes sobs. I'm tired, weak, and emotionally done. I won't quit though, not when my baby needs me. But my tears fall as I search for my son. "Cay!" I need him so much. I don't care that he's been angry or defiant, I just want him in my arms. "Cayden, please, Cayden."

Zach trots over and hops off his horse. He holds my waist and helps me down. "Look at me," he commands. "I'm going to find him."

"He must be so scared." I hold on to his arms as I tremble. "This is my fault! I shouldn't have let him go."

"This isn't your fault. *None* of this is your fault." He grips my face, and I hold his wrists. "You have to be strong. I know you're scared, but trust me, Presley. I'm not going home until we have him safe, okay?"

I believe him. He says the words with such authority, I know he means it. He presses his lips to my forehead before releasing me. "I can't lose him, Zach."

"You're not going to."

I pull myself together and muster whatever strength I can. Where else could he have gone? There are so many trails. Zach and I both drink some water, and he calls Wyatt. They talk about the areas they've searched and our search party is now the entire town of Bell Buckle. Everyone is out on their horses, four wheelers, and trucks searching for him.

Zach hangs up the phone. "Let's follow the creek. If he likes the water it would make sense to think he would stay close to the water."

I've lost the ability to make decisions right now, so I nod and pray that Zach will find my baby.

Seventeen

W e ride at a steady pace, calling his name, and looking for
anything that would give us a clue. Zach checks in with
the rest of the searchers, so far nothing. It has to have been at least
two hours of riding down this creek. My hope drains with each
passing minute.

Worry grips my throat, choking the life from me. I can't
manage anything except short breaths.

I wonder if he's sleeping, cold, scared, or if he's hurt. Memories assault me one by one. The way he felt in my arms right after
he was born. Holding his tiny little hand with my finger. How he
sounded when he said "Ma" for the first time. I remember the way
he would look at me when he would do something wrong. Cayden
was always the more mischievous one, but he was so cute, I
couldn't be mad for too long.

Growing up, my mother always said, "God only gives you
what you can handle." Well, I've reached my capacity.

Zach slows, waiting for me. "You okay?"

"Not even in the slightest."

"Do you need to rest for a minute?" he asks.

I look at him with a blank stare. I'm not stopping. There's

nothing that could keep me from continuing my search. "Every minute we waste is a minute he might need."

"At least eat something." He hands me an energy bar. "You drank a lot and need your energy if we're going to keep riding."

He's right. I grab the food, taking a few bites. "Thanks," I say softly. "I appreciate you doing this."

"I'd do anything for you," he says as he trots forward.

I pull back on the reins, stop, and wait for him to turn around. "You can't say stuff like that to me," I demand. "You can't mess with my head. Don't you see how fucked-up I am?"

Zach closes the distance. "You're hurting. You're not fucked-up."

"What are you doing?" I shake my head. "You have her. Why are you saying these things to me?"

Zach hops down and grabs the bridle, forcing me to stop exactly where I am. "Do you know that I was planning to propose the day you came back to Bell Buckle? Do you know why Felicia doesn't have a ring on her finger?"

I don't want to hear this. "I can't do this right now." Tears form as I contemplate everything that's happened tonight. It's too much.

He looks at the sky and lets out a heavy breath. "You're right. Now's not the time. When you're ready, after we find Cayden, and you want to know the truth, I'm here."

Zach lets go of the horse and walks toward the water. My chest aches for so many reasons. I want to know what he feels, but I don't at the same time. I watch him squat and splash his face with water. We're all exhausted, scared, and praying for a miracle.

I don't know why, but I get down. My feet move on their own until I'm standing beside Zach. I need to be close to him. I need to feel some flicker of hope that everything's going to be okay. His arm wraps around my back and I turn into him. "Just hold me," I request.

And he does.

He holds me close. He holds me secure. He holds me like I haven't been held in so long.

I close my eyes and rest in his safety. I try to find my center, feel the world around me, and allow the calm to wash over me. I'm so lost, weightlessly drifting and hoping for something to tether me. Right now, I feel as if I've been caught and I might be able to stand on my own. In his arms, I can fight.

My fingers grip his shirt, and I slowly raise my gaze until I find his eyes. I hold on with everything I have. I don't want to let go. I don't want to float anymore. "Zach," I whisper. "Don't let me go."

He doesn't let go as he presses his forehead to mine. We stand like this, wrapped up in each other as I beg God for my son.

Please, I need him. I've lost too much.

Zach's head lifts from mine. I open my eyes and look at him but he's searching for something.

"Presley," Zach's arms fall. The calm I had vanishes with his embrace. "Look, over there!"

My eyes go to the spot he's pointing to. There's a horse tied to a branch. "Cayden," I mumble. "Cayden!" I scream out and run as fast as my legs can move.

"Cayden!" Zach calls out looking around. "Where are you, buddy?"

We call out over and over as I rush toward the tree. "It's my dad's horse. It's Shortstop!" I say to Zach as we scour the area. "He was here." We both take off in different directions looking for where he could be.

"Mom!" Cayden's voice cracks.

I scan the area, trying to find where his little voice is coming from.

"I found him!" Zach yells as he rushes down the hill. "We're here, Cayden."

My heart pounds against my ribs as I run to them. I start to cry as my feet slide against the wet leaves. I move as fast as I can, and the second I see him, I can breathe. "Cayden!" Relief floods me. He's okay.

Zach drapes his jacket around Cayden and my arms fly around him. I pull my son into my arms as I sob. "You're okay. Oh, thank God, you're okay." I touch his face and push his hair back to make sure he's not bleeding.

"Are you hurt?" Zach asks.

Cayden cries in my arms and nods. "I fell. I tied Shortstop to the tree and then I couldn't get back up. I'm sorry, Mom."

"Shh," I say and try to soothe him. "All that matters is that you're okay." I kiss the top of his head and look at Zach, who smiles and lets out a sigh.

"I can't walk," he says.

Zach doesn't falter before he's scooping my son up and climbing the hill. "Just hold on, buddy."

Cayden's arms wrap around Zach's neck as he carries him. Once we get to the top, he crouches down and Cayden practically leaps into my arms. "I've got you, baby." It feels like a dream. I truly didn't know if we'd find him. I tried to focus on anything but the possible outcome where it didn't end with him in my arms.

Zach's hand rubs my back and the smile doesn't leave his face. "You had us worried there, man."

Cayden closes his eyes as a tear treks down his cheek. "I didn't know where I was. I remember Uncle Cooper saying to stay along the water, but I didn't know which way I was going."

"You did the right thing," Zach reassures him. "I'm going to call everyone." He ruffles Cayden's hair before turning away.

"Zach." I capture his attention. "Thank you for keeping your promise. Thank you for everything." I don't think he can begin to imagine what this means to me. He is everything I could need tonight. Protector, savior, and friend.

He nods once and walks away with the phone to his ear. I hear him in the distance letting everyone know we found him. You can hear the hoots and hollers of people in the woods. The community came out in full force, and we're all going home with a smile.

Exhaustion hits Cayden and he falls asleep in my arms. It hasn't been more than five minutes, and he's out. Between the emotional and physical things he's been through, he's spent. Zach comes back over and rubs the side of Cayden's face as he sleeps.

"He looks like you," Zach muses.

"Well, that means Logan does too." I laugh and stare at the reason for my existence as he sleeps. I glance back at Zach who moves his hand.

Zach turns his head quickly. "They both do."

"Zach?"

I don't know why he keeps pulling back. I'm not exactly giving him the clearest of signals, but he's not either. He's dating Felicia, kissing me, leaving her at the bar, but she's living with him. Plus, he scares the shit out of me. I've lived that pain. I've lived through more agony at the hands of men who love me than any woman should. Of course I'm wary. Now that he knows the truth, I'd think he would understand it more.

"We should head back. I'll ride with him if you can guide Shortstop."

"Sure."

Getting Cayden on the horse with Zach is far from easy. He's heavy and refuses to wake. After a few minutes, we get going. I ride alongside them as Zach navigates as if this is his land. It's crazy how well he knows the area. My gratitude grows as we ride in. Neither of us speaks, but we keep glancing over at each other.

I wonder if I have the capacity to ever trust again. Has Todd truly taken that from me? I'm hurt, angry, confused, but somewhere deep down, I want to be happy. And I wonder if there's a reason Zach is back in my life.

We move toward the barn and the quiet erupts in cheers and clapping. The whole town is here. I look over at Zach and he smirks. This is what country life is like. Had the tragedy I endured in Pennsylvania happened here, it would've been an entirely different scenario. My home would've been filled, food overflowing, and I would've never had time to be alone.

My father takes Cayden from Zach and squeezes him. Guilt and regret fill me. I robbed my father and mother of so much time with the boys. They never got to see them grow up, and for that I'm sorry.

"Mom!" Logan rushes out as soon as he hears the commotion. "Cayden!" He pivots, rushing toward his brother, and they fall to the ground.

My hand flies over my mouth as tears fall. As much as I don't think I would survive, we would've lost Logan too. His brother is his world. They have a bond like no other. Logan finally releases Cayden and finds his way over to Zach.

A hand rests on my shoulder, and I turn to find my brother covered in dirt and sweat.

"Pres." Shame layers his voice.

"It wasn't your fault."

"I should've been watching them better."

I place my hand on his. "I know you would never hurt them."

He draws me into his arms, kisses my cheek, and ducks his head into my neck. My brother doesn't cry, but he shakes as he holds me close. I can only imagine how scared he was too. Knowing that he had them in his care, that I've lost everything, and how it would've destroyed all of us if we lost Cayden.

"It's okay, Coop."

He shakes his head and releases a sigh of relief. "I'm going to get the horses ready for tomorrow."

Which is his way of saying he's still emotional.

"You should do that."

People hug us, get to meet the boys, and chastise me for not coming to see them. It's a long night, and the boys finally head to bed. Mama and Daddy escape not too long after them. As exhausted as I am, I can't imagine sleeping.

I migrate to the back porch to watch the sun come up. Today is a new day. I need to remind myself of that.

Each time the sun rises, I choose whether or not to dwell in the darkness, and so far I've been choosing wrong. Todd made his own decision, but that doesn't mean that my life can't find new light.

I sit on the porch swing swaddled in a blanket with faith that we can start to heal. I know it won't be easy. There's a lot of things I need to come to terms with, but last night reminded me that I still have people to try for. The boys, my parents, my brother, Grace, Zach . . . I think about him.

How he makes me feel. How he's always made me feel.

"Hey." Zach peers at me as I shake off my thoughts. "I figured you'd be asleep." He climbs the steps slowly as I get to my feet.

"I figured you'd be gone."

I walk toward him, unsure of why he's here. "I left for a bit, but wanted to come check on you."

"Oh."

He snickers. "I couldn't sleep."

"Me either." He's close enough that I can smell his cologne. Even after a long night, being in the woods, he smells like home.

I take another step.

Then another.

I'm so close I have to tilt my head to look into his eyes.

I breathe him in, feel his heat, and I can't stop myself. I want him. I *need* him. I grip his neck and yank his mouth to mine. I kiss him. I kiss him and give in to everything I've been feeling. He doesn't waste a second. His arms wrap around me, holding my body against his. My fingers grip his neck, keeping him exactly where I need him. This kiss is frantic, but God it feels good.

His tongue presses against my lips, and I gladly open. As soon as our tongues collide, I'm done. I lift myself into his arms and his hands cup my ass. He holds me as we go at it like teenagers. We break the kiss when Zach slams my back into the post, but I dive right back in.

I need this kiss. I need him to remind me of the woman I am. I've loved him my whole life, and I need to be loved right now. He moans into my mouth, and I feel it in my core. I want to drown in him. We kiss and claw at each other. I have no sense of time or anything that's not him.

After God knows how long, Zach cradles my face in his hands and pulls back.

My chest heaves as we both stare into each other's eyes.

"I—" I don't know what to say. I assaulted him, and the last time he kissed me, I slapped him. Now I'm leaping into his arms? Shit. What am I doing? "I'm sorry," I say quickly and slide down. "I don't know what the hell that was. I can't believe . . ."

He sighs while looking around. "I couldn't—I mean." He runs his hands over his face. "I can't." Another pause. "I can't do this."

"I know. I don't know what I was thinking," I try to explain. "Tonight was just so much, and I'm clearly not thinking straight."

He takes a step back and puts his hand up for me to stop. "That's not what I can't do."

I'm confused. "What can't you do?"

"Pretend. I can't do this with you. You know why."

"Know what?"

"Ask me why again, Presley," he demands. "Ask me why she isn't my wife. Ask me why I didn't propose to her!"

My heart races, and my mouth goes dry. He steps toe to toe with me. His deep blue eyes, light brown hair, and scruff take my breath away. Zachary Hennington has always been the man who ties my stomach in knots. "Why?" The word falls from my lips before I can stop it.

The wind whips my hair around and the chill in the air causes goose bumps. "Because when you came back, I knew. I knew that I could never look at another woman like I do you. Every time I close my eyes, I see you. I've always seen you, Presley."

"But you're still with her."

"No," he says. "Not anymore. It's not fair to her, even if you tell me you don't feel the same. Even if I walk away tonight knowing there's not a chance in hell of us ever being something . . . I'll wait for you."

My lips part and my stomach squeezes. "But—" I grapple with what he said. "You and her . . ."

He runs his hand across my cheek. "It's over. I'm going to end things with her as soon as it's not the middle of the night. She's not the girl I want."

"Zach," I say hesitantly. "You don't know me anymore. I'm damaged. I've been through hell, and I'm not even a piece of the girl you knew. I mean, if you don't want to be with her because she's, well, her—fine. But not because of me."

"I don't want you to say anything. Just know that I mean what I said." His fingers fall as he leans in and kisses my forehead. "It's not because of you, Presley. It's because it's always been you."

He turns and walks away. Leaving me more torn up than the last time he left me. Now it's my choice. And I have no earthly idea what to do.

Eighteen

"**M**om." I hear Cayden say from my door.

"What's wrong?"

"Can I lie with you?"

It's the second night this week he's found his way to my room. "Of course." I lift the covers and he climbs in.

Cayden rests as I brush his hair back. Cayden suffered with night terrors, and the only way to get him to sleep was to lie in his bed until he finally passed out. Todd could never soothe him for long enough, so I was the one who ended up cuddling with him. When they were little, I used to wish their time away, I wanted them to talk, walk, and feed themselves. Now, I would give anything to have those moments again.

His breathing evens out. "I miss him," he says in a hushed tone.

"Who?" I ask, even though I'm fully aware of who he means.

"Dad."

"I know you do."

I've been trying so hard to rid myself of the anger that festers inside me. Knowing that we could've avoided this pain makes it damn near impossible to let go. It's so hard to reconcile. There were no warning signs that this was what he was planning or even considering. I look back on the period of time when he was out of work, and I blame myself for being so oblivious. I should've known. I was his wife, his partner . . . I wrestle with my guilt every day.

"Was he sick?"

And this is the part I hate.

"No, not that we knew of." I dance around with half-truths. I would say that to some extent he had to be sick. But that's not what Cayden is asking me.

He turns over and faces me. His big green eyes are so full of innocence—innocence that I'm trying so desperately to save. The world is full of ugly truths; children shouldn't have to be burdened with them.

"I want to go back home," he says with tears in his eyes. "I miss my friends and my room. I miss Aunt Angie."

"I wish we could. I really do." I kiss his head. "I miss her too. But this is our home now. You have to focus on the good things about Bell Buckle." I'm preaching to the choir.

"I like my horse."

"See?" I smile.

"I like Uncle Cooper and Wyatt. He's really funny."

"He's something all right." We both laugh. "He's been my friend since I was a baby. Did you know that?"

Cayden's eyes widen. "He knew you when you were young?"

"Hey," I chide. "I'm still young."

"Whatever you say, Mom."

I tickle his sides, and he giggles without restraint. That's a sound I miss. Even now when they laugh, it seems like it takes them effort. "I'm twenty-nine. Say it," I continue.

"No, you're not."

"Say it or suffer the wrath of my tickles."

Cayden squirms and laughs as he refuses to say it. Finally, he gives in. "Fine! You're twenty-nine."

I lie back as though I'm exhausted, letting out a huff. "You're so sweet to say such nice things."

"In your dreams, Mom."

"Turd."

We both laugh a little and then settle down.

This right here feels normal. It's like having my life back. Being silly, laughing, and being in the moment. We need more of this. I need more of this. I'll never be able to go back to who I was, but that doesn't mean I can't be happy. These boys, they're my happiness.

"Mom?" Cayden says after a lull of silence.

"Hmm?"

It takes him a second before he responds again. "Can I ride today?"

I lean on my side. "Your horse?"

"Yeah, do you think we could ride together?"

It's the first time he's asked me to have any part of his horse-back riding. He usually asks Cooper, Daddy, or Wyatt. I figured he needed some male bonding, and they're all "real cowboys."

"I would really love that."

"Wyatt said you used to be a really good rider."

"Used to be?"

"He said now you suck."

I have to hold back scolding him because this is probably the most this kid has spoken to me in months. He's been so distant, so closed off, and refused to let me in. The last thing I want is for him to shut down again.

"I won a lot of rodeos."

He gasps. "You rode a bull?"

"No," I say on a chuckle. "I did barrel racing."

We spend the next half hour talking about what it was like when I was a kid here. I tell him about the creek and some of my favorite things to do. We talk a little about Wyatt, Zach, and Trent. He asks a lot of questions, and I enjoy answering them. I've been close to both boys, but Cayden has always been a tough nut to crack. I pray this is a turning point for him—and me.

～

"Presley," my mother calls from the kitchen. "Can you run into town and pick up some things I need?"

Despite not wanting to, I could never say no. "Of course."

I grab her list and my keys. The boys are off with Wyatt and Cooper mending fences or something. I love how much the men in my life are stepping up and taking my boys under their wings. Trent took them for a ride in the police car the other day, now all I hear from Logan is how he's going to be a sheriff. God help me.

I arrive at my first stop where I'm enthusiastically greeted by Mrs. Rooney. "Presley!" she rushes toward me. "Your mama said you were coming, and I'm just tickled to see you."

"I saw you the other night."

"Yes." Her lips turn up in a smile. "But so much has changed."

I have no idea what changed in two nights, but this is Bell Buckle. I have two choices, play into the insanity of small town gossip, or get what I need and leave. I go with option two. "I need to get some flour and chocolate."

"Are you baking a cake?"

"My mother must be."

I look at the rest of the list and realize she needs the oddest things. "I hear Zach is quite the hero," she says offhandedly.

Here we go. I knew it wasn't going to last long, but the last time I saw Zach was two days ago, and I haven't heard a word since. It's not like I expected to, but at the same time he sounded so sure. Maybe he and Felicia are more than he let on. Either way, I don't want the entire town thinking we're getting back together.

"He did find Cayden, but you already knew that." I smile as she nods. "Do you have the chocolate back by you?" I look around, but there's so much stuff, I can't find anything.

"It's right here, dear." She walks around and reaches for the bag. "Have you been able to thank Zach since then?"

If I hadn't known this woman my entire life, I might have told her to mind her business. However, my mother would tan my hide if I ever did—thirty-five or not. "I really should get going."

"Of course." She gives me a knowing smile and takes her time at the register, talking about her kids and the new items she's getting at the store. I listen and pray I can get out of here before the sun goes down.

After a few minutes and a lot of questions, I'm all checked out. "Thanks, Mrs. Rooney. I'll see you soon."

"You make sure of it. Also, be sure to give Zach a call. I hear he'd love to see Cayden. Careful getting home now."

I let out a short breath. "I will." She can interpret that answer however she'd like.

I get what Mama needs from the other two stores and get in my car. Once there, I take a moment to bang my head against the steering wheel. "Stupid Zach," I say, repeatedly working out my frustration—on my face. I stop once I feel a little better. It's the same questions with each person. "How's Zach? It's so great to see you two together again. Have y'all thought about getting back together? You two were always destined for each other."

They're all killing me slowly.

I put the car in reverse but stop when I see that damn truck parked across the street.

Well, I'm not going to cower over here. He can see my car. I back out and see him looking at me in my rearview mirror. My heart stammers as I look back, but instead of giving into the nerves, I wave as I drive off. I don't understand how he could say all of that and not even attempt to talk to me, it makes no sense. I literally threw myself at him. My stomach clenches when I think about the things he said. In my heart, I want all of it to come true. But I'm not the one who made a ton of promises. It's time for Zach to decide if he's willing to chase me.

Working at the ranch is by far not my dream job. I would love nothing more than to open a cupcake store in town, but it would last a whole day before I had twenty women bringing their batches of homemade goods to sell. But today, I get to leave the office for a change.

"Your chariot awaits, Ms. Townsend." Wyatt bows dramatically.

"I still haven't quite figured out why I talk to you."

"Face it, Pres. I'm the yin to your yang."

"You're the shit on my shoes."

"I'm the bread to your butter," he counters.

"You're the pain in my ass."

He slaps my ass. "Now I am."

I flick his hat off his head and climb onto the horse. "Don't mess with me, Cowboy."

Some emotion flashes across his face before he quickly recovers. "You know what field we're moving them to?" he asks, getting down to business.

"Yup." I pet the side of Shortstop's neck. This horse and I have a deep connection. I truly believe he protected Cayden that night. The horse easily could've thrown him or gone God only knows where in those woods. But he allowed Cayden to guide him. "Who else is going with me?"

I get to lead the group that's going to move the cattle from one end of the land to the other. I loved doing this as a kid. Our whole family would go out and round them up, move them, and spend the day together. Cooper is bringing the boys on the four-wheeler to the ending point.

"You've got Vance, one of the ranch hands, me, and Zach."

My eyes snap over to his. "What?"

"You know, tall, dumb, blue eyes, really bad haircut."

I shake my head with my lips parted. If he had broken up with Felicia, like he said, I would've heard by now. Clearly, what he said to me wasn't what he meant. It hurts because I trusted his word. There are still feelings lingering between us, which scares me. I don't want to get my heart trampled, and right now that's what it feels like.

"Don't worry." He shakes his head. "He's not riding doubles with you."

I want to throw something at him.

"Whatever. It's a big field." There's no reason for me to have to see him. He can lead the cows and I'll wrangle any stragglers. Plan made.

My family owns a lot of land, and Daddy has always believed that the cattle have to sometimes take a longer ride. Before the days of cell phones, and all the things we have now . . . we would spend days on a long move. It was our version of a family vacation. That is *not* happening this time. I'm not camping with Zach. Not on his life.

Wyatt laughs. "Oh, Cowgirl, one day you're going to wake up from the dream you're living in."

I just glare.

I take the horse to the trailer and get him settled. It's about a fifteen-mile ride out to where the cattle are. There's no way the horses could handle going there and back in one day. Regardless, I refuse to set up a tent with any of the Hennington clan. I'll find a way back home one way or another.

Our two-horse trailer is only half full. I have a pretty good idea who Wyatt is planning to load in the other spot, and who will be driving.

"Good morning, Presley." Zach's deep voice causes me to jump as he pops up at my window.

"Jesus!"

He smirks. "Ready for our day?"

"Wasn't aware we were having one."

"I figured you've avoided me enough. It's nice to get out of the office." Zach slaps the window of the truck and goes around to the driver's side.

This is so not going to be good.

He hops in as if he doesn't have a care in the world. I'm ready to lose it. How can he be so oblivious? How does he not think we should talk about what happened? I cross my arms and breathe out of my nose. Fine. I can play along.

"What's wrong?" he asks as he pulls out of the long driveway.

I look over as if he's gone crazy. "For real?"

"You seem like you're not happy to see me."

"How's Felicia?" I ask with acid in my tone. I said I would

play it cool, but thinking of her makes me stabby. She's a vile bitch and even if Zach and I never ended up back together, I wouldn't want her anywhere near him. Her soul is as black as her hair.

Zach fixes his hat and grins. "If you'd returned my call you would know."

"You called yesterday, and I was busy." The truth is I didn't want to call him back—I was angry he hadn't tried to call sooner.

"I figured you'd call back."

"Why didn't you come by?" I inquire. "It's not as if you don't know where I am."

He looks over with his eyes blazing. In that glance, he melts me. "I know exactly where you are, Presley."

"You still haven't answered my question."

Zach pulls the truck over and turns to face me. "Felicia and I aren't together anymore. I spent the last few days moving her out and finding her a place to live." He pauses for a second. "You see, I meant every word I said. But I had to be fair to her, and my coming over to your house after ending a five-year relationship wouldn't have been. So, you're in the batter's box." He leans back and throws the car in drive.

I let the information seep in.

Zach is no longer with Felicia.

I'm single.

He drives as I mull over all the insecurities I have and whether I can even think about this. We have no shortage of sexual attraction—we never have. I know we're compatible. I know we have the ability to love one another, and I realize I've always loved him. And if I'm truly honest, I know he loves me. He wouldn't have left her if he didn't. He wouldn't look at me like he does. And he wouldn't be here right now. Zach has hurt me though.

But we're both adults now. Things have changed.

Hell, I've changed tremendously. It's unfair to think Zach is the same. It's a lot to consider. My stomach clenches and my heart races.

He arrives at the gate where we need to enter to ride out to the cattle. As he opens the truck door, I grab his arm. "What's the count?" I ask, using his analogy. Zach communicates better in baseball terms.

He smiles as he tips his head. "Darlin'." his Southern drawl becomes apparent. "There's no strikes, no outs, and we're only in the first inning."

I cover my laugh with a cough. "You need to work on your game, Zachary Hennington. I'm not even sure I'm going to take a swing."

Zach's eyes brighten as his smile grows. "I'm pretty good at reading the batter, and I think she just might be ready to lift that bat off her shoulder." He leans close and all but whispers, "Question is, will she get a hit or strike out?"

I tap my chin. "Hmm. Depends how good the pitch is."

"Right down the middle."

"What if it curves?"

He takes my hand in his, yanking me forward. "It's the perfect pitch, Presley. It won't sink, curve, or slow down. It's not even a fast ball. It's that one pitch that only comes around when the pitcher wants the batter to hit." His lips are so close. Every part of me tightens as I wonder if he's going to kiss me. Instead, his mouth goes to the side of my face. "The pitcher is practically begging the batter to take a swing. Take the bat off your shoulder, darlin'."

He releases me and hops out of the truck whistling. I sit there frazzled, my breathing heavy. What happens if I strike out?

Nineteen

As we ready the horses, I can feel Zach's eyes on me. I fight every bone in my body from looking over at him. I have to say something, one way or another, but fear overrides my desires. My heart needs to be protected, and I need to be certain I'm ready to even consider another relationship.

I'd be lying if I said I didn't want him, though.

I've always wanted him. Now we're here, all these years later, with a second chance.

"Zach." I start to say something . . . anything, but before we can say anything else, Wyatt and the other guys come up.

"Took you two long enough." Wyatt smirks. "I thought maybe you'd stopped off for a quickie."

Zach glares at his brother, but of course, nothing bothers Wyatt. He's best left ignored. "And here I thought all the Hennington boys had stamina. Guess you're the weakest link." I shrug and climb onto Shortstop.

The irony is laughable.

"You make sure you ride Shortstop really hard, but don't let it get too bumpy." Wyatt smirks as if he read my thoughts.

"Jerk."

"Been called worse."

I hear Zach's chuckle, and I stick my tongue out at Wyatt.

"So mature." He laughs before slapping my horse's butt, causing him to rocket forward.

The barrel racer in me comes to life. I lean forward, allowing the speed of the horse to flow through me. My heart rate increases with every step Shortstop takes. I give myself this minute. The wind whips my long brown hair, my smile is wide, and my eyes finally feel like they can see the world again.

We approach the tree line, and I remember that there's no way in hell we can fly through there. I turn Shortstop to return to Zach and Wyatt. My chest heaves, yet it feels so good.

It's liberating.

"Nice try on getting the horse to take off." I smile as I come up next to Wyatt. "You forget I happen to know how to ride."

"I figure little by little we'll get our cowgirl back."

"I'm about as back as I'm ever going to be." I look at Zach as he sits on his horse looking intoxicating. His confidence and ease make his presence known. His eyes don't stray from me—making me feel like I'm the only person who exists.

For once, Wyatt is quiet, or maybe we just don't hear him. Because right now, all that I can see, hear, and feel is Zachary Hennington. I don't know how I can resist him, if I want to, if I should, but being here right now tells me I know what I'll do. I think he knows it too.

"Well." Wyatt claps his hands loudly. "I'm going up to start, you know . . . working. You two have your silent staring contest and bring up the herd from the back. Vance and I will lead."

I draw in a deep breath and nod. "Ready?" I ask Zach.

Instead of answering, he moves forward. "Take a swing, Pres. What's the worst that happens?"

"You hurt me."

"I won't."

"I don't think you will on purpose, but you don't know what the future holds."

Zach lets out one short laugh. "I do though. I know that every part of my future includes you. When you came back into town, it was like my world settled. You were always supposed to be a part of my life, but I wasn't ready for you then."

My heart aches and hope blooms deep within me. Could it really be that we were not ready back then? They say everything happens for a reason, maybe we couldn't have made it work, and that was our sign. It still doesn't answer whether I'm ready to open myself up. That wouldn't be fair to either of us.

"Hey," he says, drawing me out of my mind. "No answers now. Just know that I'll wait for you."

Zach winks and rides off toward the cattle. I look to the sky and close my eyes. "Why can't you send me a sign?" I ask whoever is up there.

I pull the reins tight and head toward the guys. It's time to work. I have at least nine hours for deep reflection today.

It takes about an hour to get the cows to actually move where we want. They're slow today. Bringing up the herd is a little more difficult, but Zach and I work well together. Each straggler gets pushed to the pack, and we find a rhythm.

I'm grateful for the fifteen or so cows between us. It gives me time to my own thoughts. I wonder if Zach is ready to even take on two boys who recently had their world crushed. They're not going to be easy to win over. They loved their father very much, and they have a lot of residual issues.

Wyatt falls back and catches my attention. "I need you over on the left."

"Huh?"

"The left. Zach needs a little help." He smirks at his own joke. Sure, he does. "He's just fine."

"Well, I'm the foreman and I say go on the left."

"I'm the owner's sister."

He narrows his eyes. "I'm still your boss."

"The hell you are. Why are you doing this?" I ask.

"Because you're stubborn. You have a good man who loves you right in front of you. And you're going to spend the next however many hours talking yourself in and out of this aren't you." His brow rises. "That's what I thought," he tacks on at the end.

I sigh. He doesn't get it. I don't know how anyone can because this isn't cut and dry. "So you think letting him push me is the right thing?"

"I think you're both scared. He knows that you lost your husband, and you have Cayden and Logan. He's aware of what all of that means. I made damn sure he did. Did he fuck up when he was a kid? No. He was given the promise of a big ass check and a chance to play ball for his life." Wyatt stops, giving me a chance to swallow that one. In the back of my mind, I've always known that. But the broken woman in me wouldn't accept it. Wyatt doesn't know everything. "If you'd rather give another Hennington a chance, I'm always here."

"You and I would never work. You know that," I say gently.

"I know. You'll always love Zach, so why are you still over here? Go love him."

I wish it were that simple.

Begrudgingly, I head over to the left. "Wyatt said you needed help on this side."

"Did he?" Zach grins. "Sometimes he's not half bad."

"Sometimes."

We both move slowly, waiting to see if we get a rogue cow. Zach takes the first step. "There's a lot we need to talk about. You said some stuff that night when we were outside. I've let you have some time, but you can't keep living like this."

My muscles tense as I see where this is going. Talking about Todd's death is the absolute last thing I want to do. "I'm doing everything I need to."

"I need to know where your head is at. You're lying to everyone, but I'm not everyone."

Since I told him the truth, I've wondered why. Why would I tell the one person who I really didn't want to know? Of everyone that I could've let it slip to, it was Zach. It made no sense other than that somewhere in my heart, I needed him to know. Maybe I knew he wouldn't wield the information against me like a sword. Zach wouldn't judge.

"No," I agree. "You're not."

That doesn't mean I can talk about this. I've buried parts of that day so deep, I don't even know where to find them. Bringing it up, facing it, could wreck me all over again. The nightmares and the visions of my husband are painful. Right now I'm angry. I've held on to that feeling to get through the days. To bring back the sadness would be too difficult.

"All I'm asking is that you don't treat me like them. As worried as you are about what our future might—or might not—hold, I'm feeling the same shit, Pres. I'm fully aware that I was the one who left. I live with that regret every damn day. But you fucking broke me."

I look over with a ton of questions. "I broke you?"

"Yeah." He looks heavenward before his gaze locks on me. "I loved you. You were the reason I was taking that position with the Dodgers. I wasn't doing it just for me!"

"I know you think that. If I had left that college for you, I would've been a fool. People already thought I was for giving up the school I wanted to follow you. I didn't want to spend my entire life chasing your dreams. There's no way we could've done another two plus years with you traveling, the girls throwing themselves at you, and me finishing school."

He rubs his shoulder as he takes a minute to respond. "We could've lasted. Or maybe not. We won't ever know because you didn't give us that chance. You think I'm the only one to blame?"

"I have for a long time. I felt like I was dying inside without you. You were such a deep part of who I was that when you left I was empty. Todd was visiting Angie that weekend and he held me while I sobbed. It's how we became anything. He held together the pieces of me that you destroyed."

There's truth in what he said before. The minute he left—I gave up. I was young and dumb too, and I jumped right into a relationship with Todd. God, I was so afraid of being alone.

But my life with Todd wasn't bad. We had love, children, happiness, and I would've grown old with him.

"I would've held you."

"Not from California," I remind him.

"No, I guess not."

We fall silent as we ride slowly. There are things that I need to deal with to move forward. Not only with Zach, but in my life. He's right to be wary. My heart is still heavy with loss but also filled with anger toward so many.

Our history runs deep, and the scars aren't superficial. They're branded into who I am and have shaped the deformity that is my heart.

I can't just move on.

I can't just forget.

Then those wounds were reopened by my husband. The man who was supposed to be there through the good times and bad. The vows we took and the life we shared are no more.

"What are you thinking?" Zach asks.

"I'm thinking about you, Todd, me, and whether I can move on from any of it," I say honestly. "There are a lot of things between us. A lot of history, and it's not as simple as just trying again."

He nods. "I didn't think it would be."

"Then what did you think?"

Zach sighs and stops moving. "Wyatt," he calls out. "Presley and I will be there in a minute."

I look over confused. "We can't . . ."

"We'll only be a few minutes," he says as he climbs off the horse. He holds my reins while looking up at me. "Come down."

His voice is commanding. I swing my leg over, but my other foot gets stuck. I almost fall, but Zach's strong arms snag me. My hands rest against his broad chest, feeling his heart beat beneath my fingers. We don't move. Neither of us do anything except look into the other's eyes. His arm tightens as he holds me even closer.

I want to kiss him and feel his lips against mine. The battle is clear in his eyes.

"We've kissed twice now." His voice is low and raspy. "Once I attacked you, then you attacked me." His brow raises and I smile. "The next time, though, I don't want either of us holding back."

"And what if I kissed you right now?" I ask breathlessly. Every cell in my body is awake with desire. Touching him, being in his arms, is everything I remember. Only he's stronger, sexier, and right in front of me.

He grins and moves his head toward mine. "Then I'll take that as your swing."

Can I resist? It's Zachary. He's always been a part of my soul. I don't know that I can walk away—even if I want to. I had lived my life without him once, I'd survive it again, but I think I'd regret not trying.

"Zach," I whisper. A part of me is stalling. The other part is asking for him to tell me what to do.

He leans in closer and my eyes close. But instead of his lips touching mine, he kisses my forehead. "I can't tell you if you're ready, Pres. I can only tell you that I've always loved you. I've always closed my eyes and seen you beside me. It was never over."

"What about all the crap between us?"

"Like what?"

"Like the fact that I have two small boys who just lost their father. I'm still fucked-up from it. That I have no money and had to move home. I've been through so much trauma in the last six months that I can't sleep. Everything hurts." My eyes fill with tears. "I'm so tired of hurting. And you scare me. You can hurt me worse than you know."

I feel the acceleration in his heart. His blue eyes are soft and warm. "I can't guarantee that this will work. I would be lying if I said there weren't obstacles. I know you have Cayden and Logan. I would never try to start something with you if I didn't want your kids to be a part of my life." He pulls me tighter. "I'll be their friend. I'll let them get to know me and see how not all the Henningtons are idiots." We both laugh as I shake my head.

"Well," I say jokingly.

"I know your husband died, and how. As for you being broke . . ." He stops for a moment. "I don't give a fuck. Your lack of money or if you were rich doesn't hold any weight here. I want to see where this goes, and if it works, I want to take care of you. There's a lot of shit we have to work through. This isn't going to be easy, darlin'."

Nothing seems to be anymore. "I don't want easy, Zach. I just don't want agony."

"I don't ever want to hurt you."

"I know you can't promise that."

"No, I can't. But I can promise that I'm not going away easily. I'll wear you down, Presley Mae. I'll remind you that sometimes the reward is worth the risk."

He kisses my nose and releases me. I stand there feeling bereft. The loss of his arms causes me to shiver.

He'll wear me down because there's not much resistance left in me.

I hope he's ready.

Twenty

"I don't think we can ride any farther today," Wyatt says as the sun sets in the distance. "We've still got a few more miles and the cattle aren't cooperating."

It's been grueling the last few hours. The pace has been agonizingly slow, and no matter what we seemed to do, we were still chasing another stray for twenty minutes.

We're about halfway, so there's no way to go back and no way to go forward. I knew I shouldn't have freaking done this. Somehow the gods have a way of kicking me in the teeth. Now, I'm going to be forced to camp out with Zach, Wyatt, and Vance, who has been riding with Wyatt. Fantastic.

"I need to call the boys," I say as I walk toward the trees. "This is the last thing I need."

Wyatt laughs. "I'll snuggle with you. There's always room in my sleeping bag for you, Cowgirl."

My eyes dart to Zach as he gives Wyatt a glare that would make any man cringe. Wyatt looks back over and flips him off with a smile. "What's the matter, Zach? Your tent isn't working properly?"

"I'll kick your ass so far you won't be able to find your way back to Tennessee." Zach's voice is low and threatening.

"Please, I've seen you fight."

"Presley," Zach says with gritted teeth. "Why don't you call the boys. I'll help Wyatt with setting up camp." He grabs the back of Wyatt's neck, causing him to shrink. "We'll get everything in order before you get back, won't we, Wyatt?"

Wyatt tries to elbow him, but with no luck. "Let go before I break your nose!"

"Stop being a dick."

"At least I have one," Wyatt says, swinging his body around.

This is a brief glimpse into my future with Logan and Cayden.

Boys.

I shake my head and walk away. Daddy answers the phone on the first ring. "Hi, sugar."

"How did you know it was me?" I smile. They refuse to get a phone with caller ID.

"I know when you need me." Daddy can sometimes make everything feel better. I've never been more grateful for that. "How's the ride?"

"Slow." I sigh. "Stubborn cattle."

He laughs. "I understand stubborn things."

I'm pretty sure he's talking about me. "I bet you do, Daddy."

"I figured you all were stayin' out tonight. This was a long move."

"I didn't think we would."

"Honey, you should know those boys are in cahoots. They picked the two farthest points on the land. I don't think they could've found a longer or more treacherous ride if they tried."

Of course they're behind this. Bastards. "You knew this?"

He chuckles, and I picture him shaking his head. "Yup."

So he's on board with Zach? That makes no sense. Daddy liked him just fine, but when he broke my heart and left me in Maine, Zach lost any respect my father had for him. He's a proud man, and his little girl was taken from him—in his mind—and abandoned.

"We'll talk about this when I come home."

"Sure, we will." I hear him laugh through his nose. "You callin' to talk to the boys?"

"Yes, Daddy."

"They're out with Cooper. He took them to his place for the night. Said he figured you'd call and to quit worrying. They're fine."

I groan. "We'll see how—" I start to say before catching myself. It wasn't Cooper's fault. And he would never let them wander off again. "Never mind. You sure you can't come get me? Keep me away from these Hennington boys."

"I tried that for half your life, baby girl. It didn't work then, and it ain't gonna work now. You let your brother spend time with his nephews without you interfering." He clears his throat, and I wait for what he's going to say next. "You be careful out there and I'll see you tomorrow." He hangs up before I can say anything.

That's one thing about Forrest Townsend. When he's done, he's done.

I check my phone and see a text.

Cooper: *Enjoy your night.*

Me: *You did this.*

Cooper: *You said you wanted out of the office.*

Me: *Asshole. I didn't mean a night in a field with your staff.*

Cooper: *Brat.*

Me: *I hate you.*

Cooper: *I hate you more.*

I laugh at the infantile text messages. I've missed my brother. He was always protective, even if he idolized Zach. He would get in his face if I cried or was angry. Zach could've beaten him to a pulp, but he would let Cooper yell and threaten him. It would make me fall more in love with Zach to see him give Cooper a sense of strength.

"Can't hide forever." Zach's voice startles me. His hands glide up my back and rest on my shoulders.

"I'm not hiding."

His fingers dig and rub into my neck, relieving the tension. "If you say so," he says and continues to massage me.

I close my eyes and let some of the stress go. His touch allows me to relax. I feel safe in his hands. Even if for so long I've told myself that's the last thing I could be. I was so young. We were so stupid to think we could have it all and it would cost us nothing. Life doesn't care if you're in love, there's always a price for happiness, we were just unwilling to pay.

"Do you think we have a real shot, Zach?"

He stops and his front presses against my back. His arms wrap around my shoulders as I hold on to him. "I think all of this happened for something. There's a reason you're in my arms right now. A reason that I didn't make choices that would've prevented it. Me blowing out my shoulder, you having to come back here, it's for something. And if it's not for us, then why?"

My hands cinch around his forearms as I mull over what he said. "I can't make sense of Todd, though."

"I don't know why either. Were you happy?" His voice strains a little.

"I thought so. I know this isn't easy to listen to." I turn to face him.

He cups my face and looks at me with so much compassion I almost can't take it. "Presley, you were married. You had two boys. I left you almost sixteen years ago. It would be ridiculous for me to think you didn't have a life or love."

My eyes fill with tears. "But to think of Felicia and you . . ." I take a step back.

"You have to trust me. The only way we're ever going to know is if we're honest. Does it suck to know another man has touched you? Yes." Zach moves closer. "Do I want to think about the fact that he was there for you because I left? No." My fingers clasp his wrist. "But God help me, Presley. I'll listen to it all. I want to know it all. The good, the bad, the happy, the sad, and then I want the rest."

A tear descends as my guard falls. "I'm afraid I'll never heal. I don't know how to heal."

The anger that lives inside me has prevented any forward progress. Todd robbed me of everything I knew. My home, my friends, Angie, any financial freedom I had. We lost everything because of him. I lost my husband too, though. It hurts to know all the things we've shared are now just memories. He wasn't mean or unfaithful. He was the man who held my hand through thirty-six hours of labor. He stood by me when I decided to open my business. There's a part of him that, no matter how angry I am, will claim a special place inside of me.

Zach has never had to love me when part of my heart belonged to someone else.

"I don't expect you to forget about him." The pain in his voice is hidden well, but I see it in his eyes. "He's a part of you. And you're already healing, you have to let it happen."

"I've loved you since I can remember. I've never been able to stop, and I never will. But you're going to have to be patient." My voice quivers. Everything inside me is playing tug-of-war. I want him, I don't want to. I love him, I shouldn't. He could heal me; he could break me. All of my thoughts contradict one another. But one thing that keeps coming to the forefront is: I don't want to have a life without him. Whether as my friend, or something more serious.

His eyes close and he rests his forehead against mine. "I'll be patient."

"Like, very patient."

He laughs and lifts his head. "I know. However, feel free to leap into my arms and kiss the shit out of me anytime."

I giggle as I shake my head. "I don't know what that was."

"I'm okay with it," he jokes.

"I bet you are."

"Like I said, I'm ready and willing."

My eyes lock on his. "I'm glad to hear it."

Zach's smile grows. "I've missed you. I've missed this. We were always—easy."

My hand presses against his cheek. The feel of his day-old stubble scratches my palm. My fingers glide back and forth against his face, reminding me he's real. Zach was always a dream to me. A beautiful hope that would never be. But this, right now, isn't a dream. "Do you know why I couldn't come back here?" I ask.

"No."

I sigh and drop my hand. It's a lot to admit. It's not something I'm proud of. I loved my husband, that was never something I doubted. But there was a part of me that knew if I saw Zach, I wouldn't be able to walk away. "You," I admit.

Zach's hands drop and he takes a step back. "I don't understand."

"I don't either." My voice shakes as I speak. "I never could understand why, when I would allow myself a moment to think of you, I would hurt. I don't know if it was lack of closure or if I was terrified the memories I buried so deep would come back." I turn and face the woods as I come to terms with my emotions. "I knew that if I saw you, if we were close again." I spin so he can see me. "You would be where my heart would find comfort again."

Zach rubs his face before looking at the sky. "Do you know how many times I wanted to find you?"

I shake my head.

"I went to your father once. I begged him to tell me where you were, but he said I'd had my shot and blew it. That you were engaged, happy, and over me."

My jaw drops at his admission. I never knew that. In all these years, my father never mentioned that. "I don't know that I've ever been over you. I loved Todd. I loved our life. I loved how happy he made me. But you've found a way to become a part of who I am. Does that make sense?"

He strides closer. "I loved after I lost you, too. But it was never close to what I felt for you."

When two people loved each other without inhibitions, the way we have, there is no chance of ever being the same again. The connection we share isn't something that can be severed. I learned to love differently, and in this instant, my soul has found its way back to him.

"Kiss me," I say in a hushed voice.

His arm snakes around my back as he draws me near. My breathing gets shallow as I realize what is going to happen. I'm going to let him kiss me. I'm going to kiss him because that's all I can think about. We've shared two very different moments, now I want this. Zach's eyes melt into pools of indigo. The pinks, oranges, and reds filter around him as the sun sets behind him. Everything is warm and beautiful around us.

"Are you sure, darlin'?"

"I've loved you since I was twelve years old, Zachary Hennington. You were my first kiss, my first love, the first man to touch me. I want you to kiss me, and I need to kiss you."

As I look into his eyes, I remember everything over the last few months. Him giving the boys their horses, finding Cayden, the way he cared for me at the bar, the way he was always watching me, and then he left Felicia to give us a chance. No guarantees that we could ever find our way back to each other, but I was worth the risk.

His hand tightens around my hip as his other holds the side of my face. He slowly pulls me in and my eyes close. As soon as our lips touch, my heart explodes. Everything inside of me tenses, and I grab the back of his neck. I feel so much all at once. I'm scared, happy, sad, desperate, and hopeful. It's as though I've found my place again. Zach is home. Zach is the place that I've always known and wanted.

We hold each other as our mouths move in harmony. His tongue slides against mine, and I moan. He yanks me even tighter against his body as he kisses me relentlessly. My arms encircle his neck, keeping him where I need him. He leads, then I lead, each giving and taking.

I don't remember the last time I was kissed with so much force.

His lips leave mine and trail down my neck. He holds my head back as his tongue tastes my skin. "Zachary." I groan as he finds his way back to my mouth.

Our arms hold each other so close it feels as if we're one person. I can't feel anything except him. He's a part of me, and I'm a part of him.

Each second that I'm in his clutch I don't think. My mind floats on a cloud as he holds me secure. I'm safe and there's no pain. He robs me of the thoughts that have haunted me and replaces them with the sun. All I feel is warmth. All I see is light. All I feel is joy.

He breaks the kiss and we both struggle for breath. "Holy shit," he pants.

"Yeah." I try to slow my heart. "Holy shit."

"Pres," he says with tenderness. I look up and his thumb brushes against my lip. "Are you—" He stops before starting again. "Was that okay?"

Another part of my heart becomes Zach's. "Yeah." I smile up at him. "That was okay."

There are no guarantees that this will work, but I don't want to live the rest of my life wondering. And if we still can kiss like that . . .

"Good."

"Zach?"

"Yeah?"

"There's a lot of things that we need to talk about. I've only been a widow for a small period of time. The boys aren't ready to see me with another man," I explain. I have to do what's right for them. "I'm not saying we have to hide, but while we're figuring things out, I don't want to rub anything in their faces."

He nods. "I'll let you lead the pace on this, but I'm going to be around a lot. I've spent half my life without you, and I'm not letting more time get away from us."

"Okay," I acquiesce. "I can handle time around you, I guess."

His eyes shift from hard to soft. "You guess, huh?"

"It'll be painful, but I'll suffer."

Zach's hand grips the back of my neck, threading his fingers in my hair. "Suffer?"

The pace of my pulse accelerates. My bones liquefy as he tugs gently, causing my scalp to tingle.

Slowly his mouth closes in, but he lands against the top of my neck. The warmth of his breath mixed with the cold trail from his tongue causes my stomach to clench.

"I don't think you know suffering with me." His low voice is seductive. "I was a boy then. I can promise you that I've grown a lot."

"Mmmm," I moan as he nips at the bottom of my ear.

"There won't be suffering. Just a lot of pleasure."

Oh. My. God.

"Promises, promises, Zachary."

"Oh, darlin'." He pulls my head back, forcing me to look into his denim blue eyes. "I promise that and a whole lot more."

Slow is going to be really difficult when he's saying things like this.

I may cave a hell of a lot sooner than I ever thought. Because if I couldn't resist a fumbling teenage Zach, I'm sure as hell not going to be able to keep away from the confident, sinful, and hot as hell man before me.

Twenty-One

ZACHARY

How the hell did I get so lucky? What did I do to deserve this chance? Nothing. Not a goddamn thing. I never thought I'd see her again. It seemed the world had decided that long ago, yet I'm holding her in my arms.

I kiss her lips once more. Since I'm waiting for her to realize she shouldn't do this, I take every chance she gives me to touch her.

"Let's head back." I stare into her green eyes and see the fear. "Pres?"

She looks away and twists her bracelet, "I just don't know where or *how* we're going to sleep."

I want to laugh at how damn cute she is. She's got nothing to worry about. Other than me sporting wood all night at the thought of her so close, I won't push anything. I promised her time, despite the fact that Presley has always been my demise. She's the one thing in this world I've always known was right.

"Relax," I say, trying to calm her nerves. "You'll get the tent and we'll all be out by the fire." I have no idea if that is Wyatt's plan, but that's what's happening. There's no way she's going in that tent with Vance or my brother, who can't seem to keep his hands to himself.

She lets out a huge sigh. "Okay. Sorry, I'm being ridiculous."

"Come on." I begrudgingly let go of her. We make our way to where the guys are, and I try to figure out a plan.

There may be a lot of good between Pres and me, but there's a whole shit ton of crap between us too. I need to be really smart with how I proceed. I can't spook her, and I can't let her think I'm not interested. Because that's ridiculous. But it's only been a week since Felicia moved out. Just like my worries about whether she can love again after her husband, she's probably worried about the same thing.

"You all right?" she asks.

Her green eyes glimmer in the moonlight. I step closer because I need to kiss her. I have to feel her mouth on mine, reminding me that she's fucking here. She's here and not some crazy dream I've been imagining. I keep moving until there's no distance between us. When her breath hitches, I step back. "Shit." I close my eyes and look away.

"Hey." Her hand presses against my arm. "What's wrong?"

I don't want to admit this crap to her. She doesn't need to know how the inkling that she's willing to give us a chance, makes me this happy. Because if there's any hope for us left in her heart, I'm going to find it and hold on for dear life. Presley is mine. Always has been. Always will be. I'll make damn sure of that.

"I was going to kiss you," I confess. It's true, and it's the only part of my thoughts I'm willing to part with.

"Why did you stop?"

"Do you want me to kiss you?"

This girl. I can't figure her out, which was never an issue. I used to be able to see into her mind no matter how hard she fought against it.

She looks away. "I don't know . . . what are we doing?"

"Let's call it dating."

"Dating?"

"Yeah, that thing where the guy tries to get the girl to see how perfect he is—which you already know partially. This is like dating with knowing we already match."

She shakes her head with a smile. "You know we're different people now, Zach."

"Yes. It's why I stopped myself." Even though I wanted to claim her again, I want to be the last man that has a part of her.

It's barbaric, I can comprehend this. But the idea of anyone else's hands on her body makes me want to beat the shit out of something.

Presley walks forward and places her hand on my cheek. I freeze, allowing her to set the pace. It takes every ounce of restraint I have not to pull her into my arms. Years I've waited for this. I haven't been the same since she walked out of my life, or I guess, since I walked out of hers.

"Sometimes when I look at you, I'm a kid again. It's like our first kiss or the first time I ever knew what it was like to be held by you. I was so sure that we'd always be together." Presley's eyes close, and I tug her toward me. Her head rests on my chest and my heart aches. I did this to her. "I don't want it to feel this good, Zach."

"What do you mean?"

Her head lifts and she stares into my eyes. "It scares me how easy it is to be with you. How it feels like the world is righted again. Like this was how it was supposed to be, yet that makes no sense. Considering how things fell apart, it shouldn't be this . . . effortless."

She's right on a few things, but I don't think this is effortless. This is painstakingly difficult. My head knows we're not the same kids, but my heart doesn't. It only knows that it's beating again. "This isn't easy, darlin'. This is hard as all hell. I'm conflicted too, but right now, holding you, is what I want. I'm not trying to jump ten steps ahead. I'm trying to live in the moment."

I look in her big beautiful eyes and get lost. I can't remember the last time I felt this calm. She's the air I breathe, and I hope to God she doesn't make me suffocate again.

"Okay. Live in the moment."

I snort. "I don't know if you've ever been able to not think ten steps ahead."

She smiles and nods. "I know. But I'm going to try."

She's always had her plans. Her goals were mapped out since we were kids. It was annoying as hell, but she needed that stability. My brothers and I did everything we could to make her loosen up. And when she did . . . it was the most beautiful thing in the world. Presley without inhibitions was intoxicating.

Her hands hold my head to hers. I battle my wants and try to remember that she's still figuring out what she's feeling. I ball my fists behind her back so I don't take control, and then I feel her breath on my lips. "In the moment," she whispers before her mouth mashes against mine.

I hold her back, pressing her against me. Her lips move with mine, and it's fucking surreal. She's been the one thing that got away, but I'm holding her now. There's no chance I'm going to let this end. I'll give her anything she wants if it means I have a chance at redemption.

For years I've told myself I'm better off. I've lied to everyone, saying that Presley and I were too young and didn't love each other enough. That was never the truth for me. I loved her too much. I loved her enough for the both of us, but I never showed her—even though I thought I did.

She shifts back.

"We're going to make this work," I state. There's no room for discussion.

"I sure hope so, Cowboy."

I lean back with a huge grin. She used to call me that when she was in the mood. "Cowboy, huh?"

"Well, that's what you are now, isn't it?"

I can see that she remembers. Her playful tone and smirk tells me all I need to know. There are some things that no matter how hard we try to forget—still live inside of our hearts.

"You're going to test me?"

I watch her come to life before me. The first time I saw her she was sad, unable to really smile. Bit by bit, she's becoming the girl I knew. It feels that way for me too. She's made me feel things I didn't realize I was missing from my life. Just being around her makes me feel whole again. It's crazy how much this girl lives inside of me.

"I think everything in our life is a test. I'm not sure if we'll pass, but I can't pretend that I don't feel things for you."

"You two do realize we can hear you, right?" Wyatt laughs from the site. We must be closer than I thought.

Presley ducks her head into my chest. "Oh, God."

"You can leave," I reply.

"Nah!" he yells back.

I run my arms up and down her back. "Let's go back before they act like idiots."

"Too late," she says.

"True."

We head over and the guys, of course, say a few things because they're incapable of being mature. Wyatt is the worst, but when he sees Presley is uncomfortable, he stops. I'll never forget the day he told me he was in love with her. I wasn't sure what the hell to do.

He's my brother.

She's my everything.

I had just lost her, and he came out to California. We were having a few beers, and he blurted it out. He told me how he would never do anything, but that he loved her, and I was a fucking moron.

He was right. I was stupid, but I'm not going to be that dumb ever again. Presley won't be able to get rid of me so easily.

PRESLEY

"I had a good time." I look at Zach, who's standing on the bottom step.

I feel ridiculous, but I can't stop grinning. Last night was everything. He was sweet and a complete gentleman. I didn't think about the ridiculous amount of debt I'm trying to pay off or the fact that I'm thirty-five living at home with my parents. I was Presley. A woman who has been through hell, but is finding her legs again. I didn't curl up and die along with Todd. There's something to be said for that, and I deserve to be happy again.

"I'm glad I went."

"Me too." I smile.

"I'll come by tomorrow to check on the boys' horses."

"Be sure to stop by the office." I bite my bottom lip. I'm a damn schoolgirl all over again.

Zach climbs the steps slowly. "I will. You can bet on it."

I take a step back, not because I don't want to be close to him, but because of how much I do. The boys could be anywhere, and I want to keep this between Zach and me. If people realize we're together, it'll be the talk of the town. I've had enough of that to last me a lifetime.

He keeps advancing, and I retreat. "I'll see you then." I walk backward and keep going until I bump into the screen door. "Bye, Zach."

The deep sound of his laugh fills my heart. "Bye, Presley."

Once I'm on the other side of the screen, I wave again, and he winks. I close the door and press my back against it. This is going to be impossible. Feelings that were six feet under have come back to life. I remember how special he makes me feel. When you're looked at like you're the only person who matters—it's exhilarating.

I take a few breaths in attempt to collect myself. Before I fully can, the boys are flying down the stairs. "Mom!"

"Hi, guys!" I say with a shaky voice. I glance back one last time, hoping to see him, but he's gone. It scares me that I wish he weren't.

"How was camping?"

"Did you see a bear?"

"Were there coyotes trying to eat you?" They rattle off their questions, and I shake my head.

"I missed you guys."

"We had too much fun to miss you," Cayden says with all the honesty in the world. Logan laughs.

"Thanks so much." I grin.

Logan shrugs. "Uncle Cooper is fun, Mom."

"He used to pull my hair and hide my dolls." I try to sway them.

Cayden rolls his eyes. "So?"

"So, he's a butt."

"Whatever," Logan dismisses me. "Is Zach coming over today to help train Flash and Superman?"

Of course they would ask this.

"No, Zach just went home."

"Aww," they whine.

"You can ask Papa to help you train Flash and Superman," I suggest.

I still can't get over the names they picked for their horses. I shouldn't be shocked, considering last month Cooper found his old comics and let the boys read them. Since then, it's all we hear about. The argument over whose horse is going to be faster is enough to make my ears bleed.

"Hi, sugar." Mama saves the day.

"Hi, Mama."

"Did you have a good ride?" she asks and hands each of the boys a cookie from her secret stash, which is the worst-kept secret ever.

"Thanks!" they both say in unison.

"Now, out of my kitchen," she demands. "Shoo."

"Come on, Logan. Let's go see if Superman has used his laser beam eyes on your slow horse!" he taunts and Logan runs after him.

"My horse has kryptonite!"

I laugh and lean against the counter. "Well?" she asks again.

"Yeah, it was good."

"You and Zachary were together all night?" she pries while trying to pretend she's barely paying attention.

I could be honest with her. As much as she gossips, she would never betray me. Mama has been on the receiving end of it and never wants that for me. Plus, she knows it's the fastest way to get me the hell out of here.

"We stayed in our respective camps. Wyatt and Cooper are going to need to knock it off."

"They want you to be happy."

I grab a cookie, and she glares at me. Why is it the boys can eat them, but I can't? "I'm hungry." I shrug and take a bite. "They can't force this. Zach hurt me really bad, and I'm still dealing with all my shi-crap." I catch myself. She has a wooden spoon and her aim is impeccable.

"He loves you. He's always loved you."

"I'm not counting my chickens. That's all."

She nods while stirring whatever is in the pot. "I see." I wait for her opinion, but she doesn't say a word.

"That's all?" I ask in disbelief. That's never all.

"You're a smart girl, Presley. I don't need to tell you things you already know. Now, hand me that rolling pin."

I place it in her hand, wondering what alternate universe I've stepped into. My mother has always made her feelings on the Hennington boys known. She begged me to date other guys, but no one even caught my eye. I believe there are people that you love so deeply they ruin you for anyone. Zach was that.

"Mama?"

"Hmm?" she asks nonchalantly.

"What did you think when I married Todd?"

She puts the crust on the pie, wipes her hand, and takes mine. "I thought you sure were broken."

"Broken?"

"Yeah, sugar. You didn't even give yourself any time. You jumped right into lovin' that boy. You would tell me all the time that he was keeping you together. But you'd cry as soon as you'd mention Zach. I think you made yourself love Todd so that your heart wouldn't hurt for Zach." She pauses, allowing me to absorb what she said. "I'm not saying it wasn't real. But for you to ask me that . . ." Mama tilts her head and busies herself.

I sit on the stool, watching her and thinking about what she said. The girl I was then was weak. I relied on Zach for everything. He was the reason I went to Maine and the reason I fell apart. Angie would tell me to "get over it" but I couldn't. I didn't know how to get over someone who was half of me.

Then there was Todd. He plugged the holes that Zach left.

"No, it wasn't the same, but I loved him," I finally say.

"I don't doubt that." She looks up. "I think you grew to love him. Which is why y'all worked. You didn't have this perfect story twisted up in the center of a tornado. That funnel lifted, leaving you and Zach in its wake. But you and Todd were strong at the base. I wish the good Lord didn't take him from you. So young." She shakes her head. "Makes no sense why these things happen."

I close my eyes and everything inside me tenses. She's said this a few times, and each time she does, I cringe. It's not God's fault. It's his. "God didn't *take* him, Mama," I say without thinking.

Her gaze lifts as she gives me a curious look. "What do you mean?"

I let out a long breath and decide it's time to be honest with my mother. "There's a lot more to this . . . to why we're here." How the hell do I say the words? I'm so ashamed and hurt.

She puts the bowl on the counter and comes around the island. "What is it?" Her fingers press under my chin, forcing me to look at her. Her kind eyes take me back to when I was a kid.

Tears fill my eyes to the brim, spilling over as I let the words come. "He took his own life. Todd got us in financial trouble, and he . . . he . . . he chose to leave. God didn't do this. God didn't take him. He took himself."

My heart hammers against my chest as she takes me in her arms. My mother holds me close, and I cling to her. Sometimes a girl needs her mama's embrace. This is one of those times. I fear the judgment, but it doesn't come. She gives me all her love and support as I let it out. I feel her chest heave as she cries with me.

After some time, she kisses the top of my head and looks at me with bloodshot eyes. "The boys?"

"They don't know," I say immediately. "They can't know. No one can." I implore her with my eyes. She needs to keep my secret.

"Okay." She nods. "Who else knows?"

"Only Angie and Todd's parents." I pause. "And Zach."

The hurt flashes in her eyes, but she covers it quickly. "I see."

"No." I grab her hand. "It wasn't like that, Mama. I was drinking, he was there, Felicia got me riled up, and Zach was calming me down. I was yelling at him, and it came out."

She pats the side of my cheek. "I'm not mad, baby girl. I'm just sad for you. I wish you would've told me. Your daddy and I didn't understand why you had no money with Todd being a big financial whatever up there."

"Yeah, he financially screwed me."

Mama sits as I spill the details. I let out every ugly piece of the truth, and it's both freeing and exhausting. My tears ebb and flow, pain radiates from my chest, and yet, through the broken parts of me, I heal. Her understanding, warmth, and touch allow me a chance to grieve a little deeper. I don't forgive him. Not for any of it. But maybe a part of me understands his desperation.

~

"I think you should come visit," Angie tries to encourage me.

"I wish I could. I have to work. You know why."

My mother offered to give us money, but I refused. It would be easier, but my need to rely on others is partially what got me into this mess. Had I been more involved with my own life, I would've known. But I went on believing everything was fine. As much as I wish the chain of events were different, I can't undo them. And I need to take care of myself.

"I miss you tons."

"I miss you more."

"You should," she jokes.

I ignore her comment. "Did you decide on the cupcake of the month?" I ask. I miss the store so much.

She laughs. "I did. It's not a cupcake though."

"Umm," I say with confusion. "It's a cupcake of the month!"

"I picked a muffin!"

"A muffin? Who the hell wants a muffin at a *cupcake* place?"

I swear this girl and her half-brained ideas.

"We've sold more this week than we have in a long time."

Huh. Well, okay then. I guess muffins are cupcakes without the frosting.

We talk about the two guys she's dumped in the last two weeks. I've always needed to be with someone. Angie, though, enjoys her space and freedom. She's the ultimate city girl. I don't think she will ever leave her downtown apartment for the suburbs.

"The boys start school soon?"

"Yeah, three weeks." I inwardly groan. This is going to be so hard for them. They don't have a clue how different this environment will be.

"They'll be fine. I talked to Cayden this week. He sounds really excited."

I laugh. "He is. But I think it's because he's finally going to be out of the house."

"He loves that horse too," she says with a hint of disappointment.

"He really does."

She can be pissed that Zach gave it to him, I don't care.

"About that—" There is a beat of silence before she continues, "Shit. I have to go. We'll talk soon, okay?"

I thank the heavens that we can avoid this topic a little longer. "Love you."

"Love you more."

We disconnect, and I flop back on the bed ready to pass out. This is going to be a fight. This is going to drive a deeper wedge between us. She'll never accept this, and I have to come to peace with possibly losing my sister.

"Did you even love me?" Todd asks with anger seeping from every pore. "Was I ever the one you wanted?"

I'm so tired of this same conversation. Of course I loved him. He was my husband. I just want him to stop doing this to me.

"How could you even ask me that?" I yell back in my own hostility. "You did this! You chose this! You! Not me!" I want him to see that this isn't my fault. But he keeps berating me every night.

He steps closer. "I loved you when he didn't. I was there. Now you're going back to him like he didn't throw you away?"

How dare he question me? "You've got some nerve! You think I should sit around crying over you? What about my heart? What about all the pain you've inflicted? You sling around your accusations as if I put this into motion."

Todd grips my arms and tears fall. It's the first time we've touched since he left me. I rip my arms away. "Presley." His voice cracks.

"No!" I sob. "No, you can't. You're gone. You're not here for me." Every piece of me breaks inside. He's a ghost, an illusion, but he feels so real. "In all the years we were together, I was only with you. I loved you. I had children with you."

He lets out a deep breath. "You and I both know that's a lie."

My eyes snap up to meet the sadness in his. "A lie?"

"You and I both know that you never wanted to have children with me. Those boys came by one drunken night when you forgot to take your pill. Let's not delude ourselves."

I walk with my fist balled and slam it into his chest. "I hate you."

"I hate me too! Why do you think I left you?"

I start to shake and fall to the ground. I have no fight left. "I'm not going to live like this."

"Just tell me why it was so easy to go back to him." *He crouches down and takes my hand.* "Why so soon? Why is he so hard for you to let go of? Did you ever let go?"

I gaze at him with tears falling freely. "I don't know."

"I do." *He sighs.* "Because it was always him."

I wake and sit up, out of breath. *It was only a dream.* I would swear it really happened, but know my mind is playing tricks on me. My heart pounds in my chest as his last words play on repeat. *"Because it was always him."*

Twenty-Three

Zach: Come meet me at the barn.

Me: What barn?

Zach: Yours.

I head outside in the stifling heat. You could fry an egg on the ground with the way the sun is beating down. I didn't expect to see anyone today, and the office only has a fan so I wore a pair of cut off jeans, a white tank, and my cowboy hat.

"Zach?" I ask, looking around.

I walk forward a little. As soon as I see him, he grabs me.

"Get in here." Zach's voice is strained as his hands grip my waist. "You," he says with a groan.

"What?" I ask, confused about what has him so upset.

His eyes travel down my neck slowly. I watch his chest heave as he continues to the deep scoop of my neckline. Zach drinks me in, and the rate of my breathing increases. I can feel his eyes, the heat from his body, and the grip of his fingers on my back. Everything else around me dissipates.

"Do you know how beautiful you are? How much I want you right now?"

Zach has been extremely patient. It's been a very slow moving train. One that he hasn't even tried to make go faster.

"Cowboy," I murmur. His eyes flash to mine, and I grin.

That's all it takes.

He looks back quickly as his hands tangle in my hair. Then his lips are on mine. My hat flies off my head from the force of the kiss. My legs wrap around his waist as he carries me back deeper out of view. I grab his neck and my hair veils us, making me feel like only we exist. I kiss him hard. He kisses me harder. When we reach the back of the stall, he uses the wall to keep me up as his hands roam my body.

I never want this to stop.

His rough fingers graze my bare skin and I fight back a moan. His hand grips both of mine, pinning them above my head. I grip harder around his hips but for a different reason now. I want more.

Zach takes his kiss away, and I whimper. "Tell me when you want me to stop, Presley."

I look in his eyes and shake my head. Right now, the answer is never.

I don't know if it's the heat in the air or the heat between us, but I'm burning.

He keeps my hands above my head with one hand as his tongue slinks down my neck. I struggle to breathe as he goes lower. His other hand cups my breast, and my head falls back against the wood.

Zach steps back, causing me to stand on shaky legs. His knee slides between my legs, and I use it for leverage. He doesn't say a word, just gazes into my eyes as he squeezes and kneads my breast.

"This is okay?" he asks while releasing my hands.

"Yes."

"Can I touch you more?"

"Yes," I say without pause.

He slides the strap of my shirt and bra off my shoulder. "You're so beautiful. You've always been, but it's like seeing you with new eyes."

Good. God.

He drifts to the other side down but doesn't expose me. His hands frame my neck and he pulls my lips back to his. We kiss as he barely touches my skin. I'm close to begging, but his mouth is what I want right now.

"Pres?" Wyatt's voice stops us both.

Zach lifts my straps back into place and puts his finger to my lips.

"Presley?" he calls again. "Where the hell did she go?"

I'm going to get caught making out with Zach in the barn. This is déjà vu all over again. Zach grins, caging me in with his arms. I want to kiss him again. I can't seem to look at him without craving it.

I hear Wyatt's footsteps get closer. I close my eyes and wait for him to say something.

Instead, he retreats.

As soon as it sounds like the coast is clear, I breathe a sigh of relief. "That was close."

"I'm pretty sure he knows."

"It could've been Cooper."

Zach presses his lips to mine, effectively quieting me. He leans back and runs his fingers through my tresses. "I'll see you tonight."

"I'll be there."

"Zach." I smack his chest as we sit tangled in the blanket. He keeps telling me about the tricks he and Trent are playing on the new trainer at his ranch. "You're so mean. You and Trent need a hobby."

"I think I've found a new one." He kisses the side of my cheek and tugs me closer.

"I'm a hobby?"

"More like a sport."

I lean back with my mouth agape. "A sport?"

"Maybe a marathon. But it's okay, darlin'. I like all the practice time we're getting."

I let out a soft giggle and lean back into him. "I might have to make you sit the bench."

Zach's lips graze my ear, and I shiver. "I'm not sure you really want that."

He's right. I don't. Each day that we spend together, I fight my feelings for him. When I'm in his arms, it's impossible to not give in. It's like falling back where we left off as kids—the good part. I feel the desire pulse through me when we touch, and it scares me. It would be so easy to lose myself to him. Allow the passion to take hold, but that would be a mistake. One that would leave me even more messed up over him. So, for now, we're taking things slow.

"Watch it," I warn as his arms tighten.

We've met the last eight nights like this. Under the stars, at the creek that separates our properties. I try to remember that we're not sixteen, but it's so easy to forget the world when Zach is here.

"Today at the barn was fun," he reminds me.

The yearning I squashed is back.

"Yeah." I let out a small laugh and jab him with my elbow. "It was fun. Maybe we'll do it again sometime."

Zach groans. "Maybe?"

"You never know."

We both fall quiet as he holds me close. I want to move things forward with him. At the same time, I'm enjoying the pace we're at.

"Sun's coming up. We should get you back home," he says against my ear. "Don't want you to turn into a pumpkin."

"I need to get some sleep too. I'm exhausted." Mostly because I don't want to dream and also because I'm staying up all night to meet Zach.

"Me too," he confesses. "Felicia was asking yesterday why I looked like shit."

Just her name causes my mood to shift. "Did you tell her it's because I'm keeping you up all night?" I say half joking, yet half serious.

Zach pulls back a little. I can tell he's trying to gauge how to answer this. He told me last night how she's trying to convince him to try again. He's also not allowed to say we're together, so he's backed into a corner. I hate her. I also know she's relentless. If she wants him back, there's not a trick she won't resort to.

"Pres," he says with an exasperated breath. "I'm doing what you want."

"I know." And I do. He is respecting my wishes. It's way too soon. Right now things are fun, but what happens when we come back down to earth?

Eventually, I'm going to have to face the unresolved issues between us.

And I don't know where that will leave us.

"Trust me." He takes my hand. "I would much rather tell everyone, but you've made it pretty clear you're not ready for that."

I look away, conflicted. I feel like every single thing in my life is some big secret. It's maddening. The secrets I keep are better left in the dark. When they come to light, they'll overshadow everything else. I need more time. "Not yet. I hope you understand, but for now, I want to enjoy this. We have a town waiting in the balance, and what if this goes south?"

"You're worried about the town?" he questions.

"Not really, I just mean that you'll have people hounding you, and so will I. Right now, there's no one up our asses. As soon as we're sure—"

"I'm sure about you, Presley. Make no mistake."

I hold up a finger to stop him. "I know that I want to try again. I'm sure that right now, this feels good." I hook my arms under his and watch his reactions. "I'm not saying we have to keep this quiet forever. But for right now, I want to have time for *us*. Without outside influence." I finish with a kiss to his lips.

He leans down, allowing his lips to ghost over mine. "I can wait for you. I can wait forever if that's what it takes."

I push on my toes closing the tiny gap. His fingers touch the small of my back as I hold myself to him. It's a sweet kiss. No tongue, no immense passion, but full of confidence that we're going to make it. If there's one thing I know, it's that Zach can make me happy. I just have to let him.

~

"You look all sorts of tired," Wyatt says as he pushes the door open to my office. "Kinda like my brother does."

I knew it wouldn't take long for him to be onto us. Especially after the almost incident yesterday in the barn. I'm pretty sure he put two and two together.

I lean back, tossing the pen on the desk. "I've been having bad dreams."

"Still?"

I forgot he knows about them. "Yeah, they're getting worse."

"Your husband?" he asks with concern.

I've mentioned them, but never gotten in too much detail. "It's like he's real. We argue, he says a lot of hurtful things . . . it's all in my head."

"It is."

"But I can't stop them."

Wyatt comes around the desk and sits in front of me. "What are you battling, Cowgirl?"

Wyatt has always been someone I can trust, but I already feel like too many people know. "Guilt, I guess."

"Because of you and Zach?"

Knowing how Wyatt feels about me, this feels so wrong. I don't want to hurt him, especially because he's one of my best friends. Yet, he's the only one I trust. "We're taking things really slow."

He chuckles. "I doubt that."

"No." I stand my ground. "I mean it."

"You and Zach have only ever had two speeds, Presley. You're all in or not. I'm not blind or stupid. Neither are the people around you. Hell," he says, letting out a laugh, "half the town has a bet going on how long it will be. He threw Felicia out slower than I thought he would."

I groan. "This! This is why I didn't want people to know. It's none of y'all's business."

He leans in close, a smirk on his face. "Nice to see you found your inner country girl."

"What?" I ask with annoyance.

"'Y'all.' I think that's the first time you've said that and acted like you belong here."

I look at him with a blank stare. "That's what you take away from what I said?"

He grins. "Just pointing it out for you."

"I appreciate it."

I don't at all. I actually would like to punch him for his smug grin. Why do people have to invade my life?

Wyatt slaps my leg. "As much as I hate to admit it, I'm going to say this: you and Zach are right. It's nauseating to be around because you can't help but watch. Every person in this world should hope for a love like you both share." He sighs while getting up. "I'm not saying you can't fuck it up—because you both have proven you're capable of that already."

"Asshole."

"I'm serious. You two don't know your ass from your elbow when it comes to fixing what you broke. How long have you been sneaking around?" Wyatt questions.

Ugh. I don't think we're sneaking around. I think we're keeping things low key. He's also missing one very important part to this equation. "And what, my friend, should I tell Cayden and Logan?"

He looks away, shrugs, and grumbles something under his breath. "They're good kids, Presley. Give them a chance to work through it."

He's right. They are good boys. "I want to be sure it's serious."

Wyatt laughs so hard he slaps his leg. "Oh, that's a good one."

"I don't know why you're laughing," I deadpan.

"You and I both know it's every bit as serious as it ever was."

All I know is that I'm hesitant. Not because of Todd or the boys. But because of Zach. If I give my heart to him, will he be able to endure the road ahead? Can he muddle through the parts of me that are so deeply broken that I don't know where the crack begins? The losses I've endured have changed me, left tread marks on my heart, and altered the course of my life.

Then I think about the past.

The mistakes I've made along the way. I've hurt myself in so many ways. Things I thought were going to bring me happiness that only turned into regret.

I was young, foolish, and thought I knew what I was doing. I was desperate to forget about him, to stop hurting. I wanted to tell him everything I was feeling, but instead . . . I ran.

My gaze latches back on Wyatt's. "I hope it can be. I just don't know if I should trust his promises again."

He comes close and crouches down. "Why are you so sure that he's going to hurt you?"

"Because the only two men I've ever loved left me. Both of them willingly."

Wyatt's eyes flash, and I wait for the follow-up question.

I implore him to ask me. If he does, I won't lie.

He closes his eyes, releasing a breath from his nose, and looks back at me. "One day you're going to realize how wrong you are, Cowgirl."

Wyatt doesn't say another word. He kisses my hand and walks out the door. I really hope that one day comes really soon because I'm pretty damn tired.

I go back to work, thinking that this conversation is done, when a knock comes a minute later. "Dammit, Wyatt."

"Well," a voice that is not Wyatt's says from the door. "I'm not that Hennington, but some say I'm the better looking one."

I lean back with a grin. "I would agree with them."

Zach walks forward with a bouquet of flowers. "These are for you."

I walk around my desk with a big smile. "You're so charming." Without a thought, I give him a sweet kiss. "Thank you."

He nods. "I'm here to meet Cayden and Logan."

"Oh?"

I didn't know they were meeting. Usually the boys are anxious to tell me. Zach has been coming a few days a week to show them how to train the horses. He's been amazing with them, and secretly it's meant everything to me.

"Why don't you ride with us?"

I look out the window and gnaw on my lip. I don't know. It's all of us together.

"Presley," Zach says with affection.

My heart accelerates at the thought of the four of us spending time together. "I . . . think . . . ugh!" I say exasperated. "Okay. One condition."

"What is that?"

"No innuendoes."

Zach chuckles. "I would never."

"Liar."

"Okay, maybe one or two, but I'll behave."

I give him a look that says he's full of shit. He doesn't know how to behave. None of them do. "We'll see."

"Do I get a reward if I'm good?" he asks with a mischievous grin on his lips.

How can I even second guess what I feel when he's like this? I don't smile half as much when he's not around. It's like Zach takes on the weight of the world so I don't have to. Or maybe this is what happiness is. Freeing.

"Maybe you'll have to wait until tonight." I wink and saunter out the door.

He groans from behind me, and I can't help but smile.

We head to the corral where the boys are already working with their horses. It's crazy how in a few months they've become so comfortable here. Cayden had a hard time with his horse after getting lost, but Wyatt and Cooper were instrumental in getting him back on. I really am lucky to have the men in my life.

"Mom!" Logan waves as he trots forward. "You going to ride?"

"I am!" I smile, and his smile grows.

"Your mom used to kick my ass in racing," Zach says with his arm resting on the rail. God he looks hot like that.

His tight jeans, hat, and the way he owns the world. Everything around him seems brighter. It's as if he's the sun, bringing warmth and beauty to things that used to feel dark and cold.

"Well." I try to control my raging hormones as I speak. "You always were slow."

"I let you win."

I scoff. "The hell you did."

"I think you know that boys are better, Mom." Logan laughs as he says the words.

I look over with my brows raised. "Is that so, little boy?"

"Oh, God," Cayden grumbles. "Now you've done it."

"What does that mean?" I ask, knowing full well what he's talking about.

I love competition. Maybe it is the racer deep inside, but even when the boys were little, I loved watching them get into whatever it was and trying hard. We would have contests for everything. I would typically win, but if Todd beat me, it was a full-on party in the house.

Cayden throws his hands up. "It means now you're in Mom-is-the-best mode. You're going to be all crazy and do your dance when you win."

"I think you should imitate her again." This from Logan, who's trying his hardest not to laugh.

I look at Cayden and give him the stink eye. "Don't even think about it."

He looks at Zach and grins. Cayden hops down with purpose and waves his hands around and shakes his butt. I laugh, he laughs, and Zach bursts out a long puff of air while gripping his stomach.

"So funny, boys."

"Zach." Cayden keeps going. "Then she does this." He totally makes up dance moves I've never seen.

Zach claps him on the back. "You should've seen when she was younger and she would win a race."

They all start pretending to be me, each impression less flattering than the last. I stand there with my arms crossed as if this bothers me. But it doesn't. Not in the least. Right now my kids are bonding with him. They've already been spending a lot of time together when he finishes at his ranch. He's been showing them how to be "ranchers."

But this is something else. Zach is showing them how to be friends. He's building something with Logan and Cayden without even knowing it. I watch with so much warmth in my soul that I could burst. There's nothing fake about this. He's not doing it because he has to or to win my heart. He's doing it because he cares about them.

It's clear now that, no matter how much I resisted my feelings, I never had a chance. My love for Zach never died.

Twenty-Four

"What do you say, darlin'? You up for an ass whoopin'?" Zach asks as the boys grin.

First, he called me "darlin'." Second he cursed in front of the kids. However, they're boys, and they've said and heard worse, so I let it go. Neither of them seem fazed by the term of endearment, but this is the South and everyone is someone's "darlin'".

I look Zach up and down, tapping my chin with my finger. "Well," I say dismissively. "I'm not sure you're a worthy opponent."

Cayden laughs. "I think he could take you, Mom."

"You do, huh?" I ask. "Did you know I happen to be Bell Buckle's most prized barrel racer?"

Logan snorts. "The whole ten people who live here? Half of which are our family."

"Watch it, twerp," I say, half joking. I think it's great they're enjoying this, but let's not go too far. "My title is no joke here."

"Were you homecoming queen too, Mom?" Cayden nudges Logan as they sit watching me. They know how to push my buttons. Todd used to make fun of my social status all the time. Like being pretty is a sin.

Zach walks over, throwing his arms around the boys. "She sure was. I'm surprised she doesn't sleep with her tiara."

"You wanna play too?" I ask with a shrug. "I seem to recall someone here with his own crown."

"I was a stud," Zach says with no pause. "Women loved me. Of course I was the king."

I clutch my hand over my heart with extra flare. "Oh, King Zach, however will your royal subjects compare to you?"

Logan bursts out laughing. "You guys are stupid."

"You're going to find yourself grounded," I say, smirking.

"You're going to lose to Zach. I bet five dollars." Logan throws his arm around Zach's shoulder.

"Yup," Zach agrees. "Me and Logan know the deal."

"Cay?" I ask as he deliberates. "You both can't abandon me for him!"

No way *both* of my boys are going to the dark side. Where's the loyalty? I won't lie to myself, though, the fact that they're bonding with him makes me smile. Zach was always good with kids, and he and Cayden have really grown close after the night in the woods. Yet, there seems to be something holding him and Logan back from connecting on that level.

Cayden grumbles before relenting. "I guess I'll pick you."

I giggle. "Turd."

"Okay." Zach claps his hands. "Here are the rules. We ride from here to the old barn and back. First one who makes it back here—wins. You remember the way, don't you, Presley Mae?"

I tilt my head and pop my hip. "I remember just fine, Zachary Wilber."

"Wilber!" Logan yells. "Your middle name is Wilber?" He laughs uncontrollably.

Zach steps closer, and I know I'm in trouble. "Now, Zach," I say, retreating. "You used my middle name. It's only fair."

"Wilber is a family name."

"Yes," I agree with my hands raised, "and a fine one at that." I look over at the twins who are giggling conspiratorially. "One I would try to denounce, but that's neither here nor there," I say as he gets closer.

"I think you need a good ass kicking."

"You wouldn't."

He glances at the boys and smiles. "You're right. I wouldn't."

He stops moving, and my heart settles. Maybe I'm not in trouble. Before I can say another word, he rushes toward me, catching me completely off guard, grabs my legs, and throws me over his shoulders. "Zach!"

The earth spins beneath me as he twirls me around. I'm going to kill him. "Say you're sorry."

"Never!" I yell as I grow dizzy.

"Say it!"

"Put me down, you giant jerk!"

He slaps my ass. "Say you're sorry and that you wish you were named Wilber."

Logan and Cayden's laughter fills my ears as Zach continues to spin. "Fine!" I yell as my vision blurs. "Sorry that your parents named you Wilber!"

"I don't think so."

I laugh and hold on to his waist as he goes faster. My light brown hair floats around me, but all I hear are the boys cheering him on. I don't care if we look ridiculous. For the first time in a very long time, we're all happy. The boys are laughing, happy, playful, and I'm feeling the same way.

"Say it, Mom!"

I slap Zach's legs, and he stops. "I'm sorry and I wish I could be as cool as you and have my name be Wilber."

"Good girl," Zach says as he puts me back on solid ground. He doesn't let go as everything around me spins uncontrollably. My feet stumble, but Zachary's arms are around me in an instant. I hold on to his broad shoulders and fight back the urge to kiss him.

I bite my lip to stop myself, but I see the desire pooled in his eyes. There's no denying the attraction between us. It's been weeks of spending the nights together, chasing away the demons.

"I'm going to fall."

"I won't let you."

I look into his blue eyes, searching for anything to tell me different, but I don't find it. "I—" I start to say, but Zach saves me.

"Now." His voice echoes. "You ready for me to show you who the ruler really is?"

Logan hoots. "Team Zach!"

"Team Mom," Cayden's unenthusiastic voice calls out.

"Cay!" I say with my hands on my hips. This kid. I gave birth to him, the least he can do is pretend to be on my team.

He shrugs. "Sorry, Mom. I want Zach to beat you."

"Kids," I say and then head over to grab the horse.

Shortstop is saddled up next to Zach's horse. I go around, checking my saddle and all, making sure no one is trying to sabotage me. I put nothing past these boys.

Zach brushes his front against my back as I'm bent over checking the horse's hoofs. "Sorry," he jests with a grin.

"Keep it up, Cowboy."

He does it again and the deep timbre of his voice vibrates. "You know how much I like it when you call me that."

I take a few steps back and peek over at the boys who are immersed in some argument. It also helps having a very large animal blocking their view. I saunter up to him, run my finger down his chest, and enjoy the way he shudders. "I do know this. Maybe tonight I'll call you it without anyone around."

Zach's head falls back, and his hands grip my arms. "You're going to make me crazy."

"Not as much as watching you right now is making me."

I'm so enjoying this. His eyes travel down and rest on my chest. I flex a little, puffing my breasts out. My tight, white tank top leaves little to his imagination, plus his mouth was on them less than twelve hours ago. We've been tempting that line for the last week, and I notice he's growing more desperate. But right now, this isn't so much sexual as part of my plan.

"Fucking killing me, Pres."

And it's working.

"Awww," I croon. "Is it going to be kind of . . . *hard* . . . to ride?"

His eyes flash to mine. Recognition flashes as he figures out my game. "You play dirty."

I smirk. "I play to win." Zach adjusts himself while grumbling under his breath. "Time to race, boys!"

I hop on Shortstop and Zach drops his chin and his lip twitches. "You're dead."

"You're not on your horse yet, Zach." I cock my head to the side. "What's wrong?"

"Some things never change," Zach mutters as he goes around walking funny.

I head over to the starting point as Zach struggles slightly to get on his horse. Well, no reason that the race can't start now. "Call it, Cayden!"

"Ready."

"No!" Zach yells.

"Set."

"Presley! Don't cheat!" he calls out as he finally gets on the horse.

"I'm not the one starting it." I smile innocently.

"Go!" Cayden says, and I'm off.

One misstep and Zach will easily catch me. I ride as fast as Shortstop will go toward the tree. Wyatt, Cooper, Zach, and I used to race all the time. Wyatt always beat us. I swear he cheated somehow. There was only one race when I actually came close. But Zach and I were pretty neck and neck. There's a way to turn and get the most traction, but I can't remember if it's left or right.

"Come on, Shortstop." I spur him on. We fly through the trail without focusing on anything but us. I need to use the time I got. Plus, I want to win.

The tree comes into my view and I hear Zach's voice behind me.

"Better watch, darlin'. I'm coming."

"Shit."

I lean forward and slap Shortstop's back, hoping he'll fly faster.

I take the turn and Zach is right on my heels. "I'm gonna get ya," he taunts.

The end is in sight. I want to win, but he'll never let me.

We come to the trail that widens so we're side by side. We both surge forward and the boys yell and jump up and down.

No matter who wins the actual race, I think I've won much more.

According to Logan, Zach won. Cayden, of course, doesn't dispute, just so I lose for once. Little shits.

Zach does his own victory dance and the boys join in. I laugh, watching the three of them behave like dorks. After they're done with the taunting and celebrating, we all go on a ride. The boys handle the horses with ease. He's done such a great job with them. They sit tall and maintain control the entire time.

"Can you guys race again?" Logan asks as we put the horses in their stalls.

"I think Zach has to work," I explain.

"He's a lot of fun, Mom."

I smile. "Yeah, he is. I've known him a long time."

He leans back against the wall. "Wyatt told me. He said you and Zach were boyfriend and girlfriend for a long time."

Oh, Jesus. Well, I guess it was going to come out sooner or later. "Yeah." I smile. "We were for a long time. Then I met your dad."

Logan nods as if he understands. I sit and wait for his next question because I see the wheels turning. His mind goes non stop and I can never be too prepared. Cayden and Zach are still in the corral, and I want to give him the answers he's searching for. Logan is a tender heart. He's missing his dad, and I've probably done a shitty job of helping him through that.

"Do you think Dad would like Zach?" Logan asks without meeting my eyes.

Hell no, he wouldn't. "I think if your dad knew Zach now, he would."

That's about as close to the truth as I can get. Todd hated Zach. But Todd had a very skewed version of who he was. All Todd saw was a man who left me in the worst way. I was broken, and Todd cared for me.

"Cool." Logan returns to quiet reflection.

"Do you like him?" I ask.

"I think he's really cool. I think he likes you, Mom."

I'm thrown off by that statement. I'm shocked that one of them picked up on it. "You do?"

He shrugs.

I don't want to ask this, but I don't know if I'll ever get another chance. "I think Zach likes you and Cay a lot."

"Do you like him?" he questions me with tears in his eyes.

"I will always love your dad. He gave me you and Cayden. No one else will ever take that away, okay?"

My heart aches as I look in his eyes. I see the pain that he hides well. My babies have been so deeply affected by Todd's absence. They don't deserve to hurt anymore.

"I love you, Mom."

"I love you more," I say as I fold my arms around him.

Logan's shoulders shake a little as he tilts his head to look at me. "I like Zach, and if you like him, then that's okay."

"You're a good kid, you know that?"

My son's eyes close as he squeezes me tighter.

Cayden and Zach walk into the barn, and Logan extracts himself.

"I think there's something in the kitchen," Cayden says conspiratorially.

"We'll see you guys later!" Logan calls out as they rush off.

I finish cleaning up the barn a little. Floating around feeling slightly withdrawn. I wonder if it's too fast that I'm even thinking about really moving forward with Zach. What would Todd think? Would he understand? Do I care what he would think? I don't know. I think he would want me to be happy. I know I would want that for him, but I also remember how he felt toward the mere mention of Zach.

How he would go to any length to avoid hearing his name.

I can't imagine that he would be happy about Zach being around his children.

Then again, had he chosen not to commit suicide, he would never have needed to worry about that.

"Hey." Zach's hand rests on my shoulder. "What's going on in there?"

"Do you think we're moving too fast?" I blurt out.

He stops moving and takes my hand. "What makes you think that?"

"Logan notices something between us, and I keep thinking that maybe this is too soon."

"Do you feel like it is?"

"Isn't that what I said?"

Zach's thumb grazes the back of my hand. "No, you said you keep thinking. What do you *feel*?"

I stand there, trying to get a grip on what I am feeling. I'm happy, able to breathe, and I want to be with him each night. The best part of my days are my nights with Zach. I long for him the minute we walk away from each other. And until Logan even said anything, I didn't think we were moving fast at all.

"Confused," I finally say.

"We're not a normal couple, Pres. We've known each other forever, and honestly, this is slow. I've been in love with you my whole life. I know you better than you know yourself. Don't you get it, baby? We're made for each other." Zach releases my hand and cups my face. "I know every part of you, love every part of you, and there's no rush on my part, but I don't think we're doing anything too fast. I think we're just finding our way back to where we always were meant to be."

I close my eyes, press my lips to his, and let his words sink in.

It feels the same way to me. I wish that we didn't have to go through the hell we've endured to find our place, though, and I pray both boys will find a way to accept this.

Twenty-Five

ZACHARY

I want to make tonight perfect. She needs to get out of her own head and allow us to be us. But Presley is an over thinker. Always has been.

"You sure about this?" Wyatt asks as he helps load my truck.

"No, but I'm tired of sleeping on a rock."

He laughs. "I doubt that's what your reason is, but I'll buy it for now. She's going to see through your bullshit though. She always does."

I've got tonight planned down to every detail. Presley will meet me like she always does, only this time it won't follow the way it has for the last three weeks. She refuses to let me take her out, so I'll force a date.

"Just load the truck." I remind him of his job. "I didn't ask for all your commentary."

Wyatt came over to grab a few things from our parents. Somehow, that turned into an hour of him, once again, saying how I'm fucking up things on the ranch. Bastard didn't want to help when my parents needed him, but now he's full of opinions. When I brought Felicia on to help me run things, he quit that day and went to work for the Townsends. Instead of him growing up and being an adult, he left me high and dry.

Dad had a stroke and could no longer work, so I did what was needed. My parents busted their asses for me, it was the least I could do. Thanks to my dad, I was able to attend any baseball camp I wanted, travel, take extra lessons. All because it was my dream.

"There's extra blankets because she gets cold." Wyatt tosses another bag in the back.

"I know."

"I don't know what you know, Zach. I hope you're ready for whatever it is you're doing. Presley may think she's ready, but you've got blinders on."

Here we fucking go again.

"You're not her brother. You're mine. Start acting like it." I shove his hat in his chest. "I love her. I would never hurt her. And no matter what you think, this isn't some fucking fling. This is me takin' care of her."

He can think what he wants. The truth is this is for her. This is about her. Not me or the fact that I have to ice my nuts every night. She doesn't sleep unless I'm holding her. There's no way in hell she's comfortable on that damn rock, so I'm going to treat her right. I could kick my own ass for not thinking of this before.

"Whatever you say, Zachary. You always know best when it comes to her."

"What's your problem?"

He huffs. "I'm sitting here watching you two sneak around. How the hell is that okay with you? If she's not ready to even talk about you both, how are you even anything?"

"I'm not sneaking around. We're not kids anymore. She's got kids she needs to protect. There's a lot more to this than what you think you know."

Wyatt needs to take his opinions somewhere else. I don't know when he became the expert on relationships. He's never had a serious girlfriend.

Wyatt crosses his arms. "I'd bet my ass that there's more you don't see. But hey, I'm just a country boy, right?"

Wyatt walks back in the house, and I let it go. Sometimes he grumbles regarding Presley. They have a very unique friendship, and I respect it. At the same time, I fucking hate it. I hate that he gets her on such a deep level.

I hop in the truck and head to our meeting spot. Only this time, our night is going to go down much differently.

Me: Head out early.

Presley: I just got the boys to bed.

Me: Perfect.

Presley: I didn't say yes.

Me: You didn't say no. I've got a surprise.

I hope that gets her attention. She's a stubborn Southern woman who likes to press my buttons. If I don't keep her on her toes, she's likely to keep going in circles.

Presley: Oh? What kind?

Got her.

Me: The kind that you need to come see. Your parents know. Just come to our spot.

I spoke with her mama this morning when I got the idea. She smiled, patted my leg, and told me I'm back on her good side. That's one Townsend down. Her daddy is going to be a whole different ball game.

Presley: What are you up to, Zachary Hennington?

I love when she calls me by my full name. She only does it when she's mad or feeling feisty.

Me: Darlin', get your fine ass down to our spot. We got us a hot date.

And hopefully one that puts a big smile on that gorgeous face. I'm going to show her how special she is and how she's always been my choice.

Twenty-Six

PRESLEY

I walk down the stairs after getting the kids to bed and Daddy is sitting in his chair. "Goin' somewhere, sugar?" he asks not looking away from the television.

"Hi, Daddy," I say as if I'm fifteen again.

He gives a short laugh. "Right. Don't think I don't know you're out every night with that boy."

"I'm pretty sure he's not a boy anymore, and I'm well past the age of curfews." I kiss his cheek and he humphs again.

"We'll see you in the morning."

I smile and squeeze his shoulder. "Love you, Daddy."

He looks over. "I love you, Presley."

There are days I kick myself over pushing my family so far away. Today is one of them. My father and mother have been the solid ground throughout these months. They've not asked for anything from me but have given everything of themselves.

I head out the back door and snuggle into the blanket I keep out on the deck. It's chilly out, and I'm barely wearing much. When I got his text, I felt like I needed to put a little effort in. I'm wearing a short, white, eyelet dress with a brown belt and a light jean jacket, I curled my hair this morning so it cascades in soft flowing waves. I threw on my cowboy boots, since trudging through the field to get to the creek isn't usually a good idea in any other shoes.

Not that I usually go looking like crap, but at the same time, I never dress up.

I get to our meeting spot and find Zach leaning against his truck. "Hello, beautiful." He walks forward, tugging me into his arms.

"Hi yourself." My smile is instant. I try to look over his shoulder, but he turns me so I can't see.

"You're trying to kill me, aren't you?"

"Me?" I ask with confusion.

"That dress."

I grin. "I might have had a plan to torture you."

"Well." His lips press to mine. "I think." Another kiss. "You're doing." And another. "A good job." This time when our lips touch, I hold him there. Zach's hands find their way to my hair, and he fists it loosely. I love the way he kisses me. Such power and strength, but never brutal. It's a heady feeling when someone makes you feel safe and strong at the same time.

Our tongues dance as I get lost in Zachary's touch. I can't seem to stop myself. Being around him makes me crazy. It's as if the time we spent apart only amplified things. When he touches me, it takes everything I have not to throw him down and feel every inch of him.

Zach's grip loosens, and he touches the side of my face. "I have a plan."

"I remember." I smirk.

He takes my hand and pulls me to the truck. This isn't his old one, this is brand new. "This yours?"

"I have two. Our truck, and this one."

It hits me that he said our truck. "You think of the other truck as ours?"

Zach starts the engine and turns with a sly grin. "Of course I do. It was where a lot of memories were made. I can still look at the passenger seat and picture you doing your summer strip down after I made the winning homerun."

There are some memories I guess we'll never forget. "I was young."

"You were naked."

"I had my bra and underwear on!"

Zach drives down the road with the biggest smile. "Pres, you had white panties on that might as well have been off. And you took your bra off if I remember correctly."

I shift in my seat as he taps the steering wheel. "You aren't wrong, babe. You took my bra off."

Remember that, buddy.

We were always experiencing this high force of sexual tension as kids. I didn't want to wait too long, but I was terrified once we had sex, he'd leave. Zach was always going somewhere and maybe I knew we wouldn't last.

"I remember. You squirmed in that seat. You kept lifting your hair, letting the wind blow it around. I also remember that was the first time I realized why road head is a dangerous act."

"Zach!" Heat burns my cheeks. "I can't believe you said that."

He shrugs unapologetically. "It was a good day."

"Where are we going?"

His fingers tangle with mine. "We're having a date."

"But everything is closed, it's already ten." I peek at my watch. "And I'm not ready."

I hate myself for saying that last part. I wish I would get over my issues. Zach has been damn near perfect. Today reminded me of that. The way he was with the boys, the race, and then how both of them rooted for him.

"I know, baby. This is a date for us. Trust me."

I squeeze his hand. "I do. I'm sorry. I don't mean that I'm not ready. I think I'm just really scared."

"Relax."

He turns onto a piece of land that the Henningtons own. It has a pond about two miles in where we used to swim as kids.

Trent would freak me out with this stories of the blood-sucking leeches that would kill me. It took me a good year of watching Wyatt and Zach not die before I'd go in. Trent lived for tormenting me—he was damn good at it too.

"The pond?" I ask.

Zach doesn't answer, he focuses on the road. The moon is bright tonight, and as we stop in front of the pond, the reflection is breathtaking.

"Zach," I whisper. All around the lake are lanterns with candles casting the most beautiful glow. There's a gazebo tent with chairs and a screen around it. I continue to scan the area as my heart swells. "It's perfect."

Zach gently takes my hand. "Come on." His voice rings with pride. He drags me in front of the truck with the lights shining on us. "Dance with me."

I don't say a word. Instead, I wrap my arms around him and let all my fear fade away. The music from the cab plays around us, but I couldn't tell you the song. I feel the music. I feel his pulse beneath my hands, but mostly I feel us. We're the music of this moment. He's the beat that I'm dancing to. And our music is a beautiful symphony.

"You're like this dream I keep waiting to wake up from," he croons in my ear.

My eyes meet his. "I know what you mean."

"I thought you were gone forever." His thumb brushes against my face. "I never thought I would touch you again."

I smile softly, leaning my head in his hand. "I didn't either." We weren't supposed to be this anymore. I learned to love with part of myself missing. It wasn't easy, but I was doing fine. Never did I expect my reality to become this.

He lifts me slightly so I have to look in his eyes. "I'm not happy about the how, but I am happy that it's this way. I missed you, Pres. You're my heart."

And I melt. "You're making it hard to resist you, Zachary."

Zach dips down and kisses me with everything. My fingers

grip his hair, holding him to me. Our lips move with passion and fervor. I want him to feel how much he means to me. How much this means to me. Dancing under the stars with nothing but the headlights and lanterns shining on us. I hate how much he knows me. He planned the most perfect non-date date.

His hands frame my face as he tears his lips from mine. "I need to stop."

I want to urge him to keep going. Every cell in my body is saying tonight is the night. We've danced around this, and he asked me to feel. I want to feel him. All of him.

But I don't. Instead, I step back.

"Sorry." He comes closer. "Sometimes I have to remember we're not there yet."

"I want you, Zach." The words come out before I have a chance to catch them.

His eyes widen. "I'm not trying to push you."

I never thought he was. There was a hope that tonight would be that, but I'm shocked I've been able to keep myself from jumping him. I know what I feel. I want to be with him.

I need to be with him.

If I never knew how incredible it could be, maybe I would hold off. But it's been a long time for me. There's a very real part of me that needs to be taken care of. I don't doubt that he'll do that. I trust him.

"What's in the tent?" I ask with a sultry undertone.

The first time Zach and I made love was in a tent. I have a feeling about what's there.

I turn, but he grips my wrist. "I promise it wasn't for what you think."

I give him a soft smile. "I know, Cowboy."

Even if he told me that was his intention, I wouldn't care. Well, maybe I would. But all I see right now is that he cared. He did everything so that our first "date" was special. Just like he is.

"We don't have to do anything. I just want to sleep together under the stars. I want to hold you all night long. That's all, Pres."

I take his hands and walk, leading him to the tent. "I want that too, Zach."

He lets out a sigh. I want all of that—after.

Once we enter the tent, I zip it shut so we have no bugs or unwanted guests. Zach faces me as I turn back toward him. I peel off my jean jacket, showing my strapless dress before turning around and looking at the interior of the tent. Once again, he's truly gone above and beyond.

It's filled with more candles and lanterns. But in the middle is a bed with blankets and pillows. Not a blow up mattress either, no, he has an actual bed. He had to have worked on this as soon as he left me.

"Tell me this is real," he murmurs.

I reach behind me, sliding the zipper down. "This is real."

He strides forward and grips my hands, stopping me from removing my dress. Zach releases my hands and holds me close. "We don't have to do anything, Pres."

My fingers graze his cheek allowing the scruff to tickle my skin. "I've never been more sure. I want you to make love to me, Zachary. I want you to give me tonight."

His head rests against mine. "I'll give you every night."

Zach's mouth fuses to mine as he lifts me in his arms. I hold on to his neck as he walks toward the bed. He lays me down with care, bracing himself above me. He continues to kiss me without hurry. We both take our time since we have all night.

His lips move to my neck, kissing every inch of my skin on the way to my shoulder. "So perfect," he whispers.

I push up on my elbows as his fingers roam my body. I shiver under his touch, but I'm far from cold. The warm summer air leaves a light mist of sweat across my skin. I close my eyes and breathe in this moment. Musk, grass, and country air fill me. Everything that is Zach.

I run my hands through his dark brown strands as he uses the position to slide my zipper the rest of the way. He leaves it that way, and he's letting me lead a little. "I want you," I reaffirm. "I want us."

"I've always wanted you."

I get on my knees, allowing my dress to fall. I couldn't wear a bra with this dress, and it seems that worked to my benefit. His eyes drink me in. Zach lets out a deep groan, and I move closer. "Touch me," I plead. "Please."

He doesn't make me wait. His hands are on me in an instant. It's not like we haven't gone this far in the last few weeks, but this is different. I feel it too. There's a barrier down between us. We both know where this is going.

Our lips find each other as his hands squeeze and pinch my breasts. He rolls my nipples between his thumb and forefinger, making me nearly buck off the bed.

I want to feel his skin. My hand presses against his chest. He moves back and looks at me, questioning, and I lift his shirt over his head. There's nothing I like more than looking at him. We may be in our thirties, but Zach is built like a twenty-year-old. His chest is broad and his abs are exactly like I remember. Every valley and peak is firm and mine to touch. I allow the tips of my fingers to enjoy the divots as I explore him a little. "You're still the sexiest man I know."

"It's because we're a perfect match." He kisses my neck. "You're the most beautiful thing in the world. Because you're made for me." Zach moves a little higher and places another peck right below my ear. "Just like I was made for you."

I recline and grab his face. "I'm feeling so much right now. I can't explain it." I want him to know, but I don't think I can put it into words. Maybe I'm not ready to either. It's so overwhelming, knowing in my heart that this is what is meant to be.

"Just feel us," Zach commands before his mouth is on mine.

His fingers descend the length of my back, and I hold on to his shoulders. He presses me against the pillow, my eyes close, and I do exactly as he said—feel.

His lips travel back down my body, lavishing my breasts and sucking on my nipples. Fire burns through my bloodstream. I have no thoughts that aren't of him and me right now. I can't remember the last time I felt so adored. Each of his touches is purposeful, branding me to him.

"If you need me to stop . . . " he reminds me.

"Don't stop."

Zach hooks his fingers in my underwear and slides them off. I lift a little to make it easier. I'm now completely bare to him, in every way. I let him see in my heart and my body. The last time Zach saw me like this I was eighteen. I had no stretch marks, cellulite, scars, or unwanted pounds. My boobs were perky, not showing the aftereffects of twins. Fear takes hold. What if he doesn't like me? I close my eyes with my head turned.

"What's wrong?"

"Nothing," I say quickly.

Suddenly, I feel his weight over me again. "Presley." He brushes my hair back. "Look at me, baby."

My eyes flutter open.

"Time has made you more magnificent than I remember. Whatever imperfections you see . . . I only see beauty."

A tear falls from my eyes. "Why do you always know the right things to say?"

He shrugs with a grin. "Trust me—I don't. I'm telling you what I feel. Showing you what I see. If that's the right thing, then it solidifies what I already know."

My heart beats against my chest and I pray he doesn't say it. I know he loves me. I see it when he looks at me, and if he's looking closely too, he sees it. But I can't say it right now. We may have established there's no right timeframe for us, and it's crazy to think we wouldn't fall back in love, considering I don't know that I ever really stopped, but I won't say it to him tonight.

I'll show it.

To ensure he doesn't utter the words, I lean in and press my lips to his. His tongue moves with mine as we pour ourselves into the moment. I unbuckle his belt, undo his pants, and slide them down. Zach kicks them off and flips me so I'm on top.

His dick presses against my core and I moan. "I need you."

He pushes me so I can stare at him. I move, giving myself

the friction I so desperately crave. My hair falls around me and he leans up taking control. He kisses me and drags his fingers down my back. I hold on to him, living each second in Zach's embrace.

Zach turns me so I'm on my back again. He slithers the length of my body, leaving a trail of kisses. This is what he was fantastic at even as teenagers. His tongue and mouth had a way of working in perfect harmony, ensuring I would lose it. "Zach," I whisper into the night.

"I need to taste you, Presley."

"I might combust."

The sound of his amusement vibrates against my skin, but he doesn't say a word. Instead, his tongue presses against my clit.

My fingers grip his hair as he does it again. My hips move, but he holds me still, continuing to lick and suck. Each swipe causes my head to thrash. I mumble incoherently as he takes me to new heights. I'm lost, floating, weightless, and I don't care if I ever come down. "Zach!" I scream out as I fall back to earth. He continues until I grow still.

He crawls back up. "I could drown in you."

My eyes open and I grin. "I could let you."

Zach pulls his boxers down and I see him fully. Every inch of him is mine again. He was the first man I ever let inside of me, and who knows if he'll be the last.

"If you want to stop . . ." He gives me the out again.

I bring my hand to his face. "I want you to make love to me."

"I'm damn glad you said that." His smile warm and assuring.

He reaches over for the condom. While he rolls it on, my stomach tightens for so many reasons. What if it's not as good as I remember? What if he doesn't think I'm good?

"Zach." Fear bleeds through my voice.

"What's wrong?" His eyes are wide as he probably senses my distress.

Now I feel stupid. "Nothing. I'm just being a silly girl."

"Presley." He adjusts his weight slightly. "I can wait."

I want to laugh. There's no way in hell that we're waiting. I don't want to wait either. I don't want this to suck. "I can't. I'm ready."

He shifts forward, and I feel him against my entrance. "Keep your eyes on me," he requests.

I stare into his deep blue eyes and see so much love it actually makes my chest ache. Everything I've lost in the last eight months has brought me here. To a man who loves me. Who has taken an interest in my kids. Meets me every night so he can hold me when I can't sleep. He's the boy who held my hand when my Nana died and I was too scared to go in the house. The teenager who punched Armando Delgado in the nose when he tried to kiss me, but then got him ice. He's the man I never knew, but has always lived in my heart.

When he enters me, everything goes still. There are no crickets, no fireflies blinking, there's nothing in this entire world but us. Our eyes stay on each other as he pushes deeper. Tears form and one spills over. It's too much. Too many emotions, thoughts, feelings, and I can't contain them.

Zach leans down and kisses my tear away. "God, Pres."

"You feel so good." I choke the words out.

"Don't cry, baby."

I need to explain, but there's no way to put him at ease. "It's happy tears. I'm so happy right now."

They continue to run down my face as we make love. Zach wipes each one away, and whispers how perfect I am. I flip him on his back and ride him, needing to feel the power of control, and I know how much he used to like it.

"I'm close," he says as I rock back and forth.

I ride him harder, enjoying the way his face tightens and his grip is stronger. I rake my nails down his chest and he clamps down on my wrists. "Let go, Zach." I move as fast as I can.

He can't hold on and he cries out my name over and over as he finishes.

After our breathing returns to normal, he takes me in his arms. I lie there with my hand on his heart. There's a lot to say, but all I want is to *be* right here. Legs tangled, completely sated, and lost in each other.

"Pres?" he asks while running his finger up and down my back.

"Hmm?"

"Will you sleep here tonight?"

I lift my head and smile. "Yeah, I think I can do that."

He yanks me so I'm flush against him, and I close my eyes. I'll stay here as long as I can, because right now, everything feels right.

Twenty-Seven

"You should curl your hair and pull it up," Grace says as I stand in front of the mirror.

"I'm so tired you're lucky I can keep my eyes open." I go back to getting ready. Emily is on her way over to go out for the night. She's going to sing at Lucky's in town, and everyone will be there because no one is driving to Nashville.

It's been three weeks of meeting Zach since we made love. I sneak out in the middle of the night and creep back to my bed in the morning. Thank God, I still remember the stair creaking pattern. Although, I think Mama has known for a long time. She's made plenty of references previously to the bags under my eyes and the grass on my clothes.

"Emily said it's mandatory you're there." She comes behind me, fixing my hair. "Let me pin it for you."

After we figure out what to wear, we head downstairs. Cooper's eyes lift, landing on Grace, and I wonder . . .

He watches her a little too long, grunts, and goes back to whatever he's reading. Interesting.

"Hi, Coop!" She slaps him on the back of the head, and I hold back a laugh. It seems the feelings aren't reciprocated.

"Grace." He rubs his head. "Going to see Emily?" he asks me, trying to keep from looking over at her.

I give him a knowing grin, I answer with, "I think you should come."

His face falls as he confirms what I suspected. "Yeah." Grace chimes in. "We should probably have a chaperone."

Cooper gives a lame excuse, but I let it go. Grace was Trent's girl for a while. And when a Hennington claims his girl, everyone backs off. Unless, of course, you're a Townsend. I can only imagine how this will play out.

"Have fun, Mom!" Logan says as he flips through the channels with my dad.

"You guys behave."

"We won't leave the house, Mom." Cayden attempts a joke.

"Good." I mess his hair.

Grace and I head out to where Zach will be, and I remind myself that I'll have to pretend nothing is going on between us. We're still keeping things under the radar, but I don't know how I'm going to be able to stay away from him. In fact, I know I won't. When he's around, I'm unable to resist being close to him. He fills me up and makes everything brighter. The dark isn't void when he's near. Plus, since we've been having sex, all I see is him naked when I look at him.

"Grace," I call her attention.

"Why does the way you say my name worry me?"

I shake my head. "It's not bad."

"Are you finally going to admit you and Zach are back together?" she says with a sly grin.

"You know?" I question, slightly flabbergasted.

"Of course I know. Everyone knows, Presley. I mean Zach is walking around town as if he just won the state championship. You're suddenly smiling all the time. Both of you look like you're staying out all night . . ." She nudges my elbow and laughs. "We're not dumb, but we did let you have your secret."

My mouth hangs open. I really thought we were in the clear. "Unreal," I mumble to myself. "I thought . . ."

"You thought nobody knew?"

"Yes!"

"Don't ever go into acting." Grace parks the car and turns to me, placing her hand on my forearm. "I'm happy for you, Pres. You've been so sad since you've been back. I know it couldn't be easy coming back here, but we love you. I've never been married, and I don't have kids, so I won't even pretend I understand what it's like to lose your husband. Just know that I'll always listen. And I won't lie . . . I'm really happy you and Zach have found a second chance."

I smile and nod. "I'm scared that I'm happy too."

"Why?"

"It's so soon."

She shakes her head. "I think it's been too long. You don't remember the Presley and Zach that I do. The ones that everyone wished they could be like. Loving each other so much that other people were jealous." She laughs at the memory. "I mean . . . I broke up with six guys because they didn't look at me like he looked at you."

"That's crazy," I chide. "You can't think that what we had is normal."

"Exactly, Presley. It wasn't. It was so special. I think we all wept when we heard y'all broke up. Don't get me wrong," she quickly adds. "I think you were right. You'd spent your entire junior and senior year waiting for him. Then he took that contract like you were irrelevant."

"Thanks." I sigh.

"You were so young, though. He was an immature boy with dollar signs in his eyes."

I get what she means. In the last few months, I've come to see that I was too naïve to even understand the situation. Do I wish that things had happened differently? Yes. Maybe. I don't know. If he had never taken that contract, then I wouldn't have my boys, and really, they're everything.

"I think that things worked out the way they were supposed

to," I admit. "I've been angry at him for so long. I don't want the town butting in either."

She laughs. "I get being angry. Those men have a way of getting under your skin and embedding themselves there." Ahh, her and Trent. I wonder what exactly is going on in this town. Grace and Cooper were definitely giving each other some lonely eyes. "Let's get in there." Grace's smile brightens.

We head into the bar where my eyes immediately seek out Zach. What I'm faced with is not what I am expecting. Felicia clutches Zach's arm as he talks to Trent. Her hands cling to him as she rests her head on his shoulder. He doesn't pay her any attention, but I couldn't give two shits. I watch her stare at him, hanging on every word while my rage starts to churn.

Is she out of her mind? He's mine. We were at his place last night and well into the morning. She needs to get her nasty hands off my man.

"Well," I say under my breath.

Grace's gaze locks on what I'm seeing and she lets out a growl. "Pres." She draws my attention away. "Listen, the only way you're going to fix this is to walk over—"

I don't let her finish. I know exactly what I have to do.

My feet travel quickly as I march toward them. Anger boils in my blood as I think about the last few weeks when Zach held me, kissed me, made love to me like I was the only woman alive. Now this bitch is touching him? Not just no—hell no. She's going to learn really quick where her hands do and don't belong. And Zach, well, he's going to learn a few things as well.

Zach's eyes follow me as I approach. He glances at Felicia and then back to me. *Yeah, you're in trouble.*

I don't slow down or pause. I stand right in front of Zach, grip his neck, and pull his mouth to mine. Right here in the middle of the town bar, I kiss him. I let every person know exactly what we are. Zach doesn't falter, his hands grab my back and he holds me tight to him. His lips move with mine as catcalls and whistles ring out around us. I don't know how long we're like this, but it feels like an eternity.

I stake my claim on the boy that has always been mine. The worry melts away about what people will think. Grace is right—we've always been special.

Once I feel my point is made, I lean back. Zach's lips form a cocky grin. "Hi, darlin'."

"You're in trouble."

"If that's how you punish me, I think I could accept this."

My head dips as I give him a no-nonsense look. "Big. Trouble."

"Felicia," he says as he pulls me against him. "I've decided I am going to go to the auction gala next week." I look at him with confusion. "Get me two tickets. Presley will be coming as my plus one."

"Be sure you get us a hotel room too," I tack on. "We'll probably need some privacy after."

She huffs and walks away.

"So we're going to a gala?"

"It made my point."

I gaze at him, remembering why the point needed to be made. "Why exactly was she hanging on you?"

He brings me flush against his body. Zach's nose rubs against my ear as he whispers. "She's drunk, and I was being nice. Nothing more. But you ousted us in one hell of a way."

I lean back so I can look in his eyes. "I guess it's time the women in this town know that you're not available."

"Presley." His deep voice grumbles as the gratification in his eyes shines. "I haven't been available since I was fifteen years old." He kisses my forehead, pulls me tighter, and goes back to talking to Trent like nothing happened.

I look over at Grace, who's standing with her arms crossed and sporting a grin.

Well, no more hiding for me.

Wyatt shows up with some chick I've never seen before. "If it isn't Mr. and Mrs. I'm-so-stupid-I-think-I-had-the-whole-town-fooled."

"Shut up, asshole." Zach jokingly punches his brother.

Wyatt rubs his shoulder. "I'm hurt. I go through all the trouble of makin' you both realize how dumb you are, get you back together, and you punch me? Dick."

"You did this?" I ask with a smirk.

"Well, yeah, Cowgirl. How else did you think you'd wake up?"

I love that, even with all the crap between us, Wyatt would never make me feel uncomfortable.

I lean in and kiss his cheek. There are so many things I want to say, but not here. Wyatt is the reason that I've been able to see past my own pain. "You're a good friend. You're going to make some woman very happy someday." I glance over at the girl he brought with him. She basically has a bikini top on and shorts that are more revealing than my underwear. "Hopefully someone else," I say offhandedly.

He laughs. "I think you've been drinking already."

"Not a lick."

"Well, then maybe you should, because no one can tame the wild beast that is me."

His humor is his defense. I see through it, but we all need our armor. I've hid behind walls for a long time, and honestly, if it weren't for him, I still would be. Safety is a luxury that should never be taken for granted. When my world kicked me in the teeth, the vulnerability I felt was unnerving. It rocked me to my core. While Wyatt hasn't had that type of horrific experience, he hurts.

"The only thing wild about you is your hair." Zach nudges him.

Wyatt flips him off, grabs his drink, and throws his arm around his bimbo of the night. "Peace, suckers."

Zach and I both grab a drink. He drinks his beer while I sip my Jameson until Grace drags me away and onto the dance floor. We giggle and dance, like old times. Songs continue to change, but we keep steady where we are. I love to dance. I love knowing that I also won't look like a fish out of water when we line dance. I can handle numbered steps.

"Man." Grace laughs. "Zach is about to pummel that guy staring at you." She spins me around and I see him watching someone.

My eyes dart to where he's watching and I giggle. It's the guy who I danced with the last time. "He's oblivious to the fact that I was making out with Zach before, huh?"

We continue pretending like I don't care until I see Zach bang his bottle on the bar and start walking toward him. "Shit." I rush off, Grace following.

I catch Zach before he can reach him. "Where you off to, Cowboy?" I smile.

Zach immediately thaws. "Going to set the record straight with someone."

"Not worth it."

"You're worth everything."

"Awww." I kiss his lips. "You're so cute."

"I like you like this," Zach says as he keeps walking.

"Like what?"

Zach leans down, the warmth of his breath tickling my skin. "Happy."

I like it too, but God if I'm not scared that this could end quickly. There's no more secret Presley and Zach. No chance of us going slow, because everyone knows. This town will probably hold a damn parade tomorrow. My kids will need to be told right away, and who the hell knows how that will go.

The song morphs into one of my favorite two-step songs. "Dance with me," I command.

His arm glides around my back and he lifts me, carrying me toward the dance floor. He places me down and grabs my hand. I love this. Right here. The way he holds me when we dance. His hand grips the back of my neck so he can lead me while the other wraps around my fingers against his chest.

Without a word, we move in harmony. The song is about falling and how he'll catch her. I can't help but imagine his voice as the lyrics speak to my heart. It's something that Zach would do. He'd be there if I fell.

Zach spins me around the dance floor, all the while never moving his gaze from mine. He leads me effortlessly, and I am completely mesmerized. He mouths the lyrics and tears form in my eyes. The bar melts away as he serenades me with words that speak to both of us. The music stops, but we stand here in each other's arms.

"I love you, Presley."

My heart stops as I look at him and know. I've fallen completely head over heels in love with Zachary Hennington, again. The boy who stole my heart as a child has done it once more. Only this time it's stronger. I knew it the night we made love. Hell, probably the minute I laid eyes on him again that there'd be no chance of resisting him. We were always Presley and Zach, and we always will be.

My eyes fill with moisture. "I love you too."

He tugs me close and kisses me.

Clapping erupts, and I push back, laughing.

I look around as one person continues to clap. I glance over, expecting to see Wyatt being his normal self.

Instead, my eyes meet a pair of green eyes I haven't seen in months.

Angie stops, wipes her face, and walks back out the door.

Twenty-Eight

"I'll be right back," I tell Zach as I rush out after her. Dammit. I knew this wasn't going to go over well, but I didn't think it would happen like this. I never could have imagined that this was how she'd find out.

I push the door open and look around. She's walking quickly away from the bar, shaking her head. I've known her half of my life and she doesn't typically avoid a fight. She's the girl who will stand toe to toe until she feels heard. Angie only runs when she's hurting.

"Angie!" I yell. She halts and then turns, giving me a look filled with a mixture of sadness and anger. Instead of waiting, she takes off, moving even faster. "Angie! Stop!" I rush toward her, but she keeps going. "Dammit! Quit walking away from me."

Angie spins and glares at me. "You're kidding me. You're going to tell me to stop? How about you stop!" Here's the girl I know.

"Don't you dare." I stand ready to defend myself. "You don't know what I've been through and you don't get to judge me."

"Zach? Zach is who you're dating?" As angry as she is, I hear the hurt mixed in her voice. She saw it all. Every horrible thing that I endured and all the nights I spent sobbing in her arms.

"Really, Pres? After everything? Zachary fucking Hennington? I mean, why don't you go back in time and be a damn kid again. Oh, well, you kind of are. So, really?"

I don't know what to say. There's so much that is fucked-up about this scenario, and I don't know which part to avoid. I'm not wrong though. This isn't seventeen years ago when I was a kid. We're adults, we've taken our time, talked, worked through any past issues. This isn't a fling. I love him.

"Yes. Really," I say with care. "We're not the same people, Angie."

"No?" She laughs. "He's not the same guy who left you when you needed him most? Or are you not the same girl who married my brother? Because that girl wouldn't go back to him."

I was trying to be careful, but she wants to bring Todd into this. I refuse to let her use him as a weapon. Her memory is a little off about who hurt me the most. "Your brother? You mean the one who saddled me with over two hundred thousand dollars of debt and then killed himself? The one who's responsible for the reason I'm back in Bell Buckle? That one?" I ask her with disdain. "The one who left his twin boys without a father? His wife without her husband? Let's not start going tit for tat."

She huffs and swipes a tear. "I can't believe this. I thought you were miserable here." Angie starts to pace. "I thought my poor sister and nephews were stuck in Tennessee, hating life. I come here to find you making out with your ex. The guy who, according to you, fucked your entire life."

"Stop it."

Her whole body tenses. I can see the struggle inside of her. "I'm so upset, but it's more that you lied to me, Presley. Me! Your best friend. The one who's been there every step of the way. How could you?"

And here is where my own anguish lies. I hate that I didn't give her the option to hear it from me. I was so afraid of what she would say. My heart couldn't take her disapproval.

"I wanted to tell you, but I knew you'd react this way." I step closer. "You've been my family for so long, and I didn't want to listen to your opinion on this."

"So you lie?"

"I didn't lie." I defend. "I didn't tell you because it hasn't really reached where we are now until after we spoke." After the words are out, I instantly hate myself. "No." I huff. "You know what, no."

"No?" She looks at me with confusion.

"No!" I grow angry. "I'm not going to make this out to be something it's not. I love him. I love him, Angie. If you love me, then you'll understand that. Because I deserve to be loved again. I'm not supposed to live the rest of my life wishing for something that Todd took away." I pace as tears begin to fall. "I'm not undeserving. And I'm damn sure not going to feel bad that Zach and I found something again."

She snorts. "Did you even love him?"

I know who she means. I fight back the urge to slap her. "Don't ever question my love for Todd."

She's hurting and upset, but I'm not wrong here. It took all of this to see that. I'm not cheating or dishonoring his memory. He chose death, and I choose life.

She grips her two ponytails as she screams. "Dammit, Pres! I was so happy to see you. I needed to hug you and make sure you were okay. I didn't expect this! Had I known—"

"What?" I challenge her. "Had you known what, Angie?"

"I could've been prepared."

"Do you want me miserable?" I ask with wariness.

"Yeah, I want you to be sobbing every damn day." Angie rolls her eyes. "Of course I don't want that. I wanted you to trust me."

I wish she knew how much I wanted to tell her. "If I thought that you would've been the least bit happy for me, I would've. Don't you see? Your opinion matters, and I knew that this wouldn't go over well."

She tilts her face toward that sky, takes a deep breath, and then faces me again. "I hate that I reacted this way. I wanted to make you smile. And I didn't want it to be Zach."

But Zach is who helped me. I was in agony until he showed me the way. Angie would've been my rock if I could've stayed in Pennsylvania. But my path didn't go that way—it came back home.

"It's not your choice."

Her anger returns. "How could you forgive him when he left you pregnant?" she screams at me.

"Dammit, Angie." I look around to make sure no one is around. "I never told him about the baby."

"So he doesn't know?" The judgment in her tone makes me cringe.

"No," I huff. "I'm . . . I have every intention of telling him, but it never seems like the right time."

She shakes her head. "You have a real issue with keeping secrets, Presley. They're going to bite you in the ass."

This isn't a conversation to have outside of the bar. "Just stop."

Angie turns, and I can sense her disappointment. I plan to tell Zach. I've said the words in my head a hundred times, but then I can't say them aloud.

"I'm working on my issues. Little by little." I feel like I've had a mountain of crap to deal with. I'm fully aware that I'm not handling things the right way. "I'm sorry." I place my hand on her shoulder. I haven't seen her in a long time. I've missed her. "I don't want to fight. Please," I beseech her.

"I don't either." Her heavy breath releases. "I should've known though. I was telling myself the whole time that this was going to happen. I should've known you'd find your way back to him."

I bump her arm. "Did you want to be my savior?"

"I am your savior. I'm the best damn woman in the world." Her smile cracks. "I hate you. I hate that even when I want to choke you, I still love you."

"I hate you too." I grab her arm, yanking her into a hug. "I missed you."

"Seems it."

I slap her shoulder. "You have to be a smart ass."

Angie leans back with a sigh. "Do the boys know about you guys?"

"Not yet," I admit. "It has all really only become serious the last few weeks. We were taking things insanely slow. I think Logan has an inkling though."

We both walk over to the bench that sits against the wall. I see her mind is wrestling with this, and to be honest, so is mine. It's all become very real in a matter of a few hours. Zach and I have been trying to maintain a slow pace, and it just got railroaded. She takes my hand in both of hers, and I'm brought back to the last time we saw each other.

"Your hair still looks like shit," I say offhandedly.

"You're too skinny."

"You really should stop being so pretty."

Angie grins. "I get it from my sister."

I rest my head on her shoulder and fight back the urge to cry. "I'm truly sorry."

"Me too."

"We should get back in before Zach and Grace come out with a search party. You know how the South feels about you Yankees."

She gives me a dirty look. "I swear. It's an alternate universe down here. Did you know there are no Starbucks anywhere around here?"

"Yeah, I'm aware."

She would die down here. Her city life is all she knows and loves. Angie almost lost it in Maine for four years. But we had a lot of bars. She found a way to swap her coffee for beer. "I think I should say hello to him," she says as her head rests on mine.

"It would mean a lot to me if you and he could be civil. For the boys too. They really like him."

"He got them fucking horses!" She laughs. "I would like him too if he got me a damn horse."

I shake my head. "Let's go."

We both get up, but when we turn, Zach is heading toward us. My stomach clenches, and I pray this is easy. Angie huffs from behind. We're off to a good start.

"Hello, Zachary," Angie almost croons.

"Angelina," he says her full name with a smile. "It's been a long time."

"Has it?" Her sarcasm is thick. "I guess it has been. I'm sure you've missed me."

"Okay," I say loudly, trying to diffuse what's building. I know Angie, and I also know Zach will step to her challenge.

"You okay?" he asks while rubbing my arm.

I grab his hand and move toward him. "I'm fine. Angie didn't know . . ."

I haven't told anyone until tonight, but I see the flash of disappointment in his eyes. He knows that Angie is truly a sister to me. They always got along until he left me. Then she loathed him.

"I'm so sorry about your brother." Zach steps forward and her head falls. "I remember that you were close when we were younger."

"Thank you," she says sincerely.

Angie may be a lot of things, but cruel isn't one. She's been through hell as well. She's not an unkind person, just a little feisty. One thing I always could count on was her being by my side. Her loyalty and friendship are unwavering.

"Let's go get a drink," I suggest.

We all head inside, and I introduce Angie to everyone. She and Grace have their love of painting in common. Angie tells her all about the museums and galleries in Philadelphia and New York. Trent and Angie also seem to instantly hit it off. He flashes his badge, and she tells him how unimpressed she is. It's hysterical to watch, and Grace loves that a woman is putting him in his place. I wish she'd try a little to talk to Zach, but stubborn is one thing Angie most definitely is.

As the night wears on, we all have a few drinks and are enjoying each other's company. Zach sits next to me with his hand on my neck, absently running his fingers up and down. My hands are on his thigh and every now and then we lean into each other.

"So, Angie," Zach says, bringing her attention to him. "How long are you stayin' in town?"

She leans back in her chair and crosses her arms. "Trying to get rid of me already, Hennington?"

"Ang," I warn. "I don't think . . ."

"I'll be here for the boys' birthdays." She stares at him with a look that makes me want to slap her. As if she's challenging him. "My brother took them to a hockey game every year for their birthday. I figured we'd drive to Nashville and see the Predators."

Todd made it a huge event for them. The older they got the more elaborate the day became. It was something special for the three of them. Back then, Angie and I would go to the spa, it worked really well for me.

"I'm sure they'll love that," I say with a smile. "They weren't impressed when I offered."

"I'm the cool aunt."

"Yeah." I laugh. "I know."

"Anyway, now that I'm here, don't be sad when the horse lessons go on the back burner." She smirks.

Zach doesn't miss a beat. "We'll see."

She has no idea how obsessed they are with their horses. Or Zach. Each day Logan warms to him more and more. Cayden already thinks he's the "coolest" of all the Henningtons. Logan still thinks that Trent is the best. For the life of me, I don't know why. I think it's the badge. Wyatt has become a brother to them. They see him as an equal, probably because he acts like it.

Angie turns back to Grace as she rolls her eyes. We're going to have a long talk.

"Cowgirl," Wyatt says, returning from wherever he and his hussy were. "Whatcha got here?"

"This is my sister, Angelina."

Angie glares at me for using her full name before looking at Wyatt. Her entire body freezes as she catches her first glimpse. Oh, shit. I think my sister is enjoying the view of another Hennington. They're like honey to flies.

"Hello, Angel." Wyatt's charm is thick, and she's done. I've seen that look before. He's getting ready to make her his next target.

"Angie," she corrects him.

"Could've fooled me."

Trent chokes on his beer and Zach bursts out laughing. "Smooth, brother," Zach says. "Real smooth."

"Like a baby's ass." Trent joins in on the ribbing of Wyatt.

Zach nudges Trent. "He's an ass all right."

"Knock it off, you two," I reprimand under my breath. "Angie, this is Wyatt."

"Oh, my God!" She stands and pulls him close. "Thank you! I've heard about you forever, and Presley says you're me—with a dick."

Seriously. "Angie!"

"What?" She looks over and shakes her head. "Oh, do we not curse here? I don't know what's acceptable down here."

"Angel," Wyatt drawls the new nickname, "you can say whatever you want round here. The dirtier the better."

"I like him." Her lips curl into a smirk as she looks between me and Wyatt.

"I bet you do." We're in so much trouble.

"Two out of three ain't bad." She tacks on while looking at Zach.

He laughs. I do not. Instead, I stand ready to drag her ass into the bathroom and stop this shit. Her anger is completely unjustified. If she wants to be mad at someone, it should be me.

Wyatt steps between us quickly. "How 'bout a dance?" he asks Angie with his hand extended.

I swear he had a date when he came in. I wouldn't be surprised if he left her ass somewhere. That man. He's out of his league with Angie. She will eat him for breakfast. Although, it might be fun to watch.

"Sounds great." She stands and shrugs.

Maybe she'll come back with a better attitude. Wyatt might help dissipate the tension.

They head off with a reluctant Trent and Grace. I turn into Zach. "Sorry about before."

"Nothing to be sorry for. Angie loves you and is looking out for you and the boys."

"She does. And I was married to Todd for a long time. I don't think she's ever envisioned me with anyone else, let alone you—no offense."

He sniggers. "None taken."

"I feel better, though."

"Oh?"

"Yeah, now we don't have to hide really. We can be Zach and Presley. We don't have to pretend once we talk to the kids."

Which is going to have to happen. Especially since their loud-mouthed aunt returned. She'll never be able to keep this to herself. And now that Zach and I have taken the next steps, admitted we love each other, I feel like the time is right.

"Presley," he says with affection.

"Yeah?"

"I love you. I mean it. No matter what happens when we talk to Cayden and Logan. No matter if Angie or the rest of the world don't like us together, I'm in. I'm committed to making this work."

He has no idea what he does to my heart. Each time he speaks, I fall harder. I lean forward and press my hand to his heart. "I love you, Zachary Hennington. From the first kiss we shared, I have been head over heels in love with you."

Our lips touch, and I hear a bunch of idiots yelling. "Kiss her like you mean it, Zach!"

I go to turn my head, but he grips my face. His lips press hard against mine, and he tilts my head. I feel his tongue glide across my lips, and I sigh into the kiss. He holds me and dominates every move. I'm trapped, lost, completely captivated by him. My heart pounds as he continues to kiss me with so much passion it takes my breath away. No woman should go through life without feeling this.

"You two about done?" Wyatt says and we break apart.

My lips burn, and I cover my mouth. "Sorry," I say, ducking my face while slapping his chest.

Zach grunts and adjusts himself. "It's your fault."

"Don't blame me, Zachary," I joke.

"So, Zach," Angie says from behind. "I feel like we need to talk."

"Ang," I warn.

"You know, bury the hatchet since you're fucking my sister again."

"Oh, God. Please stop."

Angie continues to ignore me. "It's been a lot of years between us."

I turn and look at her. "Between you and him?"

She shrugs. "I mean, I was there for her while you were off being Joe Baseball, making sure that she didn't end up in the looney bin since you left her for your glowing career." The floor drops from beneath me. I look at her, begging with my eyes to stop from saying anything more. "Have you finally seen the error of your ways by leaving our girl?"

"We've worked through it all," he says holding on to me.

"Yes, Angie." I give her a look. "We're over it. You know." I decide to stop this now. "It's late. I haven't seen you in so long. Let's head back to the house and get some girl time."

"I can take her home," Wyatt offers.

"Didn't you have someone with you?" I ask.

Wyatt shrugs. "I like this one better."

Angie looks up with a laugh. "You really are me. But I'm pretty sure my dick is bigger."

"Wanna compare, Angel?"

"Angie."

Wyatt shrugs. "Semantics."

"All right, you two." The mother in me comes out. "I'll ride with Angie since she drove."

Zach tugs me against his chest. "See you tonight?" he whispers in my ear. "I can't sleep without you."

I stare into those blue eyes I love so much. "You bet."

Second chances don't always happen, but I think Zach and I were destined to find our way back. If he had stayed, we'd never know what life without each other was. I'm grateful that with all the pain I've been through, I've been able to find my salvation.

Twenty-Nine

"Okay, so you sneak out every night?" Angie asks snuggled in my bed. She's decided we need to have a sleepover like we did before we grew up.

"It's not really sneaking out."

"Do you go out the front door?"

I huff. "No."

"Does anyone know?"

"Well, they know, but it's not common knowledge."

"Do you climb out the window?" she asks.

"No." I laugh. "I go out when the boys are asleep and come back before they wake. It's dating, only at night."

She sits back with her arms crossed. "Are you going tonight?"

I don't want to lie anymore. "Yes. I don't know if he'll be there, but I'm going down to the creek."

Angie grins. "I appreciate the honesty."

The next hour we spend talking about everything. She even laughed at the story of the race and has started to smile a little more when I mention his name. I'm hoping she'll see how much he makes me happy. How things have turned around since he's been here.

"I don't like it," she says. "But I'm happy for you."

I sit on the bed next to her and grab her hand. "I get that it's hard for you. It's really hard for me. I didn't jump into this haphazardly. He's helped me come to terms with Todd's decision in a lot of ways. I don't understand, and I don't think I ever will, but I'm not so angry anymore."

She nods. "I wish I weren't."

"What do you mean?"

"He could've done so many other things than that. I struggle a lot with reconciling it. It never had to be this way."

I close my eyes and focus on what I want to say. "No, it didn't. We would've been able to work through this, but I guess it was too hard for him. I understand pride. I really do." It is what kept me so isolated when I first returned here. I didn't want anyone to know. I hated that I had to come back here to live with my parents. I still struggle with it. "But I was his wife. I was supposed to be his partner . . . he decided on his own that he couldn't handle it."

"Yeah," she agrees. "And he fucked everyone's life up."

"Maybe," I say with a great deal of care. "Maybe he thought this was saving us."

Angie's eyes fill with tears. "I've been alone too, Pres."

"I know."

"No." She shakes her head and sits up. "I don't think you do. I talked to him almost every day. I talked to you and those boys. You were my family. He took that from me too. But most of all, he left me with so many questions. And then you didn't want to talk to me." Her lip trembles. "I get it, but it hurt."

"I'm so sorry."

"Don't be. That's the thing." Angie wipes her face, swiping away the tear that fell. "I'm not angry or upset with you. I just want you back home."

I don't know that I'll ever return to Pennsylvania. If things with Zach and me keep on this path, who knows where we'll be, but when I close my eyes at night, I don't see the city lights anymore. I see stars. I see blue eyes, fireflies, and country hills. My heart is here. My heart is with that man who is probably waiting down at the creek.

Right now she's in pain, and I don't want to hurt her more. But returning back there isn't what I want now.

Angie drifts off to sleep after we finish talking a little more. I'm late, and I text Zach letting him know. Since he didn't respond, I'm assuming he's passed out in his truck. The last two nights we've met, there wasn't much sleeping.

We won't be heading out to the pond this time, though. I want to make sure I'm home early. Plus, I'm hoping we can figure out how we're going to tell the boys. I think Cayden will take it really well, but Logan is a toss up.

I get to the creek, but there's no sign of him.

I shoot him another text.

Me: Hey, Cowboy . . . I'm here.

I sit down at the rock and think about the other night.

"I think if we work out we should build a house here," I say from my spot curled up in his arms. We finished making love and as magnificent as that is, this is better. Zach lies on his back while I rest on his chest. His heartbeat thumps in my ear as his fingers graze my back.

"Yeah?" he asks, trying to hide his excitement.

"Well, if I keep you around."

He chuckles. "Maybe I'll get rid of you."

"Ha!" I say in his face as I lean up. "You wouldn't."

Zach tilts slightly, pushes my hair back, and grins. "I don't know . . ." His hands lift the blanket. "You're hot." He reaches his hand down to my thigh, slowly making his way around the front. "But you always were hot."

"Is that so?" I ask as I part my legs for him. "You're not so bad yourself."

His lips touch my shoulder and I shiver. "All the guys would talk about how if I ever lost you, they'd be the first in line."

I shake my head. "Is that why you refused to breakup with me?" His finger brushes against my clit, and I moan.

He continues to rub in small feather-light circles. "Nope." His voice has some extra grit to it. "I would've killed anyone who touched you. You, Presley Mae, are everything to me."

I want to say something back, but as soon as he says the last word his thumb presses down and he fingers me. My head presses back against the pillow as I arch into his touch.

"Your body is mine to do this to," he murmurs before nipping at my ear. "Mine to have." He pinches the nerves, and I almost buck off the bed. My legs open wider while I hope he keeps going.

I'm climbing higher as he continues. His fingers slide in and out slowly, keeping me right at the cusp. "I need more." I lean into his touch, but he jerks back.

"I need to hear it, Presley."

I don't know what he needs, but I really want to come. "Zach," I protest.

"Say the words, and I'll make you come," he promises.

My eyes don't move from his. "What words?" I say while every part of my body is tight. "I'll say whatever you need."

Right now, I could scream with desire.

"That you're mine now."

The word "now" stands out. I adore that he feels I always was his without dismissing my life with Todd. My fingers grip the back of his neck. "I'm yours now and always, Cowboy."

Not a moment later, he has me pinned to the bed. He lines his dick up and pushes inside of me. My eyes roll back as I feel him fill me to the brink. Each thrust brings me closer. Each sound of skin slapping against each other binds us closer. I breathe him in, committing it to memory. He's the sun, the air, the beautiful touches of light that surround us. I want to live here with him forever. His arms envelope me, his love satiates me, and his voice comforts me. I know who I am when I'm with him.

I push him on his back, needing to make him feel my love. I want to show him everything that's in my heart. "Watch me," I say.

I hold his dick in my hand, guiding him inside of me. "You have no idea . . ." he says, watching himself disappear inside of me. "You're a part of me."

"And you're a part of me too."

Zach's head drops against the pillow once I'm fully seated. I wait. I want his eyes on me. To see him lose it as I'm giving myself to him is the sexiest thing in this world. The candles provide the most beautiful glow over him. His usually tan skin looks deeper, his blue eyes are warmer, and every inch of him is all mine.

When his gaze meets mine, I start to move. "Fuck," he groans.

"That's what we're doing."

"No, darlin'," he says. "We never fuck. Even when we're rough." Zach's fingers grip my hips, digging into the flesh. "Even when it's fast, hard, and completely out of control." He leans forward so we're chest to chest. He takes a fistful of my locks in his hands and tugs. "I'm always loving you."

I kiss him hard. We both collapse, and I ride him. The friction causes my climax to come fast and hard. I cry out his name over and over as I pulse around him.

Zach flips me on my back and pounds into me. We don't speak, but I feel him saying it all. He loves me. I love him. Zach finishes and pulls me back in his arms. "I think we should build that house. I could do this with you for a long time."

My lips draw into a smile. I kiss his chest and nestle in. "I could too."

And I really could. Now, it's as if the dreams that used to haunt me of Todd have changed into him watching over us. Maybe that's why the dreams were so distressing before. I was so angry with him that my mind wouldn't allow me the chance to be happy. But once I let that go, everything fell into place.

I glance down at my phone where there's still no message.

I call, but it goes to voicemail.

"Hey, babe. I don't know where you are. I'm worried. Please call me back."

A knot forms in my stomach as I go over the number of things that could've happened. Of course my imagination runs wild as it goes from car accident to him sleeping. I decide to walk to his house. I'll never sleep now.

I think back to the last time I couldn't get someone I loved on the phone.

I make my way to his house and force myself to stop connecting this to my past. He's not Todd, and it's unfair to even let myself go there. He has a good reason why he's not here—like sleeping. I head back to the creek, and wait for another hour. It's almost four in the morning now, and I'm exhausted.

He's obviously not coming, so I go back home.

Instead of waking anyone, I curl up on the porch swing and close my eyes.

"Presley!" I hear someone yelling my name. "I know you're here! Come down so we can talk!"

I open my eyes as the sun blinds me. My body is stiff from sleeping on a wooden swing, and I have no idea what time it is.

"Zach?" I look off the porch as he exits the barn. "What are you doing?" I look down at my phone and it's six thirty in the morning.

Great. A little over an hour of sleep. I'm going to be a treat.

"What am I doing?" He stumbles and slurs a little.

"Are you drunk?" I ask. He moves to the side then drops back a little. I take a look at him, and he's still in the same clothes from the bar, there's dirt all over him, and he has something in his hand. "Are you seriously at my house drunk like this?"

"Should I not be here, darlin'?" Zach challenges me.

I'm beyond confused. We were supposed to meet last night, if anyone should be angry, it's me. "No." I huff out a deep breath as I step down off the porch. "Where were you last night? I waited for you by the creek. I was worried."

He walks toward me and blows out a heavy breath. "You should be."

"What?"

"You should be worried, Presley." He leans back against the wooden barn doors. "Or you can drink until it doesn't hurt. When you're drunk, you don't give a fuck anymore."

He's not making any sense. "Don't care about what? Where the hell were you last night?"

"I was learnin'."

Oh, Jesus. This conversation is exhausting me. "Let's get you to bed. You need to sleep this off." I step closer and he moves quickly.

"I was learnin' about things you've never told me."

He takes a long swig of bourbon while keeping his eyes on me.

"Oh, yeah? Like what?" Now I'm pissed. He doesn't show last night, has me worried, and he's drunk.

He laughs. "Like you keep a lot of secrets. But I'm figuring them all out."

My heart stops. "What did you say?" He couldn't know anything. I've told him about Todd and the money. I've told him everything but . . .

"Yup." he moves forward. "Imagine my surprise. But what else are you keeping from me?"

"You need to sober up."

"Stop lying to me!" Zach yells.

I push him back inside the barn so he doesn't wake everyone. "I'm not talking to you about anything when you're belligerent. You want to have this conversation?" He looks away. "Then sober up."

Zach runs his hands through his hair, and I see the sadness in his eyes. "I loved you. I loved you so fucking much. But you . . . you don't even tell me the truth!"

I want to cry. How the hell would he have found out? This doesn't make any sense. It can't be about the baby. I'm going to tell him about it anyway. Plus, we were fine a few hours ago. "Sleep, please. I'll talk to you in a few hours. Just get some sleep."

In the one stall we always keep blankets in, I lay out a makeshift bed for him. He tosses the bottle and stalks toward me.

Zach's hand grips the back of my neck before his lips slam down on mine, holding me still. The instant our lips touch, I can feel it. Something is wrong. He's angry, hurt, and something has changed. This is a completely different kiss than any other we've shared.

Zach pulls back and stares me in the eyes. "You've ruined me, Cowgirl."

Words fail me as does my heart. I stand, fear freezing me in place. He doesn't say another word before he lies down and passes out before I can thaw out.

He knows something, and what comes next isn't going to be good.

Thirty

W hile Zach sleeps in the barn, I go back inside to get ready for the day. I feel that growing pit in my stomach festering and eating me alive. I was wrong for not telling him about the baby, but I was eighteen. I wanted to tell him. So many times, but it seemed irrelevant. I didn't know if we would last, and it was something that was so painful to remember, I couldn't say the words. Each time I'd remember what it was like when he left, I focused on that. Not the baby.

I head out to the barn, but he's not here. How could he leave like this? We need to talk.

I look around, but he's definitely gone.

No, he's not going to do this to me.

"Looking for me?" his deep voice calls from behind me.

"Zach." I turn to face him.

He moves toward me with purpose. "You lied to me."

He knows.

Zach challenges me with his eyes to deny it.

"I didn't want you to find out this way. I was going to tell you."

"When?" he bellows. "When were you planning to tell me we had a baby?"

Neither of us moves. I want to tell him everything, but how do

I explain this? I was young, dumb, broken, and then I was completely wrecked. "I-I . . . it was a long time ago."

He takes a step back. He doesn't really look at me. His eyes dart around. "I can't." Zach turns and heads past me.

I grab his arm. "Please. I was going to tell you so many times. Then . . . I didn't want to. I know that makes me a bitch, but you have to understand just thinking about it made me hurt. I was hurting so much already."

Telling him this is futile. I was wrong to keep this from him, but I had my reasons. Loss has surrounded me for the last year. All I do is lose people, things, jobs, children, life. I want to gain for once. Bringing up that baby is only reminding me of another painful checked off box.

Zach faces me. "You had a baby. *We* had a baby."

"No." I look down and this time there's a flood of tears. "I lost him."

"Him?" he chokes.

"I found out I was pregnant two weeks after you left. I carried him for seventeen weeks, and then I miscarried."

His eyes bore into mine as he breaks down. "You couldn't tell me? You didn't think I deserved to know?" I've broken his heart. "Fuck, Presley! How could you keep this from me? How could you look at me after all these years and not fucking tell me?"

I lost myself when that happened. The anger, sadness, feeling of complete failure loomed over me for months. Each night I would wake up crying, clutching my stomach, and begging for Zach to come back. My life was so dark and ugly at that time.

"I couldn't tell you. When you left, part of me died. A big, huge, aching hole was punched through me. Then I found out I was pregnant. I was so mad. I hated you for leaving," I explain.

"You should've fucking told me! I would've come back!"

This is exactly why I didn't tell him. "Not for me!"

My tears fall as my pain from seventeen years ago surfaces again. I've buried it, but it's back with a vengeance.

"What the hell does that mean?"

"It means that I wasn't enough for you! I needed you. And you left. So what? Because we had a baby that would've altered things? I lost that baby, and I lost you. What do you think I was feeling?"

"I don't know! You didn't give me a chance to find out!" He grunts and slams his hand against the barn door. "I can't believe you, Presley."

"I wasn't perfect. I was eighteen! Eighteen, Zach. I was alone in a strange new place, pregnant, with no family, and a boy who just wrecked my world. Was I wrong? Yes. But dammit, I was so scared."

This was handled wrong, and quite honestly, I was so angry I didn't care about him. I felt completely alone. I couldn't think straight, and when he got on that bus, he broke me. Everything that I thought made sense, no longer was what I thought. It was as if the shift in my universe was so severe, I was walking upside-down.

"But you had no problem blaming me for leaving?" He takes a step forward. "How easy for you to say it was my fault. I would've come back if I knew you were pregnant. I would've stood by your side, finished college, gotten married, and seen where the world took us."

There's a part of me that wants to laugh. "So a baby would've changed your dreams?"

"No." He pushes back from me. "I still would've—"

"You would've, what?" I ask, agitated. "Huh? I told you when you left I wanted a family, and you said you didn't even want to think about that. You would've given up your dream?"

As much as Zachary knows me, I know him just as well. He had two passions, baseball and me. I saw what happened when he had to choose before, I don't think that baby would've made a difference.

My anger mirrors in his eyes. "We don't get to know that because you kept it from me!"

"Here's what would've happened," I say, stepping toward him. "You would've kept on playing ball just like you already were. Nothing about our situation would be any different. You'd have taken that job, and I would have stayed in school. Were we wrong?" I pause. "Maybe. But it was the choice we made. I didn't know about the baby before you left. Maybe then it would've gone a different route, but I wanted to be reason enough for you to stay, not because you knocked me up."

"So you knew for how long?"

"I only knew I was pregnant for about four weeks."

"Four weeks!" he screams. "Do you know how many times I called you over those four weeks?" Zach steps closer. "Do you?"

I hate myself right now. Everything inside me is breaking exactly like it did all those years ago. "I was wrong, but by the time I was ready to tell you, I was bleeding!" Tears fall as I remember that day. "I lost that baby. I lost him! I called Angie, but she wasn't there. So Todd took me to the hospital. I cried for hours as they explained what was happening. I called you that day, Zach."

His eyes snap to mine. "When?"

"Some girl answered your phone. I called when I was sitting in that hospital bed getting ready for them to remove everything from inside of me."

The feeling of betrayal was so strong, I vowed never to speak to him again. It wasn't rational. I don't know that many of our choices at eighteen were, but thinking about him and another girl was the end of my rope. My hormones and emotions were all over the place.

"I wasn't with anyone." He strides closer. "It took me years to even look at another girl!"

"She wasn't the issue. It was that I needed you." He doesn't get it. "I called and some chick answers a month later?"

"Fucking hell, Presley! That was seventeen years ago and there was no one else."

"Jesus!" I throw my hands in the air. "So now the seventeen years ago is fine for you, but not me?" I cry out. "You know what? I don't care! I'm just explaining why I never called you again."

He looks away and then back to me. "It's bullshit! And not only that, but what does that matter? You ended things with me!

You chose to walk away and be done because you didn't want to wait the three years."

"I didn't think you'd move on so fast."

"I didn't! Maybe it was my agent who answered the phone, did you ever think about that?"

I sure as hell didn't at the time. And I don't care because that's not the damn point. That was the argument we could've had back then. "No, but that's not what this fight is about. I didn't think that because I was pregnant and losing a baby."

"How do two people remember the same thing so differently?"

"I don't know."

"I'm so fucking mad," he admits.

I understand his feelings, but neither of us were perfect. If I'd told him about the baby a few months ago, what would it have done? It was a million years ago, and losing that baby was the single most life-altering moment until Todd's death.

"So you get drunk and show up at my house? Decide you want to yell at me? Tell me how wrong I am? You don't think you could've handled this a little different?"

"I handled this wrong?" He chortles. "You've got to be fucking kidding me!"

"We both did!" I yell back. "I'm not saying I was right, but how is this helping us?"

This is the Presley and Zachary of old times. Two hot-headed and emotional people. Yes, he's sweet and loving, but he has an angry side. When you poke the bear, he roars loud. Funny thing is that I'm the same. He's pissed me off by coming here yelling at me.

"No, you know what's wrong, Presley?" The rage rolls off him in waves. "Getting back to my house last night, ready to see you, and then finding out we had a baby and you've been lying to me for seventeen years."

"How did you hear about this, Zachary?" Now I'm angry. He wants to be a condescending prick? I'll go right back at him. The only person who knows is Angie, and she didn't tell him. "Huh? Who opened your eyes to the lying bitch that I am?"

He winces slightly. "I never called you a bitch."

"Who told you?" My voice is eerily calm. Almost sweet, but there's nothing sweet about this.

"It's irrelevant."

"The hell it is!" I yell while marching toward him.

He buries his hands in his hair and moves away from me again. "I need to know why you didn't tell me." Zach's anger has dissolved. The hostility that was there has morphed into disappointment. "After everything we've talked about, how the hell could you keep this from me?"

There are a variety of answers I could give him. My life has been a road paved with spikes and nails. I've plugged, patched, and replaced the tire, but the car has never ridden the same. The loss of a child isn't a patch job.

Zach's back is against the wall, so I walk toward him until we're touching. "I never speak about it. Somewhere deep inside of me, it lives, but for the most part, I don't think about it ever. You were the one man I dreamt my whole life of sharing a child with. When that dream became my worst nightmare, I became hollow." His eyes lock on mine. "When I got back here, I was dealing with Todd's suicide, my debt, my boys, and the last thing I wanted to do was go back to that pain too. I'm sorry I didn't tell you, but honestly, I didn't want to live in the past once we'd made the decision to start over."

"You had no problem throwing the past in my face," he says with frustration.

He's right. I didn't. "I was wrong."

"I've lived with guilt for all these years from walkin' away from the girl I loved more than anything. I've struggled with forgiving myself. I've fought every damn day to prove that I'm better for you!" He moves forward, forcing me to retreat. "I've given you every part of me, Presley." His chest heaves as tears form in his own eyes. "Me! Only me! I've kept all your secrets! I've stood by your side. Held you when you've cried over everything that Todd put you through!"

"I didn't ask you to keep secrets," I scream. "So now you're going to use Todd's suicide against me?" I push him back. "I was leaning on you. Do you think it was easy for me to tell you that he killed himself?"

"Don't talk about my daddy!" Logan rushes forward, pushing against Zach.

My stomach drops. I don't know when he got here, but this wasn't supposed to be how my son learned the truth.

This is all my fault. Secrets come to light no matter how hard we try to bury them.

Thirty-One

"Logan!" I rush toward him.

"That didn't happen! My daddy would never! He loved me!" He slams his hands on Zach's legs.

Zach crouches down and holds Logan. "Of course he loved you," Zach says, looking at me with regret.

"You're not allowed to yell at my mom!" He continues to thrash in his arms. "You're not my dad!"

"I know, little man. I know I'm not. But I care about you."

"No, you don't! You'll never be my dad! I hate you!"

The stitches holding together my shredded heart rip apart. Again my son is hurting. I'm so inept. I don't know how to do this. How do I keep screwing up?

I grab Logan and pull him into my arms. "Stop! Logan, stop!"

He fights me away, trying to get to Zach. "Logan." Zach's voice is desolate. "Logan, I'm not . . . I . . . I would never try to take your dad's place." His eyes are filled with fear. I don't know what to do. I can't believe Logan heard what I said. "I would never hurt your mom."

I cradle him. "Zach and I . . ." I start but what the hell do I even say? We were fighting? So what? He never should have heard it like this. "I'm sorry, Lo."

"Why did you lie about Daddy? Why did you say he killed himself? He didn't." Logan begins to cry. "His heart stopped!"

"His heart did stop," I explain.

He looks at me with so much pain in his eyes. "You told me he was in Heaven. You didn't tell me he killed himself! You didn't tell me that he didn't want to be with us anymore."

I take Logan's face in my hands. "No, he loved you and wanted to be with you!"

"You're lying," he cries. "You made us move here. We didn't want to come here. We wanted to stay in our home." His tears stream as my heart breaks. "I want my dad back!"

"I know you do. I wish he never left us either."

"You can't say that!" he yells. "You love Zach!"

"Logan," Zach says, touching his arm. "Your mama loved your daddy so much. She told me about how much she misses him. She told me all about what a great man he was. How he took care of you, took you to hockey games."

"My daddy was the best!" he says with defiance.

"He had to be if he had you and Cayden."

Logan looks away with tears falling.

"Logan," I say with tenderness.

"He was yelling at you! Daddy never yelled at you!"

"What's wrong?" Angie asks out of breath with Cayden's hand in hers. She sees all of us with tears running down our faces. "Logan?"

"Tell her, Aunt Angie!" he begs. "Tell Mom that Daddy didn't kill himself!"

Cayden's body locks and Angie holds him close. His eyes dart to mine and Angie's.

"Lo," she hiccups. "It's so much more complicated than this."

Wyatt, Cooper, Mama, and Daddy arrive behind her.

"Mom?" Cayden asks.

"You're all wrong!" Logan screams. "He . . . he . . . he . . . " Logan turns his head into my chest. "He wouldn't kill himself!"

"Cayden," I say softly with my arm open.

He charges forward and wraps his arms around me. "Why?" he asks. "Is it true?"

Angie looks at me and her lip quivers. I beg her with my eyes to say something. I can't breathe. I feel like I'm losing everything all over again.

"You know that your daddy was my brother," she says as she walks forward slowly, "and that I miss him every day, but sometimes things happen that we can't explain. It's hard and it hurts, but know how much he loved you both."

"He loved my mom!" Logan yells.

This is so out of character for him. He's always been the docile one. Reasonable and intuitive.

I cling to the boys as I grapple with the wounds I've caused. I was protecting them, or so I thought. It would've been hard and hurtful if I'd told them in the beginning, but maybe it would've been fine by now. I've been dying inside from carrying all of this on my own.

Angie looks at me, and her breath catches as tears pour down her face. "He did." Her voice is low and broken. "He loved us all so much. But he was very sad, baby."

A sob breaks from my chest. "He loved you and Cayden so much!" I pull them tight. "Never ever doubt that."

No matter what Todd chose, I will never let them feel unloved. I wonder if he loved us so much that he couldn't bear to witness us suffer. I think about the man he was, and how much we were the center of his world. Someone who loves that hard doesn't choose to walk away that easily. As much as his choice destroyed things, it brought me here. It gave me my family, friends, and Zach. Todd may have broken a part of me, but he also healed a piece that was already damaged. I wish it never had to come to this.

Cayden begins to cry harder. "I don't understand. If he loved us, how could he leave?" His voice trembles.

I think he knew once all his lies were exposed, he would've lost me in some way, so he let me go the only way he could. On his terms.

"Sometimes there are no answers. Sometimes we have to love that person and find comfort that he's not suffering anymore." I wipe the tears that fall. "He'll always be in our hearts and our memories. That'll never go away."

My daddy enters the barn slowly and sinks next to me. "Do you remember what I told you boys about a daddy's love?" They both look at their granddad and nod. "Remember I told you that the why doesn't matter, it's the forever?" He reaches his hand out and touches my face and then looks back at them. "Whatever your daddy's reasons were don't matter. What you need to remember is that he loves you forever. And he'll live inside of you. He's watchin' over you, givin' you love when you need to feel it. Like right now."

The rest of my family comes around us.

"We all love you," Mama says. "More than my own life."

"But," Logan says.

"No, son." My father cuts him off. "There are no buts in this. He knew you boys needed the love of your family. He made sure your mama was taken care of. You may not understand it, but even from Heaven, your daddy's lookin' out for you. You're hurtin', but look around right now. You have all these people lovin' on you."

Cooper steps forward and drops to his knees. "No matter what happened, you're not alone," he says, looking at me and then the boys. "You don't have to keep what you're feeling inside. We're here for you guys and your mama."

A shattered cry falls from my lips as I break apart. I've held this in, letting it fester and rip my insides to shreds. I've let my own fears force me to suffer more than I had to. There's no judgment in their eyes. Just unconditional love.

I look over at Zach. The man who's been my everything for the last six months. The man who's given me more love and compassion than anyone, yet I've kept things from him. I've possibly severed my relationship for a secret that's seventeen years old.

"I love you," I say to both Logan and Cayden. "I love you so much," I say looking in Zach's eyes.

He shakes his head and looks away.

Wyatt nudges him and tilts his head. They both stand and walk toward the door where we can't hear them. His hand rests on Zach's shoulder as Zach's body slumps down. I want to call out to him, comfort him, but I don't even know where we stand.

So much has been said.

So many hearts that need healing.

He looks over at me, nods his head, and walks out of view.

"Here," Angie says as she hands me a cup of coffee.

"Thanks." I scoot over on the swing and she sits. "I really screwed up."

"Yeah." She sighs. "But then again maybe not."

I glance over waiting for her to explain, because I don't see how this could be good in any way. Angie sips her drink, oblivious to my waiting. "How?" I finally ask.

"You're learning to ask for what you need. You're not running. You're fighting for your life, Pres. There are no more secrets now. You can finally be free." She throws her arm around me, tugging me to her. "I know it's scary, but Zach needed to know. The boys needed to know the truth. And if he doesn't come around, that's okay. You're not living in the shadows."

As awful as today was, there's been so much healing and love. The boys are hurting, but they understand a lot more now. My parents and brother were instrumental in helping them. We all sat with them, talked, offered the strength they needed, and in the end, they were both a little calmer.

In no way are we all okay, but there's no lack of support to help us through.

"What if I can't get him back?"

"Well, then he doesn't deserve you."

"I was wrong," I admit.

Angie will always be on my side, but I'm aware of how she feels about this. "I think you were really young and then really hurt. I've known you pretty much my entire adult life. You're not a dishonest person, Pres. You're a runner. You never had to face shit head first."

My god, this is what they see me as? A weak woman who runs?

"Wait." She sits up and looks at me. "Before you go all stupid in your head. I just mean that you had Zach as a kid. Then me and Todd. You had someone the whole time. Then Todd pulled the rug out from under you. And with that comes some scrapes and bruises."

"I feel like an idiot."

She rests her hand on my leg. "You're not. You're so much stronger than the woman I saw last. You stood your ground, apologized, and tried to make amends. I think you've come a long way, my friend."

"I had no choice." I release a heavy breath.

"No." She stops. "You didn't. And I think that Zach is different too. You both are. It was really unfair of me to think otherwise."

Logan opens the door, and we both look over. "Mom."

"You okay, baby?" I ask as I walk over.

"I like Zach."

My lips press together into a small sad smile. "I do too."

"I want to say I'm sorry to him."

Hearing Logan say he wants to apologize to Zach makes me feel like, maybe, I haven't screwed him up completely. "I'm sure he'll come around again."

He looks over toward the corral. "He makes us laugh. He's really nice, and he makes you smile."

I don't want to hide the reality from him anymore. "Zach and I have adult problems. And whether we work out or not, I know him. He really loves you and Cayden. I don't think you'll be able to get rid of him. No matter what though." I squat down so I can look in his eyes. "Uncle Cooper, Aunt Angie, Wyatt, Trent, and everyone else in this town will be around you. Okay?"

"Do you think he's mad at me?"

His little green eyes fill with moisture. "No, baby. I don't think he's mad at you. Not even one single bit."

He nods. "I hit him hard."

Angie giggles. "I think you and I need to work on your boxing. You gotta hit him in the 'nads next time."

"Angie!" I scold her.

"Teach the kid the basics, babe. 'Nads and nose." She winks.

Logan laughs, "I missed you, Auntie."

"Oh, Bubs," she comes over and messes his hair. "I missed you more."

"Please listen to nothing she says. You don't want to hit anyone in the 'nads."

"They're balls, Mom," he corrects me.

"I'm not even going there," I say with a laugh. Boys.

His gaze returns back to the corral. "I hope he comes by tomorrow."

I want to say I do too, but he's got a lot on his mind. Zach filled a role for Logan without anyone asking him to. He became his friend and someone he relied on. Wyatt and Cooper are as well, but Zach was something special. I think Cayden thinks of him as a hero. He remembers what it felt like when Zach found him, but the bond between him and Logan was slowly forged.

Angie takes Logan's hand. "How about we all go watch a movie? I'm here for another week because someone." She looks around tapping her chin. "Is turning eleven soon. I wonder who that could be?"

Logan rolls his eyes. "You need to work on your acting skills, Auntie."

"I'll give you acting skills."

"Don't give them to me!" he gasps. "You need them."

We all burst out laughing as Angie starts to chase him. "Come here, you little monster!"

They both head inside, and I sit here wondering what to do. I feel so lost right now. The dust has settled for the most part with the boys, but Zach and I are clearly not even close. No matter what, we need to talk again.

I take out my phone and text him.

Me: We should talk.

I stare at the phone, willing it to respond. I haven't heard from him since he left with Wyatt.

Zach: I know.

That's it? I try to keep myself calm. I don't have the energy to exert on this.

Me: Tomorrow?

Zach: Yeah, tomorrow. How are the boys?

I look toward the sky and pray. "Please don't let me lose this man again. Please let us find a way to work it out."

Me: They're both okay. Logan is worried you're angry with him.

His response is instant.

Zach: Never. I'm angry with me. I'm angry with us. Tomorrow we'll talk.

I type out my response. It sits on my screen as I debate whether to send it. This isn't something we should talk about via text, but I have to tell him I love him. I need him to know that even though we're both feeling a lot, that hasn't changed.

Me: I'll miss you tonight. Please know that no matter what, I love you.

I press send and close my eyes.
I sit, holding on to my phone and waiting for it to buzz.
But it never comes.
I think I've lost the love of my life—again.

Thirty-Two

"Just when we thought all was working out for them. We didn't even have time to make them a back-together cake," Mrs. Rooney's voice filters through the hallway. "Bless her heart. She must be a wreck."

"She hasn't even been out of bed yet," Mama says.

Oh dear Lord. I better stop this train before it goes off the rails. I enter the kitchen, and it's filled with food. I'm talking a bakery's worth of cakes and pastries. Angie sits at the table, digging in and writing things down. "What is all this?" I croak.

"Good morning, sunshine." Angie tries for chipper, but it's fake. She knows I'm far from feeling like sunshine.

I look over at the four other women in my kitchen. Mrs. Rooney, Mama, Mrs. Hennington, and my third grade teacher, Mrs. Kannan. This cannot be good.

"Oh, sugar," Mrs. Rooney says with her lips pouty. "I'm so sorry about you and Zach."

I look at her with wide eyes. "What?" How in the hell?

"We heard all about what your fight was about." Her hand rests on my arm. "You must be devastated."

"Completely wrecked. I mean, she looks like it," Mrs. Kannan comments.

I woke up ten minutes ago. What the hell are they expecting? I also didn't expect a confectionary parade in my house. I rub my eyes, hoping it'll cover the eye roll as well. I need coffee to deal with this.

Mrs. Hennington steps forward. "You'll always be like a daughter to me."

"Thanks. I think." I shake my head. "We're fine, though. I mean we'll *be* fine, we just need to talk."

They talk as if I'm not there. "Do you think she'll find another man at her age?" Mrs. Kannan questions. "She's still pretty and hasn't gotten too many extra pounds, but she's not a spring chicken either."

"I'm right here," I remind them.

"Zach looked terrible last night." Mrs. Hennington sighs while turning back to her friends. "I was so happy they'd finally found their way."

I stand here like a voyeur of my own life.

"We didn't even get to enjoy their reunion before they screwed it up," Mama says. "I swear that girl has always been too smart for her own good."

"I heard she kept some big secret from him."

"Hello!" I yell. "Can hear you!"

Mrs. Rooney looks over at me then back to their little hen meeting. "He wasn't Mr. Perfect either though, Macie. I mean that boy of yours needed a good whipping a few times."

I can't listen to this but trying to get them to stop is useless. He'll call today and then this can all stop. I look over at Angie who is stuffing her face. She shrugs unapologetically. "I want to hire all of these baking goddesses." Gobs of cake fall from her mouth.

"You need a trough."

I plop down in the chair next to her. "Have you tried this?" She shoves the fork in my face. "Eat this. It's orgasmic."

I take a bite of Mrs. Hennington's cheesecake. I'd know it anywhere. It tastes like heaven. "This is why I bake."

"This would be why I would be a thousand pounds," Angie

admits while popping another forkful in her pie hole. "God." She moans. "I could die happy in this sugary heaven."

I lean back and try very hard not to listen to what they're saying. According to them, Zach never returned back home last night. Of course I slept with the phone in my hand, praying he'd call. I also went to the creek, but he wasn't there. I feel off balance.

Me: Please tell me you're okay. I want to talk sooner rather than later.

"You'll be diabetic if you stay here." I laugh through the words.

Angie eats while I wait for the phone to ring.

"Presley." Mama takes my attention from the phone. "The town wants to do something nice for you." She smiles at her friends.

"For what?" I'm so confused.

"Well." Mrs. Rooney walks over. "For your breakup of course. No woman should go through being broken hearted at your age."

The fact that I somehow manage to not make an outward groan should earn me a medal. "We're not broken up. We have plans to talk."

"Really?" Mama asks. "Then why did Macie rush over here to tell me that she saw Felicia moving boxes back into his place."

My heart drops to the floor. He wouldn't take her back. There's no way. This is insane and wrong. "Mrs. Hennington." My voice cracks. "Are you sure?"

"I'm sorry, dear." Her gaze drops to the ground. "I asked her what in the hell she was doing, but she said Zach would be letting me know soon enough. I didn't see him, but it was clear she was hauling her stuff back in." She releases a sigh through her nose. "I have half a mind to throw him off my land."

"How?" I manage to mutter. "I mean, there has to be a mistake."

She rubs my back. "I wish there were."

Well, fuck that. I'm not going to sit back this time. He can't tell me he's here for me, that he loves me and wants to build a house, and then go to Felicia after our first fight. There's no way. She has to be confused. He wanted a day, well, I wanted a life.

Thirty-Three

ZACHARY

I stare at the text from last night and hate myself for not responding. After I sent the last text, I chucked the phone across the room. I didn't want to see what she said. Between the throbbing headache from drinking so much and the ache in my chest, I knew I couldn't.

Presley has no idea how crushed I am. A baby. Our baby. The one thing I've never given anyone else because I couldn't imagine have a child with anyone but her. She never said a word to me, and for that, I can't talk to her right now.

"You should call her," Trent urges. Both of my brothers have been with me all night. I was so fucked-up, throwing things around the house, they didn't trust me not to get in a fight with the rest of the furniture. So they brought me to Wyatt's cabin where there's less of anything, let alone anything breakable.

"And say what?"

"Tell her you're sorry and that you love her. I don't know! You cried all goddamn night about how much she means to you. You know that you'll never stop loving her, right?"

I nod.

"Then don't be a dick!"

"She lied!"

"So what?" Wyatt chimes in. "So fucking what? She's Presley Townsend. The girl half the men in this town would give their left nut for. We won't even talk about what that means to you."

Trent hums in agreement.

My younger brother starts in again. "I'm not making excuses for her, I'm sayin' you know her and the shit she's been through."

"You think it's okay she kept this from me?" I throw back at him. "You'd be perfectly okay with knowing all this time spent . . ." I groan. "God! I don't even fucking know what I'm mad at right now! I just know that my whole goddamn life I've spent trying to get over her."

"So, you're over her now? You don't want her? Are you really willing to give her up?" Wyatt smiles, waiting for my answer. "Can you handle watching some guy's hands roaming all over her while she dances at the bar?"

I see red. "Fuck you."

"I don't think so. If you love her, then stop being a bitch about this. She lied to you, I get it. She's been in a really bad place." He slips into a more neutral tone. "I didn't know her husband killed himself. She must've gone through hell. It explains why she was afraid to tell you this too, man."

I grasp all this intellectually, and then there's the fact that she's been pissed off at me for a long time. I've never doubted we'd work through this, but she has. She wasn't sure that we would find the love we once had. Or if it was all in our heads. I knew though.

"What the hell does that mean? Afraid to tell me?" I ask him.

"You left her. Todd left her. She lost everything. She gets you back. What the hell do you think was the next possible outcome to her?" He cracks his neck. "Please, make the wrong choice. Let her go. See what happens."

Trent stands, walks over, and slaps the back of my head. "You're an idiot."

"You're both assholes."

"True." He chuckles. "But at least I know that if Grace ever really was going to walk away, I'd chase her."

He's so full of shit. Grace has been gone for months, he just won't see it. He's the last person I'm taking love advice from. Wyatt gives me a look that lets me know we're on the same page.

"How did you find out about the baby?" Trent asks.

"Doesn't matter."

The point is that she kept it from me. I found out, and that's the damn issue.

Wyatt stares me down. "I think it does matter."

"You would." I raise my chin. "Imagine knowing the girl you love, want to marry, would die for, kept this goddamn secret for so long. I deserved to know about that baby."

Wyatt hops to his feet and walks over. "You've always been the slowest out of the three of us. Yet, you managed to get the girl." He huffs out a frustrated breath. "I know what it's like to watch someone you love look at someone else. I lived it. I know what it feels like to not be able to say what you're thinking, because you know when you do, life will change." He snaps his fingers. "Just like that. You want to play games with her? She'll find another player. There are plenty in the lineup."

He walks out of the door of his own house, and Trent shakes his head. "He's been in love with Presley since the first time he laid eyes on her, but she found you first. I don't know what you're expecting from him. He's kept away because he'd never get between you two, but I'm not sure that if you walk away, he will anymore."

"He'd be dead to me."

"Why?"

"Because she's mine."

"Right now she is." Trent rests his hand on my shoulder. "But not if you let her go."

I lean back in the chair as Trent leaves the house. I don't know what to do anymore. It's been almost twenty-four hours since I saw her. She's consumed every moment of my thoughts since I left her. Then I think about Logan and Cayden. How broken those boys were over the truth. How broken I am over the truth.

Did she do it because she wanted to hurt anyone? No. I'm

fully aware of why she kept it from me. It doesn't hurt any less though.

I sit there, thinking back on how we'd dreamed of having a baby. So many nights we spent talking about our life and how it would be.

"Two boys and a girl." Presley looks over with stars in her eyes.

"I want all girls," I tell her, and she rolls back over with a smile.

"You would, Zachary Hennington. You would."

I'd give her whatever she wanted as long as she doesn't quit smiling like that. I'm a lucky bastard.

"How about we compromise?" I ask her.

She looks over as she contemplates. "What kind of compromise?"

The thing about her is that she knows me well enough to know that I'd cave to her. But she lets me have this for a little while. Not as if I have any control over it anyway.

"Two boys and two girls."

"Four babies?"

"Why not? I have two brothers and you have one. It would be better if we have an even number." Which is true. Wyatt is always the one that Trent and I team up against. Last night we almost got beat with the spoon because we hung him on the flag pole. Land of the free is what we told Daddy. He laughed, but Mama was yelling about boys and her hair.

Presley tilts her head and looks at the sky. "I don't know. I mean, that's a lot of names. We only have two picked out."

She's crazy, but I love her. "We know the first girl will be Sadie and the first boy is Colton."

"Right, but that was a month of fighting—"

"And making up," I remind her.

"Which was fun." She smirks. "But. Two more names would be a lot more fightin'."

I love when her accent grows strong. Presley is a siren. I can hear her call no matter where I am. On the field I go into a tunnel. Focusing only on the batter, the ball, the runners. I hone in and live in that moment. Unless she speaks. I don't know what it is, but she'll break my trance with one word. And if she's upset, her accent goes deep, and it's all I hear.

"And a lot more making up."

"If I forgive you." She cocks her head.

"You always do," I remind her.

Presley groans. "Stop being so damn cute."

"What about . . . Noah and Holly?" I offer.

She rolls her eyes. "Those are the same names you always say!"

"What are yours?"

I already know what she'll pick. "Sydney and Dawson."

"Like that damn show you watch?" Hell no. "I'm not naming my son after some guy on a creek."

"You live on a creek!" She scoffs and crosses her arm. "And I like his name. It's Pacey that I like-like."

I swear she knows what to say to get me jealous. Of course she likes some damn TV star. She forces me to sit through an hour of that crap show every week. I swear. Then we go onto another show right after it. She, Grace, and Emily have a weekly date, but somehow I get drug into it.

"We're not naming my boy either of those." I stand firm.

"Fine."

"How about Babe for a boy and Penelope for a girl?"

Presley stares at me like I've lost my mind. "I'm going to pretend that you're kidding about Babe. Naming him after a famous ball player won't make him one. And Babe is what we named the potbellied pig we just got. So, no."

"All right, you pick a girl's name and I'll pick the boy. What-ever the next name is, we go with."

"Okay, for a girl I pick Violet."

I could handle that.

"For the boy, I pick Logan."

She smiles. "I like that. Colton, Sadie, Logan, and Violet Townsend-Hennington."

"What?" I damn near lose my mind. "What the hell makes you

think you're not taking my last name? What the hell is that two last name crap?"

Presley rolls on her back, looking at me with a grin. "A woman has every right to hyphenate."

"I'll show you hyphenate." I drop down and kiss her breathless. She squirms beneath me and I fight ripping her clothes off right here in the middle of the outfield. This girl has no idea what she does to me.

I grip my phone in my hand, squeezing until my fingers turn white. I need to make a choice. Is this worth living the rest of my life without her?

"Go home and shower," Wyatt says, throwing the door open after he's cooled off. "Then find your balls and get your head out of your ass, possibly in that order. Because I promise you this." He steps forward. "If you don't go after her, I will, and I'm not going to play fair this time. I'm going to show her why I am the better brother, and why she should've been with me the whole time."

My anger rises and I go toe to toe with him. "You listen to me," I say pointedly. "I haven't let her go, so don't make me lay you out. Keep your damn hands off her."

"Then go hold on to her."

I walk past him, bumping him with my shoulder.

"Chump." He laughs as the door slams behind me.

I walk to my house while my mind ping pongs back and forth over what the right thing is. It's one thing to understand why she did what she did, it's another to accept it. Then there are the boys and what they're going through.

Maybe now just isn't the right time for us.

Maybe there will never be a right time.

I could've been there for her through it all. The part that pisses me off the most is the time we've wasted. I've spent my whole life thinking about her, even when I was trying to forget. I sabotaged every relationship because no one could measure up.

She didn't have to love anyone else. Another man didn't have to give her the comfort she sought. I would've been there.

Instead, she kept it to herself and used it as an excuse. What else is she keeping from me?

I get to my house and groan. I don't have the patience for this. Felicia stands against the door as I approach. I used to look at her and see beauty, now I see how blind I was. She's the polar opposite of Presley in every way. Felicia spent hours getting ready when we'd go out. Where Presley takes five minutes. Felicia wasn't well loved around the town, but I chalked it up to them not knowing her. I think it was me who didn't know her. She had me fooled, but now, I'm seeing things I never noticed before.

"Hey." She smiles. "I wanted to come check on you. I was worried when I heard how you closed the bar down and Brett needed to drive you home."

"I'm fine." I'm not half as nice as normal. She's having a really hard time understanding her role. "You should go. I appreciate you checkin' on me, but I'd rather be alone."

"Zach." She sighs. "Please, you need a friend."

I look at her and wonder if we could've worked had Presley not come back. I had plans to marry her because it was time. It was the right thing to do. Trent asked me if I ever loved Felicia. I did, but never close to the way I love Presley.

"I need to think, Felicia. Alone."

She puts her hand on my arm. "I know how much this hurts you. I'm glad you get to finally see the person she is. She's a liar, Zach. She's always been. How could she keep a baby from you?"

"Stop," I demand. "Stop talking, because I see what you're doing."

"I'm not doing anything."

"No?" I laugh. "Tell me this isn't part of your plan."

Felicia steps back. "Plan to what?"

I just look at her.

"We could move past this, Zach," Felicia simpers.

There it is. "No. We can't."

"Zach," she begs. "Please, I'm in love with you. I can make you happy."

And right now, I know where I need to be.

"I love Presley."

We've both spent our whole lives running. Whether toward each other or away. It's time to stand and deal with all our shit so we can move on. Loving her isn't a choice—it's who I am.

"No, listen to me. You deserve so much more." Felicia steps closer and puts her hand behind my neck. I move back, but she grabs tighter.

"I always knew that you would come back to me."

"Well." Presley's voice rings from behind me. "I guess I know why you didn't text me back."

I push Felicia away and turn to see Presley with tears in her eyes.

"I swear to God, Presley." I push away from Felicia and walk toward the girl I love. "I got home and she was here."

She shakes her head. "Your mama said that she saw Felicia moving boxes in." She crosses her arms across her chest.

"She's not moving in here," I explain.

Presley retreats. "I came here because I couldn't stand being away another second. I missed you so much my heart ached, Zach." I grab her arms but she jerks them away. "I thought it was a mistake. I thought she was confused."

I don't know what my mother saw, but it wasn't that. I look over at Felicia, wondering what her game is. "Did you tell my mother we were back together?"

Felicia takes a step back, wringing her hands. "I told her I was moving some boxes."

I turn back to Presley. "She's not who I want," I clarify. "I was coming home to shower and then coming to get you."

Presley doesn't look like she's buying it.

"And do what?" She taps her foot.

"This." I can't wait another second. I grab her shoulders and crush my mouth to hers. I inhale her scent and confirm everything I already knew. This is who I love. This is where I belong. I'll fight to the death for her. We'll fight because we're both hot-tempered. Things will go wrong, and there's a lot of shit to work through, but Presley is my life.

She came back here, and for the first time, I don't feel like I'm missing something. Just her being close makes a part of me come to life. I'll be hell pressed to let her go again.

I release her and she steps back. Great. She's going to slap me again.

Instead a smile forms. "That would've worked."

Her eyes dart behind me. "Nothing happened. Nothing ever would."

"Okay," she says.

"Okay?" Felicia yells from behind me. "Okay? Just like that? She lies about a baby, keeps the secret for *years*, makes you look like a fool, and you kiss her? I tell you the truth. I let you know all the things that have happened and it means *nothing*?"

I pull Presley against me. "It's not up to you."

Presley shrugs out of my hold and walks over to her. "It was you that told him. I figure you were lurking in the shadows, overheard, and thought this was your golden opportunity." She's absolutely correct. Felicia waited until Presley left and told me everything. "You forgot one thing." Presley smirks.

"What's that?"

"He doesn't love you."

Presley turns and heads back toward me. We're not done talking about anything, but I can't let her go. My life wouldn't work again without her.

"Screw you, Presley!" Felicia yells.

Presley turns, lifts her hand, and waves with just her fingers. "Bye, Felicia."

I'm in so much trouble with this girl.

Thirty-Four

PRESLEY

"We should talk," Zach says as Felicia's car drives off. I know we're not okay. No matter what he said in front of her, or the way he kissed me. There's a lot lying under the surface that needs to be said.

"I agree." I enter his house were the lamp is knocked over and a bunch of papers are thrown around. "What the hell?"

"I was pissed."

"I can see that."

He closes the door and starts to pick up some things. "I'm still pissed."

I figured he would be. "Can you let me at least explain myself?" I ask.

He sits down and clears a space for me. "Go ahead."

My stomach churns as I try to formulate my response. "When I was sixteen, I wanted to marry you. I remember telling my mother that I was going to be Mrs. Zachary Hennington." I smile. "I was so in love with you that I didn't even care what that meant. I knew with you being a few years older it meant that it would be hard when you graduated before me, but my faith in us was impenetrable." I was so young. "I thought if we loved each other hard enough, the rest would work out."

"Do you have a clue what it was like for me to leave you, Presley?" Zach asks, leaning forward. "I was eighteen and going off to college where the rest of my team was screwing the cleat chasers while I was counting down the days till I could see you again."

I rest my hand on his. "I know that. At least I thought I did. When you were gone and I had to be here alone, I was so depressed. Grace would come over and drag me out. I missed my prom because you had a game that week. I had nothing, Zach. I was nothing."

I stand and pace his living room. It was so long ago, but it feels like yesterday. "When I was finally coming to Maine, all I could think about was how we'd have two years together again. I would have my other half. You proposed to me on my graduation day, and I thought this was really it. I knew your dream was to play ball. I think I kept telling myself that it would happen when we were done with school. I wouldn't have to go through all of it by myself. Then you took that deal without even a hesitation. You didn't even talk to me about it first."

"If you think that it was easy to leave you." He walks toward me. "You're wrong."

"I don't think that." I shake my head.

He runs his hand down his face. "Do you know how many times I replayed that moment? I did hesitate, Pres. I wanted to talk to you, but the manager told me if I walked away, I wouldn't get that deal again. I wasn't sure what to do."

"I recognize that now. It took me a long time, but I do get it. I want to explain about the baby." I draw a deep breath and expel it.

He closes his eyes and sits back on the couch. Once I'm seated, I dig deep and feel it all, just like seventeen years ago.

"You had left, and I was beyond depressed. I thought you'd stay. I really believed that you would've gotten off that bus, taken me in your arms, and we'd be together. I was crazy, but I loved you so much." In my eyes we're back to being kids. I can see the movie play out in my head. "I started getting really sick, but I chalked it up to you being gone. I could barely eat, and I was a mess." I huff and roll my eyes. "I was so dumb. I mean, really—dumb. Angie finally forced me to the doctor, and I found out I was twelve weeks pregnant. I was already so far along. I hadn't been eating, taking vitamins, anything. I think I cried worse that day than when you left."

"Why didn't you call me?" he asks.

The million-dollar question. "I wish I could give you a better answer than this," I admit. I really regret this the most. "I didn't want you to know. I didn't want you to have any part of my life. In my mind, you left me by choice, therefore you didn't get a choice in my life."

"Wow." He sits back.

"I know," I say quickly and move closer. "I know how bad that sounds, but I don't want to lie to you anymore. I know how wrong I was. It was the worst thing I could've done. After two weeks though, it changed."

He looks up. "I don't understand."

I was fourteen weeks pregnant, I remember that I felt this bubbly feeling. Todd was visiting, and I started screaming. He and I had spent the day watching television and eating whatever I could stuff in my face. Todd was next to me when I felt the first flutter, but I wanted it to be Zach. I can remember looking at him with tears in my eyes because they weren't the blue eyes I wanted staring back.

"I knew I needed to tell you. I was building up my courage to call you. Todd had been pressing me to let you know. Things between him and me were platonic, but I could see he had feelings for me. He was adamant that you should know."

For all of Todd's mistakes and the pain he's caused me and the boys, he was never cruel toward Zach. I never understood it, but it was what I think drew me to him in the beginning. The fact that he was fair. It also could've been that he thought I was irrational.

"Presley." he lets out a shaky breath. "I can almost understand the shit we did when we were young. But we've been growing closer, making plans lately, and yet you didn't mention it."

"I was afraid. I had to go through it, not you. It was agony living through it once, bringing it up again is the last thing I wanted to do."

Zach looks at me with a mixture of understanding and anger. It's unfair to him, but losing that baby was horrible for me.

"What would you have named him?" Zach inquires.

I don't know why that matters. "Why?"

"Do you even remember the conversations we had?"

I lean back a little, trying to recall what conversation he's talking about. We had so many about what our life would be like. I smile, despite myself, thinking about the way we'd have name wars. The way he'd get so frustrated at some of my outlandish names. It was always entertaining. "Sadie and Colton," I say as it hits me.

He looks at me without a word.

Oh, my God. "Zach," I gasp. "That . . ."

"Logan and Violet." His face gives nothing away about what he's thinking, but I can only imagine. That's why he looked like he was in pain when I said Logan's name.

"I swear," I beseech him. "I didn't remember that. I tried to forget things because they hurt so much. Every time I thought back, I'd be thrown into a deeper depression."

Zach steps forward. "I feel like I failed you." His voice breaks. "I let you down, and I didn't know I was doing it. There's been this thing with you that I can't explain."

I take his hand in mine. "I didn't want to destroy what we had. I've been so worried that it was going to disappear again. Being with you makes me so happy, but it is also terrifying." I need to go deeper, but it's going to hurt. "I was happy before, and my life collapsed. But when I'm with you, I feel like I belong. I'm free to just *be* with you."

Zach's fingers tighten.

"I didn't want to lose my freedom. I didn't want to lose you. So, I didn't think about it. At all. I tried so hard to keep it buried because it couldn't touch us. I was wrong, Zach. I was so wrong." Tears fall from my eyes. "I love you so much. There are no more secrets. I promise."

I watch for him to condemn me or admonish me. We can move forward if he's willing.

He stands, without a word, and walks out of the room. Leaving me.

I sit as my insides implode. Every piece of me aches knowing that I've lost him. I truly thought we had a chance. After a few minutes without a word from him, I get myself together so I can walk out that door before he wrecks me. My heart can't handle him telling me it's over. I've done all I can, and I have to respect his wishes.

But it hurts so bad.

I stand and gather my things with tears falling. I weep quietly on the outside, but inside I'm screaming in denial.

My hand touches the cool door knob. As I turn it, I hear his voice. "Where are you going?"

"Please don't say it," I request.

"Say what?"

I turn. "Don't tell me it's over."

"Okay," he replies. "What do you want me to say, Presley?"

"That you forgive me. That you want me to stay."

Zach takes two long strides before he's close enough to touch. I step back and he follows. My back presses against the door and he cages me in. Zach's fingers glide down my cheek as he wipes away the remaining wetness. "I don't think I could ever stop loving you. I don't want to live without you again," he confesses. "We're stronger than we were all those years ago. So." He kisses my nose. "Say you'll keep fighting with me for a long time. Say you'll meet me at the creek every night. Say that you'll fall asleep in my arms and deal with my shit. Presley Benson, say you'll stay." He's holding my eyes with so much emotion in his own as he says those words.

My hands grip his shirt, holding on for dear life. "I'll stay with you forever."

The anger and sadness in his eyes is replaced with love and hope. Every word I said is true. He's my forever. His lips press down on mine and he lifts me in his arms. I hold on as he carries me through the house to his bedroom. Our tongues slowly move against each other as we pour the last two days into this kiss.

Emotions flood me as I realize that this doesn't have to end. We're not walking away this time. He lays me down on the bed, and I begin to cry. I feel a mix of joy and relief as we give in to each other. There's nothing holding me back. Every moment feels so right, even more so than before.

All my cards on the table, and he didn't fold. He went all in.

"Why are you crying?" he asks, concerned.

My girly emotions are probably scaring him. "I'm happy."

He smiles. "I am too."

"You make me happy."

His hand brushes my hair back. "I love you." He kisses me again. "So much."

My hand rests on his chest. "I don't want to lose you again, Zach."

He leans down so our noses touch. "I won't ever let you run. If you do, I'll follow you" His lips touch mine. "I'll chase you to the ends of the earth."

I slide my fingers up his chest, reveling in every muscle that tenses beneath my touch. "I think we should do some of that makin' up we used to be so good at."

Zach rubs his nose against mine, kisses the corner of my mouth, and then descends to my neck. He sucks on the spot right below my ear that always makes me squirm. He hums against it, and I groan.

I love that we still fit so well together. I love that he still can turn me on in seconds and knows what I like. It's like dating on speed—we rushed past all the awkward stuff and just fit. It could've gone very differently, though. That much time apart, other people, and the fact that we have a past . . . it might have changed the game.

He slides my straps down, kissing me along the way. Everything inside of me burns for him. "I'm going to make up with you for a while, darlin'." He looks at me with hooded eyes. The passion that simmers beneath ignites into an inferno.

I grip his chin in my hand, forcing him to look at me. "I'm counting on that. Now, kiss me."

"Yes, ma'am."

And he does. His lips move with mine as we tear at each other's clothes. I want his skin against mine. There's love to be made here, and I plan to spend as long as I need to until we're satisfied.

He rolls me under him before slithering down my body. "I need to taste you," he says with his eyes locked on mine.

Zach is always intense when we're together. He conveys everything with his eyes. There's so much spoken between us with only one look, and he'll adjust his movements based on what he sees. It's so damn sexy to watch, and it's beyond pleasurable to be on the receiving end.

He kisses my stomach and rests his hand there. I look down at him and run my fingers through his hair. "I hope, Zachary."

"Hope what, darlin'?"

"I hope that one day we can fulfill the plans we made." I rub the side of his face. "I want to have all the things we said, including a baby. I'm just not there yet."

He's not asking me to either. But I don't want him to think it's not a desire. Zach is an exceptional man. He's stepped up with Cayden and Logan without hesitation. He's the kind of man that will be the father figure my boys need, and hopefully to our own children.

He climbs back up and pulls me toward him so we're both sitting face to face. We're naked and completely bared to each other. "I never got married or had children. There wasn't anyone else in this world I wanted to do that with. Except for you." His thumb glides across my lips. "You're going to marry me someday, and I'll be anything Logan and Cayden need. A friend, a father, and a protector. I'll love the three of you with everything I have. And I know you're not ready yet, but know I was ready six months ago."

I smile and shake my head. "You're that sure, huh?"

He grins back while pushing me against the pillow. "I'm sure that I'm going to marry you, and then we're going to make a very special family."

I want to give him all of those things. "Maybe we should spend some time practicing?" I offer.

"Ahh," he says as his fingers press against my core. "So you think I need to train?"

Zach makes circles and my eyes close. "You're doing . . ." I start, but it feels too good to talk. "So good."

He goes back down, only this time he doesn't stop. His hands lift my legs as he licks and swirls his tongue against my clit. "Zach." I moan.

He keeps going as my head tosses back and forth. Holy shit. I'm going to explode. He keeps going as I grip the sheets. I writhe and moan as he bites down, taking me over the crest. "Zach!" I yell as my orgasm rocks me. My breathing is heavy, and I swear my bones liquefy.

I look down at him and he winks. "Now what were you saying about practice?"

"I think you're good," I say breathlessly. "But I think I could use a go in the batter's box."

I push him on his back and toss my hair over my shoulder. I want to watch his face. I kiss my way down to his dick, using my tongue to circle the tip. "Pres," he warns. I know what he likes, and it's not when I toy with him. But it's my favorite part. Watching him become so desperate that he is so close to losing it.

There's something so erotic about him lying here with his hands behind his head as I pleasure him. Instead of my typical cat and mouse routine, I decide to surprise him. I open my mouth and take him deep.

"Fuck!" he yells and leans up. "Holy shit!"

I smile to myself as I bob my head. I take his length while paying extra attention to the tip. Each grunt and groan that falls from his lips spurs me on. I want to please him, show how much I love him through my body.

"Darlin'," he pants. "Baby," he grunts. "Stop. You have to

stop." His hips buck, forcing me to take him deeper. "I'm gonna come if you don't stop. I want to be inside of you," he stresses.

I pull back, and he pounces. Within a second, he has me pinned beneath him. "I love you."

"I love you," I say.

"Don't ever stop," he says as he enters me.

My eyes roll back as I feel him fill me. "I won't," I promise.

We make love. Sometimes it's really sweet and slow, other moments it's frantic. I cling to him as my second orgasm hits me like a freight train. He tells me how beautiful I am, how much he wants me, and how he needs me.

I feel more tied to him than I ever have. Today we gave each other everything we have, and there's no way I can get that piece of myself back, even if I wanted to. My life with Zach will never be easy—both of us are too hardheaded—but it'll be worth every tear shed. He's where I'm meant to be.

We lie here, entwined in the sheets. "I want to talk to Logan," he states.

"About?"

"Us." Zach rolls over and places his hand on my hip. "You mentioned that he feels bad. I don't want him to worry."

I nod. "He needs that."

"I think we all do. I think Cayden and I should get a few minutes together too."

I place my hand on the side of his face. "Okay." I smile. "Let's talk to them."

"First, I think we should make up one more time just to be sure."

I giggle as he yanks me on top of him.

One more time is the least I can do to ensure we're fully made up.

Thirty-Five

ZACHARY

I 've never been so nervous about seeing the boys, but the last time was horrible. Watching them cry and cling to Presley like that pulverized me.

Knowing that I had a hand in them finding out that way is killing me.

They may not be mine, but they're a part of her, which means they're a part of me. I meant every word I said to her—I'll be whatever they need.

"Hey guys." I try to give them an easy smile and hope it looks that way.

"Zach!" Logan rushes over, and I open my arms. "I'm sorry I hit you," he says immediately.

He gives me a big hug, and I hold on to his shoulders. I want him to really hear me.

"It's water under the bridge, little man." I hate that this kid felt torn up about it. If I saw someone yelling at my mama, they'd have to deal with the three of us boys. "I think it's admirable the way you defended your mama. It showed real strength and courage."

"I didn't hurt you too bad?"

I keep my face stoic. "I had to ice my leg." I pretend to stretch it. "But it'll be fine." Logan beams with pride, and I can't help but to feel proud too.

Cayden hops down off the porch, and I wait to hear what he has to say. "Does this mean I won't be a Benson anymore?"

Presley walks over and puts her hand on my arm. I figure she wants to take this one. "You'll always be a part of your dad. He gave you life, his name, a home, and so much more. Your name will never change, even if someday mine does."

If the boys weren't here, I'd be telling her it most definitely *is* changing. Pretty soon, I'm going to make sure the entire world knows who she belongs to.

"I want you guys to know something," I explain. "I'm always here for you. Always. If you want to talk or learn some pretty cool pranks—I'm your guy. I grew up with Trent, who did it to me, and I turned around and did it to Wyatt."

They both laugh.

"But seriously, I care about all three of you very much." I hesitate a little about telling them how much I love Presley. They've had a rough couple of days, and there's still a right time for things. I would rather show them how much she means to me than say the words.

A man's words are only as true as the actions that follow.

I want to teach them the things my own daddy taught me. He's given my mother the world and treated her like she owned it. He never complains. He told us once that if she ever left him, he'd lose himself. I used to think he was out of his mind, until I lost Presley.

Presley takes my hand in hers. "I think," she says with enthusiasm. "We should team up and race again. What do you say?"

Logan and Cayden perk up. "I don't know," I joke back. "I whooped you once, it was really embarrassing for you."

"Ha!" she says in my face. "I beat you! I think your memory is going, old man."

She wasn't calling me old when I was making her back arch and cry out in pleasure. "Old?"

Presley's eyes shine as she looks at me from over her shoulder. "Older than me."

"Regardless, you're wrong. I won, right, boys?"

"You lost, Mom. I think since Cayden is the youngest, he should be on her team," Logan offers. I take it as a good sign that he wants to be on the winning squad.

"Sounds good to me." I fist bump him.

"Again?" Cayden grumbles. "I get stuck with Mom *again?*"

"Hey!" Presley jeers. "I got stuck pushing you two melonheads out, you don't see me complaining." She turns and mumbles. "I give birth to them and they like him because he gives them a horse," she gripes. "Insane."

"We can hear you." I remind her.

"I'm glad," she taunts back.

She's so cute when she gets like this. But while my girl was off in the big city, I was raising horses. I've learned a thing or two. I'm going to school her ass.

"Okay," she says as she takes out Shortstop. "Rules are there's a new route."

I narrow my eyes at her. She's up to something. "I don't think so."

"Are you going to deny me, Hennington?"

"You're in trouble."

She saunters up to me with those green eyes full of mischief. "I think." She pats my chest. "That you're the one in trouble, Cowboy."

When she says my nickname, I can't handle it. I want to throw her to the ground and make her scream it. "Presley," I warn. "You're going to pay for this."

Her lips form a straight line and my body goes still. Her fingers graze across my chest. "I look forward to it."

"I bet you do."

We race as the boys root for me. Logan and I have our own victory dance at the end. Presley swears that, once again, she's been cheated. And she thought she could win.

The rest of the day I spend time with the twins working on

training their horses. We decide to go for a really easy ride with them both. It's a slow, relaxing day for the four of us. The boys laugh a lot, mostly at Presley's expense, but she doesn't seem to mind. Each time one of them lets loose and smiles—she lights up.

She'll give me a look every once in a while that tells me how grateful she is.

"How about we cook out at my place?" I offer when the four of us get everything settled after our ride.

"Cool!" Cayden exclaims. "We get to see where Zach lives."

Logan looks at his mother. "Can we?"

"You know how to cook?" she challenges me.

"Men grill. Women cook."

She removes her hair out of the clip, letting it fall around her. God, I want her. But then I see what I said registered. Her arms cross and her eyes widen. "Is that so?"

Here we go.

"Just a different choice in words," I try to cover my slip.

"Uh huh."

"Hey, Logan," I call out. "Can you help me?"

Presley shifts from being a little hostile to curious.

"Sure!" He rushes over.

I walk over to her and pull her close. "Give me a few with him, okay?"

"Cayden," she calls out. "How about we go check and see if auntie has slipped into a sugar coma. And let her know she's coming to dinner at Zach's."

Logan and I walk the horses back to their stalls. "You think we can talk man to man?"

He sits on the bale of hay and nods his head. I choke back the laugh at how mature he's trying to be. I remember being his age. Ballsy as hell and thinking I was already a man. I won't rob the kid of that.

"I want to know if we're cool."

"We are," he says. "I like you and all."

I chuckle. "Well, that's good."

The thing that has been bugging me is what he overheard.

"Yesterday, you overheard your mom and me fighting. I wanted to know if there was something you wanted to ask me." If he didn't hear anything about the baby, we're good, but I need to make sure. It didn't even dawn on me until we were out on our ride.

"Are you and my mom going to break up because she kept something from you?" he questions.

I feel a bit of relief that he didn't hear all the shit that came along with that fight. "No, we're not."

"Are you mad that she lied?" Logan looks away with worry.

"We both kept things from each other when we were young, but it all came out. That's why we were fighting. Both of us forgave each other."

"She kept the truth about my dad from me."

"You know why, right?"

These kids should've never had to go through this. I'm glad Presley has found a way to move on from her anger, but I haven't come close. I look at these boys and rage fills me. They're good kids, she's a good woman, and he left them like this? Makes no sense to me.

He lets out a heavy breath, "I do. I'm not little though. I can take it."

"I know you're tough."

"Will you promise me something, Zach?"

Logan and Cayden both have Presley's eyes. They're identical and I find it hard to look at those boys and not offer them anything they want. "I can try."

"Promise you won't hurt my mom."

That's a promise I would do anything to keep. But these boys have had their fair share of half-truths. "I promise I'll never intentionally hurt her. I can't promise it'll never happen because sometimes we make mistakes and hurt the people we love."

"Like my daddy?"

"Yeah, dude. I don't think he wanted to hurt you."

He looks away and draws in a deep breath. "But it still hurts."

"I'm sure it does."

"Yeah." He looks back at me.

"How about we get these horses brushed and then we can do something nice for your mom?"

Logan's face lights up, and I feel better. He's a good kid with a big heart.

After twenty minutes we get everything squared away. I take Logan to the field where we grab flowers for Presley. Both of us take handfuls of whatever we can reach. We walk back as he tells me all about some game he plays with his friends from Philadelphia. We talk some more about nothing, but it's all about small steps.

"Where were you boys?" Presley asks from the top of the stairs.

Logan shows the flowers that were behind his back. "Zach and I got you these."

She smiles the smile I remember. The one that is just for me. Her eyes fill with tears, but they're not tears of sadness. "Thank you," she whispers.

Presley comes down the steps, kisses Logan on the cheek, and then heads toward me. I don't know if we're doing the whole affection in front of the boys thing. I let her take the lead and do what she's comfortable with.

She throws her arms around me, burying her face in my neck. I feel her tears against my skin, and I hold her close.

Her head lifts and she leans in, pressing her lips to mine. She tilts her head back after our brief kiss. "I'll be thanking you properly later."

I laugh and spin her around. I'm a lucky man. And I plan to make sure it stays that way.

Epilogue

PRESLEY

~EIGHTEEN MONTHS LATER~

"Are you ready yet?" Grace calls from downstairs. I've never seen the town so freaking excited over a parade. I honestly don't even know what this one is for.

"I would be if you weren't making me dig through boxes!" I yell back down.

Zach and I started construction on the house we're building by the pond six months ago. The boys fell in love with the land and immediately asked when we were moving there. Thankfully we only have two more weeks of this. I can't wait to be out of my parents' house. They've been fantastic, and since living here, I've paid off a good chunk of my debt and gotten to a manageable place. Since I don't have to pay rent or really any expenses, it's been a little easier to make extra payments.

Angie is back in town visiting, she was excited to come see the house since the boys are constantly sending her videos and pictures.

"Hurry up!" Angie yells.

I roll my eyes and fix my dress. I got suckered into riding on Grace's float. Her father is the fire chief, and he demands they have a float since the sheriff does. As if Trent and Grace need any more tension these days.

I head down the stairs, searching for the box where my boots are. "You look cute!" Grace smiles.

"It's all I could find." I laugh. I grabbed a dress since no matching was required.

"Well, it works." Angie shrugs.

"Where are the boys?" I look around.

If they got dirty outside, I'm going to lose it. I told them to stay clean because they're riding on the float with Trent. He's decided they're his deputies.

"They went with your parents," Grace explains.

"Yeah, and we need to go."

As we approach the center of town, I already see people lining the streets. I love the way the town shuts down for these events. It reminds me this isn't just a community—it's a family.

Angie groans each time someone stops us to say hello, which means she's been groaning nonstop. Finally, we make it to the staging area for the floats.

"This town needs a Xanax."

I giggle. "You need one."

"Hi, Angel," Wyatt wraps his arm around her from behind.

She peels him off before turning and pointing her finger in his face. "So help me God. I don't know what is wrong with you, but we are not—ever—going there again."

"Again?" I nearly shout. "When did you the first time?"

"Irrelevant," she says and turns back to him. "Run along."

I stand there with a smirk on my face. Angie turns and gives me a challenging look.

"Presley!" Grace yells from the float area. "We have to go."

"Yes, Presley." Angie raises her brows. "You have somewhere to be. I wouldn't want to keep you."

I point my finger at her. "We're so talking about this."

"Y'all are killing me," Grace grumbles as she pulls me to the float.

Once Grace fusses for a few minutes and gets us all situated, I glance at the boys. They're on Trent's float, standing with their chests puffed out and hands in fists on their hips. I don't know if they think they're superheroes or if they're imitating Trent.

"Hi, boys!" I wave.

They both give me a salute. "Officer Benson and Officer Benson at your service."

I bust out laughing. They're so cute. They've both adjusted really well to living here. Some days are harder than others. I field a lot of questions about their father, but the family support they receive has made the transition easier than I could've imagined.

"Where's Zach?" I ask them.

They both shrug. "I think he was talking to Coach Keeland," Logan says.

It's a very real possibility. Logan mentioned to Zach that he wanted to play baseball, which prompted Zach to leap from the dinner table, grab his glove, and practically haul Logan outside to throw the ball. Turns out that Logan is actually really good. He made the school team and Zach has become his cheerleader. I'm surprised he doesn't paint his face for games. It's hysterical to watch.

Cayden and I have been riding a lot. He finds a lot of comfort around the horses. It's great being able to bond over that.

"Grace?" I interrupt her scowling at Trent who is talking to some girl. I swear that boy has his head up his ass.

She looks over with sad eyes. "Why did you have to get the good brother?"

"I called dibs early."

"You suck," she quips.

Mrs. Rooney comes around the corner. "It's time to start! Make sure you keep your timing." Yes, we wouldn't want to mess up the order. "That means you, Trent Hennington. Don't make me get your mama over here."

I love that he may be the sheriff, but we all know who is in charge in this town.

"What is this parade for again?" For the life of me I can't remember why we're celebrating.

She laughs. "This is the parade to celebrate Bell Buckle's founding father's birthday and you and Zachary movin' in together."

"What?" I deadpan. "Are you serious?" I look at Grace.

She shrugs. "You know how your mama and her friends are. They'd do anything to throw a parade. Don't tell me you're that surprised. We had a damn parade because Mayor Peckham had his appendix removed."

I can't believe this. We're having a parade because I'm going to live with Zach? I'm going to kill my mama and her friends.

"Let's pretend this has nothing to do with me," I tell Grace.

"Whatever you want, sweetheart."

Grace checks her makeup while I look around.

"Presley, honey." Mrs. Rooney grabs my attention. "Be sure you pull that dress down a little more. The whole town doesn't need to see *those* cheeks, baby girl. You might be livin' with him, but you don't want to give the milk away for free, if you know what I mean."

"Oh, dear Lord," I grumble. I would love to tell her I sold the cow when I was seventeen, but I choose not to. "It's not that short."

She doesn't respond, but sure enough, I'm tugging it down.

The parade starts. Grace takes her spot at the front of the float, and I go to the back. Grace waves like the beauty queen she once was, though I don't think this is what she envisioned as the former Miss Bell Buckle—riding on a crepe paper float complete with a large plastic heart behind us. But she seems happy.

We ride for a few minutes when suddenly the parade stops.

"What the heck?" I say to Grace.

I look over to see what is going on and see Zach standing in the middle of the road. "Zach?" I move toward the edge.

He hops on the float with a huge smile. "Hi, darlin'."

"Hi." I give him a look that says I think he's lost his mind. "What are you doing?"

"I needed to tell you something."

"Right now?" I ask.

"Yup."

I look around, waiting for Mrs. Rooney to come beat him with a paddle or something, but they all stand there with smiles. The boys get on the float and my heart begins to race. I glance back where my family stands, all holding hands.

"You see," he says nonchalantly, "the boys and I were talkin' the other day. We all think it's time we're a family."

Tears fill my eyes. "You do?"

"Yup!" the twins say in unison.

Zach drops to his knee. "I love you, Presley. I love Cayden and Logan. I love every part of your life and want to share it with you." He takes my hand. "I fell in love with you when I was fifteen years old. I swore, one day, I would marry you. I came pretty damn close once." He winks, and I attempt to refrain from crying. "I never thought you'd find your way back to me, but here we are. I promise to love you with every piece of me. I will never betray you. I will never leave you willingly. I'll stand by your side and be all that you need." Tears now fall from my eyes without any chance of stopping. "I want to have a home for all four of us. Cayden and Logan have given me permission to ask you . . . Presley Benson, will you be my wife?"

I look at my boys, who stand behind him with huge grins. The fact that he asked them makes my heart swell. Tears of joy fall from my eyes as I look at the man I love with my whole heart. Second chances don't come along every day, but I'm eternally grateful for ours. "Of course I will, Cowboy." Zach places the diamond ring I wore when we were younger on my finger. I can't believe he kept it.

He stands, takes me in his arms, and kisses me while cheers erupt around us. Our lips part. "Looks like we finally hit a home run," he says huskily.

I smile. "I'd say this was a grand slam."

I hope that this book was as special to you as it is to me. I wrote it as a tribute to a friend who endured much of what Presley did.

If you or someone you know is suicidal, please, contact your physician, go to your local ER, or call the suicide prevention hotline in your country. For the United States, the numbers are as follows:

The National Suicide Prevention Lifeline at 800-273-TALK (8255), or message the Crisis Text Line at 741741. Both programs provide free, confidential support 24/7.

Wyatt and Angie's book is available now and this cowboy is WHOA!

Their story is sure to take you on a journey you will never forget.

Be sure to grab Say You Want Me!

***

That said, I was not ready to let Zach and Presley go so easy. I wanted to stay with them, see them through even after the Return to Me series was over and I have EXCLUSIVE access to a bonus scene if you keep swiping!

Bonus Scene

"No pressure today, Cayden," I try to reassure him knowing it won't work.

For a ball player, there's nothing more important than today. There are games in your life that no matter what the coach or your stepfather say, they're that do or die time. This will define him in so many ways. If it goes well, he'll think he's invincible . . . if it goes badly, he'll hate life.

I've experienced both. I just didn't think I'd be having the same emotions about baseball again, this time as a father. Here I am, coming full circle.

"What if I make an error?" he asks while looking over at the stands filled with fans. "What if I strike out? What the hell was I thinking?"

"Listen, you just go out there and play the best you can. It's a game. At the end of the day, someone will make an error, someone will strike out, and someone will make a play that changes the game, you don't know which you'll be, but it's a game."

I've said those words to him a million times.

Cayden releases a heavy breath, and nods. "Thanks, Dad."

I clasp his shoulder. "I love you, son. I'm proud of you no matter what."

Cayden does his best to shove down his fears and I release my grip. I may not be his biological father, but watching my boy find himself has been the most gratifying thing in the world. Seeing him take the field today . . . there's not even words.

His brother, grandparents, aunts, uncles, and cousins are waiting outside Yankee Stadium, ready to watch him start in his first major league game. I'm here in the locker hall, watching him walk toward the field for batting and fielding practice.

"Surreal, huh?" Presley's arms wrap around me from behind.

She has no idea. I don't say a word, I just nod.

"You did good just then, Cowboy."

"Yeah?"

"Yeah," she kisses my cheek. "He looks calmer. I remember when it was you all freaked out and I would try to talk to you down."

Her memory of how she calmed me and hers are a little off. There was very little talking before games. A lot of tongues, hands, and promises of what was come if I played a good game.

I turn, holding my beautiful wife in my arms. "Not how I remember it," I give her a playful grin.

Recognition hits her and I fight back the laugh at her disgusted face. "Well, I prefer Cayden's way."

"As his mother, I bet you do. What made you come down here? I thought you were up in the stands."

Her small hand grazes my cheek. "I was, but I had a feeling you two needed some support."

This has been bittersweet for me. Many moons ago, I wanted the life Cayden is living, but injuries took that from me. In hindsight, it's all gone the way it should. Had I still been playing ball, I wouldn't be married to Presley or had two boys I love more than I knew was possible.

"I gave up that dream a long time ago, darlin'. I'm pretty happy with my lot."

"Still," she smiles. "I know what it's like to lose a dream."

"And I know what it's like to gain an even better one," I counter.

She leans in, presses her lips to mine, and sighs. "I love you, Zachary."

"I'm glad since we've been married damn near fifteen years."

"I didn't say I liked you," she says as she slaps my chest. "Come on, let's go see your family before they wander the streets forgettin' this is New York and not Bell Buckle. Even though Angie knows how to navigate a city, corralling Trent is a full-time job."

I can't even imagine Angie trying to handle that group. My mother has never been anywhere except Tennessee, and Nashville is not anywhere close to this city.

We head over to the group and sure enough, Angie looks like she's about to lose her mind.

"Where's Logan?" I ask.

Angie tilts her head to a crowd of girls where Logan stands in the middle. "He's letting everyone know his brother is playing with the Yankees."

Cayden's only focus is baseball and has been since high school, whereas Logan was girls. I swear they took the two things I cared most about and split them. I loved both, I lost both, and found the one that really mattered. Funny how life works out that way.

"Which by the way," Angie tacks on. "As a Philadelphia fan is absolutely killing me to wear this damn jersey. I feel as though I'm betraying my city."

"He's your nephew who loves you, get over it. Wear it and bask in your newfound love of the Yankees." Presley says and then looks over where Logan causes a round of laughter.

I smile as Logan works the girls a little. "He does realize they want to know his brother and not him, right?"

Presley laughs. "It's Logan, he's twenty-four and more like Wyatt than I'd prefer, but it's why he transferred to go to NYU for grad school."

"Those two can't even handle being out of the same state," I note.

"Nope. Twins through and through."

They both grew up to be great men. Logan is in law school at NYU, where Cayden was drafted right out of college. Thankfully, he didn't choose to make the same mistakes that I did. He leaned on Presley and I to help with the right steps to achieve his end goal.

Logan on the other hand, took every opportunity to get in trouble just so he could argue his way out. I never doubted he'd follow this career path. He's going to make an excellent lawyer.

"They're both a whole different level of trouble," I note as I look at my other son. "Do you remember when Logan tried to sneak out but didn't remember to shut the alarm off?"

She huffs. "And then Cayden tried to tell me he was sleep walking?"

"What about when Cayden was grounded from using the car so he picked up that girl on horseback . . ."

Presley groans. "Those two drove me crazy until they left for college. I'm just glad they haven't done half the shit you and your brothers did. I swear, you Hennington boys just breed trouble."

"That's all your bloodline, darlin'."

She rolls her eyes. "They're mine when they do dumb shit and yours when they're on top of the world?"

"Basically," I smile.

At least she's catching on.

"Listen, I wanted to put a baby in you, but you were all: *I'm too old*," I say in my best impression of her. "So, I get the good parts of my boys, and you get the jacked up part."

Presley goes quiet and I know I'm in for it now. "Put a baby in me? And what jacked-up parts are you referring to, Cowboy?"

"You know, the dumb things."

She looks up to the sky before meeting my gaze. "I'm pretty sure that's learned behavior, honey. Because . . . that was just dumb there."

I wrap my arm around my wife and pull her to me. "It's okay, I forgive you for messin' them up."

"I'm going to mess you up if you don't quit it."

The gates open and my chest tightens. All of us stop talking as

dawning hits us. We're going to walk in there and watch Cayden
Benson-Hennington start as the Yankee's second baseman.

"You ready?" I ask Presley.

Her hand tucks into the crook of my arm. "I'm ready."

I love her and these boys more than I knew I was capable of. I
always thought I understood unconditional love, until Presley and
I found each other again. Cayden and Logan are a part of me, and
I'm thankful every day that I've been given the gift of them in my
life.

Being a stepparent is the choice to love another man's child
like your own. There was never any doubt that I would love them,
they're a part of her. We may not have had children together, but I
raised those boys.

They're mine as well.

And I wouldn't change a single thing because it led me to right
here.

Books by Corinne Michaels

The Salvation Series

Beloved

Beholden

Consolation

Conviction

Defenseless

Evermore: A 1001 Dark Night Novella

Indefinite

Infinite

The Hennington Brothers

Say You'll Stay

Say You Want Me

Say I'm Yours

Say You Won't Let Go: A Return to Me/Masters and Mercenaries
Novella

Second Time Around Series

We Own Tonight

One Last Time

Not Until You

If I Only Knew

The Arrowood Brothers

Come Back for Me

Fight for Me

The One for Me

Stay for Me

Willow Creek Valley Series

Return to Us

Could Have Been Us

A Moment for Us

A Chance for Us

Rose Canyon Series

Help Me Remember (Coming 2022)

Give Me Love (Coming 2022)

Keep This Promise (Coming 2022)

Co-Written with Melanie Harlow

Hold You Close

Imperfect Match

Standalone Novels

All I Ask

You Loved Me Once

Acknowledgments

To my husband and children. You sacrifice so much for me to continue to live out my dream. Days and nights of me being absent even when I'm here. I'm working on it. I promise. I love you more than my own life.

My beta readers, Michelle, Jenn, Holly, Katie, Melissa, and Sunny, I love you guys. Thank you for reading the dozens of drafts and changes I send you. I can't tell you what your love and encouragement mean to me. You're the reason that I keep going—I swear.

My readers. There's no way I can thank you enough. It still blows me away that you read my words. You guys have become a part of my heart and soul.

Bloggers: I don't think you guys understand what you do for the book world. It's not a job you get paid for. It's something you love and you do because of that. Thank you from the bottom of my heart.

Thank you to Lisa my editor for your support and guidance through my projects. Sarah Hansen, from Okay Creations, for making my covers perfect. Ashley Williams for proofreading so many times until you probably see spots!

Christy Peckham, my right hand, my friend, my tormentor-Ha! No, you keep me on track and never waver. I'm so blessed to have you in my corner.

Melissa Erickson, you're amazing. I love your face.

About the Author

New York Times, USA Today, and Wall Street Journal Bestseller Corinne Michaels is the author of multiple bestselling novels. She's an emotional, witty, sarcastic, and fun loving mom of two beautiful children. Corinne is happily married to the man of her dreams and is a former Navy wife.

After spending months away from her husband while he was deployed, reading and writing was her escape from the loneliness. She enjoys putting her characters through intense heartbreak and finding a way to heal them through their struggles. Her stories are chock full of emotion, humor, and unrelenting love.

CONNECT WITH CORINNE

Website: http://www.corinnemichaels.com
Facebook: https://www.facebook.com/CorinneMichaels
Twitter: https://twitter.com/AuthorCMichaels

Made in United States
North Haven, CT
17 July 2024

54902436R10187